THE NORTH BEYOND

PART 2 : MAESRHON

P.M. Scrayfield

Pen Press

First published in Great Britain

All paper used in the printing of this book has been made from wood grown in managed, sustainable forests.

ISBN13: 978-1-78003-490-4

Printed and bound in the UK
Pen Press is an imprint of
Indepenpress Publishing Limited
25 Eastern Place
Brighton
BN2 1GJ

A catalogue record of this book is available from
the British Library

Cover design by Jacqueline Abromeit

CONTENTS

... the story began with:

THE NORTH BEYOND
Part 1 : Numirantoro

...and continues with:

THE NORTH BEYOND
Part 3 : Haldur

THE NORTH BEYOND
Part 4 : Artorynas

III CHILDHOOD

CHAPTER 17

Tests and talk

The usual buzz of chatter, the rattle of knives and spoons, the scrape of benches on the stone floor, of footsteps passing to and fro from the kitchens, filled the small hall in Tellgard where food was eaten in the middle of the day. It was always an informal occasion, as the times of activities varied and people came and went accordingly. But today a meeting of Tell'Ethronad was scheduled for the afternoon and so the hall was clearing more quickly than usual as men left to prepare themselves and gather their thoughts for the council. It meant free time for the youngsters and many of them had already moved off; but among those who were still eating was a group about half-way down a long table, laughing and talking among themselves. From the top of the hall, Arval watched them quietly, deep in thought, turning over in his mind the conversation he had just overheard between Forgard and a member of the Tellgard staff.

'… because the boy will be ten years old at the Spring Feast.'

Arval caught the words and began to attend.

'This year? Are you sure?'

This was the other man, and Forgard's reply was emphatic.

'Absolutely. His name's on the list to begin sword-practice before summer with the other ten-year-olds, and as we all remember only too well, he was born on the night of the feast.'

'Yes, indeed. Well, ten years is long enough to wait for some sign of improvement, in my opinion.'

'More than enough! We need to keep up the pressure in Tell'Ethronad. Now's the time to take action, when the memory is fresh in men's minds. There is just the chance that we can discredit him and who knows, maybe then hope will return to us.'

The men got up from the table and moved off, leaving Arval to his thoughts. So the tide was beginning to turn his way again in the council! It had been a long ten years. As he pondered what he had just heard, his eye roved idly over the group of youngsters. He knew they had come from a science class where flight had been the topic of study: he had passed the windows and noted the diagrams on the wall as his colleague held up a specimen for practical examination: one of the collared doves that fluttered in the exercise yard, with wings and tails spread out, fan-like, as they wheeled and turned in the air. The boys' heads were together as they argued some point, pushed at each other and giggled at some joke, but as usual, the dark head was just a little removed from the rest. Arval's gaze softened imperceptibly. There was no-one better placed than he to understand the nature of that separation. It could never be fully bridged: only learning the truth would help to heal it, but such knowledge was not for a ten-year-old mind to comprehend. With a shout of laughter most of the boys suddenly jumped up and went to the kitchen door, obviously intent on second helpings; but the dark-haired lad made for the hall door, alone. He turned briefly and looked back as he left the room; and Arval, with a shake of his head, rose from his seat and went to prepare his papers for the meeting.

Later that afternoon, a small boy came trotting along the street towards the *Sword and Stars* and turned in at the wide gate that led to the inn yard. He glanced swiftly round, but seeing no sign of the person he wanted he crossed over to the service door in the corner. From within he heard the sounds of someone working a water pump, the clatter of dishes, the rap of clogs on the stone floor. He went in, the savoury smells of cooking making his mouth water, and passing the scullery on his left put his head around the open door of the kitchen.

The conversation that had been in progress stopped abruptly; a man who was busy linking sausages looked up sharply and a youngish woman at the dough-board spun round as his eyes widened on the door behind her, but relaxed again when she saw the boy.

'Hello! Looking for Isteddar? He's off with his dad somewhere, on an errand for the storeman. Like a piece of cheesebread?'

'Oh... er, no, I've already eaten, but thank you very much indeed. I'll see Isteddar tomorrow morning, then.'

He ducked out of the kitchen and went back into the yard to get away from the cooking smells. It was true that he had had his midday meal, but his portion had been small and cheesebread was one of his favourites. But, he thought, I am under orders. A man must learn to master himself. He wandered around the yard for a few moments, looking in at the stables and workshops, exchanging a word or two here and there, deliberately giving himself the chance to succumb to temptation as he inhaled the delicious smells of food. When he was quite sure he had won his private battle, he jogged back into the street and away on up to the gardens of the fountain. Every week he liked to set himself some secret task or target to accomplish. This time he had resolved that he would turn down every offer of a treat, or each chance to do something he would really enjoy. Maybe next week he would seek out some frightening challenge, face up to something that he was afraid to do. That should make this week a lot easier than next, he thought, because treats of any kind rarely came his way. Meanwhile, who could know how often in his life he might be hungry when this could not be helped, so this afternoon he must be stern with himself and go about his business without wasting time and energy thinking about cheesebread.

He headed across to the far side of the gardens, away beyond the formal area near the fountain to where a few coppices of shrubs and small trees grew. It never occurred to him that his outlook on life was rather serious for one not yet past his tenth birthday, but then sometimes he felt older than Arval, especially when he was with the other youngsters. Walking into the coppice until he was hidden from the view of anyone who might pass by, he searched underneath the thick leaves of a holly bush for the ash stave he had left there. He picked it up, testing it. It was quite slender, with the bark left on, and still flexible from having been kept underneath the damp leaves. The bigger trees around the clearing had been marked with cuts and daubs of mud. The boy used these now as targets, holding the stave like a sword, whirling around as if to meet an attacker, trying to hit the mark first time, changing from hand to hand every so often. That was another test he had set himself, to be as equally skilled and strong with either hand. Formal sword-training would not start for him until later that year, after he was turned ten, but he wanted to be the best in his group. He was already unbeatable with the sparring-stave, an achievement for which he had earned only ridicule from his father and brother.

Deciding that without Isteddar to partner him, sling-practice in the open park beyond the coppice would be too wasteful of time spent in setting up targets and too likely to attract the attention of some interfering adult, he carried doggedly on with his self-imposed exercises, ignoring the protests of his increasingly empty stomach. Eventually he loped over to the fountain to get a drink. There were three or four women sitting there, keeping an eye on an assortment of babies and toddlers and chatting among themselves. As he reached for the cup, the woman nearest to him started with fright; he always tried to move as quietly as he could and at a speed he thought he could keep up all day if he had to, and she had not heard his approach. Her companions all looked round and their talk faltered into a silence which followed him as he set off back down the street. He ran past the *Sword and Stars* without stopping or looking into the gateway. Isteddar might be there by now, and the chance of being asked in must be firmly avoided. He liked Isteddar's mother and father, but their honest, unassuming kindness hurt him twice over: it intensified his feeling of strangeness, of not belonging; and the warm, welcoming air of their rooms in the staff quarters of the inn only served to emphasise the coldness that awaited him in his own home.

He took the steps up into a handsome colonnade two at a time, waited a moment or two for a clear space between passers-by and then took them all in one flying leap down again. Leaning against the wall, he noticed that there were thirteen pillars, and an idea came to him. Climbing the steps again, he walked along counting the flagstones. One at each end of the colonnade at the top of the steps, and two between each pillar. Good! Here was another test to set himself. He would run along, putting one foot on each flagstone, and thinking as he went of a word for each letter of the alphabet. On the count of three, then: apple, barley, cockerel, daisy, evening, firewood, gold; hawthorn, ivy, jerkin, kestrel, ladder, mushroom, night; opal, piglet, quiet, ridgepole, stewpot, tillage, oh! missed a step, vixen, weather… He found himself at the end of the colonnade, leaning on the last pillar, out of breath and grinning to himself. He needed a one-syllable word beginning in 'u', to match the rhythmic pattern he had unconsciously fallen into with his other words. Nothing came immediately into his mind, which ran on automatically to the remaining letters. Funny how all the difficult ones were at the end. Yawning, yellow, yesterday, he thought; and, there must be something, yes, got it! Zest. He remembered a morning when the old dear in the kitchens at Tellgard had slipped him a lemon cake. She'd told him it was flavoured with *zest* from the lemon peel.

Underneath, upstart, untied. He sat down on the top step, racking his brains. He'd just have to cheat on 'x' and put in excite, or extreme. His eye fell on the house diagonally opposite, a handsome, dignified building in mellow stone with steps up to a porch over which a large lantern swung. It was where Valafoss lived: the boy noted, without really seeing, the broken places in the stonework here and there along the top of the courtyard wall where Heranar and Valahald had used the carving for target practice. Valafoss would be at the council meeting, he supposed, like his own father and Arval and the rest of them. The worst thing about Tell'Ethronad days was not being able to stay at Tellgard during the afternoon. But still, he thought, brightening, Arval had promised that once he was turned ten, he would be allowed to use the library by himself and work in there unsupervised if he wanted to. He knew Arval would have trusted him long ago, but understood that to show undue favour would be unfair on the other youngsters and harder on himself too. He had learnt his letters so young that he could barely remember a time when he was unable to read, devouring everything he could get his hands on. But books of any kind were in short supply at home, where in any case his studious tendencies aroused mockery.

Across the street, two women were standing in conversation watching him. Suddenly the noise of a loud splash, followed by laughter and shouting, came from the far side of the wall and caught his attention. Valahald and Heranar, by the sounds of it; maybe there was a pool or pond in the garden and one had pushed the other into it. As he looked up, he registered the stone ornament, with rather dead-looking plants in it, at the end of the wall where it turned at an angle from the street. Urn! Got it, he thought, jumping to his feet, crossing the road and setting off again. As he passed the women, they fell silent, but he caught a word or two of their conversation.

'...yes, ten years this Spring Feast is right...'

He had run on, away down towards his home, before they spoke again.

'Did you see the way he was gazing at the house?'

'I did, poor little mite. And did you see how he jumped up when he heard those two young ruffians at their horseplay? Couldn't bear the way the place has been let slide, likely...'

Family supper

Supper that evening was a tense occasion in Vorynaas' private dining-chamber at Seth y'n Carad. Vorynaas sat brooding over his meal, scarcely noticing the food but drinking heavily. The meeting of Tell'Ethronad had not gone well; there could be no doubt that he had lost some ground in the council. After all I have done for this city, he thought angrily. The servant stepped forward to offer more food, but Vorynaas waved her away.

'Give it to Ghentar.'

She moved around the table, serving the last of the chicken and almonds to Ghentar, who helped himself to the wine, adding more to the diluted mix in his cup. Vorynaas noticed the way his son was smirking at the girl and his mood improved a little. That's my boy, he thought. I could fancy that girl myself, but if the lad has an eye for her already, he's growing up fast. I think I might take him with me, next time I travel south to the old mines, let him get a feel for the business. He met his son's glance, and grinned.

'What have you been up to today, then?'

'Bored witless at Tellgard this morning, had a bite with Thaltor in the *Leopard* at lunchtime, walked round the walls for a while, did some sword-drills with the fellows in the guard.'

Vorynaas had a good idea of what Ghentar had left out of this list, suspecting as he did that the boy was gambling fairly regularly: if he missed silver from his pouch again, he would tackle the lad about it, but privately – not in front of Maesrhon. He turned to the other boy.

'And no doubt the intellectual in the family has been writing a poem, or gainfully employed in some such way.'

Ignoring Ghentar's derisive guffaw, Maesrhon spoke quietly.

'No sir, I was at classes in Tellgard this morning, and this afternoon I, I went running in the gardens of the fountain.'

He hated it when his father and brother made derogatory remarks about Tellgard, and so he schooled his face to show no expression. He was afraid that if he reacted to their jibes, he might not be allowed to attend classes at all, so he had made a secret bargain with himself. Jeering about Tellgard, about his teachers there, about what was taught, about his interest in learning, he would submit to without comment;

he would not rise, however provocative the insult; but he had sworn, taking the Starborn to be his witnesses, that if anything should be said against Arval, he would not let that pass. He loved Arval with a fierce devotion, and clung to that unswerving loyalty as to a lodestone: it gave meaning to his otherwise directionless life.

Vorynaas snorted. 'Running, eh? Well, I suppose it will come in useful once you start sword-training. You'll be able to get out of the way faster.'

Suddenly his manner changed: he shot out his hand, spun Maesrhon towards him by his shoulder and addressed him harshly.

'Why were you hanging about outside Valafoss' house this afternoon?'

'I wasn't! I…'

'Don't lie to me, you little runt, you were seen gawping from across the street. Not good enough for you here, is it? Hankering after the old days?'

Maesrhon stared in bewilderment.

'No… but I don't understand what you mean.'

'Forgotten something, haven't you?' Vorynaas' fingers bit into his shoulder painfully.

'*Sir*,' added Maesrhon, shaking a little with fright and suppressed fury.

Ghentar sniggered. 'He forgets things too often. Don't I seem to remember he's supposed to be practising serving the wine? I've got an empty cup here.'

Vorynaas sat back and Maesrhon took up the wine flask, but it seemed he was not going to get away so lightly.

'So what *were* you doing? Thought you said you'd been in the fountain gardens?'

'I was, but I had to come past Valafoss' house on my way home.'

Maesrhon's mind raced. If he told the truth, he'd be ridiculed for making up word-games; but if he lied, his father would know and suspect something worse. Maesrhon had always been a poor liar, and knowing it made him even less adept. *I wish I knew who it was that saw me and told tales to my father*, he thought. *What is it to anyone where I go? Who has been spying on me?* He turned from replacing the wine and took a deep breath.

'I just sat on the steps for a while because I had to think of a word I needed, for a, well, to fit in with some lines I was making up.'

'Ah, a poem! You were right after all,' said Ghentar to his father with a sneer. 'I bet there's never been a storyteller in the family before.'

Vorynaas turned a black look on his elder son. 'You do? And how much would you bet on it?'

The boy flushed and for a few moments the three of them were silent with their thoughts. Ghentar glared across the table at Maesrhon, blaming him for the slip of the tongue which had brought their father's suspicions onto himself; while the younger boy sat with downcast eyes, willing himself to show no emotion, desperate to escape to his own room where he could think freely. Vorynaas watched the pair of them. There was exactly three years between them in age. Ghentar was more like his father than ever, strongly built, of medium height with thick, reddish chestnut hair, dark eyes and a high colour. Vorynaas had a touch of grey at his temples now, and his beard was a little grizzled about the corners of his mouth, but he was still handsome enough, fit and energetic. If he had been honest with himself, he would have admitted that Ghentar, over-indulged as he had always been, was lazy and carrying too much weight. He lacked his father's agility of mind, too. There was no doubting Vorynaas' intelligence, even though it had been directed to some questionable ends, but his restless ambition and devious brain were completely missing in his elder son. Vorynaas however would see no wrong in the lad and favoured him in everything. But Maesrhon now, that changeling with amber eyes! Not ten yet, and as tall already as Ghentar at rising thirteen, but much more slightly built with longer limbs and narrower hands and feet. Dark, too; his hair, falling back from his face in loose, springing locks, was almost black. But Numirantoro had been dark, after all, Vorynaas reminded himself, and Arythalt also; and both of them tall… yet as he looked at the boy, the old suspicion still gnawed at Vorynaas.

A boy's heart

The following afternoon, Maesrhon was sitting in the wood workshops, slowly paring away at the carving of a robin which he was making. The craftsman in charge had wanted him to colour it, thinking it a waste not to show the bird's red breast feathers, but Maesrhon had held out against this idea. His three favourite small birds were the robin, the dunnock and the collared dove. No-one rated the dunnock because it was small and unobtrusive, not pretty or brightly coloured like a bullfinch or a bluetit; but Maesrhon had sat hidden until the bird was close by him and he had seen its neat shape and the fine grading of brown and grey in its plumage. To him, it had a quiet elegance, a quality he saw also in the doves: he loved the pink shading in the grey of their feathers, the unexpected garnet of their jewel-like eyes. But the robin… He sat back, flexing his fingers. The carving was coming on quite well; he liked the grain of the wood. It should come up nicely with oiling, and maybe he would use glass or polished stone for the eyes. There was something wrong, though. Well, not wrong, just… He held it out at arm's length and stared at it rather glumly, sighing.

'What's the matter?' asked the lad at the next workbench with a grin. 'Got a feather too many in one of the wings?'

He winked at Maesrhon, who shrugged: he was used to being teased as a perfectionist but to him it seemed extraordinary that so many of his classmates were apparently content with putting in a minimum of effort even when they were capable of doing really well if they tried harder. He struggled now to explain what he saw as the problem with his robin.

'No, it's coming on all right, but maybe I've picked the wrong bird, or something. I can't find the real robin in it, you know? It's just that now I've started, I think that what I really see in a robin is the song. Well, obviously I don't see the song, I hear it, but you know what I mean. To me, the robin *is* the song, but how could you show that in a carving?' He realised long before he got to the end of this little speech that he was wasting his time; the other boy was shaking his head.

'Do you know something, you are really *weird*,' he said. 'Look, there's Thaltor, he must be going to take the sword-drill today. Let's go and watch!'

'I'll follow you later,' said Maesrhon, staying in his place as everyone else packed their work away and rushed out noisily, leaving him alone in the room.

After a few moments he moved over to the side bench, away from the window, and took down a large sheet of rough paper and a carpenter's pencil. First with one hand, then with the other, he practised trying to draw a perfect circle freehand, measuring the results for accuracy. This was a favourite game of his and it left him free to think at the same time, ignoring the background noises drifting through the open door from the class in the yard. Footsteps approached slowly along the boardwalk outside, and men's voices in conversation; they came gradually to a halt just beyond the door. Maesrhon usually wrote with his right hand, but he had discovered long ago that he could produce mirror-image writing with his left, moving in the opposite direction on the page. Now he wondered if he could do both at once. Why not try? He smiled to himself, reaching for a second pencil, but some words from the conversation outside caught his ear and stopped him just as he was poised to begin.

'...yes, ten years this Spring Feast.'

Where had he heard those words before? Yesterday, in the street, those women talking! But this was Arval's voice; he began to listen carefully.

'Well, I agree with Forgard: ten years is more than long enough,' said the man with Arval. 'Vorynaas had his way, and look what it brought us: we were too cautious in Tell'Ethronad yesterday, we should move the council against him.'

'He can see the way the wind's blowing: it will do no harm to let him brood on events for a while. One must remember there is a child involved.'

This was Arval once more; Maesrhon heard him move as if he had stepped up to the door, then he spoke again.

'We can talk more about this later...'

The voices faded as the men began strolling away, but Maesrhon sat frozen, staring at the paper before him. Somehow he knew that Arval had realised he was in the workshop: that was why he had moved away, changing the subject. He thought over what he had just heard, wondering what was meant about the council and Vorynaas. It came to him that his father disliked Forgard; he knew they were opposed in the council. But now the boy remembered other conversations which had been abruptly halted when he had appeared, yesterday at the *Sword* and then again by the fountain. And those women, talking outside Valafoss' house! He'd heard them say something about *ten years this Spring Feast*. Was it him they were all talking about? He knew he had been born at the Spring Feast: Arval had told him. Now he began to wonder what his father could have done, and what might happen to himself and Ghentar if the council took action against Vorynaas. No, Arval had said *a child* was involved: Ghentar was nearly thirteen now. Maesrhon was so used to daily slights and unkind words from his father that he hardly noticed them any more, but yesterday evening Vorynaas had showed his dislike of his younger son more clearly than usual. Ghentar had no need to worry. It followed therefore that there was some secret concerning himself, his father and events at a Spring Feast of ten years before. Except that it wasn't so secret, was it? They were all whispering about it. He wondered if Ghentar knew. Well, nothing was more certain than that he would never, ever, give his brother the satisfaction of asking him; and approaching Vorynaas was also out of the question. That left the only person he would trust always to tell him the truth. He would ask Arval, but not yet. This was something he desperately wanted to do, so he would make himself wait until next week. And, he thought in a moment of daring inspiration, he knew just what he would set himself to do next week, that he was afraid to do!

Maesrhon had the strangest dream that night, in which he saw a huge, empty valley lie dark and barren under a moon rising at the full. Even in his dream he gazed in wonder, never having seen either moon or stars in waking life; yet as is the way of dreams he was somehow in the scene as well as an observer of it. He knew that although he seemed to stand on the near slope, staring out across that lifeless valley, he was at the same time looking back at himself from high on the far slope. He awoke to lie oppressed by the bleakness of what his mind had seen, with a weight settling on his heart like a heavy blanket. He felt chilled and alone, even his bed seemed cold and comfortless. Wondering how much of the night was left, his thoughts turned to the day ahead: lessons in the morning, then archery practice after the noon meal while the older boys did sword-drill. And next week he would talk to Arval. Warmth crept back into him with the thought. To him it seemed that he was alone in the world: but when he did well, or achieved a first place, he did it for Arval. His starved little heart loved Arval the Earth-wise, who stood to him for father, mother, teacher, friend and brother all in one person. I would dare even the wilderness in my dream for Arval, he thought, settling to sleep once more.

Questions

Since taking up residence at Seth y'n Carad, Vorynaas had made it his business to put on a good show for the various festivals of the year and the Spring Feast was no exception. Expenditure on entertainment and largesse he regarded as money well spent, binding folk to him by obligation and buying their support. But sensing as he did that the mood in council was turning against him, he resolved that this year's festivities, which fell in the week after the unsatisfactory meeting, should be particularly memorable. As usual there would be a grand civic occasion in the public hall, but this year, in addition to the feast-day food and drink which his guards, workers and numerous dependants enjoyed as usual, he had provided free entertainment for the poor: there was to be an ox-roast and barrels of ale, together with jugglers, tumblers and even a troupe of fire-eaters from the Outlands. Not so well publicised was the fact that when the merriment was at its height, and men's resistance lowest, Haartell and his assistants would move among the crowd taking the names of any unwary enough to join Vorynaas' workforce in the valley of the Lissa'pathor. Many a man who signed, or made his mark, thinking he gained security for his family, realised too late that dealing with Vorynaas was done only at the highest price.

Maesrhon loitered briefly on his way to Tellgard, watching the trestles and awnings being set up in the compound outside the east wing of Seth y'n Carad, men and women bustling about, chocking up the barrels, preparing food, erecting a platform for the entertainers. His stomach churned with fright when he thought about what he had set himself for this week's test and he toyed with the idea of postponing his talk with Arval so as to use it as a reward to himself for his daring. But no, that would be cheating, giving in to weakness. He turned away and walked on. After the mid-day meal, he and Arval sat on a bench outside the tower, but the boy found it hard to know where to begin his questions.

'Lord Arval, could I see in a dream what I have never seen in life?' he asked eventually.

'Certainly. Do you want to tell me about your dream?'

'Well…' After a pause, Maesrhon recounted his dream of the withered hillside, lying lifeless under the moon. He had been unable to shake off the memory of its desolation. He looked up at Arval for reassurance and the old man smiled down at him, hiding his misgivings.

'You have seen the wilderness, Na Caarst that lies about all settled lands. North of the forest, beyond Maesaldron, it stretches far and wide, hostile to life. Men do not journey there.'

A foreboding settled on Maesrhon at Arval's words. 'Maybe my fate will take me there,' he muttered.

'Now, now.' Arval stood up and turned towards the tower door. 'The mind is a strange country, full of mysteries. Come with me, I have something for you to see that will show you my meaning.'

Together they climbed the stair and entered Arval's study. He took down a richly-bound volume from the shelves and brought it over to the table, sitting down beside Maesrhon. Turning the pages, he stopped at a picture of a green, empty landscape lying under a wide grey sky. The wind was blowing strongly in the picture, you could see it in the way birds swept through the air against the flowing clouds, in the way the hawthorns all crouched one-sided in the same direction. But unmoving, massive, stark and stern, on a level space in the middle distance stood a circle of huge stones, their rough-hewn surfaces streaked with lichen and glistening here and there with a vein of some mineral. Maesrhon gazed at the scene, lost for words in the face of its enigmatic message. Looking at the facing page, he saw delicate writing, beautifully ornamented. He read the words: "As silent as standing stones".

'You have never seen anything like this in life, have you?' asked Arval, as the boy shook his head. 'Well, neither had the person who made the picture, yet this image came to her. Can you guess who the artist was?'

Maesrhon's eyes flew to Arval's face. 'Was it … was it my mother?' he whispered.

He is still very like Numirantoro, thought Arval, apart from those golden eyes of course; let us hope he is old enough to bear it when his other parentage begins to show.

'Indeed it was,' said Arval, 'and she asked me the same question as you have done. I see her in you, *Is-torar*.'

The child sat silent, savouring the beauty of the book, his pleasure in Arval's company and the talk of his mother, the warmth of the old man's diminutive form of address. He had never used this name before and Maesrhon fed on the affection, feeling it soak through him as a plant takes up water after a drought.

'Did my mother make all this book?' he asked Arval now.

'All of it except the binding,' said Arval, 'and there are two others here which she also made. They are too precious for everyday use, but you will be ten years old at the festival, will you not? You may look at them after that, if you would like to.'

'Oh, yes please, I would like that very much indeed! But, Lord Arval...' Maesrhon hesitated; he had the opening he wanted now, but was unsure how to use it. 'I, there was something else I wanted to ask you.'

Arval waited without speaking and eventually Maesrhon blurted out what was weighing on his mind.

'What happened at the Spring Feast when I was born? Did my father do something wrong?'

'Why do you ask me that?'

'Because I know you will tell me the truth.'

The old man looked at Maesrhon, noting how neatly the boy had used the ambiguity of his question in unconscious flattery, increasing the pressure on him to answer; and the child gazed steadily back at him. Arval felt the weight of knowledge and memories, the burden of the secrets and promises he bore. Some day all must be revealed and told, but surely not yet. He leaned forward slightly towards Maesrhon, choosing his words carefully.

'Vorynaas is an ambitious man; he rose quickly to a position of power and influence in Caradward. He gained the support of a majority in Tell'Ethronad and with it control of the city; but his support was never unanimous nor his position unassailable. There have always been those who disagree with him, but they have been mocked as reactionary and old-fashioned. As you will know, the sky has been obscured in Caradward these many years: we see the moon and stars no longer and the sun fails to shine. Our beliefs for the reason, and our methods of dealing with it, have been the source of our deepest divisions. There was disquiet in the city, and ten years ago at the festival, there was unrest in our streets. Vorynaas made a rash promise that if all would follow his lead, the light would return; but time has proved him wrong and now men wonder among themselves whether to turn again to ways they once rejected.'

Maesrhon considered these words, pleased that Arval had spoken to him as one adult to another, but feeling still that the answer somehow failed to fit his question. He thought over what Arval had said about old-fashioned ways; he would have liked to know whether these concerned the As-Geg'rastigan, but in view of what he was about to do at the forthcoming festival decided it was better not to ask. Eventually he looked up at Arval again.

'Lord Arval, thank you for telling me of this. But...' he faltered, wondering whether he dared to go on: Arval raised his eyebrows at him in enquiry and he finished breathlessly, '...but it seems to me that you could tell me more!' He looked away in embarrassment and then, when Arval laughed, turned back hopefully.

'I could indeed, but let us not run before we can walk. One day we will talk at great length, you and I.'

The boy's face was a picture of earnest entreaty: Arval was reminded, suddenly and painfully, of the young Numirantoro.

'But Lord Arval, I do not want to wait, I want to know everything you can tell me about, about everything! I want to learn, I want to know everything about the world: you say yourself that learning is the one thing a man can never regret. Please, I am old enough to understand, and if I cannot, you know how to explain things so that my mind will overcome the difficulty.'

'Listen, little scholar,' said Arval, 'and understand this! Learning and knowledge are not the same thing. With learning, you cannot begin too soon, nor is there any need ever to stop. But with knowledge, it is different. Some things are easy to learn, but hard to know; and it is better to wait a little, to let time pass and experience accumulate, before tackling truths of that kind. The mind must build its strength, just as the body exercises in order to clothe itself in muscle. I promised your mother that I would guard you and guide you. Do you trust me to do that?'

Maesrhon set his teeth against the emotion that threatened to overwhelm him; the colour came up in his face, but his lifelong habit of hiding what he saw as weakness steadied the catch in his voice. He slid to his feet, his amber gaze fixed on Arval's dark, unfathomable eyes.

'Lord Arval, I trust you completely.' He closed the book, and lightly touched the rich leather of its covers. 'I swear it on my mother's memory and on this work of her hand and mind.'

Fathers and sons

Past midnight of the Spring Feast, Maesrhon sat on the bed in his small room in Seth y'n Carad, staring at the wall. A candle burned on the chest in the corner, dimly illuminating the narrow bed with its plain cover, the washstand with bowl and jug, the high window where the unfinished robin carving sat on the sill. In spite of the lateness of the hour, Maesrhon was still fully dressed; occasionally he would stand and take a pace or two up and down the room and then sit again on the bed. Sometimes he would put his fingers through his hair, or grip the edge of the bed, or clench his fists till the knuckles whitened, as if he scarcely knew what to do with his hands. He could hardly believe he had succeeded in his plan of attending, in defiance of his father and for the first time in his life, the ancient rites in Tellgard. It had turned out to be quite easy, when the rowdy merriment was at its height in the grand public hall, to slip out and then not return: as usual he had not been included in the top table party and no-one had taken any notice of him. Meagre though its comforts were, he was glad now that he had his own room, something that had only come about because right from their infancy Ghentar had refused point-blank to share with him. He was desperate for privacy, for silence, for solitude, so that he could try to come to terms with what he had seen and heard that evening.

Of course he had received teaching in Tellgard, heard the legends, read the stories and poems, spoken with those who kept to the old ways; he had gathered all the knowledge he could, feeling his heart turn to the light and wisdom it perceived in such lore. But, he thought now, that was nothing compared with hearing Arval lead the people in the words of the *Temennis*, feeling the power of the pledge renewed, seeing flame become flower, light become leaf as fire sprang from the seed in life returning. He felt his whole being yearn for the Starborn with a kind of famished craving, as the shrivelled stomach of a starving man aches for food. Unable to rest, he got to his feet again and then whirled around in fright as the door suddenly crashed open. Light flooded into the room from the lamp that Vorynaas held in his left hand: in the other he held his riding-whip. He was wearing his rich feast-day clothes; Maesrhon could smell the mingled odours of food, wine and smoke and hear his heavy breathing.

Vorynaas moved with slow threat into the room and put the lamp down on the chest.

'Where have you been?'

Maesrhon's heart hammered in his throat. Vorynaas had rarely raised his hand to him, more usually wounding him with words as if instinctively knowing that this would hurt the boy more; it was Ghentar, though the favoured son, who had been on the receiving end of numerous leatherings for his frequent misdemeanours, but Vorynaas had always before used his belt. Maesrhon forced his eyes away from the whip.

'I have been in Tellgard to attend the rites.'

'You dare defy me?'

Vorynaas spoke quietly, but his voice was laden with menace. Without warning, he swung the whip. The lash caught Maesrhon on his upper arm as he instinctively shielded his face and he felt a line of white-hot agony drawn there.

'Take your tunic off.'

When Maesrhon, huddled in the far corner of the room, made no move to comply, Vorynaas sprang forward and tore the garment off the boy, hurling it onto the bed and pushing the child violently from him; as he staggered against the washstand, the jug fell on the floor with a crash of breaking pottery. The whip whistled again and a weal opened up across Maesrhon's back. He sensed Vorynaas losing all self-control, but even in the midst of his panic he managed a mirthless inward laugh. You set yourself a test, he thought, and by the Starborn, now you've got one – and one far worse than you bargained for. He felt a steely resolution replace his fear. I will not beg for mercy, he vowed, and turning deliberately, he faced his foe. Vorynaas looked into the amber eyes, wide in a white face, and his own narrowed in fury.

'You little changeling!'

He threw down the whip, pulling his dress-dagger from its sheath in his sleeve; but as he advanced, his right arm was seized from behind and he was pulled off balance.

'No!' screamed Ghentar wildly, struggling with his father; but Vorynaas shook the boy off with a snarl and turned again to Maesrhon.

'By my right hand! I'll make you sorry you were ever born, as I rue the day I tied myself to your mother!'

'You were urgent enough for the marriage at one time, I seem to remember.'

The dry, emotionless tones came from behind them, where unheard and unnoticed Arythalt had appeared in the doorway.

'Grandpa! Grandpa, stop him!'

Ghentar flew to Arythalt, pulling at him, dragging him into the room. Vorynaas lowered his arm and put the dagger away. He glared round at them all.

'Ghentar, you make me sick, you sound like a girl. As for you…'
He spat the words at Maesrhon, hate still distorting his face. 'Keep out
of my sight if you know what's good for you. I'll talk to you tomorrow,'
he flung at Arythalt, and stalked off.

It was some years now since Arythalt had been away, supervising
work in the valley of the Lissa'pathor. Maesrhon had not seen his
grandfather for almost as long as he could remember, but he thought
now that he looked grey in the face and unwell, old for his years.
Arythalt stood for a moment, looking at the boys.

'You should get some salve put on those weals before you sleep,'
was all he said.

Left alone together, Ghentar and Maesrhon looked at each other
awkwardly. Eventually, Ghentar spoke.

'I heard the jug break and came to see what was going on, and…'
He looked at his brother with some surprise. 'You stood up to him
pretty well.'

'Thanks. And thanks for coming in and trying to help.'

'Oh, well.' Ghentar felt rather foolish. His voice was beginning
to break and he was smarting with embarrassment at the way it
had let him down and cracked to a childish shriek in the heat of the
moment.

'He's never taken the whip to you like that,' said Maesrhon slowly.

'No, but you know what?' Ghentar saw the chance to reassert
his manly status. 'You know what I do, if he beats me? I just remind
myself why he does it, and that gives me the edge, now matter how
hard he lays it on.'

'Why does he do it, then?'

'Same reason all fathers beat their sons. Same reason I expect I'll
beat mine too, one day,' said Ghentar, with an air of world-weariness.
'Because he knows that eventually I'll take everything he's got: I'll
take his strength, his money, his land, his status; I'll take his place in
the world, and I'll take his women. And he'll have nothing: he'll be a
feeble old man that nobody listens to and no woman wants, and then

he'll be dead.' Ghentar laughed. 'Of course it happens to us all in the end, but he'll have to face it before I do, and it puts him in a rage.'

Maesrhon digested this piece of bleak philosophy. It was like Ghentar, he thought: robust, crude and relentlessly matter-of-fact.

'How do you mean, take his women? He's had no wife, after our mother.'

Ghentar laughed again, his superiority quite restored. 'I said women, not wives. You know what men and women do together, don't you? You don't need a wife for that, as long as there are women around.' He noticed the look on Maesrhon's face. 'You're such a little boy, still,' he scoffed. 'If you don't believe me, just ask the servants or the girls at the *Golden Leopard*. Still has an eye for them, has our old man.'

But from nowhere, the thought flashed into Maesrhon's mind: *Vorynaas is not my father.* And during a night rendered sleepless by pain and shock, he pondered this new-found certainty, together with the nagging question that naturally followed: in that case, who *is* my father?

CHAPTER 18

Arythalt visits Caradriggan

'You are making very good progress, I see.'

The dry, lifeless-sounding voice spoke from somewhere above Maeshron's head.

'Thank you, sir,' said the boy politely, wondering what his grandfather was doing in Tellgard and hoping he would not keep him too long from his mid-day meal.

'Yes, I have been watching your drill-class while talking to Arval. You are exceptional for a beginner.' Arythalt's head turned as Arval himself emerged from the door at the foot of the tower. 'And Arval tells me your academic work is exemplary. Do you enjoy your studies?'

'Oh yes, sir!' The boy lit up with pleasure at hearing of Arval's praise, but seemed less than thrilled by Arythalt's next words.

'It is time to eat, so let us talk together for a while.'

Maesrhon found his grandfather, whom he scarcely knew, rather forbidding. 'Sir, they will not be expecting me at home. I always eat in Tellgard at noon.'

'I am not going to Seth y'n Carad. Come with me now.'

They walked up the street in silence. Maesrhon could think of nothing to say and passed the time in wondering what had brought his grandfather back to Caradriggan from his work away in the north. As they drew near Valafoss' house, Arythalt paused. The boy sat down on a step of the portico opposite, recalling how Vorynaas had been angered to know he had lingered there. Well, he was quite safe today, in the company of his grandfather. He glanced up at Arythalt, who was standing motionless, tall and gaunt in his sombre clothes, gazing across at the house as if his eyes would bore through its stones.

Arythalt caught the glance and directed his wintry smile at the boy. 'You see them, do you? The ghosts that walk there?'

Maesrhon was dumbfounded by the question, but even more taken aback by the bitterness he saw on Arythalt's face. He looked again across the street and saw the house door open and a man, probably the steward, come out and walk off down the street. A woman appeared at an upper window briefly, adjusting the catch.

'Ghosts?' he breathed, open-mouthed. 'I see only living men and women. What ghosts should I see?'

'A young bride, radiant in the sunshine; her new husband, tall and straight; a small girl playing, visitors from a far country, loyal servants; a woman betrayed, a man wasted by grief and regret. My beautiful wife, cut down before her time; my dear daughter, lost to me. Myself, a broken man. See them there, passing up and down the steps, walking in the gardens under the blossom, sitting by the fountain, watching the little fish in the pool, talking in the courtyard, pacing the rooms and corridors.' Arythalt gave a hollow laugh. 'Let us hope their eyes see what was, not what is. The old place has lost the elegance it once wore so well.'

Maesrhon edged away slightly, shivering, not wanting to hold his grandfather's hand now that he had listed himself among the ghosts, not wanting to hear any more of this uncanny, unsettling talk. But Arythalt suddenly began to walk on again without another word, and he trotted to catch up. Soon they were turning in at the entrance of the *Sword and Stars*. Familiar as Maesrhon was with the outbuildings, the kitchen and the staff quarters, he had never been inside the public rooms of the inn itself and he was all eyes as Arythalt took him to a table in a secluded corner and offered him his choice from the day's fare. A steaming dish of sausages and beans in a spicy sauce with vegetables was set before them, together with wine and water, a basket of mixed breads and a selection of cheeses. The boy was unaccustomed to such abundance and he helped himself cautiously, afraid that if he bolted down too much hot food he would be unable to sample the bread and cheese.

Arythalt toyed with a spoonful from the dish, breaking some flatbread into it, but drank the wine readily as if it warmed him more than the food. As he reached for the jug again Maesrhon saw how thin he was, the bones in his wrists and hands showing under the skin. He pulled the boy's cup towards him.

'Here, it will do you no harm to learn what a good wine tastes like. Make sure you drink twice the amount of water to each measure. Are you sure you will have no more food? There is still plenty in the dish.'

'No thank you sir, that was wonderful. A man must learn to control his stomach. But sir, you have hardly eaten anything. Will you not have more?'

He has certainly not learnt his good manners from Vorynaas, thought Arythalt, and it sounds as though he hangs on Arval's precepts just like his mother used to. Smiling slightly, he drank again and then set down his cup.

'Well, we will have some cheese together, and maybe some of this bread with herbs in it. There. Am I right in thinking you do not know that Valafoss lives in what was once my home? No, I thought not. I was reluctant, when your father pushed for the man to become our business associate, and my unwillingness proved well-founded when I was out-voted at every meeting and ousted from the decision-making. So it was that I was set to oversee the works in the Lissa'pathor.' He gave his bitter little laugh again. 'One must concede that the arrangement has a certain neatness to it: yesterday's man in charge of labourers with no tomorrow.'

Once again, Maesrhon could think of no reply. This was not at all the kind of conversation he had expected, this monologue of regret from a man who scarcely seemed to notice that it was a child to whom he spoke. Arythalt coughed a little, his thin hand covering his mouth, then he drank once more.

'But sir, if you are not happy away in the north, why don't you visit Caradriggan more often?' Maesrhon ventured, as the silence grew between them.

'Ah, the young see happiness as a right, but when you are older you will come to know it as a spirit that wanders the world and rarely folds its wings to settle. I can send my reports by courier. Why should I come to Caradriggan, to lodge in that monument to vanity Seth y'n Carad while Valafoss, *who has a growing family and needs more room*, despoils my old home with his unruly brood? Why walk the streets of the city where my wife and daughter breathed their last?'

Arythalt stared unseeing before him, his arms crossed over his hollow chest, his hands rubbing at his arms above his elbows. Suddenly he turned to his grandson.

'Do you find it rather chilly in here? Shall we move a little nearer the fire, now we have done with the food?'

The boy was amazed; to him the room seemed warm, even quite hot from the fire which blazed cheerily in the wide hearth, but he jumped to his feet politely.

'Of course, sir; here, I'll fetch a tray from the kitchen and carry the wine over for you.'

'No, I must have something to warm me.' He called the serving-man over and ordered mulled wine, telling him Maesrhon would come with him to get it.

When the boy returned, Arythalt was settled in a high-backed chair next to the hearth, holding his hands to the flames. Maesrhon pulled up a stool and poured the mulled wine, watching the aromatic steam wisp off it in the firelight.

'Ah, that's better.' Arythalt leaned back and closed his eyes, keeping his hands clasped around the warm cup.

Maesrhon shifted a little on the stool, not feeling fully at ease with his grandfather, but after a moment he decided to ask another question.

'Well sir, what brings you to the city now?'

'Three things. It was necessary for me to consult Arval; also,

I wish to attend the next meeting of Tell'Ethronad. I have come to a decision on the topic for debate and I intend to use my vote. And thirdly, I remembered that you would turn ten years old at the Spring Feast and I have brought you a gift. No, it is not with me here,' he added, as Maesrhon sat up, wide-eyed, 'I have left it in trust with Arval for you. He is a wise man of great integrity, to whom I now realise I owe much. You cannot do better than learn from him.'

The boy could not contain himself; he had to ask. 'Oh! Sir, what is it?'

Arythalt leaned closer, speaking quietly. 'Silver. You will need money of your own, as you grow up. You may wish to buy a good sword, or to set yourself up in business after you do your year's military service – who can say what the future may bring. Arval will keep it for you until you need it. No-one need know about it except the three of us.'

Maesrhon was stunned by this generosity. He sat up, running his fingers through his dark hair, and the loose, heavy locks lifted and sprang back again. As he raised his hands, his sleeves fell back and revealed the end of the wound made by Vorynaas' first blow with the whip. Arythalt reached out and pulled the sleeve right up. The weal was mending cleanly although its edges were a little puckered where the scabbing began.

'That will begin to itch, soon,' said Arythalt, letting the sleeve fall again, 'so try not to scratch it.' He coughed a little again, and moistened his throat with the last of the mulled wine, looking directly at his grandson. 'Your father will not raise his hand to you again. Now, I have purchases to make, and no doubt you have had enough of an old man's company.'

'Oh no, sir. And sir, thank you for my meal, and especially for your gift to me.'

Arythalt stood for a moment, looking down at Maesrhon with his wan smile. 'You're a good boy. You don't have to keep saying *sir* to me, you know. You can call me grandpa, if you want to.'

The boy was rather embarrassed, and wanted to look away, so instead he made himself hold Arythalt's eyes while he used the name for the first time. 'Yes, I would like to do that, grandpa.'

He ran off, hurrying to reach the sanctuary of his secret coppice in the fountain gardens so that he could think things over in private. It occurred to him that Ghentar had called Arythalt grandpa in his panic the other night, and he noticed that Arythalt said 'your father' and not 'Vorynaas' like Arval did. I have a brother and a grandfather, and a man who calls himself my father, he thought, but they are not a family like other boys' families. They do not deal with me as a brother, a grandson, a son: why is that? Vorynaas calls me changeling: why? What is it that is different about me?

Daydreams and disagreements

A few days later, he was sitting in an angle of the walk that topped the city wall, on the north side where the ramparts were highest. From here he could see, if he lined up the gap in the buildings correctly, the main door of the chamber where the council met, and he was keeping an eye on it, watching for the members of Tell'Ethronad coming out. If he ran fast, and used all the short-cuts he knew, he could still be back home before he found himself in trouble because Vorynaas had missed him. But mostly he was looking out to the north, wondering about the world beyond the walls, and especially the forest. It was too far away to see across the dim and gloomy miles, but there it lay. He had seen maps during his lessons and knew of the rivers that ran through the forest, flowing southwards into the great river, Lissad na'Stirfell. Everyone feared the forest, and yet it was in the valley of one of those forest rivers that Arythalt was in charge of Vorynaas' most recent, and most risky, enterprise. He had tried to find out more from his grandfather, but without much success. One phrase ran through his mind though, words which had lodged there and fired his imagination. *Dark, but full of secret life.* That was what Arythalt had said, when he had asked what the forest was like.

He would love to see the world! Ghentar was to go with Vorynaas, the next time he travelled south to the mine workings in the Red Mountains. Maesrhon knew he would not be included. Ghentar would run the business one day, and before that he was set on a career in Rigg'ymvala as soon as he was old enough to go off to Heranwark for military training. As the second son, Maesrhon would be required to do a year's compulsory service and this would most likely be spent with the border patrols. Musing on this, his lip curled in a slight smile. Ghentar had not been pleased by his younger brother's rapid progress in swordsmanship. Maesrhon felt no inclination to become a professional soldier, he simply strove for excellence in all he did. But how would he occupy his adult life? He thought of all the things and places in his own country which he had never seen: the southern regions, and Staran y'n Forgarad; the Ellanwic with all the developments in the Cottan na'Salf; the Lowanmorad, even Heranwark. In his mind's eye he saw the many rivers and roads winding through villages, towns and cities; the mountains and moors, the valleys and plains; and then he thought of what lay beyond the borders: the Outlands, Gwent y'm Aryframan, the wilderness he had seen in his dream. But how wide was the world? What lay beyond Na Caarst? Were there other peoples who lived beyond the Gwentarans?

Maesrhon sighed a little, poking at some moss between the stones with his finger. He thought of the silver that Arval held in trust for him. He supposed he would need money, eventually, but at the moment he could think of nothing he wanted to buy. Ghentar had an expensive knife and two bronze arm-rings, and had been promised a horse of his own; but for himself he had never been particularly interested in possessions and other trappings. He loved books, though. Perhaps one day he would be as skilled with the pen as his mother had been. Maybe he could spend all his life in Tellgard like Arval, teaching and studying? But it came to him that even if he lived as long as Arval – and Arval was still learning all the time, he had often said so – even then, that was not what he wanted. He struggled to put shape to his thoughts. I want, I want to look at a leaf, or a stone and see *inside* it, be able to see how it works, what it is made of; I want to look down on the world as a bird does; I want to see *through* the mountains to the lands beyond, and the mountains beyond that. I want more than knowledge and understanding. I want to *be* the leaf, or the stone, or the bird. I want to hear the scent of spring, taste the sound of the wind, touch the lamplight on falling rain, see the savour of salt and the sweetness of honey, smell the caress of velvet on my hand. He threw the little piece of moss over the rampart with a laugh. Imagine trying to explain all that to Ghentar and the other boys! They would never let him hear the last of it. But remembering recent words of Arval, he thought of something else to add to his list: I would like to see the sun and the stars. He stood up, stretching, and then suddenly noticed the group of people milling about outside the council hall. How long had they been there? He leapt down the steps and ran off as quickly as he could.

He feared the worst when he arrived panting at Seth y'n Carad to see Vorynaas with a crowd of other men already approaching the main door to the west wing of the hall. Noting out of the side of his eye that Valestron, Thaltor, Haartell and Valafoss were among the group, he made a dash for the service door, shot through the kitchen and up the back stairs, slipped across the dais of the deserted public feast-hall and so gained the corridor leading to his own room. Quickly washing his face and hands he headed for the family dining chamber; but long before he got there he could hear raised voices and much slamming of doors. He found Ghentar in furious dispute with Haartell, who was barring his way. Ghentar rounded on Maesrhon, looking for a softer target.

'You're late! And he,' gesturing at Haartell, 'he won't let me in! You're just an *employee* of my father, you can't tell me to eat in the kitchen,' he yelled, attempting to elbow the young man aside.

The door of the room was yanked open and Vorynaas appeared, glaring blackly at the two boys. Clearly, he was not in a mood to be trifled with.

'Get down there, the pair of you,' he spat, 'and do it quickly, if you want to eat this evening and be able to sit down to it. And,' he added, his own voice rising to an angry shout, 'I am conducting an important meeting in here, so keep the noise down!'

He crashed the door in their faces. Ghentar turned on his heel and made off, Maeshron following, as Haartell snickered maliciously. After they had turned a corner or two, Maeshron ventured a whisper.

'What's going on?'

'You heard him, didn't you? *He's* having a meeting, so *we're* supposed to eat in the kitchen. Couldn't even take the time to tell me himself, had to let that Haartell throw his weight about.'

'As long as I get some food, I don't care where I eat it.' Maesrhon was more interested in what was happening upstairs. 'What are they having a meeting about? And where's grandpa?'

Ghentar turned to his brother. They were outside the kitchen door now. 'Well, *I'm* not eating with the servants. You do whatever you like, little goody-goody. I'll choose what I want and they can take it up to my room for me.'

He eyed Maesrhon with dislike. The brief moment of comradeship they had shared in the face of Vorynaas' rage was over now and would not be repeated. Ghentar had tired of Arythalt's affection at a very early age, and had barely seen his grandfather since he was a toddler; but he retained vague memories of a time when he was the longed-for boy child, indulged in his every whim, and he was envious of the interest Arythalt had shown in the younger boy.

'*Grandpa* has gone to Tellgard to beg lodging for the night. Father told him he wouldn't have him under this roof, after what he did at the council meeting.'

Maesrhon stood amazed. 'Why, what did he do?'

'Wouldn't you like to know,' taunted Ghentar, who had no idea but was not about to admit it.

Public remorse

Word was not long in leaking out, however: in no time the story was all over Caradriggan that Arythalt had spoken out against his marriage-son in the council. In an increasingly acrimonious debate, many who as younger men had supported Vorynaas turned against him. Forgard had seized his chance to urge a collective change of heart. Let us extend the hand of friendship once more to our cousins in Gwent y'm Aryframan, he proposed; let us honour the As-Geg'rastigan again, let us heal the divisions which we have allowed to open up among us. Vorynaas responded scornfully, but failed to move the majority his way; vainly his supporters urged patience, to allow more time for the Cottan na' Salf to reach their full potential, to trust the findings of the assays from the workings in the Lissa'pathor valley. Back came the cry from speaker after speaker, bidding Vorynaas remember that he had promised them food, wealth and light if they did his bidding, and that ten years was too long to wait. The first vote had been evenly split, causing Arval to ask whether any man had further words to add for the council to consider, and Arythalt had risen to his feet in response.

'I am into my seventh ten years now,' he began, 'and I have lived long enough to discover what each generation finds out in its turn: that if I could turn back time, there are many things I should do differently. The nights are black and long in the darkness of Maesaldron; my health is failing and I do not sleep well. During the wakeful hours in which I have sat listening to the waters of the Lissa'pathor running south, I have resolved to take my place once more in this council, to speak to the members of Tell'Ethronad now since my future days seem likely to be short.'

Men shifted in their seats, exchanging glances with their neighbours. Some of them were old enough to remember Arythalt's younger days and saw how he had declined, and all experienced a shiver of unease at his mention of the forest; but complete silence fell as he continued.

'What I am about to say does not come easily to me. I urge you therefore all the more to consider my words carefully.' He paused, but then after the momentary hesitation went on steadily. 'I was too ambitious for status and success to heed my wife's welfare: she left her own land for me, but I turned my face against her kin. I was too greedy for wealth to trouble over much about how I obtained it: moderate voices have been heard in this chamber, but I dismissed them as outdated. I was too selfish to deal kindly with my daughter: she begged me not to make her marry against her wishes and warned me what would follow, but I compelled her and took away her happiness. I was too proud to reconsider my position: Forgard spoke me fair, but I spurned the offer of reconciliation. I was too ashamed to admit I may have been wrong: my marriage-son and his associates treated me with contempt, but I clung to their policies even after I ceased to believe they were right. I was too afraid of ridicule to stand up for the truth: Arval urged reason and moderation, but I voted against his policies. I was too cowardly to stand against what I knew was wrong: whether Arymaldur was of the As-Geg'rastigan or no, he was falsely accused, but I looked aside when we assailed him. But now, I care no more for wealth or success, pride or dignity or status. My integrity is forfeit and my shame is enduring, but at least I have courage enough to acknowledge before you all my change of heart. I have two young grandsons. I want them to have a chance for life in a land renewed, a land where light shines once more. I say to you now, remember the words of wisdom we have heard in past debates from Arval, and from Lord Arymaldur while he was among us. I have voted once already today for Forgard's proposal and I am about to do so again. I urge you all to do the same.'

He sat down, but no-one spoke. Some were watching Vorynaas as he glared with hatred in his face at Arythalt; others looked to Forgard for a lead, but his eyes were fixed on Arval; many stared in mute astonishment at Arythalt himself, who sat with blank gaze, a spasm of coughing bringing a slight flush to his wasted cheeks. At length Arval, his expression unreadable, stood and called the company to order for a second vote. This time, there was a large majority, and Forgard's supporters carried the day.

Old men

That evening, as Vorynaas and his cronies raged in Seth y'n Carad, licking their smarting wounds, Arythalt sat with Arval in his private chamber, warming his hands over a small brazier. He was dismissive of Arval's concerns for his safety.

'Vorynaas may say what he likes about me, he knows that he can neither compel nor persuade any other man to take my place. Those who labour in the valley of the Lissa'pathor think they go there of their own will, but soon find that the terms of the bargain they have made are as binding as fetters. While they work on, their families are fed and housed. If they stop, they starve; and they cannot leave, for they dare not face the forest alone. So they stay, resentful and afraid, living the life of slaves in dwindling hope that when we do strike the seam, there will be a share of the gold for them.' Arythalt laughed briefly, quelling the cough that followed with wine.

'By the time that happens, they will need more than gold to keep them alive, as they should guess each time they see me. But though there are those among them who may be lured by greed to oversee the work, none can be trusted enough to be put in overall charge. Who but myself would Vorynaas find who would be willing to go into the heart of Maesaldron and stay there?'

Arval sat silent for a while, adding some powdered herbs to the embers to create an aromatic pungency for the ease of Arythalt's chest. He knew well enough that the gold would flow eventually: he had seen the results of the assays and indeed supervised some of the tests himself. But he was also familiar with the history of a previous attempt to mine in the forest, having read the report of those who made that attempt: the secret report which Haartell had stolen some years before for Vorynaas to study. The southward-flowing river had not been named for defeat without reason, but in bitter acknowledgement of the wasting sicknesses that had, sooner or later, claimed all who had worked in its valley. Exploratory levels had been driven at the headwaters of the Lissa'pathor and also at the more westerly Lissad na'Maes. It was the eastern lodes that had promised best, but all those early speculators had paid a high price for their prospecting. Vorynaas, with his usual callous eye for the main chance, had got around the problem by using expendable labour, readily available to him as a result of his other policies. As the days darkened in Caradward and the Cottan na'Salf expanded, as shortages of food and land began to tell and money to be concentrated in the hands of fewer, more powerful and more unscrupulous men, so the number of those ever more desperate for help increased; and Vorynaas, secure in Seth y'n Carad with his guards about him and Arymaldur gone, had been ready with an offer that few of them had been able to resist: join my enterprise in the forest and enjoy free food and housing for yourselves and your families, and when gold is found you will all be rich men. He failed to add that they would all also be dead men, thought Arval, noticing Arythalt reaching again for the wine. Arval's trained medical eye had seen the mark of death in Arythalt's face too; it would be a while coming, but the tread of its feet could be heard.

'For the good of your health, you must follow my advice,' he said now, 'or why come to me for guidance at all?'

With a wave of his hand, Arythalt dismissed this. 'Heeding your words is what has kept me alive through seven years in Maesaldron, but if I never went back to the forest, the damage has already been done. I have followed your counsel and never drunk from the water of the Lissa'pathor, although it shames me to say that others do so because they must. We have sunk wells, and sought other streams that flow into the main river, but think, Arval, where the water must come from. It finds its own level and its ultimate source must be higher ground, and that means the wilderness beyond. The rain falls there too, I have seen it; and the wind blows across it. Who knows what rides invisibly upon the air?' He shuddered slightly. 'From our cradles we have heard of blindworms, but they are just a word, a legend, to those who have never seen Na Naastald with their own eyes. I have looked upon it, and I tell you I sense horrors unknown lurking there. The evil is not in the forest, it stems from the waters, from the very air itself, that comes from the Waste beyond the wilderness, which beyond the mine workings draws so near Maesaldron.' Arythalt's voice was low and tired. 'I have avoided the headwaters so far as I could, but I must breathe the air. You think I take too much wine for my own good, I know. But Arval, the seeds of death have been planted in me, and I feel their icy tendrils growing. A slow death, that creeps upon me in a tomb-like chill, freezing my blood. Wine at least warms me a little and with luck may kill me quicker.'

Arval stood up abruptly and walked to the window, turning away from Arythalt so that the other man should not see his distress. Crossing the room again, he gripped his shoulder in passing, noting with a shock how the flesh had fallen from the bones. Resuming his seat, he searched for something cheering to say.

'You spoke bravely in Tell'Ethronad. There is no need now to denigrate yourself for decisions of the past: men will remember your words today, and honour you for them.'

Again Arythalt waved this away, shaking his head almost impatiently. 'I told the truth when I said I care no longer for honour. I cannot know how long I have left, I had to speak before it was too late. Arval …' He hesitated, drawing his chair a little closer to the glowing embers. 'Arval, I am afraid that Vorynaas may send Maesrhon to take my place, as soon as he is old enough. He always favoured Ghentar as the first-born son; though regrettable, this is not unusual, but he harbours some peculiar, ugly resentment towards the younger boy.'

'Listen, Arythalt.' Arval leaned forward, his dark eyes intent; and Arythalt lifted his own at the urgency in Arval's voice, their vivid blue now faded and sad. 'I swore to Numirantoro that I would guard and guide her son, that I would keep him safe, and love him for her. I called the As-Geg'rastigan to be my witnesses, and I will keep my promise.'

Silence fell between them, broken only by a tiny rustle from the brazier as it cooled slightly. At length Arythalt spoke again.

'Arval, there is something I must ask you. Was Arymaldur truly one of the Starborn?'

'Yes,' said Arval quietly. 'Yes, he was indeed.'

This time the silence lasted a lot longer, but eventually, with a small sigh, Arythalt shared a memory with Arval.

'I remember Salfronardo telling me, many years ago when Numirantoro was still a small girl, that her hope was to see one of the Starborn. It seems, then, that my daughter may have been granted her wish.'

Arval smiled a little sadly. 'Oh yes, Numirantoro had her wish,' he said.

Unforeseen developments

Maesrhon sat on a stool in a corner of the big kitchen in Seth y'n Carad, bolting down the last of his supper. At first he had tried to make the food last, toying with a chicken leg while straining his ears to catch what the staff were whispering about as they saw to the evening tasks. He could tell by the way they muttered together, casting occasional glances in his direction, that some rumour of the day's events must have reached them. Then voices raised in animated discussion had been heard outside the door leading to the compound, and suddenly it had burst open to reveal the man who oversaw Vorynaas' brewhouse.

The fellow was married to the housekeeper, and it was obvious that he could hardly wait to pass on his news. Not even bothering to shut the door behind him, he was already calling out to everyone, his eyes roving over the scene in search of his wife.

'Hey! You are not going to believe what I've just heard, up at the *Sword*! What a come-down for Vor…'

He broke off abruptly, seeing the boy, and turned away towards the cellar stairs. Maesrhon began swallowing down his radishes and cheese at top speed, then cramming the last of the herb bread into his mouth, he sopped it down with water, grabbed an apple and made a dash for the outer door, which was still swinging loosely. As he loped around the perimeter of the compound, approaching the gate at an angle, he heard laughter from the guard-room and saw Ghentar outlined against the light within; but no-one made any attempt to prevent him leaving and he headed up the street as quickly as he could.

Half an hour later, he and Isteddar were up in the hayloft over the stables in the inn-yard at the *Sword*. Isteddar was the same age as Ghentar and had begun his Tellgard days at the same time. But coming from a family of modest means, his attendance was irregular as he was often called away to work alongside his father; he was small for his years, rather wiry in build with a plain, open face. To Ghentar he was of no account as being socially inferior, but a bond of affection had grown between him and Maesrhon. They sat in silence now, the mice rustling and squeaking in the loft around them, Maesrhon turning over in his mind the implications of what Isteddar had told him, and the other boy trying to gauge his companion's mood.

Truth to tell, Isteddar was slightly in awe of Maesrhon without being able to say exactly why. By rights, he reflected now, you'd think he was a tiresome little swot, always with a nose in his books, always has the right answer, always asking questions in class. Yet there was no side to him at all: more than once he'd helped out when classmates were struggling to understand. What about that time when Arval had set them to write lines of their own in the style of the old stories!

Isteddar could remember with painful vividness his doomed attempts to produce something reminiscent of *Carad y'm Ethan nad Asward*. Maesrhon had amazed him, and a couple of the other lads, by reeling off one suggestion after another; they had gratefully written all this stuff down, Isteddar feeling guilty in case Maesrhon had spoiled his own chances of success, only to discover that he had been able to draw on an even deeper well of inspiration for his own work. And it wasn't just bookish stuff, either. He's better than me already with the sword, thought Isteddar ruefully, and he only started this year. Still, I reckon we're about even with the bow. But there's another thing. Why does he need to be able to use a sling? You can bet Vorynaas' sons will never have to catch their own supper – imagine Ghentar wanting me to help him out with sling practice!

Isteddar picked up some loose straws from the floor and began plaiting them into a twist, taking a sidelong peek at Maesrhon. Was he unhappy about something? Sometimes Isteddar thought an air of sadness seemed to cling around his friend. He would laugh and play with Isteddar's two younger siblings and the baby, and was scrupulously polite to his parents, when he spent time with them in their quarters at the inn; and yet it was as if in some way he was a stranger among them, a traveller making just a passing visit to daily, family life. Maybe it was because he had no mother. Isteddar threw the straw plait away and shifted to a more comfortable seat on the rough floorboards.

'So, what're you thinking about?'

'My grandfather,' said Maesrhon slowly. 'You know, Arythalt. He says the strangest things, and I think he's ill. He's always cold.'

'I don't remember my grandfathers, they both died before I was born,' said Isteddar. 'But, what about the news from the council meeting? What do you think about that? What do you think will happen?'

'I think anything must be right, if Arval advises it.'

'Yes, but what about your father? Has he told Ghentar yet?'

'No, not before I came up here to the *Sword*, anyway. He was closeted with Thaltor and the rest of them, they went straight from Tell'Ethronad into a meeting of their own. I was late for supper, but by then he'd already shut the door on my grandfather. Grandpa told me the other day that he'd come down to Caradriggan to see Arval, as well as to vote in the council. I'm glad he's in Tellgard tonight. But anyway, I could see Ghentar didn't really know what the row was about.' He gave a short, rather mirthless laugh. 'I shall wish I was in Tellgard myself when he finds out. Look, Isteddar, are you sure you've got this story right?'

'Yes, honestly! The inn was packed, they had me helping out carrying orders in from the kitchen and taking the dirty pots back for washing. I was in and out for over an hour, I must have served every table and they were all talking about the same thing. Forgard was there with both his marriage-brothers, and old Woody from Tellgard with some of the other craftsmen, a man from the horse-market I know by sight; that fellow you told me about, what did you say his name was, who came into the kitchen at Seth y'n Carad when you were having your supper, he was with a big group from the border patrols; then there were more who by their accent must have been from the Lowanmorad, and Issigitsar was there too, even Poenmorcar – not that he had much to say that I heard, but there was a crowd of Outlanders and people from Staran y'n Forgarad who were all with Issigitsar. And all the talk was about the vote to change the policy of the council. They're going to send a message, or maybe even a delegation, to Val'Arad in Framstock, and they're going to send foster-kin again – well, I know some people never broke that tradition, but it was mostly among ordinary folk like us. But now they say that it was carried in council that the top families must do it too, starting with Vorynaas and Valafoss! They can't go against a vote of Tell'Ethronad, can they? So Ghentar and Valahald will have to go off in the autumn, if the Gwentarans will have them, of course.'

'What about Heranar?'

'He's still too young. You've got to be fifteen, if you're a boy, and girls go at thirteen. I say, Maesrhon. Do you think you'll go, when you're old enough?'

It was almost completely dark in the hayloft now. Isteddar never brought candles or a lantern up there because of the risk of fire, but through the tiny gaps between the boards and a missing knot-hole here and there just enough light filtered up from the lamps in the stables below for him to dimly see the hunched-up shape of his friend beside him. Eventually Maesrhon turned, and Isteddar saw the spark as his golden eyes were touched by the glim from below.

'Heranar is older than Ghentar. If my brother is to go, it must mean that the council's move was mainly directed against Vorynaas.'

A long silence followed this. The council may have brought Vorynaas to heel, thought Maesrhon, but when you shorten the leash on a dangerous dog, you bring yourself within the reach of its jaws unless you also muzzle it. He wondered what revenge was being hatched behind the closed doors in Seth y'n Carad. Then another unsettling thought occurred to him. When Ghentar is away, what will my life be like here? I may have only one tormentor then, but I will be the sole target for his wrath. He shifted his shoulders slightly to ease the itching of the weal from the lash, wishing he could share Arythalt's confidence that Vorynaas would not assail him again. Maybe his grandfather had said something to Arval. Maesrhon moved abruptly at the thought that both witnesses to Vorynaas' murderous attack would shortly be gone from Caradriggan, and the mice that had crept closer in their foraging fled in a scutter of scampering feet.

At the sound, Isteddar looked up from picking at a loose thread in the hem of his tunic. As the conversation had progressed, he had once more become acutely aware of the difference between himself and Maesrhon, of a gulf that friendship somehow could not bridge. Worried that he had caused embarrassment for the younger boy by drawing attention to the move against his father, he cleared his throat and spoke hesitantly.

'Yes, I'd forgotten that Ghentar's still only thirteen. Like me. Right. But, you know, when you're a bit older, I mean, do you think they'll send you as well? Later? It would be good, wouldn't it? Would you want to go?'

'Here.' Maesrhon gripped his uneaten apple with both hands, twisted them sharply, and split the fruit neatly through the core. He handed half to Isteddar and began to eat his own portion.

'In a way I'd like to, but it would mean leaving Tellgard and I wouldn't want to do that, I want to learn all I can from Arval. But why even think about it?' He threw his apple core into a far corner with a laugh, and immediately squeaking and squabbling broke out as the mice fastened on it with frantic nibbling. 'I won't be going. Vorynaas will assume I want to, and that's the best reason he could have for stopping me. I'd better be getting back, it's really late.'

Isteddar knew enough about Maesrhon's home life to be concerned for his friend.

'You'll never get in tonight without being stopped. Stay here, I'll get you one of my blankets. Then if you go back early and slip in through the kitchen they might not miss you.'

'No, it's all right, I know how I'm going to get in. Look at these.' Maesrhon unfastened his belt-pouch and handed two small objects to Isteddar. He turned them over, his fingers identifying metal and leather, but he looked up baffled.

'What are they? I can't see properly up here.'

'Come on down to the stable, I'll show you.'

They climbed down the ladder and went over to the wall under a lamp.

'I made them in Tellgard,' said Maesrhon, showing Isteddar two concave metal objects, each with three sharp spikes projecting forwards and with holes drilled at the edge through which leather thongs were threaded. Isteddar shrugged, still puzzled.

'Look.'

Maesrhon slipped the objects over the ends of his shoes, and tied the thongs securely behind his heels. Then he unbuttoned his tunic and pulled out a length of rope from where it had been wound around his waist on top of his undershirt. At each end of the rope there was a loop worked into the weave. He put his hands through the loops and gripped the rope.

'I can climb like this, however high the tree before the branches start, so long as the rope is long enough to go around it. My weight is spread between my arms and legs, and the spikes dig in, so I lean back on the rope and just sort of walk up.'

'That's amazing! Could I have a go?'

'Of course. Meet me up in the fountain gardens some afternoon, you can try them in the coppice.'

Isteddar grinned with pleasure, but the smile began to fade as the next thought struck him. 'How are you going to use them to get into Seth y'n Carad, though?'

Maesrhon laughed slightly; he had gone rather pale. 'Do you know that inn, the *Sun of the South*? It's empty now, gone out of business, but it's in a narrow alley just at the back of the hall, and the sign is still there. The pole is quite close to the wall. I'm going to climb up the pole like I showed you, get on to the cross-beam where the sign hangs, and jump across onto the wall.'

Isteddar was aghast. 'In the dark? Have you done it before? How wide is the gap?'

'No. But I know I can jump that far, I've measured it out and practised it.'

'But that's on the ground, this must be twenty feet up! What if you get up there and then lose your nerve? Maesrhon, don't! If you slip you'll fall onto stone...' Isteddar left the sentence unfinished; he was white to the lips now, paler than Maesrhon.

'I have to: I have made a vow and set myself to it.'

'Are you mad? Why are you doing this?'

Maesrhon laughed again. His eyes were golden in the lamplight, a strange exaltation in his face, at odds with his tender years. 'I am afraid to do it, so I must. I must always conquer my fears.' He looked directly at Isteddar. 'I must be ready, as far as a man can be, to face what must come, one day.'

'What will that be?' whispered Isteddar; he felt sick.

'I can't say, I don't know. But I know there'll be something.'

Isteddar swallowed and wiped clammy hands on the sleeves of his tunic. 'Look, I'll come with you. Let's just go to the gate and get the guards to let you in, I'll say it's my fault you're late. Or if you won't do that, let me come with you when you climb. We'll bring a bale of straw, then it won't be so bad if... I mean, I'll be there to help if anything...' He tailed off helplessly.

'No, I've got to do it alone. But thanks, Isteddar.'

CHAPTER 19

In the south

Ghentar walked along the gritty trackway, little drifts of dust spurting out from under each footfall and settling again behind him. The air was dusty too, but Ghentar scarcely noticed how it stung his eyes, which were smarting already from unshed tears of humiliation, anger and bitterness. From away up the slope to his right, distant noises could be heard, thuds and the rattle of falling stones as work went on even through the night. He gave no heed to this either, trudging along with his head down, occasionally kicking savagely at a pebble to vent his feelings. At last he slowed down a little. He had walked quite some distance, but there was no point in going too far. After all, where was there to go in this barren landscape? But Ghentar could not bring himself to return, not just yet. He saw a boulder a few paces ahead, and went to sit on it. Rage surged over him again as the uneven surface of the stone brought a painful reminder of the beating Vorynaas had given him. He stood up, shrugging off his cloak and folding it to make a softer seat. It was warm enough, here in the south, for him to do without it. He sat on the stone, staring at the ground before him, giving in to his black mood.

If Ghentar had paid more attention to his lessons, or been a boy who enjoyed reading, it might have occurred to him to look up and regret, or at least to imagine, the stars of the south that once would have blazed above in the summer darkness. The sky was blank now, except where a hint of the louring cloud cover reflected the lights on the hillside. These shone out, a couple of score of them, bright but with a hazy ring around each where the dust hung in the air. Ghentar sat with his back to them and felt a sharp discomfort where a stone in his shoe was hurting his left foot. He poked at it with his finger to no avail, then with an exclamation of annoyance began to undo the straps of his summer sandal. Everything seemed to be purposely vexing him, he thought, full of self-pity, as he emptied out the stone and dropped the sandal on the ground, returning to his brooding. Suddenly he leapt up, hopping on his right foot, yelling.

'Hey! Drop it! Bring it here! *Here!*'

Unseen and unheard by him, a small skinny dog had crept up, grabbed his sandal and made off with it. The dog stopped at his shout, turned with the sandal in its mouth and pranced gleefully. Ghentar picked up a stone and hurled it at the dog.

'Drop it, you mangy flea-bag!'

The dog watched the stone miss by several yards, put the sandal down, shook itself vigorously and then, with the merest glance at Ghentar, picked up the shoe again and trotted away. Now Ghentar saw what he had failed to notice previously, a group of people walking by in the distance. *Sigitsaran*, he assumed, heading south-west for the Outlands beyond the Red Mountains. They had come up from behind him, walking soundlessly, half a dozen pack animals among them burdened with goods, tents, sleeping children. The dog headed towards them and Ghentar set off in pursuit, but he was not used to going without shoes and his bare foot hampered him. He stopped and fired more stones at the dog.

'Leave it!'

He stood helpless and suddenly his whole being flooded with hate. 'Nomad bastards!' he screamed. 'Filthy Outlanders! Why don't you clear off where you belong! Get out of our land and...'

He broke off, his insides contracting in sudden fright, as the small caravan of *sigitsaran* halted. Dimly he saw faces turned towards him and then he heard a series of whistles. The dog immediately trotted back a few paces, put the sandal down and then loped away to join its unseen master. Mocking laughter floated quietly on the night air as Ghentar, hating himself too, now, for the brief moment of fear he had felt, hobbled over to retrieve his shoe. It was slimy from the dog's mouth and he handled it with disgust, pulling up some scrubby leaves to clean it off as best he could. He walked back to his seat on the boulder, unable to prevent a couple of tears from trickling slowly down his hot and dusty cheeks.

He had so looked forward to this trip south with his father, but it was all going horribly wrong. Who cared about boring mines and stuff? The business would be his one day anyway; he could pay other people to run it for him when the time came. And by my right hand, thought Ghentar, won't I make sure they are all too afraid of me to even think of cheating me. But that only made him remember the blow that had been dealt to his cherished plans of a military career. How could his father have agreed to send him to Gwent y'm Aryframan? Ghentar rubbed his eyes angrily as fresh tears of frustration welled. So what if the council had voted for it, why hadn't Vorynaas just refused to send him? The messages had gone off to Framstock before they left Caradriggan, and none of his horrified begging and pleading had made the slightest difference. Condemned to exile among peasants, Ghentar thought dramatically; by the time I get back I shall be a yokel myself, I'll be too out of practice to be accepted in Rigg'ymvala! And now he had been humiliated in front of Haartell, by tomorrow everyone would know... I hate Haartell, thought Ghentar. I hate my father, he's only taking it out on me because the council made a fool of him.

There was an element of truth in Ghentar's reading of Vorynaas' motives, but he was his father's son in being unable to acknowledge his own faults. He had been warned, privately, that Vorynaas was aware of his gambling activities, and left in no uncertainty of what would follow if he stole from his father's purse again. Fright had kept him away from the dice for a while, but on the night of the fateful vote in Tell'Ethronad he had given in to the temptation to visit his friends in the guard-room. While Vorynaas raged behind closed doors with Thaltor and the others in Seth y'n Carad, and Maesrhon talked with Isteddar at the *Sword and Stars*, the young men of the guard had encouraged Ghentar to run up a tab. Eventually it had come down to himself and one other, and he had gambled and lost again. In desperation he had promised that if he could not raise the money, he would pay with one of his arm-rings, and shortly before the inspection party set off for the south, he had been forced to make good his pledge. Any hope that his father would not discover what he had done had evaporated after supper that evening, when Vorynaas, irritated beyond endurance by the boy's sulky behaviour and constant pestering to be excused the exchange of foster-kin, had dragged his son from his stool by the sleeve and missed the ring. Ghentar could not decide what was worse: the beating that followed, witnessed by that smirking Haartell and the others who were present, or the loss of the thing he valued most in the world.

'Now, listen to me,' Vorynaas said as he buckled his belt, breathing heavily. 'You will buy that arm-ring back, as soon as we return to the city. And since you have no means to do so, we will sell your horse to raise its price. And,' he added as Ghentar protested, 'I shall stop your allowance until I have recouped the cash.'

Ghentar looked up in despair, his usual high colour mottled with pallor. He had managed not to cry out during the beating, but the blow to his heart hurt more than the bruises to his body or his pride. The promised horse had been purchased for him shortly before they left Caradriggan, and had gone a little way to assuaging Ghentar's outrage at his imminent exile.

'Oh please, not Traebenard,' he begged; and then suddenly shock, pain and the effects of an overlarge supper combined in a wave of nausea that swept over him, and he hunched over, vomiting helplessly.

Vorynaas looked at his son with distaste, gesturing for a servant to come forward and deal with the mess. The boy was a problem, no doubt about it, but maybe this would a lesson he learnt for once. It would do no harm to hammer it home, though. He stroked his beard, glancing around at the other men who were present.

'Well, how about this for a wager. I'd say your backside will be more than tender after tonight – too sore for you to ride for a couple of days at least. But if you can manage to stay in the saddle tomorrow without complaining, I'll buy the ring back and you can keep the damned horse.'

An outburst of laughter greeted this, in which Vorynaas joined heartily; Ghentar, wiping his mouth with the back of his hand, left the company without a word and stormed out into the sullen night. And now, standing up gingerly from his seat on the boulder, he set his teeth. I'll show him, he vowed. I'll show them all, him and Haartell and those peasants across the border too.

A confession

Velvety darkness settled gently over Salfgard. The last few visitors, guests, friends and helpers, had straggled off to their homes, calling final farewells and good wishes, and still Ardeth lingered outside. Just beyond the buildings of the farm and home place he leaned on the pasture fence, enjoying a warm glow of reminiscent pleasure at the Midsummer Feast now over, but already letting his senses re-adjust to the sounds and scents of the fragrant summer night. From behind him came an occasional rustle as roosting swallows moved in their nests under the eaves and he fancied he could just catch the tiny flutter and squeak as bats hunted overhead. Small watery noises floated up from the valley where the river, shallow in the dry weather, chattered on its pebbly beach; from the woods a blackbird, roused in sudden fright, gave its alarm call and then settled again. A drift of air brought him the sweet smell of tedded hay, a suggestion of rich earth as the dew began to fall, even a hint of elderflowers and the first hedge roses. Ardeth drew a deep breath and looked up at the sky; here in the north-west the summer nights were short and it would not be long before the first signs of dawn appeared over the mountains even though the last traces of the sunset could still be seen beyond Gillan nan'Eleth. Stars shone above, steady and blue overhead, seeming almost close enough to touch, but remote beyond guessing near the horizon, twinkling and trembling in the haze where earth and sky met. A light footfall approached and Fosseiro joined him; Ardeth put his arm around her shoulders and for a while they stood silently together.

At length she drew him away and they began to walk slowly back towards the house.

'I know what you're thinking about,' she said.

Ardeth laughed softly and pulled her closer. 'You usually do.'

They passed inside and Ardeth latched the door while Fosseiro lit a small lamp and set a shallow pan over the charcoal burner. She sat down with Ardeth at the old kitchen table, passing him a steaming cup of milk warmed with a spoonful of clover honey in it.

'Here you are. Sip it slowly now, you've had a lot of rich food today. You don't want a disturbed night.'

With a smile, Ardeth did what he was told. 'My, what a doddery old man you've got on your hands these days,' he teased, 'but there's nothing wrong with my memory yet, you know. Weren't you going to tell me what I was thinking about?'

'Well, that's easy, isn't it? By the time Harvest-home comes round, we'll have the youngsters from Caradriggan with us.'

'Yes. I think we've done the right thing. Someone has to make a start to repair matters between the two countries although I don't think Val'Arad would have agreed even then, if I hadn't said I would have them here.' Ardeth leaned back in his chair, stretching his arms and shoulders. 'It'll be quite like old times, what with Heretellar and Ancrascaro still here, and more new ones coming up from Framstock and the Rossanlow. But considering who's in the party from Caradriggan, it will be hard on Geraswic, poor fellow. We'll not see much of him in Salfgard while they're here.'

Fosseiro glanced across at her husband. 'I suppose not. I hoped once that something might come of it, after he got friendly with Mag'rantor's marriage-sister, but...' She tailed off, shaking her head a little. 'Maybe I should never have persuaded you to let me interfere, when he first met Numirantoro.'

Putting down his cup, Ardeth took Fosseiro's hand. 'Now look, that wasn't interfering, the damage was already done there, before we ever tried to help. It might have worked out with Numirantoro – it wasn't your fault that it didn't, how could you know what would happen in Caradriggan? And anyway, you were right all along about Geraswic: don't you remember how you said he wasn't the hail-fellow-well-met we all took him for? You're a shrewd judge of character, to spot that. I must say, it's an unusual man who will hold to a lost ideal all his life, like he has done.'

Ardeth hesitated, running his fingers through his hair in the old gesture and looking down at his hands. 'But that's not all I was thinking about, outside there.'

'Well?' prompted Fosseiro, after a lengthy silence.

'The world is so beautiful,' said Ardeth eventually, 'and sometimes, like tonight...' He shifted in his chair and cleared his throat awkwardly. 'If it's true, what some say, that the Starborn need never leave it, then they are fortunate indeed. But one day, *I* must leave it. Fosseiro, we're almost into our seventh ten years now. We both have health and vigour still, but time runs a little further every day: one of us must go first and leave the other behind. I find myself thinking, let it be me! You're stronger than I am, you would still be able to hold your head high and carry on... but I... though I love this earth with my whole heart, I think I couldn't bear it without you.'

He ran his hands through his hair again, his eyes still cast down. 'I'm a very selfish man, to wish for this and to tell you of it.'

This time the silence lasted so long that eventually he looked up, to find Fosseiro watching him with a smile. As she leaned forward, the silver strands in her hair shone in the lamplight.

'Ardeth of Salfgard, selfish? I don't think so. There's no need to blame yourself for your wish; indeed if I'm to be honest with you as you've been with me, I've had similar thoughts myself.'

As Ardeth smiled back, Fosseiro stood up, came round the table to Ardeth and raised him to his feet; he put his arms about her and rested his cheek on her hair.

'Well, well, here's another who's not the plain farmer he seems,' she said. 'Ardeth, why spoil the present by worrying for a future we can't know anything about? Come on now, it's late, let's go up to rest.'

Their embrace tightened; Ardeth could not trust himself to speak. Finally with a sigh they broke apart and Fosseiro went to pinch out the lamp. She too said nothing further, but into her mind came an old memory: Numirantoro, eight years old, looking up at Ardeth in the doorway. *Arval says we should be very careful of what we wish for, because wishes can come true in ways we least expect.*

Happiness

Maesrhon opened the door of the study room next to the library and went in. There was no-one in there, and for a while he sat on a seat looking out through one of the high, narrow windows rather than reading or taking down any of his current work from the shelves. He was enjoying the happiest weeks of his life. With Vorynaas and Ghentar away, the oppressive atmosphere had lifted from his home: not that he was spending much time there except to sleep, the chance to stay longer in Tellgard day after day was one he had seized immediately. Valestron was still around, but took little notice of him, and while Ghentar was away in the south, his brother's cronies Heranar and Valahald did not bother him either. He had even been able to attend the Midsummer rites at Tellgard without fear. The boy's face changed subtly as his thought rested on the memory. He loved the beautiful words, the ancient symbolism, the way in which a deep, calm solemnity was somehow charged with life so intense that he almost felt it spark in his hair. He stood up suddenly, as if lifted to his feet by the way his heart seemed to lighten within him. Maybe, when Ghentar was away in Gwent y'm Aryframan, he could come to the other ceremonies at Tellgard too! With the thought, he took a jerky pace or two, wanting to run, run until he took flight on the wings of the energy that filled him. But as he turned away from the window, his eye fell on several books lying neatly piled on the shelf next to the place where he kept his own work. They were beautifully bound, and surely he recognised one of them? Going closer, he saw that he was right: the book at the bottom of the pile was the one that Arval had shown him in his study – the one his mother had made. Maesrhon looked at his hands to make sure he had washed them properly when he cleaned up after spending time in the wood workshop. Arval had said he could look at all his mother's books after he turned ten, and he would soon be ten and a half, so… carefully he lifted down the top volume, carried it over to the table and sat down.

Time went by unnoticed as he turned the pages, poring over the words and pictures they contained. It was difficult to decide which he liked best. This one for instance, seemed more straightforward than some of the others: *V is for vixen: voracious and venturesome, vital and vivid.* He enjoyed the selection of words, approving how they matched their subject, feasting his eyes on the picture of the animal: bright-eyed, intent on the hunt, determined however audacious the quest to find food for her cubs. Maesrhon went back to the beginning of the book and considered *A is for apple tree: ancestor of all our autumns.* This, he understood, had layers of meaning beneath its words. And there were other entries with a similar undertow of significance, he realised as he looked again at *P is for ploughland: proud, plain and plentiful, the parent of people* and *O is for oak: old, older, oldest: outlasting oathtaking, outliving ourselves.* The pictures were beautiful: the apple tree laden with blossom, standing at the edge of woodland clothed in all the different greens of spring; the oak, massive, ancient and enduring, was alone on a slight rise with a village at the foot of the slope. Maesrhon remembered that his mother had spent her foster-years in Gwent y'm Aryframan. Was that where these images had come from? If so, it must be a lovely country, he thought. Ghentar was lucky to be going there; he would feel silly later, when he thought back on the huge fuss he had made about it.

Suddenly boy-like, he hugged himself with slightly malicious pleasure at the memory of Ghentar being forced into something he badly wanted not to do. But there, Ghentar had come out on the right side in the end. It was to soften the blow that Vorynaas had bought him a horse of far higher quality than he would otherwise have been given. Traebenard, Traebenard, thought Maesrhon dreamily; as soon as I saw him the name came to me, only fitting for his dark, smoky-grey coat, the flame-shaped white blaze on his forehead, the light way he moves and handles, the brave, fiery spark in his heart and eye. Privately, he was astonished that Ghentar had used the name that he had suggested, but he still thought the horse was wasted on his brother. He wondered whether, while Ghentar was away in Salfgard, he would ever be allowed to ride it. Probably not, but even the chance to help look after it would be good. He glanced down again at the book before him, now open at *H is for harvest: heavy and hearty, hauled home in happiness.* This time, he felt sure that the picture was inspired by scenes his mother must have known during her time in Salfgard.

Maesrhon had noticed how Vorynaas was displeased when the delegation returned with the news that Val'Arad had said Salfgard was the only option open to the party for fostering from Caradward. Why was that? He knew his mother's uncle Ardeth lived there and he looked more closely at the people in the illustration, wondering if any of them were based on real life. Could the man with the pitchfork be Ardeth? He screwed up his face, working out the relationship. This Ardeth, he must be the brother of his grandfather's wife, about whom he could remember hearing very little except that she died young and was very beautiful. Arythalt was away back to his work in the forest now, but it occurred to Maesrhon that Arval must remember Salfronardo, so maybe he could tell him about Ardeth too? He went over to the window again and looked out, but there was no sign of Arval; he must be still busy in the medical wing. With a sigh, Maesrhon closed the book and replaced it. Time was running on, he had better head for home. Arval had promised that they would talk together at length, one day: I wish that could be soon, thought the boy.

Inside Thaltor's mind

Thaltor called time out, and walked over to the conduit in the corner of the exercise-ground at Tellgard to get himself a drink. He splashed water over his head, shaking the drops from his hair. The day was warm, and beads of sweat broke out again on his forehead; he wiped them with his forearm and poured another beaker of water over his face, tilting it back with his eyes closed. Coming out from the colonnade, he called the boys to order.

'All right, that's enough sitting about, let's see what you've learnt. You beginners there, I hope you've been paying attention because if not, you're in for an unpleasant surprise. You lot!' he barked at the older lads. 'Get yourselves sorted, I want you each to pick a partner from these young ones and give them a practice workout. And to make it more interesting, there's a silver quarter for the first novice to win his bout. Some hopes! Come on now, let's have the first three pairs matched up here.'

He sat down on the bench, letting his thoughts run on after his own exertion, occasionally calling out in correction or encouragement as he watched his charges demonstrate their abilities. Vorynaas and the rest of them were due back in Caradriggan today. He was glad he'd not joined them. Like Ghentar, he rated the attractions of industry and business very low compared with the entertainment on offer in the city; and besides, after what had been said, he'd have found being cooped up with Valafoss and Vorynaas day after day hard to take.

'Next three pairs!' he called, his mind still running on the divisions that had opened up between them in the aftermath of the vote in Tell'Ethronad. Vorynaas had been ranting and raving at the ingratitude of those who had turned against him in the council, and then Valestron had put his spoke in.

'You've only yourself to blame.' Valestron had a light, rather knowing voice, he always sounded as if he was on the point of laughing at some secret only he knew. 'You made a bad mistake, the night we got rid of Arymaldur. Promising that the sun would return, that was rather reckless, wasn't it? The one thing that wasn't in the plan, the one thing you couldn't guarantee – and it's come back to haunt you, because it hasn't happened and now they're all blaming you for it. Not like you, Vorynaas, to lose control like that.'

And before Vorynaas had had a chance to respond, Valafoss had felt called upon to have his money's worth. 'He's right, you know. You used to laugh at Thaltor for getting so worked up about Arymaldur that he couldn't think straight, and then you did it yourself!'

The memory still rankled. Thaltor sat fuming at the thought that they had been laughing at him behind his back all these years and then came to with a start as whoops and clapping broke out among the watching youngsters.

'Come on, sir, pay up!'

'Yes, a silver quarter you said, and Maesrhon here's won his match!'

He looked up; an older boy was grinning sheepishly, acknowledging his defeat. It just *would* have to be Maesrhon, wouldn't it, thought Thaltor with annoyance. 'I didn't see, sorry,' he said dismissively. 'Match up with somebody else and let's see if you can do it again. I'm not paying up on a fluke.'

This time he paid more attention, but his thoughts were still elsewhere. Vorynaas had tried to patch things up between them, wanted him to travel up to Salfgard several times a year while Ghentar was there, use the excuse of checking on his progress with the sword as a chance to see how the land lay in Gwent y'm Aryframan. Yes, Valestron was more the type for that kind of work, but he'd already got on the wrong side of this Ardeth and some of their other leading men, and Vorynaas wasn't sure he trusted him completely; but Thaltor now, didn't the two of them go way back, and anyway, he wanted the best for Ghentar, and Thaltor *was* the best, no question about it. He scowled as he watched the six boys now in action, noting with half an eye that Maesrhon was proving a very creditable match for his new opponent. After what had been said, did he trust any of them, even Vorynaas? Maybe he was going behind Thaltor's back to Valestron, telling him there were special duties lined up for him that no-one else was good enough to do. Divide and rule. I'd give a lot, thought Thaltor, to get one back on Vorynaas.

Suddenly, cheering erupted again and a foil flew through the air and bounced ringing on the ground. The other two pairs stopped sparring, congratulating Maesrhon and teasing his disarmed opponent. Thaltor looked at the boy standing there, foil lifted before him, the other arm still raised in counterbalance. Who did that remind him of? He stood up slowly, eyes narrowing as he measured the lad with his gaze, seeing him properly as if for the first time. So, he thought, you little cuckoo! What will it be worth to you, Vorynaas, to keep me quiet about the evidence of another occasion when it seems things didn't go all your own way? With a burst of laughter, he began digging in his pouch.

'Here,' he said. 'Twice is no fluke, so I'll pay twice what I wagered. Never mind the quarter, here's a half-*moras* for you.'

He flipped the silver coin across to Maesrhon, and caught another boy by the arm. 'All right, that'll do for today. You, put away the equipment and bring me the store key. I'll be in the small hall, I'm just going for a quick bite.'

He strolled off, and the boys milled around, laughing and bantering as they gathered up the foils.

'What're you going to do with it?' said one of them to Maesrhon. 'How about drinks in the *Sword*?'

'No, let's go up to the *Golden Leopard*,' said one of the older boys, nudging a friend.

'Oh, that's not fair!' protested a couple of the younger ones. 'They won't let us in there!'

'Don't worry,' said Maesrhon, 'I'm not going to do anything with it.'

They stared at him. 'How do you mean? Going to keep it all for yourself? Not going to *save it*, surely?'

'I don't want it.' Maesrhon stood looking down at the half-*moras* where it lay in his hand. Thaltor tried to cheat me at first, he thought; he knew I'd won the quarter, and he tried to get out of giving it to me by making me fight again. But he didn't give me the half because I won twice, he gave it to me when some idea came into his mind. I saw his face change when he looked at me. He closed his hand on the coin and his strange, golden eyes lifted to his classmates. 'I'm going to give it to Arval, for Tellgard.'

'Oh, trust you! I don't believe it – who but Maesrhon, eh? Come on, let's leave him to it. Just a minute, I've got to take the key back to Thaltor...'

The various comments, half-joking, half-exasperated, hung in the air as the group dispersed, leaving Maesrhon alone, uncomfortably aware of the shadow of disquiet which the incident with Thaltor had thrown over his last day of freedom.

Shattering news

The following evening, he sat with his brother and Vorynaas at supper, doing his best to enjoy the food that was set before them. He had been spared the ordeal on the previous day, as Vorynaas had taken the opportunity to catch up on events in the city with Thaltor, Valestron and various other associates. Tonight, as he ate his meal, he thought he detected a change in the relationship between Ghentar and Vorynaas, but could not quite put his finger on what it was. Maybe it's because of that business with the arm-ring, he thought. His brother had told him the story, placing great emphasis on how he'd ridden Traebenard the whole day after his beating, even though by evening he was bleeding and in such pain that for the following three days he'd had to walk and been unable to sit down even for meals. Vorynaas had kept his promise: the horse had returned to his stable and that afternoon he had bought back the arm-ring for his son. Ghentar was wearing it now, flaunting it a little by making sure it showed below his sleeve, but he was complaining again about having to go to Salfgard in the autumn.

'Ghentar, *will* you be quiet!' said Vorynaas in exasperation. 'Here, have some more wine and stop whingeing about what you can't change.' He refilled both their glasses. 'I've already said you can take the horse with you, and Heranar is going as well, so what more do you want?'

'I don't want to go at all! It's not fair for me to be stuck up there in the backwoods while he,' Ghentar pointed with his knife at Maesrhon, '*he* stays here in the city. Why can't he go instead of me?'

Vorynaas turned to look at Maesrhon. 'Him? What makes you think he's staying here? I can't be doing with him moping about the place on his own. I wouldn't be responsible if I had to see his changeling's face looking at me day after day. He's going too, and they can like it or lump it in Salfgard: they'll have to put up with him and Heranar, even if they are under-age. You've not got much to say for yourself tonight,' he added, directing a snort of sardonic laughter at the younger boy.

'No, sir.'

'Not going to tell me about the half-*moras* I hear Thaltor was fool enough to give you yesterday? Thought you'd say nothing and spend it on the quiet, eh? Where is it?'

'I gave it to Arval, for Tellgard.'

'Oh, how typical! See what I mean?' said Vorynaas to Ghentar. 'You, if you've finished, clear off. I've got things to talk to your brother about.'

Maesrhon looked down at the uneaten venison and savoury dumplings that still lay on his plate. It was good, and he'd been hungry, but the food had been untouched since the shattering news that he was to be sent away with Ghentar, taken from Tellgard, parted from Arval. His hands were clenched, hidden under the table, his stomach contracting upon itself, his heart pounding. Without a word, he got up and left the room.

Vorynaas watched him go, and when the door closed behind him he turned back to his elder son.

'Now see here, Ghentar,' he said with a man-to-man air, 'don't think I'm going to take this snub from the council, and condescension from those peasants in Framstock, lying down. I want you to keep your eyes and ears open while you're in Salfgard; you might get the opportunity to travel around the country from time to time and I want to know everything you can find out. Thaltor will be coming up every few months, you can report through him. Keep your head down, don't antagonise anyone, and say nothing about this even to Heranar, understand? I'm going to tell you now something no-one else knows: I swore I'd get rid of Arymaldur, and I did. When I make a vow, I keep it; and I'm going to have the last word with Tell'Ethronad, and put the Gwentarans in their place once and for all. It may take some time, but I can wait. Knowledge is power, so I'm relying on you, son. Gather all the information you can, *stay away from any gambling*, and when you come back, I'll be planning the next moves. By my right hand, there are those who will live to rue the day they opposed me.'

Solace

A piercing whistle penetrated Maesrhon's gloomy thoughts as he squatted at the side of the courtyard, putting off the hour when he would have to go back to Seth y'n Carad. He turned slowly, vaguely aware that shouting had preceded the whistle, and saw one of the kitchen staff from Tellgard, a cloth over his arm, gesticulating in his direction. He got up and hurried over, following the man who disappeared back through the door as soon as he saw the boy move. In the kitchen all was noise and bustle as the hour approached for the evening meal; appetising smells wafted around as the meat sizzled and new bread was brought out of the ovens. Maesrhon suffered a bitter pang of envy when he thought of those who had the good fortune actually to live in Tellgard, either because they were on its staff or because they lived too far away to travel to their homes during their studies. The man who had hailed him was over at a side bench, beckoning him impatiently.

'Come on, come on, hurry up, boy! Are you daydreaming, or asleep, or what? Don't stand loitering there, I want you to take this tray up to Arval. He's got a guest with him tonight, they're eating privately in the tower. Mind now, the tray's quite heavy, don't you dare drop it.'

His face was red and sweaty from the heat as he glowered at Maesrhon: a busy kitchen was a stressful workplace. Then suddenly, as the boy pushed back his sleeves and took hold of the tray carefully, he laughed and ruffled Maesrhon's hair.

'Now, don't look so down in the dumps, I didn't mean to snap at you. Here, have these for later.' He took half a dozen sweet biscuits from a nearby plate, and popped them into the pouch at the boy's belt. 'They're good, they've got spice in them. Just mind how you go on the stairs, all right?'

In Arval's study, a table was set for two, with wine in a flask and a water jug already waiting. Maesrhon unloaded his tray: a tureen of broth, two sticks of onion bread, a vegetable tart, a small loaf with a slab of butter and a little crock of honey. There was no sign of Arval's guest; perhaps he was still washing. Maesrhon stood back, behind one of the chairs, waiting for the signal to leave and wondering why Arval remained standing himself. A little trail of steam escaped from the lid of the tureen, bringing a hint of beans, roots and herbs in a rich meaty stock.

'As host, I cannot begin to eat before my guest,' said Arval, 'so perhaps you would serve him with the food?'

Maesrhon looked about him in some confusion: how could he know how much the man might require? He looked apologetically at Arval. 'Sir, where is your guest?'

'At the moment, he's standing right behind his chair. I wish he would sit down, then we could get started,' said Arval with a rather mischievous smile.

The boy gaped at him, his face lighting up as he realised this was going to be a day to remember, after all. 'But, Lord Arval! You can't mean me?' He looked down at his clothes. 'I'm not dressed properly, I've not yet been home to change.'

Arval waved this aside and sat down; Maesrhon followed and self-consciously helped himself. He nodded when Arval remarked that he understood Vorynaas and Ghentar to be out that evening, telling the old man that they had been invited to eat with Thaltor at the *Sword and Stars*.

'My grandfather took me there too, once,' said Maesrhon, 'and it was very good. But this is better.' A thought struck him. 'I think they don't know in the kitchen that it's me who's your guest tonight?'

'Possibly not. It seemed to me an excellent opportunity for us to have that talk we promised ourselves earlier in the year. But that can wait until after the meal, and I'm telling you now, I don't want any of this food left. They can get very temperamental about that sort of thing in the kitchen.' He caught Maesrhon's eye conspiratorially and the boy giggled with delight. 'Have plenty of this honey, I think you'll like it.'

The honey was thick and golden, heavy with the scent of flowers. Maesrhon ate it with the soft new bread and felt his mouth tingle with its sweet, fragrant taste.

'Sir, thank you for my supper, it has been an honour for me. I've never tasted anything as good as this honey.'

'Would it surprise you to learn that it comes from Salfgard?'

'Oh …' He dropped his eyes at this reminder of his troubles.

'I want to ask you something,' Arval continued, apparently changing the subject and ignoring Maesrhon's change of mood, 'about the time you spend here in Tellgard. What would you say you enjoy the most?'

Maesrhon considered this carefully. 'I like everything, really, but maybe learning is what I like best. Apart from the ceremonies, of course, but that's different. You wouldn't say you liked them or enjoyed them, they're too important: I'd need different words to say how I feel about them.'

'Not your sword-practice, then?'

'Oh, the famous half-*moras*! No,' said Maesrhon, who was beginning to relax and feel more at ease, 'I enjoy the classes, and I do try hard because, well, to be truthful I always want to be the best, but I don't see that sword-skills will be much use to me. I mean, who would I be likely to fight? It's Ghentar who wants to go to Rigg'ymvala; I'll just be in service for a year, which probably means time on the border patrols. I'm more interested really in improving with the bow and the stave, and Isteddar – do you know him, his people work at the *Sword* – he and I practise together with our slings.'

'Hm. Now, tell me why you don't want to go to Salfgard.'

There was a long silence, but eventually Maesrhon gave part of the answer. 'I don't want to leave Tellgard.'

'If I said I wanted you to go, would that make you feel any better about it?'

'No, but it would make me feel different. If you say I must do it, then I will go without a word, I would think it was my duty. But Lord Arval, why do you want me to go away?'

Try as he might, the boy could not quite prevent the note of plaintive hurt sounding in his voice, and Arval spoke gently to him.

'I don't want you to go away, *Is-torar*, that's not what I said. But I think it will be good for you to see more of the world, to meet Ardeth, to know what it is like to live with other youngsters. These are all things you would never have, if you stay here. And there are many things you will be able to learn in Salfgard which you cannot study properly, even in Tellgard; for there you will see the sun and the stars, and the blue sky over all; and the best storytellers are found in Gwent y'm Aryframan: you will hear all the old tales told as they should be, and see the rites performed on feast-days as they were in the old times.'

He paused to take a drink, smiling inwardly at the look which was stealing on to Maesrhon's face: Ardeth would see Numirantoro in the lad. 'You were telling me you had spent some time recently with Arythalt. Did you get on well together?'

'Grandpa? Oh, I think so, yes. But I think, well, I think he's not an easy man to know. I liked him, but he's very strange. I mean, he says strange things. He's difficult to talk to. He seems sad, and I wondered whether he was ill.'

'He was always a reserved man, but you are right, these days his melancholy is profound. And you've a shrewd eye for symptoms, I'm glad to see you must have made good use of your time in the medical wing! If Arythalt will heed the advice I have given him, he may live for a few years longer; but his illness is fatal, and he has lost interest in life: a combination that tends to speed the approach of death. I hope indeed that the two of you will see each other again; but, little son, he, with Ghentar and Vorynaas, are all the family you have known. Ardeth and his wife Fosseiro have no children, but in their home you will find friends of your own age; and don't forget that Heretellar and Ancrascaro are already there. Ardeth and Fosseiro will be as a father and mother to you: they will love you not only because they see your own mother in you, yes, and Ardeth's sister Salfronardo too, but also for yourself. Your mother loved Ardeth dearly, as he did her; the years she spent in Salfgard were the happiest of her life as I know because she told me herself. The air of Salfgard is sweet, Maesrhon; the skies are wide over Gillan nan'Eleth, the far peaks of the Somllichan Asan glow in the sunset, Ardeth's house is warm and welcoming. You should breathe that air, see the mountains under the sky, take this chance for earthly happiness. One day you will be faced with a difficult choice, and you will find it easier to make, if you understand it better; your time in Salfgard will help you to reach that understanding. Now,' he got to his feet, taking a swift glance at the boy as he sat lost in thought, 'it's getting late. Time you went home.'

The boy was still solemn; he looked up directly into Arval's deep, dark eyes. 'You said just now I would have to make a choice, one day. What choice is that?'

Arval shook his head. 'Remember what I told you about learning and knowledge being two different things? You are only ten years old, there will be time enough for us to talk again when you come back from Salfgard.'

'But I will be gone for so long! For years and years!' Panic gripped Maesrhon as he gazed up at Arval. 'How do you know…'

It was impossible for him to voice his fears: if he spoke the words he might give them power. Arval was so old, what if he was dead by the time he came back to Caradriggan?

'Listen, *Is-torar*. I promise you we will talk again, by the As-Geg'rastigan I swear I will be here when you return.'

'How can you know, Lord Arval?'

Arval smiled. 'You'd be surprised at just how much I know, let me tell you!'

'No, I wouldn't,' said the boy with stubborn devotion.

'Well, maybe not. But anyway, run along now, young man. I don't want you climbing that tavern pole again.'

Maesrhon gave a little gasp of astonishment as the words registered. 'How did you know about that?'

Then catching the amusement in Arval's thin face, he began to laugh, and the old man joined in heartily as they moved towards the door, quoting together *"You'd be surprised at how much I know!"*

CHAPTER 20

Waiting in Salfgard

A rather subdued air hung over the breakfast table in Ardeth's house, in marked contrast to the cheerful bustle that usually accompanied the meal. Fosseiro was sipping at a hot drink but most of the others were just sitting about, exchanging a word now and again but showing no inclination to begin the day's work. Heretellar alone, who had been rather late to come downstairs after the previous day's festivities, was still eating, ploughing methodically through a hearty plateful in a steady, appreciative manner much in the Ardeth style. Ardeth himself was staring somewhat vacantly out of the window, tapping his fingers on the arm of his chair. Eventually Heretellar came to the end of his meal, pushed his plate away and looked up in some surprise at his table companions.

'Bit quiet this morning, isn't it?'

'Welcome back!' said Ancrascaro. 'When you've got food in front of you, I don't think you'd notice if a thunderbolt fell in the farmyard.'

'I like to concentrate on Fosseiro's cooking and not spoil it with talking. But one thing I have noticed is that there's still no sign of anybody arriving from Caradriggan.'

Ardeth swung back to lean on the table. 'Yes, I wonder what's keeping them. I hope nothing's gone wrong; I thought they'd have been here in plenty of time for the harvest feast.' He stood up, stretching, and then ran his hands through his hair with a huge yawn.

'Well, I suppose we'd better get on with things. My head's a bit sore this morning. I don't seem to be able to stand up to these late nights like I used to.'

Fosseiro and Ancrascaro both laughed at the same time, but only Fosseiro's amusement was directed at Ardeth. Ancrascaro was thinking how strange it was that even though all of them had mixed feelings about the expected newcomers, somehow they felt let down by their non-arrival and the day had a sense of anticlimax to it. Neither she nor Heretellar had ever been very friendly with Valahald or Ghentar, although they had been careful in what they had said in front of Ardeth and Fosseiro, who after all were related to the younger boy. Fosseiro had picked up on this in her perceptive way however and had talked to Ancrascaro privately.

'Apparently the boy's the image of his father,' she told Ardeth later. 'Not like Numirantoro at all, according to what Ancrascaro says.'

'Mm. But don't forget she hasn't seen him for quite a while. What else did she say?'

'Well, I gather the lad's been allowed to do pretty much whatever he wants all his life. And I don't think Heretellar is all that keen on Valahald, although Ancrascaro says maybe he was just in with a bad crowd when they were all youngsters together in the city.'

'The thing is though, it's going to be such a mix of ages. This Valahald should have already been here, if he was coming at all, so he's going to be older than the other boys coming up from Framstock; yet Ghentar's only thirteen. I don't know how they're all going to fit in together.'

Ardeth was mulling all this over in his mind later in the morning, as he sat in a patch of autumn sunshine mending a pile of wattle hurdles. He looked up at the sound of hooves approaching at speed, and into the yard came Cunoreth, riding in his usual flamboyant style and whooping with delight when he saw Ardeth. He was in his late teens now, popular throughout the district and warmly regarded by both Ardeth and Fosseiro. Not much sign now of the skinny little lad who arrived here in Mag'rantor's arms, thought Ardeth. Almost all traces of the Caradward accent had vanished from Cunoreth's speech, and he had grown up to take a place in Salfgard almost like that which Geraswic had once occupied, although he was a much more extrovert young man with a strong line in strange hairstyles. Ardeth looked up at the braid which dangled down at one side of Cunoreth's face, although the rest of his hair was loose, long at the nape but cut short on top where his brimless, pointed cap was rakishly perched, and shook his head.

'Honestly, your hair! And now all the lads will be wanting these ridiculous pig-tails… oh, all right, you can laugh; I suppose I'm getting old and past it, eh? Well let me tell you, young man, if you keep on riding my horses like that, you'll find yourself going on foot for a while. What's the huge hurry about?'

'News, Ardeth, news.' Swinging himself down from the saddle, Cunoreth hitched the horse to the rail and dropped on to the bench. 'It's all right, I only ride him like that for the last furlong or two.'

'Yes, I know you like to make an entrance. Got your public to think of, after all,' said Ardeth grumpily, but the two of them grinned at each other all the same. 'Go on then, what's the news?'

'Well, the first thing is, the youngsters coming up from Framstock should be here by tomorrow. They waited in the town, thinking the Caradriggan party would come there to join them, but when there was no sign of them, they decided to set off separately. However, I can now reveal, thanks to my unparalleled knowledge of what's going on in the world and my wide network of reliable contacts on the roads, the whereabouts of our other missing guests! Hang on, I'll be back in a minute.'

He jumped up and ran over to the house, emerging shortly with ale, two chicken legs, a leek and cheese turnover and a large hunk of bread.

'I'm absolutely starving, it's amazing how hungry you can get when you're riding.'

Ardeth laughed heartily as he helped himself. 'I never thought I'd meet anyone who was keener on his food than me, but you're in a class of your own,' he said. 'Come on now, finish the story.'

He knew from past experience of Cunoreth that if he wasn't quick, his young friend would clear the lot. Maybe it was a legacy of his brush with starvation as a child, but Cunoreth could eat anyone under the table and yet he was as thin as ever, tall though he'd become.

'Well,' continued Cunoreth through a mouthful of bread and chicken, 'obviously they must have decided to avoid Framstock. They've come up the side road, but it seems they've been making very heavy weather of it. They've got as far as Rihannark, where they've had to stop for a spot of running repairs; then the word is they're going to use the bridge and come on up from there by the main road. I reckon they'll be here in about three or four days.'

'Why is the side road such a problem? The weather's been good, and it's not that late in the year,' said Ardeth, thinking he could guess the reason for the party's avoidance of Framstock: no-one likes to be gawped at when they've had to humble themselves. However he wondered whether he was right when he heard the next thing Cunoreth had to tell.

'Because there's such a lot of them, with two wagons. Apparently there's children, and horses and I don't know what all travelling, armed guards and all sorts. Do you want the rest of that pasty?'

'Go on, finish it up, you young pup. Armed guards, really! You didn't happen to hear whether anyone by the name of Valestron was with them, did you?'

Cunoreth shook his head. 'No, that's all I found out from a friend of mine who saw them all in the *gradstedd* at Rihannark. He passed me as I came up and gave me the news. Who's this Valestron?'

'Oh, a young trouble-maker I used to know. I doubt he'd want to come back here. But how can there be children in the party? We're only expecting the two lads.'

'Couldn't say. I'd better see to the horse, Ardeth.' He moved off towards the stable and then turned back. 'Got any idea what Fosseiro's cooking for mid-day?' he asked, ducking into the doorway with a laugh as Ardeth threw a piece of broken hazel after him.

Welcome home

Maesrhon never forgot any details of his long journey from Caradriggan, and his arrival in Salfgard was printed for ever on his mind. The party entered Ardeth's lands and approached his dwelling half-way through the afternoon: a calm, sleepy afternoon of golden autumn sunshine. Enjoying the warmth on his back as he trudged, Maesrhon nonetheless detected a hint of the frosty night that was likely to follow. As they got further north, he had noticed the changing climate and several times had been wakeful with the cold. He shivered a little, hoping there would be somewhere warm for him to sleep when they arrived. There was a pause while the captain of the escort set them all in order, telling Maesrhon to get into the second wagon and ordering Ghentar curtly to make sure he was in control of his horse. And so they came up the last slope of the road: Valahald, Heranar and the servants in the first wagon, Maesrhon in the second with all the tents, gear and stores; three guards at the rear and three in front, with the captain and Ghentar, riding on Traebenard, at the head. They came to a halt in the wide courtyard, and got down from their seats in front of a silent and, to Maesrhon's eyes, surprisingly large number of people who had come out to greet them. He identified Ardeth immediately, recognising him from the man he had seen depicted in his mother's book, and spotted Heretellar and Ancrascaro too, although he could see they had not noticed him.

All Maesrhon's senses were at full stretch, sampling and savouring each of the new messages that came to them: he could see smoke rising not far off, where he guessed the village must lie; its scent drifted to him, mingled with the earthy farm smells and a tantalising waft of something savoury cooking. His eyes darted everywhere, taking in the byres and outbuildings, a forge, barns, the large handsome home-place with gardens beside it; but his gaze was drawn most of all to the distant mountains, now beginning to be touched with the sunset. He dragged his attention back to what was happening. Ardeth had shaken hands with the captain of the escort, and with Ghentar, and glanced admiringly at Traebenard, giving him a rub on the nose. He appeared friendly but it seemed now that he was unable, or unprepared, to accommodate such a large party himself, and clearly had not expected Heranar.

'He's my friend, and Valahald's brother, and my father said he could come,' announced Ghentar.

'Did he now. And I suppose it was him who said you could bring your horse, too?' I must warn Cunoreth off this animal, thought Ardeth, what a beauty!

'Yes, it was,' said Ghentar, his voice performing an upward leap of nerves and causing him to glower defiantly.

'Well, we can talk about that later.' Ardeth ran his hands through his hair in a gesture Maesrhon was to come to know well, and turned to the leader of the party. 'Look, I think the best thing is this. You've brought tents, and cooking gear and all, you say? Well if you take the wagons on up to the village, you can park them beside the inn. Tell them in the *Malt Shovel* that I sent you. They'll probably be able to find beds for you and your six fellows, and the others can pitch in the wagon park. There'll be no problem about the horses.'

Several moments of activity followed, while baggage and bundles for those who were staying were unloaded from the wagons, and then with much creaking and jingling they turned and made off in a cloud of dust. Ardeth turned to Ghentar. 'Now about this horse of yours. We'll find a place for him in the stables but you'll have to look after him yourself, all right?'

Ghentar shrugged. 'I suppose so. My brother can muck him out, I'll see to his exercise.'

Maesrhon saw Ardeth's face change as Ghentar's words registered. 'Your brother? Is he here as well?'

'Of course. My father's a very busy man, he couldn't do with him staying at home. That's him there, his name's Maesrhon.'

For the first time, Ardeth noticed the slight figure standing apart from the others behind the heap of baggage, where the dust from the turning wheels had drifted on to him. He walked over and Maesrhon saw the shock leap into his eyes, followed by a swift spasm as if a sudden pain had pierced him; he put his left hand momentarily to his chest and winced a little. Ardeth was only of middle height, and Maesrhon was tall for his age; when he lifted the boy and set him on top of the pile of bundles, they were face to face. They looked at each other in a moment of silence, then a wide, delighted smile spread over Ardeth's features. 'Welcome to Salfgard, little son,' he said. 'Welcome home.'

Maesrhon thought he would never be able to sleep that night. He lay in bed in the loft room he would be sharing with the other boys, his mind still racing as it ran over everything that had happened and all the people he had met since he arrived. He could see already why Arval had wanted him to come here: he had taken to Ardeth and Fosseiro immediately and never in all his life had he either eaten such a meal as Fosseiro had served that evening, or been welcomed into such a large and friendly gathering of people of all ages. It would surely be impossible to sort them all out or remember their names! He was glad there were other new youngsters apart from the group from Caradriggan. Ethanur and Framhald were both fifteen, but seemed younger to him: Ethanur was from Framstock, but Framhald hailed from the Rossanlow as did Cottiro, who was thirteen, and all three of them had arrived only a few days earlier to begin five years of fostering at Salfgard. A large number of people seemed to live on Ardeth's holding, as well as working there. Maesrhon remembered a smith and several apprentices, a carpenter and a wheelwright as well as the farm workers, but their names had escaped him. Oh, there was that very thin, tall young man with the braid, Cunoreth, and his uncle Mag'rantor from the village, but he had forgotten the names of Mag'rantor's wife and three children and many more besides who lived in Salfgard itself. He turned over in bed, wondering if the other boys were asleep, or lying wakeful like himself, hearing an owl hoot as it hunted overhead and a dog barking in the distance. Apart from that, it was so quiet compared with the city. Briefly, before the doors were closed for the night, he had looked out and seen the starry sky: that was another thing Arval had promised him. If only Arval could have been here too! Remembering what Arval had told him of Gwent y'm Aryframan, he was already looking forward to hearing the storytellers and he resolved fiercely to learn everything he could in this new place, so that Arval would be pleased with his progress when he returned. The next thing he knew, roosters were crowing and the other boys were jumping out of bed to see what was happening in the farmyard below. Maesrhon looked out to see a pale blue morning sky and frost sparkling on the thatched roofs in the early light, sunlight which was still such a wonder to him each day. Life at Salfgard had begun.

Dawn in the hills

A hint of woodsmoke curled around Ardeth's dreams and caused him to open sleepy eyes; finding himself alone in the small tent, he poked his head out to see Maesrhon sitting beside their camping fire. The boy had stirred it up from its overnight slumber and fed it, and water was heating, but his face was tilted to the early morning sky. He turned with a smile, but Ardeth had seen the rapt look, the golden eyes drinking in the sunlight. Maesrhon was past thirteen now, and three years in Salfgard had seen quite a change in him. He was stronger and taller, half a head above Ghentar these days, and as his face began to show its adult bone structure, so the resemblance to Numirantoro was not quite so marked as when he was a child. Smiling back as he took the cup of warmed water the boy held out to him, Ardeth nevertheless still saw the likeness and marvelled as he frequently did at the difference between Maesrhon and Ghentar. Surely, there were never two brothers so completely unalike, in appearance, character, manner; Ardeth sometimes had difficulty even thinking of them as siblings at all.

'I think I will remember this journey into the hills, and especially this morning, all my life,' said Maesrhon.

That was another way in which he reminded Ardeth of his mother: Numirantoro too had often surprised him by the unexpected things she said when she was a child.

'Before I left Caradriggan, Arval talked to me,' the boy went on, 'and said my mother's years at Salfgard were the happiest of her life. Now I can see why that was.'

Ardeth sipped his drink, screwing up his face against the early sunlight as he gazed down the valley and blaming the dazzling rays for the way his eyes watered. 'I would be honoured if that was so, but sad to think it means she was less happy after she left us. She was like one of the Starborn, your mother; everyone here loved her dearly. You are very like her, little son.' Standing up suddenly, he pulled Maesrhon to his feet. 'Come on, let's have a bit of a splash and wash away the night.'

The stream that ran down the valley from the heights behind them swirled into a deep little pool just below their camping place. It was too small for swimming, but the volume of water was sufficient to give buoyancy and an exhilarating sense of the motion of the current as it swirled and babbled over the stones of the stream bed. It was cold from the snows above and after a few moments of laughing and spluttering, Ardeth and Maesrhon climbed out and pushed the water off themselves, letting the warm air dry them. For a man into his seventh ten years, Ardeth was still strong and hale, tanned and muscled from years of hard work in the open air, with just a hint of thickening about his waist and ribs. His glance fell upon two healing scars on Maesrhon's side and he hid the frown of disapproval and misgiving on his face as he pulled his shirt over his head. It was bad enough having to put up with a visitation from that oaf Thaltor twice a year, without him leaving the marks of his sword on the boy. And if that wasn't an old whip-cut right across the lad's back, he'd never seen one. For the hundredth time, Ardeth wondered just what was afoot in Caradriggan, what kind of home Maesrhon had there.

The two of them sat by the fire and ate their breakfast of bread and cheese.

'I wish you hadn't let yourself in for that bout with Thaltor,' said Ardeth after a while, 'especially when he was just egging you on to do it. Why did you let him talk you into it?'

'No, that wasn't the reason,' said Maesrhon. 'I agreed because I realised I was afraid to do it. And it turned out well in the end, didn't it? I was only slightly hurt, so he didn't beat me by much; and now I won't be afraid again, so I won the real fight after all.'

'Well, I don't like having to put up with him, even if it is only twice a year, and I don't like him either. He's arrogant and unintelligent, a combination I find particularly unpleasant. I don't care how good he's supposed to be with the sword, there's nothing wrong with the training we provide at Salfgard. If he was as good as he's cracked up to be, there'd have been no need for him to hurt you at all.'

'Oh, he did that on purpose. I don't like him either, but believe me,' said Maesrhon, noting that his great-uncle was more perceptive than perhaps he had given him credit for, 'if we've got to have anyone coming up from Caradriggan, rather Thaltor than Valestron. Or Haartell – if he was expected, Ghentar might even have learnt to swim to get away from him! He hates him.'

Ghentar had flatly refused to join in when their first summer at Salfgard had brought swimming and diving in the waters of the Lissad na'Rhos. Just below the village there was a series of small falls in the river, which then broadened out to be wide and slow-flowing with water-meadows beside it. Neither Maesrhon nor Ghentar could swim, but as soon as he saw all the local children disporting themselves, paddling about in the pool among the ducks and the boys daring each other to dive over the falls, Maesrhon had been eager to join them. By midsummer, when picnics and games were afoot in the meadows, he was at home in the water as anyone else.

But as he sat there on the hillside finishing his meal, Maesrhon was thinking rather of what Thaltor had said to him. It had been on the last day of his most recent visit when he had produced two real fencing swords, light and sharp, and challenged anyone to take him on. Even Ghentar had had the wit to know he was outmatched, but Maesrhon had known, somehow, that the challenge was for him alone. He and Thaltor had stripped to the waist and faced each other without shields or face-guards; he had been sick to his stomach until their eyes locked and they began circling, then the world had contracted to a six-yard space in which there was no room for fear. Of course Thaltor had disarmed him in the end and had him at his mercy, but he had learnt from the experience.

And Thaltor had looked him over, flipped him a full silver *moras* this time with a crack about the rate having gone up and said, 'Not bad. Keep it up, and you could be as good as your father was. And he was the best in Caradriggan, in his day.' Then he'd looked at Ghentar, who was glowering sulkily, and back at Maesrhon, and laughed in a most peculiar way before walking off, leaving Maesrhon to give the silver to Fosseiro and get a scolding for his hurts while she dressed them.

The boy dragged his attention back to the present. Ardeth was beginning to pack up their camp, picking up on the mention of Valestron to agree that even Thaltor was preferable as a visitor.

'Valestron and another lad were the only two I ever sent packing, but he was the worst of the pair. Geraswic threw him out of my parents' house, made him wait for the wagons from Caradriggan at the *Salmon Fly* in Framstock. There was no love lost there, I can tell you.'

Maesrhon sat back on his heels where he was collecting the tent-pegs into their bag, and pushed the loose dark locks back from his face. 'Uncle Ardeth, everyone talks about Geraswic, but he never comes to Salfgard. Why have we never seen him since we came? Is he too busy in Framstock?'

'Well, it's a sad tale to tell. Geraswic's my steward, as you'll know; he was with us at Salfgard from when he was younger than you are now, a grand fellow. He never looked at another girl after he met Numirantoro, but she had to go home a year early when her mother, that was my sister Salfronardo, died unexpectedly. You know Fosseiro and I have no children of our own, so we took Geraswic for our son and I made him my heir. He went off down to Caradriggan to ask for your mother's hand, but when he got there, she was already married to your father. Poor fellow, he's never told me more than the bare bones of what happened, but it changed him. He's never been the same man since. He never married, and he wanted me to disinherit him because of that, but I wouldn't hear of it: I told him, he's the son of my heart. But when he knew that you'd be coming here, he couldn't bear the thought of seeing you. Of course, we thought it was only Ghentar who was coming, and there's nothing of Numirantoro in him that I can see, but if Geraswic saw you...'

'Was it that she didn't want to marry him, or she wouldn't wait for him?'

'No, no, it was an arranged marriage: your grandfather and Vorynaas wanted a closer tie between them. But as to Geraswic, who knows now? When they were youngsters together here, we all regarded them as pledged, and he obviously expected to bring Numirantoro back from the city. I can see him now, setting off all spruce in his courting clothes.' Ardeth sighed. 'It was a different story when he came back.'

The boy digested this for a few moments. He had always assumed that Numirantoro's death was the reason for the name he bore, but now a new idea had formed in his mind, one that could explain many mysteries. 'Was Geraswic ever,' he asked slowly, 'was he ever in Caradriggan again, after that time?'

Ardeth glanced up in surprise. 'Oh no. That was the first and only time. He swore he'd never set foot there again.' Wondering why Maesrhon seemed a little crestfallen, Ardeth finished folding the tent into its carrying straps. 'Well, we have got ourselves into a gloomy frame of mind! We can't sit about here yarning all morning, so let's get moving, little son.'

Not looking up from buckling his pack, Maesrhon said shyly, 'Arval sometimes calls me *Is-torar*.'

'Does he indeed!' Ardeth laughed as the lad turned and his amber eyes glowed with sunlight. 'One can see why he might, but then again, he might have reasons he doesn't tell. There's no man wiser than Arval na Tell-Ur.'

'Did Arval teach you, too?'

'He certainly did, and my father before me.'

'But… your *father*… how long ago, I mean, how old do you think Arval must be, then?'

'Who could know? But there, I've thought for a long time that old Arval might be one of the As-Urad. It would account for a lot, when you think about it.'

Maesrhon was staring at Ardeth, his business with the day's preparations forgotten. '*Really?*' His mind raced, spinning with all he would ask Arval when the time came. Why, why did Arval have to be in Caradriggan; if only Tellgard could be moved to Salfgard! 'That's how he knew he would still be there. He promised me we would talk when I go back to the city.'

'Well, you won't go wrong if you stick by Arval. Your mother thought the world of him.'

'He showed me some books she'd made. There was a picture of you in one of them!'

Ardeth sat down again, sensing that this was a moment to let the boy's talk run on.

'I think a lot of what she put in them, the words as well as the pictures, came from her time here. Arval asked me what I liked best about my studies in Tellgard, and then he told me why he thought it would be good for me to come to you in Salfgard. He said knowledge and learning are not the same, that a man can't begin learning too soon, but you have to train yourself before you are strong enough for things that are easy to learn, but hard to know.' Maesrhon glanced across at Ardeth, remembering what Arval had said about the choice which he would one day have to make; his great-uncle was picking at his hands, not looking at him, and he decided to leave this from his tale as he continued.

'He told me he had promised my mother that he would guard me and guide me, and he promised me that one day he and I will talk at length. He has been like a father to me, he has always told me the truth, he was right about Salfgard and about you and Fosseiro. You've given me a home here such as I never had before.'

So Numirantoro must have lived to see the child, at least, thought Ardeth. *Easy to learn, but hard to know*, I wonder what that means. There's a mystery here somewhere, if I could just put my finger on it. When it seemed that the boy had no more to say, he decided to turn the conversation. 'Well, I'm no Arval, but I'm going to ask you a similar question. What do you like best about Salfgard, now you've had a fair while to get used to it all?'

He grinned in anticipation: most of the boys said the food, or the hunting, or the games at the festivals; some of the older ones occasionally mentioned the freedom of being away from their own fathers, and the bolder spirits sometimes voted for girls they'd taken a fancy to. Maesrhon had picked a bloom of the sweet pink upland clover and was absently sucking the nectar from the petals, staring into the distance.

'I love it all, I hope you and Fosseiro know that without my telling it. But the best things ... I think the best is what I can't get in Caradward: the chance to study the open sky by day and night, the old stories and traditions, the ceremonies in their seasons, the light, the space, the air. Everything that's special to Gwent y'm Aryframan, everything from trust in the As-Geg'rastigan to skill with the sling and the sparring-stave. Please don't misunderstand me if I say that the farm isn't so important to me, because I love that too. I do like working there, I want to learn all the tasks of the turning year, to understand growing and rearing, to absorb the patience and wisdom that comes from the earth; but somehow I know that my life won't be spent among the fields. That's why I wanted to come away with you for a few days, to see the wild places and learn how a man must live when he has only himself to rely on in finding food and shelter. Of course I realise you can't be away from the farm for too long at a time, but if there's anyone you know who would be willing to take me, I would be keen to learn more of the wayfarer's skills.'

Ardeth lay back on the warm grass and laughed. 'I walked into that one, all right,' he said, 'but I suppose I should have known what to expect from a serious young man like yourself. Do you know what Ethanur said, when I asked him? "Fosseiro's spicy sausages." Oh dear, oh dear.'

'Well, he has a point. They're pretty good,' said Maesrhon, standing up with a smile as Ardeth wiped a tear of mirth from the wrinkles round his eyes with the back of his hand. He got to his feet too, and looked about him.

'I know just the man for you, *Is-torar*,' he said, 'and we'll work our way westward and look him up. Old Torald, lives a couple of valleys away in the heart of Gillan nan'Eleth. What he doesn't know about fieldcraft isn't worth knowing. He's a man of very few words, but he'd have some to say for sure if he'd seen us sitting about half the morning like this. Come on, let's get moving.'

They set off, climbing steadily and saying little as their way became steeper and stonier. As they walked, Maesrhon was turning over in his heart the old stories and lore he had learnt since coming to Salfgard, and when eventually the two of them stopped at noon in the shade of a twisted hawthorn, he asked the question that was uppermost in his mind.

'Uncle Ardeth, what lies to the north of Gwent y'm Aryframan?'

'The wilderness, so far as I know. It stretches beyond the forest too. Even north of Caradward, Na Caarst must lie waiting, but who would go there to prove the truth of the tale?'

'My grandfather Arythalt has seen it. He works in the forest at the mines. I asked him what Maesaldron was like, and he said it was dark but full of secret life.'

Ardeth shivered. 'He must be very different from the man I remember in our youth. The Arythalt I knew was a city-dweller through and through.'

'Yes, Arval says he's a changed man these days. But anyway, surely men must once have dared the wilderness, or how did folk come to this land from Rihannad Ennar?'

'Who knows, now? Tradition says the Nine Dales lie to the north, but tells no tale as to where the road may be found. Look, little son, this living off the land is all very well but I for one have no objection to my wife's cooking if I can get it. We've got one link of the famous spicy sausage left. Do you want to share it with me?'

Learning with Torald

Torald turned out to more than match Ardeth's description of him. They found him at his home-place, a short distance away from a small hill hamlet, nestled in to a south-facing slope on an acre or two of level ground. He was of middle height and wiry build, with not a pick of spare flesh on him; leathery and tough and so tanned by wind and weather that the corn sign on his arm was barely visible. His hair was greyish and receding somewhat, but neither this nor anything else about the steading gave a clue to his age or status. Maesrhon saw another man dealing with some ferrets, a woman at a water-pump and a couple of youngsters in an outbuilding, but never found out whether they were family or servants, or indeed any details about Torald's domestic arrangements. Ardeth outlined the reasons for their visit, explained who Maesrhon was, invited the boy to summarise his request in his own words, and finally asked directly whether Torald was agreeable to the idea. The man heard them both out in silence, and then sat on beside them for a long while without comment as the sun gradually turned west. His face was expressionless, but his eyes, almost hidden among the folds and wrinkles, observed Maesrhon closely. The youngster, noticing that his uncle seemed unperturbed by the long silence, waited quietly himself, feasting his gaze on the valley opening below him and letting his mind rove far away, beyond the heights towards which the sun was sinking. Eventually Torald rose and signed to Maesrhon that he too should stand; turning him directly towards the sun, he looked into his eyes. Finally he spoke.

'I will take the boy for half a month and send him back to you for Midsummer.'

So Ardeth tramped off alone, taking most of their gear with him, for the first thing Torald did was to go through Maesrhon's equipment and provisions and reject most of it. He was left with his knife, sling and staff, plus water-bottle, meal-bag and an assortment of fish hooks. Disconcerted, but determined not to show it, he embraced his uncle with words of love and greeting for Fosseiro and then turned all his attention to whatever he could learn from Torald.

He soon found that not much time would be spent on hunting and food-gathering. Torald put him through his paces with the bow and sling, inspected his snares, tested his tracking abilities and skill at gutting, skinning and cooking, and pronounced himself tolerably satisfied while recommending constant practice on the grounds that there were also plenty of areas for improvement. He concentrated rather on imparting the signs of sky and landscape, showing Maesrhon how to acquire a feel for a change in the weather, how to pick out the best way through strange country, how to read the lie of the hills for a likely pass. Skills of improvisation and camp-building were a speciality too: how the same basic technique could be adapted to produce a windbreak, a firescreen, a fishweir, a shelter, a basket, a trailtrap; how to make a fire, whatever the circumstances; how to keep it alive from one camp to the next if necessary; how to ensure a water supply even if no spring or stream could be found. He taught mainly by practical demonstration, but when he had instruction to impart, it was terse and memorably direct.

'A man in the wild dies as easily as a little bird on a winter's night, but the dying is harder for a man because he knows what awaits him. He has only one advantage that will keep him alive, his wits. This is what makes a man, the ability to reason, to plan, to weigh up risk; so keep your wits sharp, and keep them awake. If possible, never take a risk. If you must, think it through first and be ready to deal with the different ways it may turn out. Never be parted from your pack; but just in case, always carry a separate wallet of basic tools, preferably two of them. Never get wet or cold, and especially not both together; but be clear in your mind what you will do if this happens, and do it immediately. Keep yourself and your camp-sites clean. Pace yourself. Make sure of shelter first, then a water source, then food supplies.'

So the time with Torald passed; and the days took them through thick woodland, across bare passes, around the heads of valleys above the field line, up steep slopes, and into many a stony little dale with only birds and the sigh of the air for company. One evening they sat together by the fire enjoying half a dozen small trout and Torald showed Maesrhon a new method of cooking meal: instead of seething it in the pot, he produced a shallow metal plate, heated it over the fire and then poured a stream of gruel on to it. In seconds, it had firmed into a thin disc that could be flipped from the plate and eaten hot; it was crisp and brown and went well with the fish. Torald lifted a wry eyebrow at Maesrhon's appreciation.

'Getting bored with plain meal, eh?'

'No, it's not that exactly, but it's good to know how to vary it occasionally.'

'I've told you before lad, the difference is in here.' Torald tapped his forehead with a brown finger, and seeing Maesrhon's expression, leaned forward for emphasis. 'Wits. A sheep eats the same thing every day. It stays alive and healthy so long as there's grazing for it, and it never gets bored or wants anything different because it hasn't got the brain for it. Now a man, if he eats the same thing every day, doesn't matter how well-nourished he is, his brain starts telling him he's not content. So as I've said before, make your wits work for you. If your stomach's satisfied, don't let your head tell you different. But if the chance comes for a change, there's no need to be like the sheep that eats grass all its life. Wits, boy: they're your best weapon, so keep them sharp; your best defence, so keep them strong; your greatest wealth, so see you enrich them every day.' He cooked another couple of meal-cakes and then set the plate aside to cool.

'And another thing. There's some kinds of food need watching, like this, which can burn in a couple of minutes if you don't heed it. And there's food that makes a smell when it cooks. Even meal makes more smell when it's griddled like this than if you just heat it in the pot; and if you get grease in the fire from meat or fish, you'd be surprised how far down the wind the smell of that can drift. So if you're on your own and you think there might be danger, stick to basics. Wits: don't waste them on cooking when you need them all for keeping watch.'

Maesrhon thought all this over carefully. Torald had so little to say that when he opened up like this it made quite an impression, as was no doubt intended. They finished their supper in silence and Maesrhon cleaned up, but before they withdrew into their shelter for the night, he had a question to ask. 'Torald, is it true that there are blindworms in the wilderness? What are they?'

A little spark of light showed for a moment in Torald's deep-set eye as he turned a shrewd gaze on the lad. 'Who knows? Do you know any man who has walked there to try the truth of such stories?'

'No, but I thought you would know.'

'I have seen Na Caarst, and to me it seemed barren and hopeless. A man who walked in the wilderness would be alone, maybe beyond even the help of the As-Geg'rastigan. If any creature could live there, doubtless it would be suited to survive in that pitiless waste; but whether there are such beings, or whether men have begotten them in the dark corners of their minds, who can say.'

As the half-month drew to its close, they began bearing in a slightly easterly direction but had travelled further north than Maesrhon had ever been before. Each day he expected an open view to stretch before him as they climbed to the crest of the next ridge, only to find further heights beyond. One morning they awoke to find a dusting of frost crystals crisping the short grass, and breakfasted on bowls of steaming hot beans to drive away the dawn chill.

'The poor man's meat,' said Torald, handing Maesrhon his portion. 'All the nourishment of flesh, without the expense of rearing it or the risk of hunting it. And that's not the only advantage. What does this tell you?' In the one hand he held a bag of dried beans, in the other his bowl of hot food. 'Feel the difference in weight? When they're dried, they don't weigh much, and they keep well. You can carry enough for a long march. And there's something else you might want to bear in mind.' He ate a few mouthfuls, glancing about as the day opened in the sky. 'The plants are hardy and they grow quickly. If you ever have to set out without knowing the hour or the place of your journey's end, it could be worth sparing the time to rest on the way while you sow and harvest a crop to keep you on your feet through another season. A wayfarer's staff can make a serviceable digging-stick.'

Their eyes met in a hint of wry amusement at the mutual lack of surprise from both teacher and pupil. When the meal was over and the camp dismantled, Torald took another glance around the sky and then hoisted his pack to his shoulders.

'This is about half-way between my place and Salfgard. We should both be home for midsummer.'

'May I spend time with you again?' asked Maesrhon, taken aback by the suddenness of this parting.

'You know where to find me. Give my greetings to Ardeth.'

And with that, he nodded farewell to the lad and set off at a steady pace, not looking back. Maesrhon stood alone on the hillside, excitement and apprehension coursing through his veins. He was unable to completely quell the little flutter of fear at the thought of making his way alone through country he had never seen before; but there was only a small difference between this emotion and the thrill of anticipation at the prospect. Torald obviously thought he was up to it, and Ardeth clearly trusted them both; so what was he waiting for, with the morning still fresh before him and the earth so sweetly untrodden beneath the blue sky? And he had a lot to think about too: his days with Torald had left him with much to mull over, as well as new skills to try out, for which quiet and solitude were needed. Settling the weight of his pack so that the straps would not chafe, he started walking, remembering Torald's advice about pacing himself. Then he checked, and on a sudden impulse, bent and picked a harebell where it trembled in a cranny. With a smile of delight at the day, the world and his place in the sun, he tucked the flower into his hair behind his ear and walked on.

Attack

A couple of days later, the sun was hot on his head and back as he scrambled up a steep, rocky slope. It was nearly noon, and a foolish time of day to be climbing, but he had promised himself just this one last day of travelling north before turning decisively for Salfgard. He reckoned there was still enough time before midsummer for him to do this, and the temptation to continue heading north after he left Torald, although it was a yearning he did not understand, had been too much to resist. Hot and hungry, he clambered over the last few feet of scree and boulders and then stared in amazement. Below him lay a little dale, enclosing a small lake glittering blue under the sun. It was fringed with reeds, golden below where last year's dry stalks still showed, green and graceful above where the new growth swayed in the breeze. The waters reflected the pliant branches and fluttering leaves of a group of birch trees, their bark showing silvery-white. But it was the flowers that astonished Maesrhon most, as he began slowly to descend into the valley. Flag-lilies were beginning to open along the shores of the tarn, but the whole hillside below him was a carpet of small yellow daffodils and delicate blue irises spangled with gold.

Of course, thought Maesrhon, they would flower later here in the north; but how do such flowers come to be here at all? He eased his pack from his shoulders and set it down, together with his staff, bow and quiver. Treading carefully so as not to bruise the flowers, he went down towards the tarn where he could see a small stream flowing into it, looking forward to a drink and the refreshing feel of cool water. He paused beside some rocks, looking about him. It almost seemed as though the flowers had spread up the slope, and around the lake, from this point. Their faint, bewitching scent rose in the warm air.

Suddenly the profound peace of the scene was brutally shattered. The boy leapt up in fright as a furious yell rent the air. He spun round, his heart pounding, to see a man leaping down the hillside towards him, arms whirling to balance himself as he bounded recklessly down the slope, trampling the flowers, shouting incoherently. Maesrhon had trained himself to deal with fear: he had seen the murder in Vorynaas' eyes, had faced Thaltor's sword, but there was something about the maddened rage of this stranger that filled him with blind panic. Without stopping to think, he fled away before him, down to the lakeshore and up the further side of the valley. Climbing desperately, he heard the man stumble as his foot turned on a stone, heard the heavy splashing as he pounded through the stream. A glance over his shoulder showed him he was moving the faster of the two: the man was losing ground by wasting his breath shouting. Maesrhon could make no sense of the words, but the very tones of the voice, shaking with an anger and pain beyond control, horrified him. He gained the crest of the ridge enclosing the valley and stared aghast at the prospect that stretched endlessly northward before him. Na Caarst! He hesitated, but looking back again he saw that his pursuer had not: he was closing the gap between them. There was only one thing to do, and maybe if he lived beyond this day, it would prove to be a risk that had saved him. He ran wildly down the far slope, on and on into the barren landscape, hoping his pursuer would not dare to follow. When he could run no more, he hid himself among some huge grey boulders, his breath sobbing in his throat.

After what seemed an age, during which he crouched listening for any sound of pursuit, he decided to hazard a peek from his refuge. Cautiously lifting his head, he looked about him and was dismayed to see that the man had indeed ventured into the wilderness after him. He was barely fifty yards away, far too close for comfort, but looking about him as if baffled. Maesrhon watched him for an instant too long, and the stranger turned and saw him. For a moment they looked at each other and Maesrhon saw shock of some kind register on his assailant's face. The man began to run forward again, his hands held out before him almost as if in entreaty, but Maesrhon was quicker and flew from hiding and away again.

'Come back! Stop, I won't hurt you. Come back, oh, come back!'

Taking no heed, he ran on; and then as the distance increased, an outburst of grief and loss, of pain in which anger was swamped by despair, reached him faintly; the words were lost, but there was no mistaking the anguish in the cry. More shaken by this even than by his fear, Maesrhon ran, and hid, and ran again until he could go no further. The sun had long disappeared behind the peaks in the far west, and the shadows were cheerless and cold. 'Never be parted from your pack. Never take an uncalculated risk. Don't let yourself get chilled. Make sure of shelter first, then water, then food.' Maesrhon shivered as he remembered Torald's words. All his gear was left behind in the little dale; he'd been thirsty even then, before running miles into the wilderness, and now here he was with no food, no water and no means of protecting himself. He was alone in Na Caarst, with the night coming on.

CHAPTER 21

Successful strike

When Thaltor arrived back at the border crossing on his return from Salfgard in the early summer, he found a sealed message awaiting him from Vorynaas. Damping the dust of the journey with a tankard of ale in the guardroom, he ripped it open and glanced through it. The text was short and intriguing, bidding him dispense with his travelling-fellows and get himself to Caradriggan as soon as possible. Resenting Vorynaas' high-handed tone, but curious nonetheless at the hint of momentous news, he scribbled out posting orders despatching his three companions to stations further south along the line, requisitioned a fresh horse and set off at a smarter speed. In due course, refreshed from a leisurely session in the bath-house of the *Golden Leopard* and looking forward to the arrangements he had made for the evening with one of their girls, he presented himself at Seth y'n Carad. Vorynaas was alone, and though he was as scornful and sarcastic as ever, Thaltor detected a suppressed excitement in his manner. As usual however their meeting began with questions from Vorynaas on whatever Thaltor had to report.

'He's doing all right,' said Thaltor in answer to an enquiry on Ghentar's progress. 'He's fitter, the country life must be doing him some good at least. He's taller now, and he's shed some of the weight. If he keeps it off he'll be a man to be reckoned with by the time he's twenty or so. He's strong, he fights well. Now the other lad, he's a different case altogether.'

'Did I ask you about him? It would have been better if he'd died with his mother, which he would have done if only that interfering old fool Arval hadn't meddled.'

'Ah now, Vorynaas, you've not seen him these nearly three years. Ghentar is dogged and determined, but the other boy's a natural with the sword, a pleasure to watch. And you'll be glad to hear he's less like his mother as he gets older.'

Vorynaas whipped round at Thaltor's words; there was something suspiciously bland about his tone but his face was invisible behind the raised wine cup. Draining it and putting it down again, he now changed the subject. 'So what was all the big hurry to get me here?'

'I'll come to that in time.' Vorynaas was still brooding darkly; he determined to string Thaltor along, make him wait. 'There's a lot more I want to know first. What goes on up there during the rest of the year? Is Ghentar keeping his eyes and ears open? What's his word to you? And surely you've something to report yourself?'

'All right, all right! No need to bite my head off.'

Thaltor launched into an account of what he'd gathered about the brothers' activities: how Ghentar had been taken along with Ardeth on several trips down to Framstock and had also participated in trading and hunting parties with Cunoreth and the other men and lads from Salfgard; how Maesrhon by contrast seemed content to stay up in the north and had in fact disappeared off into the hills with Ardeth on the day he'd left Salfgard to travel back to Caradriggan; how Ardeth insisted that all the youngsters kept up with the traditions of their foster-land.

'They're an ill-assorted bunch, by what I can see, and there's been some friction between ours and the Gwentarans – real bumpkins, they are. I should really say, *some* of ours, because Ancrascaro, well she was middle-aged when she was just knee-high; still as plain as ever, there'll not be much mirth for whatever man she may wed, and Heretellar's getting more like his father by the day, so worthy he can hardly move under the weight of it.' Thaltor broke off to laugh derisively and then continued. 'Ghentar though, he seems to be doing what you told him, keeping his head down and getting on with things. In fact you'd never get him to admit it, but I think he's finding it not nearly so bad as he expected. They want for nothing in Salfgard, I can tell you. But it sticks in my throat to see the way that Ardeth resents my visits, much though he might try to disguise the fact.'

Vorynaas' dark brows drew down. 'What makes him think he's so superior?'

'Well, he makes a big play of being just a plain farmer, but the way he has things set up at Salfgard, he's effectively lord of the manor. You can see that all his people love him and he's a leading light in Val'Arad. If he got any, how can I put it, big ideas, there would be nothing to stop him doing pretty much whatever he wanted.'

'So it would be prudent to stop him before he starts having the ideas, eh? Where does Geraswic stand?'

'I've never seen him, all the times I've travelled up. The locals all shut up shop when I tried turning the conversation in the *Malt Shovel* in Salfgard, but from what I gathered at the *Fly* in Framstock, and a word or two dropped along the road in the *gradsteddan*, it seems he's determined to keep out of the way while your lads are there. He never goes up to Salfgard unless they're away, and word seems to reach him if either of them's due in Framstock. Then he leaves the estate in charge of his fellow Gillis, and takes himself off somewhere. Still the thwarted lover, evidently.'

Vorynaas sat back in his chair. 'I'll never forget the look on his face that day when he turned up at Arythalt's place. I'm just sorry I was the only one there to enjoy it.'

'Well, no doubt the tale's gained in the telling, but many's the laugh about it I've had over the years,' said Thaltor, laughing again as he spoke. 'Doesn't seem you'll get a rise out of him again though, because apparently he's sworn never to set foot in Caradward again, not of his own volition at any rate.'

'Hm.' Vorynaas raised a thoughtful eyebrow, and poured another drink for both of them. 'Anything else, or is that it?'

Thaltor drank deeply and helped himself to a handful of almonds before he spoke, almost unwillingly. 'No, there is something else I wanted to say. I've made five trips now, and there are three things that strike me particularly. One is that they're doing very nicely in Gwent y'm Aryframan. It's all a bit basic by our standards, yes, but they're living off the fat of the land. You'd have thought the reduction in trade and traffic would have made more of a difference, that there'd be more signs of make do and mend... but no, as far as I can see the place is prospering mightily. But then, they've got the benefit of the climate, haven't they? When you drop back down to the border again and get the first distant sight of the dark clouds hanging over Caradward, it makes you realise how much you've enjoyed the sunrise of a morning.'

'Ah, the seductive charms of country life! Maybe you should try a day in the fields with a hoe and see how you like the sun beating down on you then. Thaltor, you disappoint me.'

'You know that's not what I mean. You did what the council voted for, what old Arval and his cronies droned on about, sent your sons away where you swore they'd never go; I've travelled up and down where I'm not wanted, we've all swallowed humble pie; and *still* we're stuck under this gloomy darkness, while up there the Gwentarans have all the flowers and brightness.'

Vorynaas stood up and went over to the corner of the room. Thaltor watched him in some surprise, having expected an outburst in response to his words; but far from showing signs of anger or impatience, Vorynaas seemed curiously serene. He produced a key hanging on a chain around his neck and inserted it into a lock high up in the wall. A section of panelling swung open to reveal a small dark chamber. Removing a metal-bound box from within it, Vorynaas returned to his seat and held Thaltor's eye with a slight smile.

'You seem a little depressed, but I've something here which should cheer you up,' he said, placing the box on the table between them. Turning the combination on the padlock, he lifted the lid and took out two leather bags. 'You like to see brightness? Then take a look here.'

And loosening the laces around the necks of the bags, he opened them both where the light from the lamp fell on their contents. Thaltor saw a sparkling glimmer as Vorynaas dipped his finger into several ounces of gold dust and then held it up, glittering; a scatter of small chunks and nodules of ore spilled from the other bag, their rough surfaces glistening with rich veins.

'We've done it, Thaltor,' said Vorynaas. 'We've hit the main seam.'

Thaltor stared, feasting his eyes, and then looked up. 'You've done it, you should say. You were the one who found out about the Lissa'Pathor and planned the whole thing.'

'You've stood with me, though. Didn't I tell you, we go back a long way? Here.'

They gripped hands and Thaltor looked in fascination at the gold particles now clinging to his own fingers. Suddenly he laughed wildly. 'Oh, yes! Listen, Vorynaas, you can bring the boys home now, we don't have to go through with this fostering charade any more!'

Vorynaas shook his head. 'Let them stay, it's only another couple of years. Why give myself the bother of dealing with them when the worthy Ardeth can do it for me? I'm going to be more than busy here, I don't have time to waste on children.'

Turning over the pieces of ore, Thaltor spoke without looking up. 'You should have married again, brought in a woman to run the household and raise them for you.'

'What! Listen, I've had two wives and both of them were more trouble than they were worth. Another is the last thing I need – you've got the right idea, never married at all. I'll come over with you to your place this evening, we'll share your girl from the *Leopard*. No, from now on, anybody or anything that gets in my way or tries to cross me – *that* to them!'

He clicked his fingers, and a shower of gold dust fell on the table in a glittering cascade. With a little cry, Thaltor instinctively moved to gather it up, but Vorynaas stopped him with a laugh. Tying up the bags again and putting them back in the box, he bent and blew at the dust; it rose once more and drifted about the room in sparkling motes.

'Don't worry about a few grains like that, because I'm telling you, Thaltor, if you saw the lodes, well…' he turned back from locking the wall panel, '…well, let's just say that the quality, and the quantity, are richer than my wildest dreams.' His voice became quiet, almost reflective. 'We can do whatever we want, now. Anything.' Suddenly a thought came to him. 'What was the third thing?'

'What?'

'You said three things struck you about Gwent y'm Aryframan, but you only mentioned two.'

'Oh, yes. Honestly, Vorynaas, at a time like this!'

Thaltor traced patterns on the table where the dust had settled once more, grinning with delight; but noticing the look on the older man's face, composed his own and returned to business. 'Well, it was just that the border areas seem almost abandoned these days. You know how at one time there were fields and farms all the way down from Framstock, flocks and herds moving on the drove roads, villages and *gradsteddan* – but all the folk have drifted away. There's an inn or two still, very down at heel, on the main routes, and a few travellers, but there's hardly a hamlet and the fields are either fallow or gone back to the wild. You can be two or three days' travel over the border now before ever you see another face.'

'Interesting. And possibly useful to know.' Vorynaas sat thoughtfully for a moment or two and then headed for the door, taking Thaltor by the arm. 'But now, I think something to eat for us, preferably at the *Sword*. Come on, we've got something to celebrate.'

Business in Framstock

'Well, see you in a couple of weeks, then. Take care, and Ardeth, just a minute,' Fosseiro gave her husband a pointed look and indicated with a jerk of her head that she wanted a word privately. Throwing the reins to Heretellar, Ardeth paused in the act of climbing to the driver's seat and turned back. Their conversation was easily masked by the noise all around them, as the party made ready to set off. The festivities for Harvest-home were over now and a large group of people was leaving Salfgard. Heretellar and a few others of his age had come to the end of their time with Ardeth; the youngsters were all travelling first to Framstock from where they would disperse, Heretellar heading back to Caradriggan with Thaltor and the rest of them going to their homes in other parts of Gwent y'm Aryframan. Ancrascaro had decided to stay on until the following spring, travelling at May-tide. The rest of them, still part-way through their fostering, were going along for the excitement of the trip and the chance of a short stay in Framstock. Ardeth was to attend a session of Val'Arad and also wanted to visit the biggest livestock mart of the year; he was less than pleased to have Thaltor and escort as companions of the way, but this was unavoidable as one of Thaltor's twice-yearly visits to Salfgard had coincided with the feast. At least it would be another six months before they had to put up with him again and meantime with luck he might turn off for Rihannark and not ride all the way to Framstock with them.

'Ardeth, you're not listening to me.' Fosseiro was pulling at his elbow, making him turn round so that he faced her with his back to the travellers.

'Yes I am, I just want to keep an eye on...'

'*Ardeth*. This is exactly what I mean. You've got to stop fussing round Maesrhon all the time. It's difficult enough for him already, being so different from the others, without you drawing attention to him by clucking like an old hen.'

Running his hands through his hair, Ardeth began to protest. 'Well, I like that! You know you were beside yourself when he went missing – the Starborn know where he really was, I don't think the boy is ever going to tell us, but if anything ever happened to him I'd never forgive myself.'

'Ardeth, will you *listen*. Don't single him out, especially while Thaltor is with you. Thaltor is watching him. In fact you can be sure he's watching all of us, and reporting what he sees. I don't believe for a moment he travels up twice a year just to hold a week of sword-drills. And that's another thing. Please don't take Maesrhon on with the stave again, no matter how hard Ghentar and his friends try to talk you into it. Promise me?'

Looking down at her, Ardeth tucked a wisp of hair, all silver now, behind her ear where the little amber drop swung. He knew what was worrying Fosseiro. He and Maesrhon had squared up during the harvest games, and while he'd given the lad a fair drubbing, he'd been beaten in the end, for the first time since he himself was a boy. That was no matter, but more significant was the crushing pain that filled his chest before he could get his breath back. It had eased eventually, after he'd rested, and he'd passed it off as indigestion as a result of the rich festival fare; but he knew the problem was more serious than that, and Fosseiro knew it too. What he had never told her was that the pain had visited him before: the first time in the shock of meeting Maesrhon and then repeatedly, although not so severely, when the boy had been missing at midsummer. He met his wife's eyes, and smiled a little.

'Yes, I promise.' He kissed her forehead. 'And I won't cluck either, I know what you mean. We'll talk about it when I get back.'

To Ardeth's extreme annoyance, although he did his best to hide it, Thaltor and his three fellows rode with the party all the way down to Framstock. There was a change in the man on this visit, thought Ardeth without being able to decide exactly what it was. The high-quality horse, the rich clothes and trappings: all these were noticeably more expensive, but it was something in his manner that was subtly altered. Ghentar rode beside him on Traebenard, showing off by sporting the new sword that Vorynaas had sent him with Thaltor. This was another thing Ardeth disliked. It was only sense for travellers to have the means for self-defence, but there was no need for an open display of arms such as Thaltor and his men, and now Ghentar, were making. Arriving in Framstock, Ardeth directed Thaltor firmly to the *Salmon Fly* while the rest of them settled into the old home-place. Forewarned of their visit, Geraswic was away; but they were welcomed by Gillis, now a young man in his late twenties, married with two infant children. He and his wife Asaldo ran the estate with Geraswic and deputised in his absence. Asaldo was homely and kind and her cooking skills were sufficiently similar to Fosseiro's to send Ardeth happily to bed in the little room of his boyhood, where the hen and chicks were still visible on the wall although much faded by time.

During the next couple of days, Ardeth renewed acquaintance with several old friends at the mart, taking Framhald and Ethanur with him each time, showing them what to look out for and how to judge a beast in the ring. Heretellar went along too; he was fond of Ardeth and knew he would miss him when he went back to Caradriggan. He wandered off among the trading stalls, looking for something he could buy as a gift to show his gratitude for five years of friendship, influence and guidance. Ghentar, Valahald and Heranar had little interest in livestock, although Ghentar swaggered along the horse-lines comparing what was on offer unfavourably with Traebenard. He had already been involved in a heated exchange with Ardeth, who had insisted that the new sword was left in the house, and as they all sat in a sheltered corner to eat their noon meal, further words passed between them.

'Our fathers are rich men,' said Ghentar, waving a grilled pork rib about with a dismissive hand and glancing at Heranar and Valahald. 'It's just a waste of time for us to be trailing about looking at pigs and ewes, we'll have servants to do all this kind of thing for us.'

The other two smirked and Heranar turned the new gold ring he was wearing around on his arm. Ardeth tried to siphon off some of his exasperation by biting hard at his chicken pie and chewing vigorously in silence for a moment to two. Swallowing, he turned to the youngsters.

'No doubt. But you'll want to be able to tell if they try to cheat you, won't you? Knowledge is power, doesn't matter what the subject is. And there's more than one kind of riches,' he added, noticing now that all three young men were wearing new arm-rings; Thaltor must have brought them along with the sword. 'You can't eat gold. Knowledge is treasure of a kind, too. You don't want to let any day go by without adding to your store of learning.'

Valahald sighed loudly, causing Ethanur to glare back: Ardeth was a great man to him and it had been a dream come true that he had been able to go to Salfgard; he was determined to make the most of every minute of his five years there. Framhald and Cottiro shuffled their feet, embarrassment spoiling their enjoyment of the food, but then Cottiro looked up and brightened.

'Oh look, here come the others!'

She jumped to her feet and waved, and Heretellar waved back to show that he had seen them. Ancrascaro and Maesrhon were deep in conversation, but she took her cousin Heretellar's free arm as they approached. He was clutching a parcel under the other arm and the two of them squeezed on to the end of the bench, laughing at some joke, while Maesrhon sat slightly apart. The awkward atmosphere soon dispersed as the youngsters chattered among themselves, but Ardeth noticed that Maesrhon had little to say. The boy was habitually quiet and reserved in manner, but since the summer he had been much more withdrawn and silent. Ardeth watched him covertly as he sat, golden eyes surveying the scene before him, his expression giving nothing away. As he grew older, his face often showed the same inward quality that Numirantoro's had sometimes worn; but maybe because he was a man, in him it was more marked. His features were stronger, but there was an indefinable sadness that seemed at odds with their increasing sternness. What was he thinking about, wondered Ardeth; how had he passed the morning? Above all, what had happened to him at midsummer?

Had he but known it, Maesrhon's thoughts were running along at least partly similar lines. He and Ancrascaro had been paying a visit to Framstock's most renowned storyteller. Arval had been right when he promised that the best were to be found in Gwent y'm Aryframan, and Maesrhon had many memories to treasure of evenings spent listening to the man who kept the rites for Salfgard; but he in turn acknowledged the master of Framstock, who had now promised to consider spending the Midwinter Feast in the north. Like Maesrhon, Ancrascaro was fascinated by the old tales, and sought out all the lore she could concerning the As-Geg'rastigan; she was always ready to discuss such matters with Maesrhon, who found her easier to talk to than many of the other youngsters. She retained some memories of Numirantoro from her early years and he liked her to share these with him; but now as she sat with Heretellar on his last day before he returned home, and as Maesrhon's eyes roved over the bustle and business of the market before him, he felt more of an outsider than ever. He loved Ardeth for his steadfast truth, and Fosseiro for her tender kindness; the learned man with whom he had spent the morning, the artisans of Salfgard, old Torald, all these he acknowledged for their particular mastery; to his grandfather Arythalt, to men such as Forgard, he offered respect; but even with Arval, to whom his devotion was still given unswervingly, where was the closeness, the easiness, the companionship that others daily took for granted? I walk apart, his restless thought said to him, so folk think I need no warmth, but which came first? If there was another mind that opened to mine, would I hide my heart?

Maesrhon shifted in his seat as his thoughts took a darker turn. Why look wistfully on the small joys which the daily round might bring? Who would yearn for the life of men, who knew as he did now what suffering they could endure? A shiver ran through him as unwillingly he recalled the unknown man from whom he had fled at midsummer. Not even the fear of finding himself alone in Na Caarst, not the terror of what might assail him there, not the panic of realising he had cast all Torald's rules of survival to the winds, none of these had been as bad as the anguish, the anger mixed with pain and sorrow, the longing and loneliness and loss that had followed him in the stranger's cries. The horror of that raw emotion had stunned his ears and still it haunted his mind; in nightmares it stalked even his hours of sleep. It seemed unbearable to him that a man who had voiced despair such as he had heard could yet drag out his existence from day to day. How could *he* live, if ever he were wounded by a hurt so dreadful? Even deliberately daring the wilderness would be less terrible. He was roused from his musing by someone digging him in the ribs.

'Are you coming with us?' Framhald was on his feet, and the others were moving off. 'We're all going to the *Fly* to have a quick drink with Heretellar, to wish him a good journey for tomorrow.'

'Oh, right. Yes, of course.'

He found himself walking with Heretellar as they turned the corner into Water Street. Cobbled and winding, it led down to the river and the *Salmon Fly* was about half-way down, an old stone building with gardens at the rear which extended to the river bank. Some of the houses had kept the hop-garlands on their doors from the Harvest Feast, and even though it was autumn, flowers still bloomed in window-boxes here and there. At the foot of the street, the afternoon sun was shining on the river as it flowed down from the bridge; Maesrhon could see children running about in the water-meadows on the further side, gathering horse chestnuts. Mellow, homely old Framstock, thought Maesrhon: friendly and welcoming, but my feet are set on a different path. He glanced up at the sky, where clouds blew over on a fresh westerly breeze. The north, the north calls out to me, but I do not understand why. Into his mind came memories of Arval, of the choice Arval had said he must some day make, of how he must be older before Arval told him what he needed to know. On the threshold of the *Fly*, he turned to Heretellar.

'Would you give a message to Arval for me, when you get back to Caradriggan?'

'Surely. What is it?'

'Tell him ...' Maesrhon hesitated; he wanted to say: tell him how much I miss him, how I wish he could be here too; but the words sounded childish and immature in his mind. 'Tell him, I am training my mind as he bade me, so that I'll be ready when the time comes for him to speak. And tell him, I am counting the days until that hour arrives.'

Heretellar raised his eyebrows in curiosity, but smiled in his straightforward, friendly way at the younger boy. 'Yes, I'll tell him that. No need to ask whether he'll understand! You and Arval are two of a kind, I think. Now, you can do me a favour too. You're close to Ardeth, and he's your great-uncle, so have a look at this and see if you think it's suitable.'

He drew Maesrhon into a snug behind the door of the *Fly*, and opened the package he was carrying. 'I like Ardeth, indeed I respect and honour him for the way he has dealt with me these past five years. I'm returning to my father a better man for his guidance, and I'll always be grateful for it; but I don't think, somehow, that Ardeth and I will meet again after tomorrow, and I want him to have something in remembrance, so I've bought this to give him.'

He showed Maesrhon a two-handled cup, made from horn so fine and thin that the light showed through it, picking out the colour of the grain; it sat in a silver holder intricately worked with interlacing patterns of foliage and strange beasts whose tails formed the handles. Around it were set six pieces of polished amber, arranged to form the centres of flowers.

'He likes to have a hot drink at night now, quite often,' said Heretellar, turning the cup around so that it caught the light, 'and I know he's very partial to Fosseiro's mulled wine and spicy possets, who wouldn't be! What do you think?'

'It's beautiful, I think he will be honoured by your gift,' said Maesrhon, 'although he won't be happy about how much you must have spent on it! I can see it's very old, it must have been very expensive.'

Heretellar shrugged. 'Well, I've been saving my allowance for a while now, hoping I'd see something special to get him. And here, look at this.'

He held the cup to the lamp on the table between them, so that Maesrhon could see one of the amber pieces more clearly. 'There's an ant or something inside, can you see it?'

Maesrhon craned and then suddenly saw what Heretellar meant. 'Oh yes, I see now! It's a little fly, isn't it?' He peered more closely. 'Look, you can see its wings and feelers and everything. How could it possibly get in there? What do you think amber really is? Feel how warm it is, not like garnets or opals or other gems.'

'I don't know.' Heretellar began wrapping the cup again. 'I'll ask Arval, when I give him your message. Come on, let's join the others.'

'Just a minute. Heretellar, you've been at Salfgard for five years and I wanted to ask you whether, well, whether Geraswic used to visit and if you'd ever seen him – before we arrived, I mean.'

'Yes, I've met him a few times.'

'What's he like?'

'To look at, or as a person?'

'Well, both I suppose.'

'Oh, fairly tall, medium build, brown hair, blue eyes. Very quiet man, doesn't have a lot to say. He must be in his late thirties or thereabouts. He's pleasant enough, and fair-dealing, but... there's something; I don't know quite how to put it.' Heretellar paused, frowning in concentration. 'You know if you have a mirror and it gets broken, you can put all the pieces of it together and it still reflects, but what you get is a distorted image, fragmented like the mirror itself. Well Geraswic is like that: there's nothing wrong that you can see, but he's damaged inside. The broken pieces hurt him, so his view of the world is splintered too. I think that's about the nearest I can get.' Remembering what he'd heard about Geraswic's past, he added, 'I wouldn't seek him out, if I were you.'

'No,' said Maesrhon, mindful of the dread that visited his dreams, 'no, I wasn't going to.'

Quarrels

After supper that evening, the young folk sat on late in the main hall of Ardeth's old family home-place. The meal had been merry enough, and afterwards Framhald had managed to persuade Ardeth to entertain them with his legendary *Farmer and Maiden* routine, which he'd done with the assistance of a furiously blushing Cottiro. Asaldo came back in to the room just as the story ended, having gone to put her little boys to bed, and surprised both Ardeth and her husband by reciting *Rhonad y'n Rhos ap Aestr'escan* for everyone. This was new to the Caradwardans: even Ancrascaro had never heard it before, and it set Maesrhon's mind running once more on the mysterious call of the north. But not long after Heretellar stood up to present Ardeth with the cup, Gillis and Asaldo excused themselves and retired to rest, and Ardeth himself lingered only for a short while. Maybe the room was too full of old memories for him to feel totally at ease; perhaps the exchange of gifts at Salfronardo's wedding long ago came back into his mind, or he heard in his heart other voices once young and now gone for ever; or was it that, like Ethanur, he had noticed Valahald and Heranar exchange glances when Heretellar pledged him and had not liked what he saw in the brothers' faces? At any rate, he wished them all a good night and left them to it.

'I'm for bed now. I know there's no point in telling you young folk not to sit up too late, but I'll just remind you that the party for Caradriggan will be setting off soon after dawn, so don't stop Heretellar if he wants to get some sleep. Good night then: the Starborn keep you all.'

He left the room to a chorus of good nights in return, and then a short silence fell in which Valahald threw another log on the fire and Cottiro, though yawning mightily, continued her petting of one of the household cats. If everyone else was staying up, she was determined to do the same. Ghentar was swirling the drink around in his cup, fighting temptation. He'd seen a set of dice and a gaming board in one of the wall cupboards: surely a friendly game could do no harm? He could say they'd make it a rule not to play for money. He willed himself not to speak, knowing he would be unable to leave well alone if once he started again, forcing himself to think about his new sword. Would he put that at risk, as once he had so nearly lost Traebenard? What a sword! He saw it in his mind's eye, remembered the feel of the grip in his hand. Thaltor had told him there was sky-steel in it; his father must have paid a fortune for it. That would be the gold strike. He smiled behind his hand in the Vorynaas manner and then frowned down at the table. How could he endure his remaining years up here in the backwoods? Why did it have to be Heretellar who had the luck of returning to Caradward tomorrow...

'I know, let's play *Wordwheel*,' said Framhald suddenly. 'Here, I'll start you off. "Silver: sleek, subtle and spotless, shining like sword-blade, sparkling like star-fire, slanting like sunrise". Not bad, eh?' He laughed with pleasure at his effort. 'Now, Valahald, over to you! Give us "boar"!'

Heranar snorted in derision and Ghentar began to protest, but Valahald lifted an eyebrow.

'Yes, I'll give you boar,' he said. 'See how you like this. "Boar: all brawn and no brain, barging and belching like a blundering bumpkin".'

As Heranar sniggered, the colour rose in Framhald's face. 'Just what was that supposed to mean?'

Before Valahald had a chance to reply, Ethanur broke in, speaking quietly although the anger could be heard in his voice. 'What makes all you Caradwardans so arrogant? By the Starborn! I don't know how Ardeth keeps his temper and puts up with you. Do you think he doesn't see you smirking to yourselves, or hear what you say behind his back?'

'I really have no idea; and what's more,' added Valahald coolly, 'I really couldn't care, either. We're only here at all because it's what Tell'Ethronad wanted – we didn't volunteer, I can assure you.'

'That's not true. We're here because Val'Arad agreed to the council's request to let us come, you and Ghentar at any rate. Heranar and I were packed off without so much as a by-your-leave, and yet Ardeth has made us all welcome.'

They all turned in surprise as Maesrhon spoke; and Heretellar, the flush of annoyance showing through the sallow complexion he had inherited from Forgard, leaned forward, jabbing his finger on the table for emphasis. 'Yes, and I'm not here under protest, my fostering was arranged from years back. I'm here because my father is true to the traditions of our land, and if I have children of my own, I shall honour the old ways too.'

'That goes for myself and my family also. Valahald, don't spoil Heretellar's last evening! Let's not quarrel – and Ethanur, you're a bit unfair on us Caradwardans. We're not all arrogant, you know.' Ancrascaro spoke up in her steady way, smiling round to include everyone, calming things down.

'No, I suppose not, you're right.'

Ethanur muttered his acknowledgement and Valahald shrugged in an off-hand manner, making partial amends by going round and refilling everyone's glass. Then the bickering broke out again, started up this time from a most unlikely source.

'Well maybe not, but *generally speaking*, I think Ethanur was right.'

Cottiro was blushing nearly as brightly as when Ardeth had played up to her during *Aryfram ac Herediro*, but she stuck to what she wanted to say in spite of Ancrascaro's attempts to stop her and Heranar's jeering interruptions. 'Look at the names you give to places and people, for one thing. We have Framstock, and Rihannark, or even just Cottiro and Ethanur. But you've got to go for *Carad*ward, and *Carad*riggan, and *Heran*wark and *Heran*ar. Not to mention Tell'Ethronad where we just have Val'Arad. And Thaltor,' she added with a final defiant flourish.

Framhald jumped in. 'Yes, and look at the difference in the poems and tales we tell. You always call for **Carad** *y'm Ethan nad Asward*, or **Carad** y'm Inenellan, you never want a comic one like *The Farmer and the Maiden* or even something beautiful like Asaldo gave us earlier with *Rhonad y'n Rhos ap Aestr'escan*.'

'That's because we like something good and strong, not all this wishy-washy stuff,' said Ghentar. 'My favourite's *Warriors of the Sun*, but you never hear that here.'

'Why would we need to listen to that? We have the real sun in Gwent y'm Aryframan.'

'Whereas we have the real warriors.' Heranar sat back in admiration at his own quick wits, ignoring Ghentar who was glaring at him, having belatedly remembered his father's admonition to keep his head down and behave himself.

'Oh, shut up, Heranar,' he said. 'Let's all have another drink and talk about something else.'

Heranar flared with resentment. 'That's good, coming from you. You were the one who said all these old countrified stories were rubbish, you're always telling me you don't want to waste your time listening to any more stuff about the Starborn. "I'm not going to be dragged along to any more of these tedious rites and ceremonies, it's all just superstitious nonsense." Your words exactly, I seem to remember.'

They all shifted about uncomfortably; Maesrhon and Ancrascaro exchanged glances and then Heretellar spoke. 'So when the pledge is renewed, you deny it and stand silent?'

Ghentar pulled himself together. 'Heranar's exaggerating. I don't mean... If anyone wants to go along with all that, well, let them, it's nobody's business but their own. The words are... the rites are quite impressive in their way and if you like that kind of thing, the words are memorable. Traditional. Yes, I'm sure it's all, well, sort of comforting, if you believe in it at all. And, er, it seems that quite a lot of people up here still do.'

Valahald continued before anyone else had a chance to speak. 'Yes, and I do have to say I personally find that rather surprising, because in Caradward we're more... *rational*, I think is the word. Certainly, if you go in for history, and literature and so on, then I can see you might find all these traditions about the Starborn very interesting; but it's mythology, isn't it? If you actually listen to the words of the *Temennis*, how could you possibly take them at face value? *As-Geg'rastigan*, really! Men rule the world. Where are the Starborn, who has known one? If they ever existed, they're gone now and needn't concern us; but surely we can see that in fact they belong in the legends which men made in the old times: today we know better.'

Framhald had been shaking his head as Valahald spoke, and now he burst out in furious opposition. 'No, that's not true! If that's what you think, you don't know better, you're just wrong. The Starborn *do* still exist. I know they do, I just know it. You're wrong.'

'Surely you've proved my point for me,' said Valahald. 'That's not a reasoned argument, shouting at me that I'm wrong and you're right. That's what I mean when I say we're more rational about things in Caradriggan. Explain to me how you know you're right, then I might believe you.'

'I just know.' Never the most articulate of young fellows, Framhald sat glowering, conscious that his lack of skill with words was being exploited to make him look foolish, but uncertain how to dent Valahald's condescension.

Ghentar now spoke up again. 'Well, leaving aside the question of the past, what about the present? Where are the Starborn? If we saw one, maybe we'd all think differently, but which of us ever has? You say they do exist, so why don't they make themselves known? Are they invisible, or hiding, or what? I think Valahald's right, they're just a myth from the old days.'

'Look, just because you've never seen something doesn't mean it doesn't exist. You can't see Salfgard from Framstock, but that doesn't prove it's not there.' This was Ethanur, determined to show he could be as rational as anybody from Caradriggan.

'I think some of the people in the old tales might have been As-Geg'rastigan, or maybe *as-ur* anyway,' said Cottiro thoughtfully, 'and maybe folk just didn't realise it at the time. Ghentar says why don't they make themselves known, but what we were taught at home was that when they walk among men, they must fulfil the image men put upon them. They don't show themselves, it's for us to recognise them for what they are.'

Maesrhon, staring into the embers as he remembered Ardeth speculating on whether Arval himself was *as-ur*, missed the way Heretellar and Ancrascaro had their heads together in a brief exchange of query and agreement; but snapped back to attention when Ancrascaro spoke.

'Cottiro's teacher spoke wisely. Some of you here from Caradriggan are too young to remember, but when I was a small child, one of the Starborn walked in the city calling himself Arymaldur. But not all recognised him for what he was and after a few years he left us.'

A confused outbreak of heated comment greeted this, in which astonishment and derision were loudly mixed.

'That's rubbish! My father got rid of him, he was...' Ghentar had raised his voice above the babble but suddenly stopped, realising this was not a moment when he could accuse Arymaldur of being an agent of Gwent y'm Aryframan, and finished instead with '...nothing but a troublemaker!'

'You're wrong there on several counts.'

Heretellar was speaking quietly but he had got to his feet, which had the effect of imposing a sudden silence. 'My own father was standing next to Arymaldur once as the members of Tell'Ethronad left the chamber and he heard what he said to Thaltor: that he would return whence he came at the moment of his own choosing, however differently matters might appear on the face of it. He warned the council to heed Arval, but they would not; and at the Spring Feast they falsely accused him and tried to put him to death. My father was there; he saw the sun rise – the last sunrise ever seen in Caradriggan. When it faded, Arymaldur was gone.'

Heretellar glanced round the room. Ancrascaro's dark eyes looked into his; the Gwentarans were gaping at him, and so was Heranar, while Ghentar and Valahald glared in open hatred. But Maesrhon was white to the lips, staring directly at him although Heretellar could tell he saw nothing of what was before him; it was an unsettling look and Heretellar briefly hesitated about going on with what he had to say. Then he remembered the recurring distress which visited Forgard and determined to continue.

'My father clings to Arval's assurance that no man in Caradriggan could kill a lord of the As-Geg'rastigan, but that's cold comfort to a man who saw what he saw and has had to live since then knowing that though he tried, he failed to prevent it happening. Arval believes it was the deeds of men that drove the As-Geg'rastigan from us in ages past – after the bad time. Now we in Caradward have raised our hand to them again. You three, Framhald and Cottiro, and Ethanur: stay true and maybe the Starborn will indeed walk again in a land where the pledge is still renewed. Tomorrow I must go back, back into the dark to stand beside my father and offer Arval my support. So for now, good night; and like Ardeth I say, let the Starborn keep you.'

He left the room in a ringing silence. None of them could ever remember Heretellar making a speech of this length before, and certainly not of this kind. After a moment or two, Ancrascaro stood up with a glance of enquiry to Cottiro; she too rose and the two girls moved towards the door but stopped suddenly as Ghentar began ranting.

'Arval this, Arval that! I am *sick* of hearing about Arval. Heretellar and his father are just the type to be his supporters: boring, old-fashioned, out of date! *My* father's got no time for Arval, he says it used to drive him mad the way my mother was always quoting him, he says…'

Maesrhon leapt to his feet. 'Don't say any more, don't ever insult Arval in front of me! I mean it, I'm warning you,' he said, breathless with fury as he stood over his brother.

'Oh, now I'm really terrified,' scoffed Ghentar. 'Ready to do battle for the old boy, are you?'

Maesrhon was calm on the instant with the uncanny self-control he sometimes showed. 'Name the time and the place, Ghentar,' he said, 'and I'll be ready for you. Any terms you care to specify, you can be sure I won't pass on them. I'm telling you again, never insult Arval in front of me.'

Temporarily taken aback, Ghentar did not answer and Maesrhon left the room without another word.

Unlatching the garden door as quietly as he could, Maesrhon saw Heretellar pacing up and down in the darkness under the damson tree. Hearing a footstep, the young man turned, startled, but relaxed when he saw who it was. He sat down on the bench and waved Maeshron over. Looking up at him, he spoke softly. 'Look, I should apologise if I've offended you by speaking harshly to your brother. He's not to blame for whatever happened, he was only an infant at the time. Here, sit down, let's talk for a while and calm down before we go to bed.'

'No, no, it's all right.' Maesrhon hesitated, not wanting to snub Heretellar, but desperate to get away by himself for a while. 'I think I'll just go for a walk. I won't be long.'

Leaning alone on the old stone parapet of the bridge, he listened to the water hurrying beneath him and was somehow comforted by the fact that this was the same river that ran through Salfgard. He wondered how long it took for each drop to flow down from the distant mountains past the falls and the pool, away down the valley, through the town, under his feet as he stood and away, far away to the distant sea. There had been no need for him to ask Heretellar which Spring Feast he spoke of. So Vorynaas tried to have one of the Starborn killed, but instead it was my mother who died – and I was born, he thought. Surely this tale is one that deals in things that are easy to learn, but hard to know! He looked up at the bright stars trembling in the cold sky, seeming to match the frost crystals that winked and sparkled on the earth below. Arval was denied all this beauty, steadfast amid the gloom of Caradriggan, waiting for him to return. Maesrhon beat his fist on the parapet before him. I am ready, you must speak and tell me what it is I need to know! He saw a cat drift silently past the end of the bridge, turning a brief glance of its night-sighted eyes on him, and with a sigh he pushed himself off from the stonework and set off back to Ardeth's house.

CHAPTER 22

Gossip

With the corner of her eye, Ancrascaro caught a lightning-fast movement and stopped to look up; but the sky was empty. Surely though she could still hear a faint twittering and chattering, the merest thread of sound to tease her ears in the wake of that hurtle of wings? She walked on slowly, and suddenly there could be no doubt: there was another, no, two, and then six or seven little birds were turning and diving through the air above her, forked tails spread to steer them through impossible twists of direction, wings glinting metallic blue in the sunlight. The swallows were back! She smiled with pleasure, only realising as her heart lifted to the little messengers of longer, warmer days that she had been feeling slightly downcast. She was heading back to Ardeth's home-place, having been helping out with the children in Salfgard. A small schoolroom was attached to the timbered hall where the rites were celebrated, and she had been more than pleased to take part in teaching the younger pupils who were newly started on their years of learning. The memories of her time spent in Tellgard with Numirantoro had never faded and Ancrascaro had it in mind to ask Arval on her return whether she too could be numbered among his colleagues. She was looking forward to this, although she had wanted to stay on in Salfgard for an extra half-year or so. But it had to be admitted, rather a cloud had descended upon her since last autumn.

It was since that argument they'd had on Heretellar's last evening, she thought now; things had never been quite the same since then. And she missed Heretellar, and now even Maesrhon was away. After Heretellar had gone back to Caradriggan, she and Maesrhon had become closer. He seemed much older than his years, so the difference in their ages scarcely mattered; and both were of a studious cast of mind. The two of them had spent hours in discussion with the visiting Framstock storyteller at the Midwinter Feast, but shortly after that Maesrhon had gone off to spend time with Torald again and he had still not returned. Ancrascaro wondered how he had managed to persuade Ardeth to let him go. They had tried to hide it, but she had seen how desperately worried both he and Fosseiro had been when the boy went missing after his first trip with the old backwoodsman. Still, at least Valahald would be leaving once Thaltor's imminent visit was over. Ancrascaro cheered up a little at this thought. She had made up her mind to stay on at Salfgard until May-tide was over, to avoid having to travel with him in Thaltor's party. Cunoreth had agreed to go down to Framstock with her, and then Heretellar was to come over and escort her home from there. Looking round as she heard someone calling her name, she saw Cottiro running after her, waving, and waited for the younger girl to catch her up.

'Has Mag'rantor's marriage-sister had the baby yet?' asked Ancrascaro as Cottiro panted up, out of breath.

'Yes, last night, I've just …' Cottiro put her hand to her side, '… I've just been to see them, it's a girl. Ooh, I've got such a stitch! Fosseiro asked me to take the shawl and cot blankets she made for them.'

'Why didn't she go with you?' asked Ancrascaro in some surprise.

'She's busy at home. Thaltor and his men arrived in the early afternoon.'

Ancrascaro pulled a face. 'I don't suppose Maesrhon's come back, has he?'

'He hadn't when I left. Ghentar will be pleased, you can see he hates the way Maesrhon's better than he is, even though Thaltor brought that sword for him and nothing for his brother.'

'If Ghentar had more brains he'd be stupid.'

Cottiro giggled with glee at this uncharacteristically spiteful jibe from Ancrascaro, who added, 'He can't seem to see that Thaltor is deliberately trying to push the two of them into rivalry.'

Cottiro looked up at her companion. Ancrascaro was much the taller of the two and was one of those girls who, although plain as a child, was becoming more striking with maturity. She was rather stately in bearing, very dark like Heretellar and now showing signs of an adult beauty that would stay with her until late in life. Cottiro was fair, and not unlike Fosseiro at the same age. Her round, open face had freckles scattered across the nose and cheeks. 'Thaltor could save himself the bother. I think there's trouble brewing between Maesrhon and the others as it is.'

'You could be right.'

They walked on for a while in silence, then Cottiro spoke again. 'For one thing, Ghentar has been pestering some of the girls in the village, but they don't like him.' Cottiro giggled again. 'And you know Escurelo from the mill? She said Maesrhon was like one of the As-Geg'rastigan, and then Astirano said maybe he *was* Starborn! Mind you, I think she really likes him, if you see what I mean.' More giggles.

They were walking down the lane between Ardeth's fields now, and the buildings of the farm were in sight; but Ancrascaro stopped and stood still, giving weight to her words by her serious tone.

'Listen Cottiro, I remember Maesrhon's mother. Folk used to say she was as lovely as the Starborn, but she was the daughter of Arythalt of Caradriggan and Salfronardo of Framstock, Ardeth's sister. And believe me, if you'd ever met Vorynaas – well, let's just say Ghentar's a real chip off that block, so that tells you all you need to know about him. Don't let the girls talk like that about Maesrhon, it will do more harm than good.'

A change of plan

In the event, Maesrhon failed to reappear at Salfgard during the span of Thaltor's stay there. One afternoon Ardeth was talking to the wheelwright, looking over a new wagon that was almost finished, when to his surprise Thaltor put his head round the workshop door and asked if he could spare a moment. Wiping the oil off his hands on a rag, Ardeth came out into the sunshine, and Thaltor addressed him curtly.

'I can't hang around here waiting for the boy to turn up when it suits him. I'm leaving the day after tomorrow, whether he's here or not.'

The Starborn be praised for that, thought Ardeth to himself; but all he said was, 'Right. He'll be sorry to miss your instruction, but you've said yourself that he's ahead of the standard for his age.'

'He was, the last time I was in a position to make a judgement. His father won't be pleased that I can't give him an up-to-date report. Why is the boy spending time roaming around in the hills anyway?'

'Because there's much he can learn there, he's with an old friend of mine. He loves the solitude and the wild places. And if he enjoys it, I'm all for letting him go. It strikes me he has little enough to look forward to when he returns to the city.'

Thaltor shrugged; in view of what he had come to say, he thought it better not to rise to this bait. 'Well, as I say, I'll be setting off the day after tomorrow. Do I take it that Ancrascaro will be travelling with us?'

'No, she's staying on until May-tide. It'll just be Valahald going back with you.'

'Ah, well now that's what I wanted to talk to you about. We want him to stay on for another year and come back when his brother and Vorynaas' boys are finished here.'

Ardeth looked at Thaltor in astonishment. He knew the Gwentarans were only with him as a result of public policy, against their fathers' wishes, and Valahald had made it plain enough himself that he thought he was wasting his time, so why this sudden change? 'He's of an age to return now; surely he should be taking up his place in Caradriggan?'

Thaltor smoothed his hair; he was wearing too much jewellery and the gold gleamed about his fingers. 'The timing will be better in another year. If you must know, just now his father and Vorynaas and I are at full stretch with all the new developments we're working on, and the changes they've brought. Vorynaas sends you this in payment.' He held out a leather bag, clearly heavy for its size.

Ardeth's face darkened. 'The boy is here to be fostered; there has never been any question of payment. Why has his father sent no message of request?'

'Because Vorynaas speaks for all of us; he's the first man in Caradward. You'd get no more than this from Valafoss, if that's what you're thinking. There's six gold bars here, each one worth twenty full silver *morasan*, more than generous enough to cover a year's board and lodging if you feel you've been imposed upon.'

'What I'm thinking is my own business, but here's some of it. Vorynaas can keep his gold. If he wants to throw it about, you can leave it with Val'Arad as you pass through Framstock. Don't insult me by mentioning it again.'

Ardeth turned on his heel and disappeared into the woodshed, but rather than working off his anger by splitting up some more firewood, he sat down on the logpile, feeling the familiar pain tightening in his chest. Thaltor watched him go, smarting with resentment. Enjoy your righteous anger while you can, Gwentaran, he thought. You may win a battle of words with me, but when the time comes for action, I will have the upper hand. And if Vorynaas will listen to me when I get home, that time may come sooner than you realise. Calling over one of the young lads working about the farm buildings, he left a message bidding Valahald to join him that evening in the *Malt Shovel* in Salfgard, and strode off.

By the time the inn closed for the night, both Valahald and Thaltor were in considerably better moods. Infuriated at first to hear that he was not after all to go home that spring, Valahald had been sullen and inclined to drink his way through the contents of Thaltor's purse in mulish silence; but after listening to the ideas that Thaltor breathed into his ear, he began to brighten in spite of himself and had a suggestion or two of his own to contribute. By the end of the evening they were laughing together and when last orders were called they raised their cups to each other.

'To the autumn, then,' said Valahald, as they drank.

'Yes, to the autumn – and beyond,' added Thaltor, grinning.

Then they headed back under the stars, Thaltor to sleep in the guest chamber which he thought plain and homespun, although other visitors had found it rich and comfortable enough; and Valahald to grope for his bed, hampered by the dark and made clumsy by too much ale.

Young emotions run high

In spite of what Ardeth had said to Thaltor, he was uneasy in his mind all the time Maesrhon was away. When the boy had come to him and asked for permission to spend time with Torald again, he had refused at first, even when Maesrhon explained that the reason for his request was to take advantage of what he could learn from Torald during the harsh time of the year when cold and extreme weather conditions would have to be endured. Eventually he had proposed a bargain.

'Tell me the truth about what happened last spring, and I will let you go to Torald once more.'

'I have told you no lies, uncle Ardeth.'

'Maybe not, but we both know you've stayed silent and left parts of the tale unspoken. Tell me now, if you want my leave to journey again.'

So reluctantly Maesrhon had outlined the story. 'I deserved the hardship for my foolishness in forgetting Torald's wisdom so soon after I'd heard it,' he said, coming to the end of his account. 'If all my gear had been to hand, I wouldn't have suffered so badly in the wilderness. As it was, I had to travel slowly because the only water I had was what I could collect each night, and my only food was what was left in my meal-bag: thank the Starborn I kept that with me. After I'd worked my way into the foothills of the Somllichan Torward, there was plenty of water and I could hunt for other food; but that took time, as did the longer journey I had to make.'

He looked directly at Ardeth, a line drawn between his amber eyes and a determined set to his jaw, although he was rather pale. Ardeth could see, as clearly as if the boy had told him, that he would have preferred to look away and to leave unsaid what was coming next.

'I risked the days in Na Caarst rather than face the man who pursued me: whoever he was, I will never forget the anger and sorrow in his voice.' Maesrhon left unspoken the night-fears he had endured in the wilderness, dreading the silent approach of unknown horrors, and the guess that his assailant had been Geraswic. Bringing his tale to its end, he finished simply. 'Once was enough, I've learnt my lessons well and won't make the same mistakes a second time. You need have no fears for letting me go to Torald again.'

No fears, thought Ardeth as he looked for the hundredth time northwards out of the hall window; what do young folk know about that! Ah, little son, these weeks and months without you seem so long. He buried his face in his hands as another wave of concern swept over him. The boy would be going back to Caradriggan all too soon as it was, let him not be lost to us as his mother and my sister were! With a sigh, Ardeth pulled himself together and tramped off to find Ethanur and Heranar, who were supposed to be spending time with the smiths. Ethanur was shaping up really well at the forge: his wrought-iron work showed great promise, and Heranar had actually expressed an interest in learning the crafts of enamelling and inlays. This had quite taken Ardeth by surprise, but he was determined to encourage the lad: like Maesrhon and Numirantoro, he was a firm believer in Arval's precepts about learning. He would work alongside them, it would be a good opportunity for him to get ahead with the knife he was making as a gift for Maesrhon.

At last, after almost four months away, late one evening as the bats began to swerve and swoop overhead, Maesrhon re-appeared out of the spring dusk. As she hugged him, Fosseiro teased him about his weather-beaten appearance and ragged haircut, and Ancrascaro smiled with pleasure to see him again.

'I was afraid you wouldn't come back in time for me to see you before I go home, and if you hadn't, well,' measuring her shoulder against his, 'I don't think I'd have known you by next year. You must have shot up another half-head while you've been away! What does this Torald feed you on? And really, look at your hair!'

'Well, I had to trim it myself with a knife,' said Maesrhon, running his hands through it with a grin. 'It'll be all right once Fosseiro has done it properly for me.'

'Don't let Cunoreth see you, he might decide to have his the same,' laughed Cottiro. 'He's got his in narrow braids all round his face now, back about a hand's width, and then loose after that. He's let it grow really long.'

'He looks ridiculous,' said Ardeth, 'and I don't care how old-fashioned he thinks I am, I shall tell him every time I see him until he does something about it. Maesrhon, welcome home.'

They wrapped their arms around each other, relief spreading through Ardeth and the tension of worry melting away.

'Look at the height of you, and you just turned fourteen! What will you be like when you're twenty?'

Suddenly he remembered that by then Maesrhon would be gone from Salfgard and unknown to him; the thought was more than unwelcome and he hastily pushed it from his mind.

'I know what we'll do! You were away when it was your birthday, so we'll celebrate it now and make it a feast-day to remember: May-tide, and a farewell for Ancrascaro, and a double birthday all rolled into one – I'll bet you won't mind marking your birthday twice over, Ghentar?'

'If you like. Whatever.'

Ghentar's ungracious response, compounded of jealousy at Maesrhon's return and anxiety over whether Ardeth meant anything significant when he mentioned betting, was lost in the general enthusiasm for Ardeth's proposal.

At May-tide the weather turned so warm and sunny that it seemed summer had taken the place of spring at Salfgard. On Ancrascaro's last day, she was sitting in the water-meadows with Cottiro and some of the village girls. A sweet smell of bruised grass filled the air and around them flowers opened in the sun: daisies and buttercups, clover and delicate pale little flowers that the local children called milkmaids. Here and there were families enjoying the rest from work, boys shouting as they matched up with sparring-staves, girls playing with balls, other youngsters splashing about in the river with shrieks at the cold water as they pushed each other in and swam races across the wide pool. Cottiro's friend Escurelo had been picking buttercups and holding them under her chin in the old game, and was now busy making a daisy-chain. They looked round when someone called Ancrascaro's name, and saw Maesrhon approaching; he had been swimming in the river but now dropped down on the grass beside them.

'You're still all wet,' said Cottiro, picking daisies for a chain herself.

'It's only my hair,' said Maesrhon, shaking his head vigorously, causing Cottiro and Escurelo to squeal in protest as they were showered with water, but Astirano turned her face away. Her heart pounded; she wanted to look at the way small drops still clung sparkling to Maesrhon's long dark lashes, but was afraid her eyes would betray her thoughts.

'Have a good journey,' Maesrhon was saying now to Ancrascaro, 'and give my regards to Heretellar when you see him. Will you ask him for me whether he gave my message to Arval? I'm sure he did, but if not, perhaps you would remind him about it.'

'Of course I will,' said Ancrascaro, 'and if there's anything you want me to pass on to Arval, I can do that for you. I'll be going to see him in Tellgard as soon as ever I can when I get back.'

Maesrhon gazed into the distance; Astirano risked a peek at him while his attention was elsewhere.

'Tell him I miss him,' said Maesrhon; somehow it was easier to send this message with Ancrascaro rather than Heretellar. 'And say, with every day that passes, I am even less surprised than I was before at how much he knows. It's an old joke I had with him, he'll remember what I mean.'

Escurelo felt a little left out of things at this exchange, so she leaned over and put her daisy-chain on Ancrascaro's head. 'There! It's your last day, so we'll make you queen of the May!'

'Oh yes! And I tell you what, we'll make Maesrhon the king!'

Cottiro scrambled to her feet and settled her daisies into Maesrhon's dark, flowing locks, still damp from the river but beginning to spring back from his face as they dried. He and Ancrascaro smiled awkwardly at each other as the others laughed and Astirano bit her lip, hoping no-one would notice how she blushed; but the moment was spoiled by a jeering laugh. Ghentar strolled over to them, flanked as usual by Valahald and Heranar. It struck Ancrascaro for the first time how curiously colourless Valahald was: his hair was a mousy brown, but his eyebrows and lashes were paler, and as he was clean-shaven his face, with its rather pointed nose and chin, seemed oddly featureless. Even his eyes were some indeterminate shade, although narrow and calculating. His younger brother tended to the pink-cheeked with gingerish hair and small teeth somewhat widely-spaced; the two of them contrasted markedly with Ghentar, who at seventeen would have been strikingly attractive if his nature had matched his looks. Although only of medium height, he was powerfully built and his colouring suited the dark trace of beard that emphasised his lips and jawline. His black brows arched over large brown eyes, chestnut-tinted like his hair but smouldering with a temper all too ready to flare. A bad enemy, but probably an even worse friend, thought Ancrascaro.

'You should just see yourself, sitting there,' said Ghentar to his brother, 'sitting there like a girl with flowers in your hair. Ah, but then I'm forgetting: no doubt this is the way they do things here, the *old* way, the *traditional* way, the proper *Gwentaran* way!'

Maesrhon ignored him, sitting with his forearm across his knee, his eyes apparently resting on some distant prospect beyond the river; but Escurelo jumped to her feet.

'And what's wrong with that? Just remember you're in Gwent y'm Aryframan now, so watch your mouth, *Caradwardan*. When we want your opinions, maybe we'll ask for them!'

'Come on.' Ancrascaro stood up, beckoning to Cottiro and Astirano. 'You too, Escurelo. Don't waste your breath on him, it will only upset Ardeth and Fosseiro.' She pulled at Escurelo's arm and they walked off, Cottiro turning back to glare at Ghentar as she went. He and the brothers sat down beside Maesrhon, who had never moved.

'Well, that's something we've got to avoid at all costs. Can't risk ruffling the feathers of the worthy Ardeth,' said Ghentar with a glance at Heranar.

'No, because he might come after us with his great big sparring-stave. I'm frightened even thinking about it,' said Heranar, sniggering. 'But no, we'd be all right. Maesrhon would look after us, he's good with the stave too. I think he prefers the stave to the sword, but I expect it's because it's the *Gwentaran* way, is that right? Hey Maesrhon, I'm talking to you, are you deaf?'

Valahald chipped in. 'Maybe he thinks he's so good with the sword as well that he doesn't even have to bother turning up for Thaltor's classes. Wait till they know about that in Caradriggan, that you were running around up in the hills with some peasant when you should have been here.'

Maesrhon got to his feet in one sudden, supple movement and the other three stood too, crowding around him. Valahald returned to the attack.

'What's the big attraction out there in the backwoods? You can bed down with animals here any time you want. Why don't you ask Ardeth if you can move into one of the byres?'

Ghentar pushed up close to his brother and then took a step back again when he realised he would have to look up at him. 'You need some manners putting on you. Our father sends Thaltor up here twice a year, specially for our benefit, and you don't even have the courtesy to present yourself for his instruction. You'll get like Ardeth if you're not careful, not fit to be seen in civilised company.'

They began to jostle Maesrhon slightly, and a daisy fell from his hair. As it slipped down his cheek with a feather-light touch, he felt a shiver run over his skin.

'Thaltor comes here for your benefit, not mine, as we both know well.' This was addressed to his brother, but with a glance at Valahald he added, 'And I don't doubt he has other purposes too.' Ignoring Valahald's reaction to this, he turned back. 'I don't care what you say about me, Ghentar, but if you know what's good for you, don't say one more word about Ardeth.'

They all laughed at this and Ghentar put his head on one side, pretending to consider. 'Oh, have I got it wrong? I thought it was Arval you were all set to champion. Now you want to defend Ardeth! It's all very confusing.'

Maesrhon shoved the brothers aside and stood over Ghentar. 'I've warned you before about Arval. This is the last time.'

'Right. Tomorrow morning, first light. I seem to remember you said any terms I cared to name? Well, as you're so keen on all things Gwentaran, how about your stave against my sword?'

'Certainly. But not tomorrow, Ancrascaro will be leaving for Framstock and we'd be missed. Make it the next day, and name the place.'

'Upriver past the falls, where it's shallow. We'll go across to the island.' Ghentar hesitated, baffled by Maesrhon's lack of reaction. 'You agree to stave on sword?'

'I've already said so. But if you don't believe me, I'll swear it. Look up, and we'll take our oath on the sun.'

Ghentar chewed the inside of his cheek, looking to Valahald and Heranar for support, but they seemed taken aback by the speed of developments. He hitched at his belt uncertainly and then nodded. 'All right.'

The sun was almost at the noon, and by the time the words were spoken, Ghentar was wincing with discomfort, dazzled and blinded with streaming tears; but Maesrhon's amber eyes were wide and golden, full of light but as scornful as the voice with which he dismissed them as he walked away. Passing between family groups without a glance, he realised suddenly that he was catching up Ancrascaro and her friends; Astirano looked over her shoulder and saw him. Maesrhon slowed down, not wanting to talk to anyone for a while, and then with a change of direction he picked up speed again, striding off towards the farm. He would climb up the side valley where the small stream flowed down and spend a few hours collecting his thoughts about the forthcoming encounter with his brother.

Escurelo and Cottiro were still fuming with anger, but their tirades on the subject of Ghentar were cut short when without warning Astirano stood still, put her face in her hands and began to weep.

'What is it? Don't cry, Astirano, tell us what's upset you,' said Cottiro, putting her arm around her friend's shoulders, but Astirano sobbed helplessly, unable to speak. Eventually she rallied sufficiently to say she wanted to talk to Ancrascaro and the other two moved off and left them together. Ancrascaro waited for a while, but Astirano sat staring blankly at the ground in silence except for an occasional catch of breath as tears rolled down her cheeks. Eventually Ancrascaro decided to speak first.

'It's Maesrhon, isn't it? You can tell me if you want to.'

Astirano's hands flew to her mouth in embarrassment. 'Oh! Does everyone know? Are they all talking about me?'

'No, no, it's not that. But I can read the signs, you know. You don't have to worry, Maesrhon won't have noticed.'

'Oh, I love him, I really do, and I'm so miserable. What will I do when he goes back to Caradriggan?'

Ancrascaro knew she was wasting her time by saying it, but said it none the less. 'Look, Astirano, please don't think I'm trying to belittle how you feel, but you and he are only fourteen. You're far too young to be upsetting yourself like this.'

Her companion mopped at her tears, shaking her head stubbornly. 'Everyone knows that Ardeth and Fosseiro were promised at fourteen. Even though he was away for five years in Caradward, they kept the pledge they made and no-one told them they were too young.'

'That was long before even your parents were born, how can you know what people said then? And anyway, Maesrhon isn't like Ardeth and Fosseiro.'

Ancrascaro paused, trying to explain what she meant in a way that would not be hurtful to her young friend. 'I know you're in love with him, you won't ever feel quite the same about anyone else; but your memories should give you joy, not sorrow. Because they will be memories, Astirano, and here's why. You're in love with Maesrhon because you don't really know him, because in your heart of hearts you realise that you'll never truly know him, so you can cherish your ideal without the risk of ever losing it. You can only truly love someone if you truly know them, too – that's how Ardeth and Fosseiro have kept their promise all these years. And listen, Astirano: I remember Maesrhon being born, I have known him all my life; but even I don't feel I really know him. The only person he's at all close to is Arval the Earth-wise – you've heard us talking about him. I don't know whether this is any consolation to you, but all my instincts tell me that Maesrhon will never love anyone like you will, or I might, because his whole heart and mind is turned away to some distant vision only he sees; his eyes look far away.'

She pulled up a piece of grass and then threw it from her with a half-laugh of exasperation. 'I expect you think that's all a lot of nonsense. It's very difficult to explain what I mean.'

'No, I sort of know what you mean, but it doesn't make any difference.' Astirano smiled bleakly. 'I wish you weren't going home tomorrow, then we could talk about him again. It does help, a bit.'

'Well, I hope so. But if you want, talk to Fosseiro, not the other girls. I know she must seem old to you, but she's really kind and she does understand things. She's always ready to listen and help if she can.'

'Mm. Ancrascaro, there's something I want to ask you. You don't think Maesrhon could be one of the Starborn, do you?'

'No, definitely not,' said Ancrascaro as firmly as she could, hoping to stop this rumour before it ran any further. 'I've told Cottiro before, I know both his parents – well, his mother died when he was born, but I knew her when I was a little girl.'

'Well, maybe he's *as-ur* then. Cottiro told me you said there was a lord of the Starborn in Caradriggan one time.'

Ancrascaro's heart turned over. Arymaldur! With a shock, she realised that her analysis of Maeshron and his effect on Astirano had been influenced by long-forgotten childhood memories, scarcely understood at the time, of Numirantoro's reactions to Arymaldur. Now she remembered hearing how Vorynaas had hated him; was that why he hated Maesrhon too? Could it be possible? All this flashed through her mind in an instant, but she kept her voice as steady as she could.

'Yes, there was. But would he have gone from us if he had a son not yet born?'

Astirano had no answer, not knowing as Ancrascaro did the manner in which Arymaldur had left Caradriggan. Thinking of this, after a moment Ancrascaro continued slowly, almost as if she would rather not have said more.

'You know the story of *Maesell y'm As-Urad*, don't you? Well, should Maesrhon be truly *as-ur*, then most likely sorrow awaits him in life. Don't add to that burden by laying your love on him when he can't return it, Astirano. Remember him, keep him in your heart, but make your life among your own people. Maybe when Maesrhon goes home next year, you could go and stay for a while with Gillis and Asaldo at Geraswic's place down in Framstock. Get to know some of the young fellows there, and meanwhile go to Fosseiro if you need a shoulder to cry on.'

A difficult conversation

All this was still very much on Ancrascaro's mind during the journey down to Framstock with Cunoreth. They rattled over the cobbles through the town and turned in at the wide gateway of the old family home. It wore its mellow grace with careless charm and it was easy to see why Ardeth loved it so well; easy, too, to understand how his boyhood years there, guided by his father of whom she had heard much, had formed the mature man. How sad it was that he had no children and grandchildren to live here and love the old place in their turn, that his hopes for even his adoptive son had been so thwarted. Geraswic now emerged to greet them, followed by Asaldo and the little boys, and she wondered whether it would be Gillis who stood to inherit in the end. For very different reasons, there was no need to even consider the question of either Ghentar or Maesrhon taking up their heritage in Gwent y'm Aryframan.

Ancrascaro found herself beside Geraswic that evening; Heretellar had not yet arrived, and Cunoreth, who was set to return immediately to Framstock the next day, was laughing and joking with Gillis and Asaldo and playing noisy games with the children. It occurred to her that Geraswic and Astirano might have found solace in each other, if only the difference in their ages had not been so large. He must be in his late thirties, she thought, surreptitiously eyeing him; pleasant-looking enough, but for the bitter lines in his face, and now here was Astirano with a cloud on the sunshine of her youth. Sometimes she could understand why Maesrhon seemed to avoid the warmth of human contact. Ancrascaro thought Geraswic must be one of the most silent men she had ever met; however, she was little given to small-talk herself, so they sat together companionably enough. But she realised that he was gradually turning their sporadic conversation towards events at Salfgard; he asked about this and that without ever mentioning Numirantoro's boys, but surely these were the names that must be uppermost in his mind. She decided to help him out.

'Do you know a man called Torald, who lives away up somewhere in Gillan nan'Eleth?' she asked.

'Oh yes. Many's the time I went out with him ferreting, when I was just a youngster, before ever I went to Ardeth in Salfgard.'

Ancrascaro took the plunge. 'Well, Maeshron's been up to stay with him twice; I mean, they've travelled together in the wild country.'

Geraswic had started slightly at the name, and was obviously ill at ease; Ancrascaro almost wished she had not said anything, but gamely carried on with a brief account of Maesrhon's recent doings. Having sat for a long while in silence once she had finished, Geraswic eventually had a question of his own.

'What does Maesrhon look like?'

An even longer silence followed her answer, a silence in which Geraswic stared down at his hands. Eventually he spoke without looking up. 'You said he's been to Torald twice, including this winter just past. So the first time was in the spring of last year, about a year ago as of now, just coming up to Midsummer?'

'But how did you know?'

Abruptly, Geraswic got to his feet, making Ancrascaro jump in surprise. 'I'm just going out,' he said, speaking as if at random, looking at her with unseeing eyes. 'I might be late back, there's no need to wait up for me.' And leaving her too startled to think of any reply, he hastened from the room.

Heretellar arrived in the morning, and in the business of welcoming him, and getting all her bags and belongings ready for travel the next day, there was little time for Ancrascaro to reflect on this strange conversation. But as they all stood together in the courtyard at the point of departure, she felt she should make some amends for upsetting Geraswic, however unintentional it may have been. After embracing Gillis and Asaldo and lifting the children into her arms for a farewell kiss, she took his hand.

'The Starborn keep you, Geraswic of Framstock; may you never know sorrow.' Then abandoning formality, she hugged him too. 'Would you think of visiting us in Caradriggan some time? My parents would be pleased to welcome you, and Heretellar and I would both love to see you again.'

Geraswic smiled, although they could see it cost him an effort. 'I appreciate your kindness; having known you, I'm sure I would be honoured to know your families also; but the Caradward road is one I'll not willingly travel again.'

The challenge

Maesrhon arrived first at the place he and Ghentar had agreed upon. Above the falls the river was wide and shallow, running in many channels with banks and beaches of water-worn pebbles which in one place were high enough above the water for grass to have established itself and make a small flat island about forty paces by twenty. Usually in the summer time it was possible to jump from one dry spot to another and to arrive on the island without the need to wade, but the weather had broken in a heavy thunderstorm the night before and the river was higher this morning. Maesrhon splashed across without bothering to remove his footwear and walked slowly up and down waiting for his brother. The dawn was damp and muggy, the air heavy with moisture, and the noise of the current seemed louder than usual.

It was chilly and dank and Maesrhon wished Ghentar would hurry up. Eventually he heard voices and to his surprise his brother emerged from the mist accompanied by Heranar.

'He's here as my witness, of course,' said Ghentar in answer to his brother's question.

'What's the need for that? We're not going to hurt each other, we agreed that the winner will be whoever has the other at his mercy. And let there be no doubt, Ghentar, if I disarm you, you will say no word against Arval again in my presence.'

'Oh, let's get on with it. Give me my sword, please.'

Smirking, Heranar presented the weapon to Ghentar with a flourish. Maesrhon, not bothering to hide his low opinion of this farcical routine, swung his stave into readiness. He was confident of the outcome of their bout, having on many occasions stated his belief that a man skilled with the sparring-stave could hold off a swordsman if he kept his nerve. He knew he was by far the best in the district, having beaten even Ardeth; and in spite of having missed Thaltor's last visit, was sure he was still better with the sword than Ghentar, with more height and a longer reach to compensate for his lack of weight. Speed, co-ordination of hand and eye, and a cool head would win the day here, especially as they were not out to injure each other; and Ghentar could not match him in any of these, so the fact that their weapons were so different would not count for much. Maesrhon's main concern had been whether Ghentar's new sword would harm his stave. His brother had not allowed him to handle it, but he had heard it contained sky-steel; so he had not brought any of Ardeth's iron-hard oaken staves to use, but rather a newish one of ash wood that he had cut and fashioned himself. He thought it unlikely, given its scarcity and cost, that there would be more than a token core of sky-steel in the sword; but if there was any on the edge of the blade it would certainly be capable of removing sizeable chunks of wood even from an oaken weapon, so he would not risk damage to any that belonged to Ardeth.

For some time they circled, Ghentar probing, feinting, coming forward aggressively and Maesrhon parrying his every move, light on his feet, the heavy stave as quick in his hands as if his weapon weighed no more than his brother's. The colour was up in Ghentar's face and he began to breathe more heavily as he lost control of his temper. He had expected Maesrhon to be cowed, to back off until he was easily brought to the sword-point; and to see him so calm, so controlled, so unreachable, enraged him. How was it that a stupid ash-plant could hold him off like this? Baring his teeth, he lunged forward again, maddened by the way Maesrhon whirled the stave, by the jarring as his sword bit harmlessly time and again on the wood, by the look in his brother's strange golden eyes. Heranar squatted well back on the shingle at the edge of the little island, watching the two of them; and all three were so intent that they never saw a face peeping at them from thirty yards or so upstream where, in a place where the eddies had made a deep little pool, a small boy crouched under the bank staring in fright, his fishing forgotten.

It was all over very suddenly. Ghentar pushed on too recklessly, Maesrhon moved aside and with an almost languid turn of his wrist the stave circled whistling through the air and seemed actually to pluck the sword from Ghentar's hand. Turning as it rose, it fell ringing to the ground, bouncing once and coming to rest on the pebbles at the water's edge. With a laugh, Maesrhon let his stave rest into the crook of his arm and put his foot on the sword. He held out his hand to his brother.

'My win, then, Ghentar.'

As he took the proffered hand, Ghentar could not bring himself to speak. Maesrhon stepped back and stooped to pick up the sword, and at that something cracked in Ghentar: rage coursed through him at the very idea of being handed his own sword by the opponent who had just won it from him.

'Don't touch it!'

The words were spat out, almost snarled, as swiftly he bent and grabbed the hilt. Maesrhon had not had time to straighten up before Ghentar, sword in hand once more, sprang upright, aiming at his brother's face. The point sliced through Maesrhon's top lip; he felt a sensation almost like a sudden burning sting and put his hand to his mouth, but it was only when he saw the blood smeared on his fingers that he realised what had happened. For an instant the brothers stared at each other, Ghentar aghast as he took in the red drops welling from Maesrhon's face and beginning to spatter on the pebbles at their feet. Then sudden, piercing screams set their hearts racing and they heard heavy footsteps running towards them; a yell rang out, though the man who shouted was still hidden by the mist. Panic gripped Heranar.

'Run!' he gasped, grabbing at Ghentar, and the two of them dashed across the island and plunged splashing into the river on the far side, slipping and stumbling as they forced themselves through the fast-flowing water. Gaining the bank at last they disappeared into the trees, as Mag'rantor, dropping the basket of fishing-gear he had been carrying, raced down to the bay where his son was still screaming. He snatched the boy up into his arms.

'What's the matter? What's happened?'

'Oh, daddy, they were fighting! Look at all the blood, it's Maesrhon, he's hurt!'

'By the Starborn!'

Mag'rantor's day was lurching into unexpected action. He'd been quietly walking down in the early morning to join his lad for a promised day's fishing, and now... He set the boy on his feet and crashed through the shallows to the island. Maesrhon was still standing there, the blood pulsing from his lip and running off his chin. Turning back, Mag'rantor shouted to his son.

'It's not as bad as it looks, but Fosseiro will need to stitch it. Run straight down to the farm and tell her to get the things ready, but make sure you get Ardeth out of the way somehow before you speak to her. He's not to see Maesrhon until he's cleaned up, understand? Go on now, run as fast as you can!'

In the big farm kitchen, many pairs of eyes watched Fosseiro in silence as she finished working on Maesrhon. Ardeth was there now, with Mag'rantor and the boy, Cunoreth, Framhald, Cottiro, Ethanur; and Valahald, standing slightly apart from the others. There was no sign of Ghentar or Heranar. Maesrhon was sitting on an upright chair, rather pale from the fumes that had been held under his nose, the same as those they used on the hives when it was time to stun the bees. Fosseiro, who was accustomed to dealing with small matters of first aid, tied off the last neat stitch of finest thread, made as clean as possible by being held in boiling steam. She had washed out Maesrhon's lip with spirit, and he had never moved or cried out; but whether that was from bravery or the effects of the smoke she neither knew nor cared.

'Give him a drink now, Ardeth,' she said, and then turned to Maesrhon. 'Sip it through the straw, the stitches will make your lip clumsy for a while. I'm afraid you're going to have a scar for the rest of your life, but I've tried to make sure it will be as small as possible.'

Ardeth handed the boy a beaker and cleared his throat. 'Now I want to know what's been going on.'

Maesrhon's expression gave nothing away. 'Ghentar and I had a point of honour to settle. It's done with now.'

'He used the sword his father sent him.' Ardeth broke off, listening; stealthy footsteps could be heard on the stairs. He pulled the door open roughly and shouted.

'Get in here, you two.'

In shuffled Heranar and Ghentar, their eyes flickering from one face to another as Ardeth turned back to Maesrhon. 'Where is *your* sword?'

'He agreed to the terms!' Heranar burst out. 'Valahald was there, he'll tell you. Ghentar said stave against sword, and Maesrhon agreed.'

'Yes, I did. The winner to be whoever had the other at his mercy, no hurt to be caused.'

Ardeth rounded on Ghentar. 'I take the Starborn to witness that I want to love the sons of Numirantoro, but you have made this more than difficult. What have you to say?'

133

'I, I didn't mean it. The shingle is wet from the rain in the night and the river is high. We both went to pick up the sword, I slipped when it was in my hand, and I caught Maesrhon's face by accident.'

'That's not true! I was there, I saw it all! Maesrhon won; he knocked the sword out of Ghentar's hand, and then when he would have given it back to him, he took it and struck him!'

As the child's voice rang out, high and accusing, Ghentar's intake of breath could be heard. He banged his fist on the table. 'What does he know? He's only a little boy, he wasn't near enough to see!'

Frowning, Ardeth looked from Ghentar to Maesrhon. 'What was this point of honour?'

Maesrhon looked directly at his brother. 'That's between the two of us. It's settled now.'

Ghentar began to hope he was going to get away with things. 'Yes, that's right,' he said, 'it's settled now. Maesrhon won, and it was just an accident that he got hurt.'

But burning with a child's sense of justice, the boy spoke up again. 'It wasn't, he did it on purpose! If it was an accident, why did they run away?'

Heranar and Ghentar spoke together, two sets of lies at the same time. 'We heard someone shouting, we didn't know who it might have been, we went to get help.'

Ghentar stared round defiantly at them all. 'Maesrhon knows I wouldn't hurt him. It *was* an accident.'

There was a moment of complete silence. Maesrhon stood up and moved away, turning back at the door. 'Yes, that's right. A mistake, that's all.'

Amid the buzz of conversation and comment that started up, Ghentar relaxed a little, not seeing the look in his brother's eyes as he left the room; and leaning unregarded in the corner, Valahald wondered whether he, or anyone else beside himself, had noticed Maeshron's use of a different word.

CHAPTER 23

Changes in the south

Meanwhile Ancrascaro and Heretellar were well down the homeward road, and as evening fell one day they arrived at the *gradstedd* where Heretellar had left the wagon in the care of his attendant while he went on alone up to Framstock. Apart from a heavily-armed merchant caravan parked under guard outside, all the custom at the inn was local except for themselves and a noticeable quiet fell on the company as they entered. But then young Meremvor jumped up to greet them, and the inn-keeper recognised Heretellar; on the outward trip his easy ways and good manners had made a favourable impression despite his Caradward accent, and now the man's wife came forward with a smile to make Ancrascaro welcome also. The other customers resumed their business and conversations as Heretellar made the introductions.

'This is Meremvor,' he said, drawing the young man towards them, 'who works with me on the estate in the Ellanwic; there's no one better with horses, mules and such, so he's the one I wanted with me on this trip.'

Removing his pointed Gwentaran cap, Meremvor coloured slightly as he took Ancrascaro's hand. But when he made to stand back, Heretellar would have none of it.

'No, we want you to join us,' he said, moving across to sit in a vacant booth where there was a table and space for four or more to gather round. 'We'll eat together and then we can catch up with all the news.'

Bit by bit, that evening and over the next few days of journey, Ancrascaro gathered that Heretellar had taken over the running of his father's lands in the Ellanwic away south in Caradward.

'It's best that I live there most of the time,' he said. 'Better for our people, to see me there working with them and looking out for them, and better for me than to stay in the city. I only wish I could persuade my father to spend less time in Caradriggan, but he won't leave while Arval stays; he feels he has a duty to support him in the council and to be close at hand if trouble flares. And Arval will never leave Tellgard, or give ground to any man on his convictions and teachings.'

'Did you give Arval the message from Maesrhon?' asked Ancrascaro.

'Yes. It's strange you know, you'd almost think the old man was just waiting for Maesrhon to return. There's a bond between them although it's hard to define it.'

'Two of a kind, I think,' said Ancrascaro, remembering her conversation with Astirano but not elaborating further. 'I hope Arval will have a place for me in Tellgard.'

Meremvor suddenly spoke up. 'If it wasn't for Arval, I wouldn't be here today. I mean, I wouldn't be able to do a man's work. I came to the city as a boy, to work with my uncle who had a business supplying the mule-trains. Then my arm got broken, and they mended it in Tellgard – Arval did, and Lord Arymaldur, too. The both of them, for a mule boy.' His voice trembled slightly, but after a moment or two, he continued. 'And then I got hurt again, at the Spring Feast when Lord Arymaldur... when Vorynaas... and Arval kept me in Tellgard until things quietened down.'

Ancrascaro looked at him, noticing the mark of an old wound cutting through one of his brows across his forehead. His eyes were bright with memories and he sat proudly as he rode. Here is another who has been touched by Arymaldur, she thought. For a few moments they jogged along in silence broken only by the rumble of wheels and the clop of hooves on the hard road.

'What happened after that?' she asked eventually.

'Well, my uncle's business had hit hard times already, before then, and he hadn't been able to keep me on; so I'd been working on the mule-trains themselves, mostly the ones from the quarries. I was hoping things would get better so I could go back to him eventually, but it wasn't to be. He struggled on while I was in Tellgard, a good two years that was: the Starborn be praised for Arval's goodness to me, he found me work to do and saw me fed and housed – but in the end my uncle had to sell up. He went back to his home village here in Gwent y'm Aryframan, and I went back to the mule trains. I was raised in a *gradstedd* myself you know, just like the one where we stayed, but somehow I didn't want to go back to it. I kept hoping that maybe... well anyway, one day I had an idea. I remembered that when Lord Arymaldur... at the Spring Feast, when the fighting broke out... what I mean is, it was your father who saved my life.' He nodded at Heretellar, and went on.

'Yes, I think Thaltor would have killed me, as he killed others that day, and to tell you the truth, I wouldn't have cared. But somehow Lord Forgard gathered me up and brought me to Tellgard, and gave me to Arval to keep safe. So thinking about this, I went to his house and explained who I was and asked if there was work for me. And Lord Forgard, there's a man who's stood by what he believes in and acts accordingly, he remembered me like I was sure he would, and he found a place for me. And after a while, when he saw where I'd be most use to him, he sent me down to his lands in the Ellanwic which is where I was when Lord Heretellar came home and now I'm working for him.'

'How many times do I have to tell you not to bother with all this formality? I'm just Heretellar to you, I'm working for my father too you know.'

The two young men grinned at each other, then the smile faded from Heretellar's face as he turned to his cousin. 'You'll find things have changed quite a bit during the time we were away, Ancrascaro.

I don't know that your parents will be keen on you joining Arval. They've the boys to think of, after all.'

Heretellar was an only child, but Ancrascaro had two brothers, born only a year apart although the elder of the two was some ten years younger than herself. As the miles passed, she began to see the first hints of what Heretellar might have meant. The country on either side of the road gradually changed from cultivated fields and pasture to neglected tracts of abandoned land. Empty farms and hamlets were interspersed with an occasional shabby inn and villages where only a handful of houses were still inhabited among buildings falling into disrepair. Scrub was already beginning to invade the ploughland, in some places already sufficiently established to form wide thickets of willow and birch. Ancrascaro looked about her, amazed at the change that had taken place during the years of her stay in Salfgard.

'What has been happening here?' she asked. 'Where have all the people gone?'

'Don't you notice how it all gets more deserted, the nearer to the border we are?' replied Heretellar. 'Would *you* want to live within sight of forts and checkpoints, where you could be seen by troops and overlooked by armed men? While there is fertile land to spare, and kinsmen with a welcome, then folk will drift away up-country towards more open skies. Look there, where the gloom begins. Why stay here, when every time you lift your eyes you see that brooding darkness?'

Away before them, and nearer with every turn of the wheels, the sky was grey and louring, obscured by thick clouds that seemed to reach towards them, drawing them on and under. Ancrascaro bit her lip as their heaviness seemed to settle on her heart. Regretful though she had been to say goodbye to Ardeth and Fosseiro, she had been looking forward to going home, but now doubts began to nag at her mind.

'What is it like on our side of the border?' she asked, and was disconcerted by a new bitterness she heard in Heretellar's voice.

'You'll see, soon enough,' he said shortly.

And Ancrascaro did see. On their final night in Gwent y'm Aryframan, she slept in the wagon while her two companions pitched a small tent; the last *gradstedd* was miles behind them. Before them stretched an endless line of lights marking the border. They pricked the darkness, some moving, no doubt carried by men engaged on manoeuvres of some kind, others clustered so brightly that they were reflected in a sullen glow by the clouds above. Ancrascaro moved restlessly in her blankets, unable to sleep. Her bed was hard and not particularly comfortable, true, but she had slept peacefully enough in the wagon many times before. What kept her wakeful was her own unease. She felt she could see the lights even through closed eyelids; somehow they seemed to pollute the darkness. And it was so airless; she felt stifled, apprehensive, fearful of what the day would show her. Dawn came, but the lights still burned, more threatening than in the full dark, imparting a sterile glare. Approaching the outer checkpoint, Ancrascaro saw that the blockhouses and troop accommodation she remembered had changed beyond recognition. Ugly though these had been, they were plain, comparatively small buildings. Now barracks, depots, fortified permanent stations stretched as far as she could see to left and right; and on the Caradward side of the border a wide area was given over to drill squares, practice ranges, stables, armouries, through which straight paved roads ran up and down.

She was so taken up with staring at all this, at the soldiers she saw everywhere, more than she had ever seen before, marching, riding, standing on guard, and all of them, even those who simply lounged and stared at the travellers, expensively equipped and heavily armed, that at first she scarcely paid attention to the business of actually passing through the earthworks. But then she noticed Meremvor. He was not wearing his Gwentaran cap today; he sat blank-faced on the driver's seat, his head lowered so that none could catch his eye, leaving it to Heretellar to do the talking as their documents were examined by the patrolman. Of course, thought Ancrascaro with a sudden chill, he doesn't want them to hear his accent! Anger flared in her, but she had more sense than to show it. At last they were waved on, and passed without speaking down the road through what she now realised was effectively a military zone. Behind them, the man who had watched their progress, standing well back from a window, sat down with a satisfied smile to put his signature to a small pile of documents. Thaltor intended to waste no time: long before the travellers were anywhere near the city, his chosen troops were moving into position on a northward sector of the border.

Waiting until they were well clear by a couple of miles, Ancrascaro turned to her cousin. 'This is just… it's so… it's just *horrible!*' she said, unable to find a word that adequately described what she felt. 'What on earth is it all for? Who is paying for it?'

'I told you you'd see, didn't I?' said Heretellar with a rather tight little smile. 'But as for your questions: well, you asked me two things, but I think there are three answers. The money flows from the gold mine – Vorynaas' gold mine. As for the purpose of it all, in one sense it's not for anything because as you rightly imply, it's completely unnecessary. What concerns me more is what use it might all be put to – and I find that a worrying thought, when I remember that Vorynaas is the paymaster.'

Busy with their thoughts, none of them gave a second glance to a man who passed them, heading towards Caradriggan at speed, just one among many armed riders cantering up and down the posting-track which ran alongside the road.

Ancrascaro soon realised why Heretellar wanted his father to spend less time in Caradriggan. The veil of antique beauty which the city had once so lightly and gracefully worn was being rapidly torn away. In street after street, a fever of new building was taking place as men made newly rich constructed large mansions to show off their wealth. Seth y'n Carad now had gilded turrets, and its massive doors were gold-studded; folk whispered that behind them were gates reinforced with sky-steel. The old horse-market was gone, its site cleared and levelled and made into a parade-ground. At one end was a high reviewing-dais sheltered by a permanent pavilion, elaborately-adorned and expensively finished yet somehow overdone: too garish, over-decorated, ostentatious and tasteless. But this was preferable to what faced it across the square, where a low, grim-looking stronghouse brooded behind barred windows. Down both sides were tiered stands flanked by barracks, and at each city gate new quarters had been built where troops were stationed. Rising to the height of the walls, they straddled the street on their upper storeys so that all who came and went had to pass a close and prolonged scrutiny. Even the walls themselves, with their fabled strength, had been torn down on the north side and rebuilt to a taller, thicker gauge; and here, where men and horses came up and down, wagons and mule-trains, soldiers, labourers and overseers, all the traffic from the gold mine in the forest constantly moving on the road, they were now extended into a mighty barbican.

If this was what Caradriggan had become, what must Heranwark be like, thought Ancrascaro in dismay. Although she was too young to remember a time when the sun shone clear above her homeland, she had grown accustomed to the unsullied skies of Salfgard and Framstock; already it was borne in on her how much she would miss them. And now, even as there came to her mind childhood memories of bright silver lanterns, sweet fountains playing in the lamplight, deference offered to Arval and Tell'Ethronad as of right, cheerful daily commerce in streets thronged with colourfully-clad citizenry, now as she looked back with newly-adult eyes, she remembered signs that the child had missed, the tarnish already falling on those silver lamps of old. Words from a long-ago day came back to her, something Forgard had said when he escorted Numirantoro home from Tellgard, something about a sickness creeping to the heart of the city as the weevil bores into the lily bulb. Yes, she could picture the scene now: herself, carefully carrying the water she had been sent to fetch, while her uncle paced up and down and the anxious words passed breathlessly over her head between him and Numirantoro. She had not really heeded at the time; but as a child will, she had picked up the mood of the moment and now, years later, it returned to her with fuller understanding.

She came out of these gloomy thoughts to find that they were drawing to a halt outside her parents' house. This, she was relieved to see, appeared unchanged: it was surely just her imagination that made the wall facing on to the street seem so blank and secretive. They had arrived in the early evening; with a pang it struck her that it would be hours yet before they lit the lamps in Salfgard, but here the lantern burned already above the door and lights glowed in the small upper windows. Meremvor handed down her luggage and got up again to the driver's seat; Heretellar had embraced her and was turning away too, ready to head off. Suddenly she took hold of him and pulled him round again.

'Heretellar, don't go, I wanted to ask you something.'

Her cousin looked at her, surprised at the urgency in her voice, and waited. 'Well, what is it?' he asked eventually.

She stood, downcast, unsure of how to go on, having spoken on impulse. 'I just wanted to know whether Tellgard is…' She hesitated and started again. 'Whether you think that Tellgard has… I mean, so much has changed here… Is Tellgard still the same?'

Their route had not taken them that way and she was afraid of what might have happened: Heretellar's warning had not really prepared her for the changes in the city, he had not tried to describe what she was about to see; perhaps there was some unpalatable truth about Tellgard which he had hidden from her?

Heretellar began to smile, but his face was serious once more as he saw the fear, the need for reassurance in Ancrascaro's eyes. 'Don't worry! The old place is looking its age these days, but its heartbeat is as strong as ever. And always will be, while Arval is with us,' he added, glancing up as the doors opened.

Out rushed Ancrascaro's two young brothers, and her parents appeared at the top of the steps, followed by other members of the household. Heretellar realised that Ancrascaro was still gripping his arm tightly.

'Don't go back to the Ellanwic straight away! Quick, promise me you won't go before we've talked again!'

'Yes, all right, I'll call round in a day or two,' said Heretellar, rather startled, before the two of them were swept up into the family reunion.

Misgivings

Across the city, Vorynaas was just sitting down to supper. It was a lavish spread, even though he was dining alone, but he felt he deserved to celebrate the moment. Below in the kitchens of Seth y'n Carad, the runner from the west gate who had brought word that the party from Gwent y'm Aryframan had entered the city was finishing his meal and fingering the gold pieces in his pocket. In the courtyard, the rider who had been held in readiness since the message came in that they had passed the border was saddling up before riding back to Thaltor who had sent it. The man carried a secret token of authenticity, but no other identification, and was charged with a brief instruction which he was to pass on by word of mouth to Thaltor alone: 'Proceed as soon as possible with the agreed first move'. Vorynaas dismissed the house-servant and helped himself to food from the dish; tonight he wanted no silent menials hovering in the background. Staring into the middle distance, savouring equally the tender braised lamb and the dark unfolding of his plans, Vorynaas smiled.

That autumn, Thaltor arrived in Salfgard a little earlier than usual, with a week still to go before the festivities of Harvest-home. To everyone's surprise, he showed interest in the preparations, and announced that he thought he would prolong his stay, deferring his days of instruction until after the feast so as to enjoy the holiday more. This was a new, more genial Thaltor, who praised Fosseiro's cooking and strolled around the farm chatting to Ethanur and Framhald. Up at the village inn, he bought drinks for the locals and joined in the banter as to the likely winners of the coming contests; and when a hunting-party was made up, he went along and gave his share of the bag to Fosseiro for the kitchen. But though everyone noticed the change in him, not all were convinced it was genuine, and there were some who wondered what the mask of friendliness concealed. Mag'rantor reported that for all the laughter in the *Malt Shovel*, Thaltor was still as thick as ever with Valahald, and that the two of them were whispering with Ghentar, their heads together in a corner. Cottiro complained to Fosseiro that she thought Thaltor was always staring at Maesrhon.

'Smirking because of the scar on his lip, I expect,' she exclaimed indignantly, 'as if he was anything to turn a girl's head himself! I don't care how much gold he can afford to wear. And anyway, you did a really good job on Maesrhon, the scar is tiny and it hardly shows unless you know where to look.'

Fosseiro laughed this off, but privately she and Ardeth were uneasy too. Well might Thaltor stare: Maesrhon was half-way through his fifteenth year now and already the child in him had been overtaken by the man. He was taller than any of the other boys, rapidly catching up even Cunoreth who towered over everyone; though gentle and quiet in manner, he yet had an air about him which set him apart from his fellows and which could be quite intimidating, although Fosseiro thought this was not always what Maesrhon intended. It was partly to do with those strange eyes of his, so golden and unwavering, but there was something else that Fosseiro could not place. Somehow the boy was unreachable behind invisible armour, always alone even in a crowd of friends. She looked up from her work with a sigh, only to see him heading towards the stables with that light, loose stride. Although the resemblance was still there to see, as he got older his likeness to Numirantoro became less marked. Could it be that he now favoured his father more? Ardeth had never met Vorynaas, and Fosseiro retained only the vaguest memory of the one time she had seen him, years ago in Caradriggan, long before Numirantoro grew up to be forced into marriage with him. Her recollection was of a powerfully-built young man, good-looking but somehow unpleasant, a description which now exactly fitted Ghentar but not his brother. Although Fosseiro had promised to say nothing to anyone, she thought she would have to share with Ardeth something Cottiro had recently passed on to her from Astirano.

But somehow, in the bustle of getting things ready for the feast, there never seemed to be time to talk quietly on their own; and then there was all the clearing up to do afterwards while Thaltor was busy putting the boys from Caradriggan through their paces in his swordsmanship classes. Sitting with Ghentar and Heranar as they waited their turn, Thaltor watched Maesrhon and Valahald in action. He was finding it more of an effort with every day that passed to keep up his pretence of goodwill, fretting to be away and discover what success his forces had met with. Surely if anything had gone wrong, rumour of it would have reached Salfgard by now, but he could detect no hint that these slow-witted peasants had noticed anything amiss away south there. His attention shifted back to the scene before him. Look at that young cuckoo! Given the difference in their ages, Valahald should be an easy winner, but he was getting nowhere while Maesrhon simply toyed with him. For some years now Thaltor had derived a good deal of private amusement from his suspicions about Maesrhon, imagining the pleasure to come from baiting Vorynaas when it suited him. But these days, his feelings about the boy were beginning to change.

He remembered how as a child Maesrhon used to hang around Tellgard. What if he was still Arval's man when he returned to the city? They'd gone to enough trouble in the past to snuff out the threat from that quarter and it would be all to do again if another faction was to build around Maesrhon. Thaltor was shrewd enough to see that there was something about him that could attract a following, and gripped the edge of the bench as resentment and dislike rose in him: yes, he knew where the boy got that air of his from, and his skill with the sword. I am the only opponent who can still outmatch him, he thought, but for how much longer? Must I put up with hearing men whisper behind my back "Maesrhon is the best in Caradriggan"? He adjusted his broad gold collar and fiddled with one of his arm-rings, forcing himself to be calm, thinking how Ghentar had marked his brother's face with his sword. His mind ran on to what Valahald told him of what Maesrhon had said afterwards. A promising lad, Valahald: much brighter than Ghentar, without the sly ways of Haartell, who Thaltor absolutely detested; more independent of thought than his father Valafoss, and skilful enough to pass muster in Rigg'ymvala, even if he couldn't get the better of Maesrhon. Thaltor straightened up with sudden exasperation, calling a halt to their bout. He needed to think this through, but maybe it would be best if Maesrhon could be disposed of; and if so, what better time or place than now, up here in Salfgard? When they had finished for the morning, he made an opportunity to mutter in Valahald's ear.

'Tell the others you and I are going to ride out on exercise tomorrow. Get yourself a horse and food for two and meet me by the oak tree where the road forks, an hour after dawn. I want to talk to you alone.'

A week later, he took the road for home, proposing in a friendly manner to journey as far as Framstock with Mag'rantor and Ethanur, who had trading to do at the market. Disguising their lack of enthusiasm as best they could, they set off early one morning at an easy pace. As Mag'rantor said afterwards, 'What else could we do? It's Ardeth who's had to put up with the man twice a year, and when he said this was his final visit, we felt we had to keep up appearances for Ardeth's sake.'

In Framstock they stayed with Geraswic as usual, but seeing Thaltor strolling about the markets on several occasions they realised that he was still in the town, quartered at the *Salmon Fly*, where by all accounts he was spending freely, standing drinks for other customers and inviting others who were staying at the inn to join him for meals.

Eventually he left for Caradriggan, having attached himself to a large party of fellow-travellers: local traffic from the mart, making for outlying villages further down the road, and a caravan of trading-wagons going all the way to the border. Mag'rantor had been chatting to an acquaintance at the roadside below the old bridge and had seen them set off.

'What's he up to?' he asked that evening, as they sat at supper and he described the scene to Ethanur and the others.

Geraswic shrugged silently, but Gillis spoke up.

'I can tell you it's the first time he's ever travelled in a party. In fact in the past he's had plenty to say about making better speed on his own, not wanting to be delayed by slow-moving wagons, not needing the kind of conversation he'd get from Gwentaran companions. That's the kind of thing he used to come out with when he'd had a drink or two in the *Fly*, from all I heard.'

Heard from his brother Rossanell, I expect, thought Mag'rantor. The fellow was never out of the *Fly* himself, a real waster. Mag'rantor had seen him slumped on a corner bench, and hanging around the edge of the market on unsteady legs.

'Well, if Thaltor has had a real change of heart, it's not before time,' he said now. 'But I wouldn't trust him, no matter how would-be friendly he is.'

A little snap of laughter signalled a rare contribution from Geraswic. 'Money talks. If he keeps throwing his gold about freely enough, no doubt he'll buy his way into men's favour eventually.'

Both Mag'rantor and Gillis protested vehemently at this, feeling uncomfortably conscious of their Caradwardan origins. 'No, no, not in Framstock, it's not like that in Gwent y'm Aryframan.'

His face settling back into its habitual bitter lines, Geraswic shrugged again, but Ethanur, who had been frowning to himself, now had something to say.

'Surely the important thing is not what Thaltor has been saying and doing, but why. Think about it: he was in Salfgard longer than he's ever stayed before, then he hung around here too. In both places, he went out of his way to seem friendly in word and deed. Then when he did leave, he made sure he had company on the way. So what does all that achieve? It means as many people as possible saw him, spoke with him, took away a favourable impression, can vouch for his presence. It means he's got all the proof he needs of where he was, and what he was doing, for the best part of a month.'

'But why would he need that?' asked Gillis, puzzled.

Ethanur shrugged in turn. 'I don't know. Maybe there's something happening that he doesn't want to be associated with. Or no, more likely something that it's important other people don't connect him with.'

They exchanged glances, Mag'rantor noting for almost the first time that Ethanur, rising twenty now, was no longer a boy. With a sinking heart he acknowledged his suspicion that the young man might have put his finger on something – but what? He turned to Gillis and Geraswic. 'Have you heard anything? We've had no word of trouble in Salfgard.'

They shook their heads. 'No, not in Framstock. Not so far as we know.'

Mag'rantor could not be rid of the unease that had settled on him. 'Well look, keep your ears open and let us know if there is any talk, will you? Now I'm for bed. Ethanur and I need to be on the road first thing tomorrow.'

Atranaar's report

Thaltor stuck with his travelling companions all the way down the road, tolerating the slow rate of progress for the sake of the chance it gave him to strike up a rapport in which he might pick up a rumour, a stray word, any hint that suspicion was beginning to spread in Gwent y'm Aryframan. Before they passed into the deserted lands nearer the border, they stopped for the night in several *gradsteddan* and here he would make himself agreeable in the public rooms, standing his round and joining in if there was gaming or a wager. But he heard nothing untoward, continuing with the party for several miles into Caradward before turning south at a road-meeting with many expressions of goodwill. He passed a couple of days at a training-camp, working off all his accumulated exasperation by putting some new recruits through a nightmarish regime of extreme endurance tests and verbal abuse. Then, finally, the time came for him to turn north, making top speed at last by changing horses at every post; and on the agreed date he arrived at one of the larger troop stations situated mid-way between crossing points on the border. Turning his horse in, he gave orders for a private room to be made ready for him, with food and wine for two; and as men scurried to obey him he took himself off for a much-needed soak in the bath-house. By evening he was sitting waiting, drink in hand; then he heard the guards exchanging passwords outside and the man he was expecting entered the room.

'Reporting as instructed, sir.'

'Atranaar, come in.'

For a moment Thaltor looked the newcomer up and down, wondering as he had done in the past whether the man was perhaps part-Outlander. He had dark, inscrutable eyes, but stood taller than was usual for the *sigitsaran*. His weapons had been left outside the room and he was without body-armour, being dressed in hard-wearing fatigues adapted as worn by the scouting patrols.

'What a name to be saddled with! Did you bring a map?'

'No sir, I never carry any incriminating documents. If you have a map here, I will be able to show you on it everything you want to know. As for my name, it came to me at my birth and I think no man can be held responsible for the actions of his parents.'

Hm, we've got a cool customer here, thought Thaltor, and then suddenly burst into laughter as the significance of what Atranaar had said struck him. 'No, indeed! Well, sit down, help yourself to wine. We'll eat first and get down to business afterwards.'

He put his head round the door and told the sentry to send orders for the food to be brought in. When all was done and cleared away, he turned up the lamp and spread a map out on the table. 'Now, show me on here the positions your men have taken up.'

Atranaar leaned forward, pointing. 'All this area here is derelict, now; your map is slightly out of date. May I mark it? Well this, where I'm shading, is the extent of the abandoned land; and here, where I show heavier shading, is where the scrub is thick and beginning to take hold as new woodland. These settlements,' and he put a ring around several names, 'are all completely deserted now, but retain buildings still serviceable enough to use as cover. Now here, and here, and here, are the first bases we established; and when we were sure we were undetected, we advanced further and spread out. Our forward positions are now *here*. You'll see we've secured both sides of these roads leading to Framstock and Rihannark, to stop any possibility of escape; these other routes that I'm marking in now are just seasonal tracks which are in sporadic use as short-cuts. Our lines of supply and communication run like *this*. Everywhere that I mark with a small circle is a base for twelve men, of whom two are specialists: one medically-trained and one a signaller. The small squares are the larger holds, each with three dozen troops. And moving about between all these are the scouts who operate alone: they all carry the means to make sure they obey their orders not to be taken alive.'

The map was now a network of lines and symbols, stretching far into Gwent y'm Aryframan from a starting-point on a northerly sector of the border. Thaltor studied it closely, deep in thought. 'You are sure your presence is unknown?'

'Quite sure, sir. We are well dug-in and camouflaged, but we have proceeded with extreme caution and by stages, as was agreed. Only when we were sure it was safe did we move further and bring up more men. All the troops are trained for this kind of action, self-reliant and well disciplined. For the first month we used the subsistence rations we carried with us, then gradually and in different places we have risked the taking of a sheep or two here, an ox there. We've seen no signs of alarm and I have placed scouts among travellers using the main roads. They report no rumour of disquiet in Framstock or any of the *gradsteddan*.'

'Have you now? Don't you think I can keep my own eyes and ears open, stuck among those peasants for twice as long as usual?'

'Of course, sir. But where possible I prefer to obtain confirmation from a second source. It struck me as possible that your rank and status might cause men to be silent in your presence where they would speak freely elsewhere.'

Thaltor grunted non-committally. 'And you've been in position for a full three months now?'

'Yes, into the fourth in fact. And may I assume, sir, that you did not in fact hear anything untoward yourself, during your time in Gwent y'm Aryframan?'

Irritation with Atranaar's cool manner battled in Thaltor with respect for the man's obvious confidence in his own expertise and ability. And after all, he thought, I picked him for this assignment myself; his success only reflects my own good judgement. He looked up with a grin.

'Not a thing. I think we can move on from cows and sheep now, and round up rather more useful livestock. There won't be anything in writing, obviously, but you can take this conversation as your go-ahead to make the next moves.'

'Are we to take able-bodied men only?'

'No, no, have sense, man. We don't want womenfolk running about raising the alarm. I'm happy to leave the circumstances to your judgement, but the main thing at this stage is to make sure that when you do strike, *everyone* is either taken or – well, disposed of, shall we say. You can rely on suitable arrangements being made, once captives reach this side of the border, be they man, woman or child. Any other questions? No? Good, now let's drink to your success.'

The first whispers

Early in the following year's spring, Ardeth travelled down to Framstock taking Maesrhon, Framhald and Ethanur with him; Valahald too was in the party, having surprised Ardeth by asking at the last moment to be included. The two Gwentaran lads were both turned twenty now, and approaching the end of their foster-years. At the Spring Feast they would be going back to their homes, but before that happened Ardeth wanted them to accompany him to a meeting of Val'Arad, which they were now old enough to attend as observers; their full induction would come later, when they were introduced by their fathers or another close family member. Maesrhon of course was ineligible to attend as being both too young and of foreign birth, but he wanted another chance to talk with the Framstock storyteller and Ardeth, although he tried to hide it from himself, was keen to seize every chance of keeping the boy by him. He was dreading their parting, which must come later that year when all four Caradwardans would be leaving his care. Even the fact that Thaltor need visit Salfgard no more failed to lift the shadow on his heart. Arriving at his old home late one afternoon, Ardeth left the youngsters seeing to the baggage and animals and settled down in the small parlour next to the kitchen for an exchange of news with Gillis. He sank into a battered armchair with a sigh of content.

'What a relief to be able to sit on something that doesn't move! The springs in that wagon aren't what they were, or else I really am getting old. Everything all right with you here? The old place is looking as well as ever, I'm glad to see.'

'Yes, most things are fine. It's a pity Geraswic won't stay when you come down, though no doubt Fosseiro will make him more than welcome.'

'Oh no, we're not expecting him up there. Remember Ghentar's not with us this trip, he stayed in Salfgard. I sent Geraswic a message to explain all that.'

Ardeth was just about to ask why Gillis seemed so concerned about this when the door burst open and the two little boys tumbled into the room, bursting to show off their new puppy to 'Uncle Ardeth', and the moment passed. By the time he set off next morning for the meeting of Val'Arad, he had completely forgotten about it; but what he heard in the debates brought Gillis's worried frown back into his mind. At supper that evening Ethanur and Framhald were full of talk about their first experience of council business, regaling the others with an account of the proceedings; Framhald, whose family hailed from the Rossanlow, had been surprised to encounter a couple of relations in town for the meeting and was explaining to Maesrhon who they were, together with what he planned to do once he was back at home; but Ethanur, noticing how Ardeth and Gillis seemed preoccupied, gradually dropped out of the conversation. Thinking over what he had heard that day, he eventually turned to Ardeth.

'What do you make of what we heard in Val'Arad? About the rumours of people disappearing, I mean.'

Ardeth sighed. 'I don't know what to think. On the face of it, it seems so unlikely; but …' He left the sentence unfinished. 'In one way it sounds like rumour feeding on rumour, each story wilder than the next; and after all, no one has gone missing from Framstock, in fact everything we heard today was third-hand at best. But each case is so similar, and if it's true that these so-called vanishings have been happening since the autumn, well that's a long time – time enough for the whispers to die out, if there was no truth behind them.'

Ethanur moved closer to Gillis, speaking quietly. 'You and Geraswic promised to send us word of anything untoward, when Mag'rantor and I were here before. And that was last autumn, but we've had no message.'

Gillis was slightly put out by this. 'Steady on, young man. Whatever might lie behind it, the talk itself didn't start up until getting on for mid-winter. By the time it seemed sense to heed it, you were due down here in person too soon to make sending to Salfgard worthwhile.'

'Yes, but think of how this could all fit in, Gillis. You know what I mean, you must remember who we talked about.'

Ardeth looked from one to the other, baffled and then alarmed as he saw how Gillis was trying to hide his unease, realising that both his companions took seriously what they had heard and had their own suspicions about it. But before he could speak, Valahald joined the conversation.

'I know I wasn't present at the debate in Val'Arad, but I really don't think you need be concerned,' he said. 'I've made a few friends around the town you know, and I've been chatting to them while you were all out. It's true that rumours are flying, but most of the people I've spoken to think that's all they are. One of my acquaintances was saying he thought the significant thing was that no-one seems to actually know any of these folk who are supposed to have disappeared. He thinks if there's any truth in the stories at all, it's probably just a case of a few wasters doing a moonlight flit from a neighbourhood where they weren't wanted, and the tales have grown in the telling.'

He smiled easily, leaning back in his chair, but Gillis made no response. He knew who Valahald spent his time with, hanging round the *Salmon Fly* plying his brother Rossanell with drink, and was embarrassed for the shame it brought to his family. Ethanur however was not so easily quelled.

'What wasters? We don't have *wasters* in Gwent y'm Aryframan.' He glowered at Valahald, but he, it seemed, was intent on avoiding a quarrel this evening.

'Come on now, be realistic, Ethanur. Your loyalty to your homeland is laudable, but we all know not everyone here is as prosperous as Ardeth. Or, may I say, as sensible.' He inclined his head towards Ardeth in a way that fairly set Ethanur's teeth on edge, and continued. 'He's just made the point himself that no-one has gone missing from Framstock, that the stories are all third-hand, that no-one can put names to the rumours. I'll wager you'll find that everyone is present and correct in Rihannark too, and anywhere else you care to think of.

Not to mention that if anyone vanished from a *gradstedd*, the news would be all over the country in no time.'

The other three said nothing. They had been disconcerted to find that Valahald had been listening to them, and Ethanur in particular was mindful of what Mag'rantor had had to say about how Thaltor and he had been so close and secret on the latter's last, strangely prolonged, visit.

After a while Valahald attempted to engage Maesrhon in conversation, hoping to discover his plans for the next few days. Time was passing by and he was still no nearer to working out how he was going to achieve what Thaltor had suggested. But getting nowhere by this means, later as he lay wakeful in bed he thought things over and wondered if it might be wiser to do nothing until he saw which way the wind blew in Caradriggan. Valahald had a much cooler head than Thaltor, and though he disliked Maesrhon just as much as the older man, he was more able to stand back and evaluate the consequences of possible courses of action. He remembered what Maesrhon had said after Ghentar had wounded him in the face and was sure that there was more trouble coming between the brothers sooner or later. Why interfere when Ghentar might do the job himself? And after all, Thaltor would be nothing without his connections to Vorynaas. Why risk his own future advancement by tying himself too closely to a subordinate rather than to the leader himself? It was of course possible that the idea of eliminating Maesrhon now had originated with Vorynaas, but that the suggestion had been put to him by Thaltor so that no suspicion would cling to the boy's father. Valahald, wondering fleetingly why Vorynaas hated his son so much, toyed with this theory for a while and then rejected it as a product of his own devious mind. Yes, on balance he thought it would be better to leave well alone, at least for the time being. And if Thaltor cut up rough about it, or if it turned out that Vorynaas did know, and was angered by Valahald's failure to act, well he had the perfect excuse.

Three things at least were clear to him. Obviously, Thaltor's whisperings of last spring had been trustworthy: it was apparent that the secret force had infiltrated Gwent y'm Aryframan and had begun to take prisoners. Second, he could see that alarm was increasing as word of disappearances began to spread. But third, and most important from his own point of view, it seemed no blame was being attached to Caradward yet. To that extent, Thaltor's carefully-laid smokescreen of goodwill had been successful. Valahald could say, if necessary, that he had been afraid to undermine all this by risking any action that might turn feeling against Caradward, that might make men speak of abduction rather than disappearance. And, he thought, settling to sleep as he came to this decision, if Vorynaas does want me to see to Maesrhon, once we are all back in Caradriggan, then that will be another matter altogether. He smiled to himself in the dark.

CHAPTER 24

Rewards of bad faith

Catching sight of a familiar figure some distance in front of her, Ancrascaro crossed the street and hurried in pursuit. She was almost sure it was Meremvor, and if so, maybe Heretellar too was in the city to visit his father now that spring was at hand once more. For a moment or two she lost sight of him among the passers-by and wondered if he had gone into a shop or an inn, but then she spotted him again as he waited before crossing a side-street. Running the last few yards, she called his name and tapped him on the shoulder.

'It *is* you! I thought I recognised you. Is Heretellar with you?'

Blushing slightly with the shyness he had never quite overcome, Meremvor smiled at her. 'Oh, you made me jump! Good day to you, Lady Ancrascaro. Yes, Heretellar and I arrived yesterday.'

'How long will you be here? Would you both come and eat at my father's house one evening? And Meremvor, I wish you would just call me Ancrascaro. Would you do that for me? Please?'

'Well, if you put it like that... Actually, that's just where I'm heading for now. Your house, I mean. Lord Forgard has sent me with an invitation for you and your parents to have supper with him tomorrow. Heretellar will be in the city for the rest of the week.'

'Oh, well in that case,' Ancrascaro broke off, suddenly noticing what had delayed Meremvor and others from walking on. Along the narrow street in front of them came a group of about thirty or forty men, shackled in pairs and followed by a separate smaller group of women. They were escorted by armed guards who were clearing a way for them to pass as swiftly as possible along the street, not being over-particular about who got shoved aside in the process. Ancrascaro's and Meremvor's eyes met.

'Let's go through here, it will be quieter and we can talk.'

She led the way under a slender stone arch that marked the entrance to a narrow alley. After a few paces it opened out into a small square, paved, with a fountain in the centre. Several seats were arranged about it, and lanterns hung from each of the four surrounding walls. Two women were chatting together on a stone bench, feeding crumbs to half a dozen doves that fluttered and preened, and Ancrascaro led Meremvor over to the opposite corner where there was a curved wooden seat in the angle of the wall. The central area around the fountain was spread with light-coloured gravel, carefully-raked; it sparkled here and there where a crystal of quartz or some other mineral caught the lamplight. Ancrascaro sighed. It was a serene and elegant place but she remembered that in her childhood it had been tended as a beautiful garden. She turned to Meremvor.

'They must be going to the slave-market. To think that there should be slaves in Caradriggan! It's not so long ago that we would never have believed such a thing could happen.' He made no answer and after a moment she went on. 'What I was going to say before was, I'll deliver your invitation from Forgard; I was on my way home when we met. I'm sure we'll be able to come tomorrow evening, but if there is a problem, I will make sure a message is sent to him this afternoon.'

Meremvor nodded. 'Right, I'll tell him.' He looked at her. 'And not only in Caradriggan. If any of that lot had come from the Open Hall – what a joke! – they'll be for the mine. I wonder if any other poor wretches are on their way to Arval. I tell you, if it were me, I'd rather go to Arval even so, than be condemned to the mine.'

Ancrascaro sat silent: she knew what being sent to Arval meant, these days.

The following evening, as Forgard's guests left the table and made their way back to his living-room, she glanced out at the street while passing a window. She paused, looking more carefully, and then followed her companions. A selection of almond biscuits and lemon cakes, crystallised fruits, toasted nuts and mixed small savouries was laid out on trays. Forgard was presiding over the choice of drinks and asked her with a smile what she would have. Going over to where he stood in the corner, she asked for a chilled herbal infusion rather than dessert wine and spoke to her uncle quietly.

'There are two men outside, across the street beside the fountain in the gardens. They were there when we arrived: I noticed them watch us. And I've just glanced out of the window, and they're still there.'

'Oh, they're old friends.'

The sardonic tone was not lost on Ancrascaro, nor the way the smile had faded from Forgard's face.

'Two of Haartell's night-shift from Seth y'n Carad, I expect. He keeps me under constant surveillance. Good luck to him! If they don't know by now exactly where I stand, that I make no attempt to conceal either my opinions or my comings and goings, then all I can say is, they should do. But then, Vorynaas has gold and to spare these days: if he wants to waste it, let him.'

They moved to sit down, joined by Heretellar and Ancrascaro's mother Eirenello, who was Forgard's sister. Her father and aunt were talking with Meremvor and another young man who had turned out to be a son of Poenmorcar. The land Forgard had sold to the distinguished engineer bordered the estates that Heretellar was now managing away south in the Ellanwic and a friendship had grown between the families. Ancrascaro sipped her drink and admired the beauty of the flowers whose scent filled the room; Heretellar had brought them from his own growing-houses. She listened as the talk turned to domestic matters: the doings of Ancrascaro's two young brothers, Heretellar's work, the new cook who had recently joined Forgard's household staff.

'If tonight's supper was an example of her arts, you're a lucky man,' said Eirenello.

'Yes, I'm more than pleased, on several counts. She came to us from the *Sword and Stars*,' said Forgard, 'where her husband lost his position because of failing heath. We've taken the whole family in; I can find light duties for her man to do, and the youngsters are still just children. There's time enough to sort something out for them, and meanwhile it's nice to have them about the place.'

'Not Isteddar's family?' asked Ancrascaro in surprise. 'Is he here too? Maesrhon used to be quite friendly with him.'

'No, Isteddar works at the *Sword* full-time now he's a man. It's a good place to have a pair of ears: you can pick up interesting stuff in the *Sword* and he hears more than I would. People who would watch their tongues in my presence often speak freely in front of him.'

Heretellar leaned forward. 'Yes, but when, *when*, will we be able to actually use any of the information that might come our way? There are not enough of us to take action, there will never be enough when Vorynaas' gold flows so freely! Was there ever a proverb truer than the one that says: *the worth of the heart is laid bare in the work of the hands when the will has its way unchecked*? His troops and spies are everywhere; those whose support he has not bought outright he has corrupted so that they stand by and let him push through laws which he uses to condemn men out of hand. They have swallowed his gold as surely as his mine swallows slaves. I thought all would be well once more after Tell'Ethronad followed Arval's counsel, but it is almost five years now since Vorynaas and Valafoss sent their sons to Salfgard and our darkness is deeper than ever. Is there no hope for us, after all?'

'Listen, *is-gerasto*. In that long-ago dawn when Arymaldur was taken from us, I gave in to despair, but Arval comforted me. "There is always hope, if men know where to find it," he said; and he told me he had the words from Lord Arymaldur himself. And before that, on another black day, Numirantoro counselled me to stand by Arval. We must continue to trust him.'

With a glance at the lines of worry etched permanently on to her brother's face, Eirenello now spoke quietly to Heretellar. 'Your father may never have told you this, but when you were still just a little child he tried to persuade Arythalt and the others to think again. Arythalt refused to listen, and Vorynaas went unchecked.' She looked across at her daughter. 'That was on the day when he asked Numirantoro to bring you with her to Tellgard, Ancrascaro. We cannot falter now. Who would wish to be consumed by an over-late regret like that which eats at Arythalt?'

A faint drift of fragrance from the flowers reached Ancrascaro again and with it a sudden insight.

'I can remember going to Arythalt's with uncle Forgard that day,' she said, 'and although of course I didn't understand all I heard, bits of it come back to me now. Didn't you tell Arythalt and Numirantoro that you thought part of Caradward's trouble was caused not so much by what its people did, as by why they did it? And now Heretellar asks why we still walk in shadow even though we complied with the resolution of the council. I will tell you why. Vorynaas and Valafoss sent their sons to Salfgard, yes, but under protest; and no others of his party have followed suit either willingly or not. Our gesture of goodwill to Gwent y'm Aryframan was void, rendered meaningless by the lack of grace with which it was made.'

'Yes, I think you're right. And let us hope I am wrong, but I can't help suspecting Vorynaas of more bad faith,' said Heretellar.

Ancrascaro saw in her mind's eye the borderlands of Gwent y'm Aryframan lying deserted and waste, almost as if the pall of Caradward's betrayal stretched over them; the troops massed along the line and at the crossing points; and she shivered as she remembered Heretellar's foreboding as to their possible use.

A prisoner

Atranaar sat staring into space, chewing on a toothpick. He appeared lost in thought, but this was deceptive. His mind was methodically working through a memorised list, mentally ticking off the various stages of a phased withdrawal of his forces. In his specialised branch of the military, instructions were passed on verbally; he and his men were trained to commit even lengthy and detailed orders to memory. The previous week, word had come in that he was to begin pulling his men back over the border, but to do it gradually behind a screen of protective outposts. He had established his headquarters in a network of dugouts tunnelled into the side of a low hill, screened by thick scrub in which two or three free-standing temporary structures were well camouflaged. Here he was a few miles in rear of the foremost positions, a network of holds which were now being emptied and carefully dismantled in a set sequence. He checked over the names in his mind: Grey Rock, Alder Valley, Broken Cliff, Dead Tree, Barren Hill. The last two had been main outposts: they would now become bases for twelve men only until all the rest were removed behind the second line, then they too would withdraw and his own headquarters would be pulled back in turn. Digging with his toothpick at a stringy piece of meat lodged stubbornly between two molars, Atranaar ran through the time-scale of the operation. He could have completed it in a week, had it not been for the orders that all traces of their temporary occupation were to be obliterated as they went.

Standing up and stretching, he reached for the jug and poured himself some water. Atranaar never drank any form of alcohol when on active duty and his men were likewise forbidden under pain of instant dismissal. In the corner of the room there was a locked cabinet where double-strength wine was kept, along with a small quantity of raw spirit. These were mainly used medically, either to clean out wounds or to dull the pain of any emergency surgery that might be necessary. Atranaar glanced round the dugout. It was small, sparely equipped and scrupulously neat: he found untidiness intolerable. His bed was folded down to make a stool, on which his blankets were set; the water jug rested on a table that also folded. A lamp burned on top of the cabinet, and two earthenware pipes had been forced through the roof to ensure a flow of fresh air. Wooden duckboards covered the floor, keeping the contents of the room out of the damp and improving the temperature slightly, but contributing little else to its sparse comforts. The chamber was barely four paces square and Atranaar would carry its entire contents himself, when it was time to move out, which he estimated would be in two to three days' time.

Atranaar ran through the tally of prisoners in his mind, the convoys of human cargo destined for sorting in the Open Hall at Caradriggan. It had all been very easy. Their quarry had been practically sitting targets: they had made only the feeblest attempts to run from their captors and very few had tried to resist. Those who did had been quickly overpowered, their knives and hunting bows being no match for his special forces. There had been only a couple of serious injuries and the wounded prisoners, together with any who were aged, babies or toddlers, had been separated off, killed and buried in well-concealed graves. Atranaar wasted no remorse on this, nor concern for the children sent stumbling under guard to bondage in a strange land. Thaltor had been correct in suspecting Outland blood in him: his father was part-*sigitsaran* and had been in service to a lord in Staran y'n Forgarad until he had got the man's daughter pregnant. Thrown out and disgraced, they had both turned on the child, taking out on him the misery of their descent into a mire of poverty, bitterness and mutual recrimination. Atranaar had enlisted at Rigg'ymvala as soon as he was of age, blanking his young years from his waking mind, although they haunted his dreams. He could never decide which he hated more, the children who suffered as he had, or those more fortunate.

Briefly he wondered what was the purpose of their present exercise. He knew from the reports of his agents that ripples of alarm had been spreading since around midwinter, but so far he had no reason to think that any in Gwent y'm Aryframan suspected that their country had been partially occupied by a covert force, even though the number of prisoners taken had been quite large. And clearly, if they were to remove the evidence of their presence as they withdrew, the idea was to ensure that the enterprise remained a secret. He could see no particular point in it unless – his mind suddenly focused on this new idea – yes, unless the whole thing had been a trial run for some future occasion? He considered this theory for a moment or two, and then stood up abruptly, annoyed with himself. First he had probed the raw wounds of his childhood again, now he was wasting time and energy on fruitless speculation. Why should he care what plans the rulers of Caradward made? He had resolved long ago to be the best at the harsh discipline he had chosen, to obey without question any orders he was given, to eliminate all weakness and emotion from his life. And he was the best, otherwise he would never have been put in charge of such a difficult task. With narrowed eyes, he silently renewed the vow he had made to bring this commission off successfully with all orders carried out to the letter.

Drawing aside the heavy leather drape that hung in the doorspace of the dugout, he went out to begin his regular check of headquarters. He passed from man to man, treading softly and speaking quietly. All was orderly and correct as he entered a small wattle-built shed among birches and young ash trees. Inside on high racks, away from the damp of the dugouts and out of reach of marauding animals, was where they kept the perishable stores and foodstuffs. The guard stood to attention: his post was a duty assigned to the most junior of their band, but it was typical of Atranaar's thoroughness that he always looked in here on his rounds and the young man was keen to make a good impression. He was in the middle of detailing what supplies he held, and what arrangements he had made for their disposal and transport when the time came to break camp, when Atranaar's head turned sharply. A second later, the soldier heard it too: a strange sound, coming closer;

heavy footsteps, occasionally stumbling; ragged breaths interrupted by exhausted coughing and retching; muffled cursing. The young guard's first thought was that one of his comrades was drunk, and catching sight of Atranaar's face he felt a thrill of apprehension at what might be in store for anyone who had been so foolish. But edging out behind his superior as Atranaar, waiting until the steps had passed the door, emerged silently with a sudden challenge, he was confronted by something very different, and quite unexpected.

Two scouts were half supporting, half dragging, a wounded man between them. His clothes were torn at the shoulder, where blood from what looked like a severe head wound had run down. His face was roughly bandaged and fresh blood showed through his sleeve from what was presumably another injury. One leg was twisted and as the scout nearest wheeled around to face Atranaar, it gave way under him and he slid from the other man's grasp to fall on the ground, his chest heaving.

'Well?'

'A spy, sir, so we've brought him in for interrogation.'

Atranaar turned to the other scout. 'Get him some medical attention, and keep him under guard. You, go with him to help and come back to your post here as soon as you're no longer needed.' The young soldier moved forward. 'You, come inside with me while I hear your report.'

The first scout followed him into the stores shed, wondering what on earth his commanding officer had been doing in there. You just never knew where Atranaar was going to turn up next! He hoped it had not been obvious that his sudden appearance had taken him by surprise, and made up his mind to give a good account of himself. He was sure the captive was a prize worth taking. At a nod from his superior, he launched into the tale.

'We spotted him this side of where Grey Rock camp was, heading towards Dead Tree. We could see straight away he was up to something and not just a lone traveller, so we kept him under observation and trailed him. He uses the country well, seems to have had some practice in fieldcraft because our fellows have left not a sign an untrained eye would see, but he must have picked up a trace or two. He left his horse and crept right up until he was within sight of Dead Tree, and we watched him. He lay hid without moving for a good half day, long enough to see men and activity, then he made off back to where we knew he'd left the horse. So we closed in to intercept, and what did he do only leap on the horse and ride off as if every creature that haunts the waste was at his heels. Well, we couldn't let him get away back to Framstock or wherever after what he'd seen, so we shot the horse to stop him, and he hurt his leg as it fell. And the strange thing was, although he was armed, he never even drew his sword as we ran up: just stood there with a kind of blank look on his face. But it can't have been that he was dazed from the fall, or that he was afraid to take on two of us, because as soon as he realised we were going to bring him in rather than finish him off, he drew his sword and fought like a madman, hampered by his leg though he was. We called on him to surrender, but he yelled back that we'd never take him alive and he got roughed up a bit in the process of being proved wrong. We could have killed him then, of course, but in view of what he'd seen, and the way he looked for death rather than capture, we thought you might like to have a little chat with him first.'

'How seriously injured is he?'

'Nothing life-threatening, I'd say, although he's taken a sword-cut to the face which will have spoiled his looks for good.'

'Right, I'll talk to the medic later. Send that young fellow back here to his post; I'll wait for him.'

'Sir. Er, there was something I thought I should say about the prisoner, sir. If he'd rather be dead than captive, I doubt he'll be interested in buying time by talking and it occurs to me that he might try to do away with himself. Best to make sure he doesn't have the wherewithal to try it.'

Atranaar raised his eyebrows slightly although his voice stayed quiet and level. 'You can rest assured I've thought of that, soldier.' After a pause to let this sink in, he went on. 'You've done well, you and your fellow-scout. If all goes well, I'll pass your names on and who knows what may be in it for you. Come and see me when we're back in Caradward.' With a nod, he dismissed the man and settled to wait for the stores guard to return.

Later, he listened as the medical orderly gave his report.

'I've done what I could for him here in the field, sir. His shoulder injury is just a flesh wound; I've cleaned it out and it should heal to nothing worse than a scar. There are no bones broken in the leg, but it's badly bruised and his knee has taken a kick from the horse. It's difficult to be sure yet, but I suspect there may be some permanent damage there. He'll maybe always have a limp, not be able to walk with ease or for long distances. The facial injuries are severely disfiguring. He's obviously caught a sword-point in the right eye, then the blade has cut down through the cheek and nose; the whole thing is a real mess. The right nostril, and part of the nose, is sliced off completely and the eye is finished. He'll be blind on that side, if he lives.'

'Is he going to recover?'

'Well, of course there's the risk of infection, especially if we have to take him with us when we move out.' A faint suggestion of query crept into the man's tone, but Atranaar made no response and after a moment he continued. 'If you want him to live, naturally I shall employ all my skill to keep him alive.'

'I do want him kept alive, at least until I've had the chance to speak to him, which means he's got to survive our withdrawal to a new camp. Can you manage that?'

'I can't guarantee it, sir. If a patient has lost the will to live, sometimes there's nothing more one can do.'

Atranaar mused in silence for a few moments. 'It seems our mystery man has a death wish. The fellows who brought him in had something similar to say. Has he spoken to you?'

'Oh no, sir. He was barely conscious when I began to work on him, and now he's heavily sedated.'

'Well, I want him kept under constant watch. If he begins to recover, see he has no means to harm himself. If he deteriorates significantly, I must be told at once. After I have questioned him, I'll decide then whether to grant him his wish or not. That will be all for now.'

Interrogation

Two days later, with their usual silent efficiency, they dismantled the hold, obliterating all signs of occupation and melting away to a new position in rear of the retreating forward-line. The wounded man was strapped to a stretcher and shared among pairs of carriers: not a popular move either with those who had brought him in, who began to wish they had managed to kill him outright; their comrades, who had heard a rumour of possible reward for his captors; or the medical orderly who assumed he would be called upon to put the man down in the end but was meanwhile fully occupied in keeping his fever under control. Atranaar had been furious when the captive began shouting in delirium during the first day of their march and had left no-one in any doubt as to what would follow if any more noise put their position at risk; but he took his own turn with the bearers nevertheless, not letting it be said that he ordered any man to do a thing he would not do himself.

As he worked with his men to establish their new camp, he pondered the impending interrogation. He had examined the gear that had been taken from the prisoner and could see from his clothes, equipment and sword that this was no peasant or journeyman artisan. And he had been alone, so clearly not a merchant or trader. His belongings, while not ostentatious or of luxury grade, were nevertheless well-made and of high quality; and according to his captors, his horse had been of similar sort. But there was nothing that would identify him: no letter, token, message, or jewellery; nothing except the sign of the springing corn above his elbow. His brown hair was beginning to show a strand or two of grey above his ears and they had estimated his age at around forty. The orderly had reported that the man's body bore no signs of scarring or injuries apart from his new hurts, and the calluses on his right hand did not match the sword-grip, so clearly he was not employed in military duties; but he was strong, muscular and fit-looking, with a tan on his upper body that was most noticeable on his face and forearms. Someone who spent his days outdoors, then; maybe a farmer, thought Atranaar. Yet why would a middle-aged, seemingly prosperous farmer leave his land to undertake a risky spying mission, alone?

He was no nearer to a theory when the two of them finally met. Supporting himself on a crutch to take the weight off his injured leg, and with his face partially covered in a clean dressing, the prisoner was escorted into Atranaar's quarters, a dug-out room identical to its predecessor except for the extra stool which was brought in for the captive. They looked at each other for a while and then Atranaar broke the silence.

'What is your name, and where do you come from?'

There was no response. This was not unexpected, so he put his third question.

'The men who brought you to me thought you were spying on us. Is this true?'

Still the man refused to speak, but Atranaar thought he saw hate wake in the one good eye; a muscle moved in the man's jaw as if he had clenched his teeth. Time to change tactics, maybe. He stood up, poured water for both of them, resumed his seat with a deceptively relaxed air. Suddenly he leaned forward aggressively. 'How do you know Valestron?'

This shaft hit the target, for the man moved sharply before regaining control of himself. No doubt realising there was no point now in remaining silent, he spoke for the first time. 'Who is Valestron?'

Atranaar smiled slightly. 'You tell me. My men have had to carry you from our last camp. You've been delirious, shouting his name out.'

'A man in a fever may say strange things.'

'Listen friend, we both know you're lying to me. In a fever, men speak truths they would otherwise conceal. You woke, you saw soldiers, Valestron's name came to your mind and lips. Do you want me to take you before him, so that he can tell me who you are? Give me your name.'

Atranaar waited a few moments in vain and then tried a different tack. 'Well then, I'll call you by your new name. Vigurt, that's what they'll call you in Caradward.'

A bitter laugh broke from the man before him. 'That suits me well, I think. "He who used to live." Why bother to drag me all the way to death in Caradward, why not finish it here? It makes no odds to me.'

Atranaar could hear, when the man spoke, how the injury to his face and nose distorted the sound of his voice. Now we're getting a reaction, he thought.

'You misunderstand me. Of course, they may decide you should die, when you are brought into the Open Hall in Caradriggan. But if you are to live, the sentence will be *ha vigu*. A slave has no life of his own, Vigurt, so has no need of his name.'

'Death or slavery? A wide choice, in your Open Hall.' The captive shrugged, his head turned aside. 'I have walked in Na Caarst, and thought it barren, but it blooms with life compared with the wasteland that passes for justice in Caradriggan.'

Atranaar could not disguise his astonishment. 'You have looked on the wilderness? What took you there?'

The man turned in his seat, facing him directly. 'A man without future will run in pursuit of the past. But no man can turn back time, and now the present is lost to me also, thanks to you. You will get no answers from me. What do I care if I have a twisted leg, and a twisted face to match it? I have no interest in living, and no fear of dying. Those who are hurt badly enough, young enough, are fortunate in a way, for nothing can touch them again. There is nothing you can do to me, Caradwardan.'

The words, quietly spoken, hung in the air between them as prisoner and interrogator looked at each other in silence. Abruptly, Atranaar went to the door and called the guard.

'You'd better think things over,' he said curtly to his captive, 'and you'd be well advised to be more co-operative next time.' He nodded to the guard. 'Take him away for now.'

But time passed and Atranaar did not send for him again, busying himself instead with other duties to blank from his mind the brief moment of mutual bleakness that had so disconcerted him. Withdrawal successfully completed, the forces moved into permanent quarters on their own side of the border to await further orders. Atranaar sat reading through the orderly's report, which stated that the prisoner had recovered well, was walking unaided although limping badly, and would shortly be able to do without the dressing on his wounded eye. He heard footsteps outside and the door opened to admit one of the scouts who had made the capture.

'You wanted to see me, sir.'

'Yes.' Atranaar pulled a piece of paper towards him, glanced through it briefly, added his signature and folded it. 'Here's your authority to get an escort together,' he said, handing the man the document, 'and a permit allowing you to requisition anything you may need for the journey. I want you to take the prisoner north and hand him over to custody in the Lissa'pathor. One eye and a lame leg won't matter there: he's fit and strong otherwise, there's plenty of work in him yet. They'll be able to use him at the mine. Report to me again when you return.'

Leavetaking

As mid-day approached, Maesrhon removed the leather apron he was wearing, folded it and sat down on it with his back against the wall he was repairing. He was high up the valley side, where the pasture was short and wiry and the wind carried a faint scent of peaty water, heather and sheep. The fields were divided by dry-stone walls, snaking up the slopes until they met the bare fells where the cuckoos were already beginning to call, flying hawk-like from one patch of ash and hawthorn to another where the streams tumbled down off the heights in steep, rocky ghylls. Ardeth would soon be moving up the ewes with lambs at foot, but as usual during the winter the walls had deteriorated here and there. Maesrhon had spent the morning methodically sorting the stone, building the wall back up to its original height, taking pride in making as good as job as he could; for although the skill of selecting the right stone for the right place, strengthening his work by laying the throughbands, levelling the top for the coverbands and coping, was something he had enjoyed for itself ever since he had been taught how to do it, today the thought was also in his mind that the better he could make the wall, the longer it would stand after he had left it, left Salfgard for ever to return to Caradriggan, as soon he must do.

Brushing his hands on the grass to shift some of the stone-dust, he stretched out for a moment or two to ease the ache in his back and arms. It was hard work, and lonely too, but it suited him. It developed his strength and endurance, improved the accuracy of his eye, and gave him time to think. Sitting up again, he opened the packet of food he had brought with him and ate his noon-meal, gazing into the distance. Then he took from his belt the new knife, his birthday gift from Ardeth, and looked it over closely for what must have been the hundredth time. He grinned to himself, realising how carefully Ardeth must have listened to what he had told of his time with Torald. His great-uncle could be a sly old fox when he wanted! And he was a true craftsman: the knife was beautifully made. The grip was a single piece of turned yew wood, hard-wearing and polished smooth. Maesrhon admired the colour in the graining and the way the tang passed right through to the end, with no risk of breaking half-way along and no rivets to cut the hand. But the chief glory was the blade, two handspans in length and the width of his thumb at its mid-point where it curved slightly. Just as Torald had recommended, there were three working areas to it: two finer, sharper edges and the more robust section at the middle where it was at its widest. Maesrhon hefted it, feeling the perfect balance, and then replaced it in its sheath, turning that over in his hands too. It was made of pigskin, tough and waterproof. There was a pocket on it for a sharpening-stone; this and the loops that secured the handle were fastened with horn buttons. Completely without adornment though it was, the knife had the beauty of total fitness for its purpose.

Maesrhon drew up his knees and rested his chin on them. He would give himself just until the shadow of that elder-bush reached the outcropping rock, and then he would start work on the wall again. His eyes roved over the scene before him as he contemplated returning to Caradriggan. It would surely be only a matter of a couple of weeks or so before the escort arrived and they would have to leave, and then he would never see Salfgard again. Somehow he was quite sure of this. He looked at the sweep of the hillside below him, the blue heights misty with distance, felt the new warmth of the sun waking the earth to the life of another season, heard the cuckoos calling over the gurgling stream and the whisper of fresh green leaves. He thought of all he had learnt from Ardeth and Torald, the fun and laughter with the other youngsters, the warmth and comfort of Fosseiro's care. Would he miss all this? Yes, the pain in his heart told him he would miss it all, every day. Then he thought of what he would be returning to: the oppressive gloom, his year of military service, the daily friction of life in Seth y'n Carad with a father who hated him and a brother whose sword had marked his face. Maesrhon's hand went unconsciously to the scar on his lip as his thought paused here. Why was he not more downcast at the prospect? Remembering how he had wondered once whether Geraswic could be his father until Ardeth's tale had told him no, and remembering too the outburst from Heretellar on his last night in Framstock, his thought turned to Arval.

I am ready now to hear what Arval can tell me, he said within himself. I know he has secrets he has waited to reveal. I will tell him myself that the time has come, that I am strong enough for the knowledge he holds in trust. A ripple of anticipation ran through him like a shiver over his skin. Everything Arval had told him about Gwent y'm Aryframan, about Ardeth, about Salfgard, had turned out to be true. Arval had always told him the truth and dealt truly with him: to talk with him again would be worth the price of returning. He stood up and looked at the heap of stone beside the wall, his eyes automatically seeking for the correct size and shape of the next pieces he would need, and another thought struck him. Just as I am a misfit in Caradriggan, so also I do not belong here. I love Ardeth and Fosseiro and I know they love me, yet Ardeth has never suggested that I might return, or follow Geraswic as he will follow Ardeth when the time comes. He picked up two stones, still pursuing this train of thought. Gillis will probably inherit from Geraswic in Framstock now, and maybe Cunoreth in Salfgard. It must have been hard on Ardeth, to see so little of Geraswic while Ghentar and I have been here. I wish them all good luck and good health, may the Starborn keep them. A foraging bee buzzed loudly as it passed Maesrhon's ear and recalled him to himself. He realised he had paused, the stones in his hands forgotten, as his eyes stared unseeing far away to the north. The north! What was it about those words that had always so strangely stirred his heart? He had trudged all the way from Caradriggan to Salfgard, wondering whether he was at last answering that insistent call; he had looked on Na Caarst, and even ventured into it, but neither Gwent y'm Aryframan nor the wilderness had been the north he sought. Frown lines appeared between the wide golden eyes, eyes filled with a longing he could not explain, as Maesrhon bent to fit his stones into the wall.

So stone by stone he worked, and one by one the days wore away; the evenings were longer, the noons warmer, the crops sprang up in the fields; and the afternoon came when the yard rang to the sounds of hooves and wheels and strangers' voices as the escort from Caradriggan arrived. Beside the richly-decked entourage from Caradward, the wagon taking Ethanur, Framhald and Cottiro back home to Framstock and beyond looked plain enough; yet Cunoreth, who was to drive it, was his usual flamboyant self, his hair flying in braids as he ran around joking and laughing, doing his best to keep tears at bay with mirth. Many people had turned out to wave and call farewell and soon they caught Cunoreth's mood of fragile humour, shouting jests and messages for kinsfolk and friends. But in that hour of parting, silence possessed Ardeth and Maesrhon in the midst of the noise and confusion. Both were men of few words, and both knew there was nothing the other could say. Ardeth stood smiling, though the tears ran unchecked down the wrinkles in his weathered cheeks, but Maesrhon's face was set and still. As the crowd moved and shifted, he caught a glimpse of Fosseiro with a comforting arm around Astirano and the pain stamped on the girl's face hurt him like the grief of the stranger who had besought him in the wilderness. He had already said goodbye to Fosseiro; now he embraced Ardeth for the last time and climbed up to his seat on the wagon. The wheels began to turn and the dust of their going rose about them. Maesrhon turned once and raised his hand, but though he felt his heart would break, he then looked back no more.

The wooden robin

For the next few days, Mag'rantor made it his business to be about the place more than usual, often bringing his children with him; his wife called down also, with her sister and others from the village. Ardeth and Fosseiro knew their friends were trying to ease their loss and appreciated the kindness shown to them. They sat talking to one another quietly by the fire one evening as they had done so many times over the years, Ardeth drinking from the cup Heretellar had given him, and turning over in his hands a little wood-carving of a robin. It was a tiny thing, worn to a smooth, glossy patina with much handling, for Ardeth liked to have it by him always. When he thought of the difference in Maesrhon, from the downtrodden ten-year-old who had brought the robin with him as the only thing from his home that he had to cherish, to the tall young man who had begged him to take the little carving as a keep-sake, he hoped that the years in Salfgard had done the lad some good. He set the robin on the shelf over the fire, but a moment later reached up and took it down again. It was strange, the way something so small and simple could bring him such comfort, but when the wood warmed to the touch of his fingers, Maesrhon seemed close by again.

'If you keep on doing that, you're going to forget where you've put it one of these days. You know how you'd hate to lose it.'

'I won't lose it. I wish I knew more about what goes on in Caradriggan. I'm certain that scar on the boy's back was made by a whip-cut.'

Fosseiro put her stitching down on her lap and looked up. 'There's not much of the boy about Maesrhon now. I think whatever befalls him in the future will be of his own choosing. Maybe you should worry more about his brother.'

'Ghentar? You must be joking.'

'No, far from it. Think for a moment of the man he might have made, if Numirantoro had lived, if he'd been born here, if he'd had a different father. He's strong and healthy, and very good-looking; I could imagine the two of you, working and laughing together, enjoying a drink and a joke together, planning for the future together. But as it is, he came to us already ruined; I don't think his years here have done anything except put off the inevitable, and now he's away back to where he'll only go from bad to worse.'

'But what about...' Ardeth broke off, not sure exactly how to put into words what he was trying to say. Fosseiro had waked an unease in him, something he could not quite pin down. He gave it up. 'Do you think either of them will ever come back as men, in years to come I mean?'

'No, I don't. And as regards when they're men, Cottiro tells me there's a rumour among the girls that Maesrhon is *as-ur*.'

Ardeth sat staring, the wood carving of the robin forgotten in his hand. His mind raced: the obvious difference between the brothers which everyone had noticed; a long-forgotten memory of Salfronardo telling him how much she disliked Vorynaas; Numirantoro's forced marriage to this very man; her yearning for the Starborn; the hints he himself had picked up that Vorynaas hated his younger son, that Arval was protecting him... and then his thoughts leapt to further, more painful conclusions. The Ghentar that Fosseiro had described, the Ghentar who might have been, such a son could have been born to Numirantoro and Geraswic: not so Maesrhon. And Geraswic, bitter though his fate had been, at least had the comfort of knowing that Numirantoro had been taken from him against her will. But if he ever knew, or suspected, that one of her sons had been conceived in love... Ardeth found Fosseiro watching him, and leaned forward to give emphasis to his words.

'Geraswic must never hear anything about this. You must make sure none of the girls ever speak of it when he's here.'

'I've already told Cottiro, in case she runs into Geraswic in Framstock any time, and Escurelo has some sense underneath the flightiness. I think I can rely on her to stop the rumour running too far up here and I doubt we'll see another contingent from Caradward.'

'Yes, come the autumn the new youngsters will likely all be Gwentaran. Quite like old times it'll be, especially with Geraswic around the place once more. We'll see him regularly again now, like we used to. That's something I'm really looking forward to.'

As evening fell a couple of nights later, up in Salfgard village Mag'rantor and his wife were on the point of going to their rest when there was a soft tapping at their door. Cunoreth was standing there, his face unusually serious.

'Ah, back from Framstock! Come in,' said Mag'rantor, but the smile soon left his face as Cunoreth came in and sat down, and then immediately stood up again, wandering round the room with a distracted air.

'Yes, got back this afternoon. I've been trying to keep out of Ardeth's way until I could slip up here to you. Mag'rantor, you'll have to help me with Ardeth, I don't know how we're going to – but wait a minute, maybe there's no need…'

Mag'rantor and his wife exchanged baffled glances as Cunoreth turned to them with desperate appeal in his voice.

'Has Geraswic been here since I left for Framstock with the others?'

'No, we've not seen him, have we?'

'Not just *here*, I mean at Ardeth's place, in the village, at the *Malt Shovel*, up in Gillan nan'Eleth, anywhere around the district?'

'No, not that I know of. He's definitely not been with Ardeth, and no-one else has mentioned seeing him. Why?'

'He's gone. We've got to break it to Ardeth before he hears it from anyone else, that's why I came to you.'

'Gone? What do you mean?'

Cunoreth beat his fist on the table in frustration and distress. 'How *would* I mean! He's gone, like all those others! He wasn't in Framstock when Ardeth and the others went down early in the spring for the meeting of Val'Arad, and he didn't come up here, because Ghentar stayed in Salfgard… but when we got down there this time, Gillis said he'd never come back! It was the first thing he asked me, he'd been hoping against hope Geraswic had been up here in the meantime. He left no message, only seems to have taken his horse; the only things Gillis and Asaldo can be sure of that are missing are some clothes and food and a small pack. He can't have gone away on business or to a market and anyway he'd have said. He's just gone, he's another one that's disappeared! What are we going to say to Ardeth, how can we break it to him?'

IV   YOUTH

CHAPTER 25

Return to Caradriggan

Evening was approaching as the riders and wagons drew near the west gate of Caradriggan and halted outside the walls while the leader of the escort dismounted to speak with the guard who came forward to meet him, bearing some message. After a moment he swung himself into the saddle again and turned his horse.

'Lord Vorynaas sends word we're to enter the city by the south gate, so let's get on with it. I could do with a wash and a meal.'

There was some subdued muttering, but no open comment as they headed off to the right. All four young men were busy with their own thoughts. Heranar and Ghentar had been greatly impressed by the new barbican, and Heranar, who was expecting to have to do his year's military service more or less immediately, was wondering whether it would now be possible for him to serve in the city rather than in some far-flung outpost. Meanwhile it had not escaped Valahald's notice that the order that greeted them at the west gate had come from Vorynaas and had applied to them all, not just his sons. Clearly, his intuition that it was Vorynaas whose word was law had been correct; he was very glad he had ignored Thaltor's hints and made no move against Maesrhon yet. He stole a covert glance at him, thinking how much older than his years he looked, with an oddly purposeful air about him. I wouldn't be making too many plans if I were you, young man, thought Valahald with a secret smile.

Ghentar, who was already feeling increasingly apprehensive at the impending reunion with his father, had not been pleased at being diverted to the southern gate. It was not so far from here to Seth y'n Carad and the opportunity for showing off to gaping passers-by would be much reduced. His bad humour was not improved by a further message, for himself and Maesrhon alone this time, that they were to proceed straight home and await Vorynaas there. He urged Traebenard forward and addressed the gate-guard angrily.

'What's the idea behind all these orders? What do you think we are, children or servants, or what? Why is my father not here to greet me?'

'My orders are from Lord Vorynaas, sir. It's not for me to question them.'

The man's voice was level and his face carefully neutral, but he stepped hastily out of the way as Ghentar, digging his heels into the horse's flanks, pushed roughly past him through the archway, followed by the others. Rain began to fall as they went, but surely that was not enough to clear the streets like this? The faces Maesrhon saw, peeping at them from windows here and there, were all children; and the few passers-by were either servants hurrying on errands or furtive figures who melted into doorways or around corners out of their way. Heranar and Valahald went on to their own home as the rest of the party swung into the compound at Seth y'n Carad. Here they discovered that Vorynaas was presiding over some event or ceremony in the city and had left word that he expected his sons to attend him at an early breakfast the following day. Leaving Traebenard to Maesrhon, Ghentar flounced off indoors, where he ran straight into Haartell: it did not improve his temper.

'Today is an Open Hall day,' said Haartell in answer to his questions, 'and there have been reviews at the parade-ground. You'll see that there are certain kinds of business which require your father's presence.'

'What business? What's this Open Hall?'

Haartell gave the well-remembered smirk that always made Ghentar want to hit him in the face. 'I'm sure you'll hear all about it tomorrow from Lord Vorynaas. You'll find there have been big changes here, while you've been away.'

Ghentar left him without comment and went up to his room. He was mollified to see that this had been refurbished with many luxurious touches; the closet and chests were full of handsome new clothes and a casket beside the bed contained expensive gold jewellery. A new door, screened by a rich hanging, had been inserted into one of the walls and when he opened this he found it led to a smaller, much plainer chamber with two narrow beds in it. A young man sprang to attention and introduced himself as one of two servants from the household staff now permanently assigned to wait on him. Ghentar returned to his own room and glanced out of the window. He saw Maesrhon crossing the courtyard carrying Traebenard's saddle towards the tack-room, exchanging greetings with the servants who were scurrying about in the aftermath of their arrival. Yes, thought Ghentar, better get used to it, little brother: no Ardeth to fuss over you now. Here *I'm* the one who counts. He sat down on his bed, savouring the fact that now he had servants of his own. It struck him that perhaps he should ask his father for a new horse. After all, he'd been riding Traebenard for more than five years and although the animal's quality had stood out up in Salfgard, now that he was back where he belonged, surely it was necessary for him to keep up a certain style. And Vorynaas owed him, he'd stuck it out up there for five years, never so much as placed a wager at the games on a feast-day. Without warning, a touch of Ghentar's earlier nervousness returned. His father was going to ask him questions: would want to know what he had to report, would probably be critical in some way of the messages he had sent back with Thaltor. He chewed at his nails briefly. Some home-coming this had been! Then his face brightened; jumping up, he called the servant.

'Bring me hot water, I want to wash. I'll wear the blue house-robes, and send word down that they're to serve my supper in an hour's time.'

Next morning, he and Maesrhon were waiting as instructed in an ante-room to the main hall in Seth y'n Carad. What neither of them knew was that when the building was under construction, Vorynaas had stipulated that a squint be incorporated into this room and another over the dais in the public hall. Both communicated directly with his own private suite, so that he could observe men unseen. The room where his sons waited was often used for confidential meetings and it suited Vorynaas well to watch who gathered there; even when it was his own associates, he could learn much by noting their faces and body-language before he joined them. So now he watched his sons as they sat waiting for him while the servants moved around the room setting food for three on a low table, comparing what he saw in reality with what he had seen in his mind's eye after listening to Thaltor's twice-yearly accounts. He stared at Maesrhon. What was it Thaltor had said? Something like "You'll be glad to know he gets less like his mother as he gets older". And just what was that supposed to mean, wondered Vorynaas. Maybe it was nothing more than a memory of Salfronardo about the boy, or perhaps that quiet, reserved air had reminded Thaltor of Arythalt. Vorynaas gave an irritated snort as he made for the door to the stairs: what gave that dried-up old bore, or his grandson either come to that, the right to be so damned haughty? As for Salfronardo, how wrong he'd been in hoping to find a spark of her fire in her daughter! By my right hand, he thought, I paid a heavy price for setting my feet on the ladder of success.

Dropping down the last four stairs two at a time, Vorynaas turned into a short approach corridor and swept into the room. As he closed the door behind him, the elaborate pleatings in the skirt of his expensive day-robes swirled and then hung in heavy folds. The two young men stood politely to greet him, Ghentar gazing avidly at his father's luxurious clothes, at the gold buckle in his belt and the broad gold rings on his left arm. Both he and Vorynaas were dressed in deep emerald green, a shade which set off their own colouring, although Vorynaas noticed that Ghentar's hair was now not so much chestnut, like his own, but more a dark, burnished red. Father and son embraced, well-matched in height and build: we could almost be brothers, thought Vorynaas, not seeing how Ghentar had marked the spread of grey at his ears and lips.

'My son, you are a man now!'

He held Ghentar off by the shoulders, smiling, and Ghentar grinned back as his confidence grew. Turning to Maesrhon, Vorynaas forced himself into a brief handshake, nodding at the two of them to sit down. Vividly the memory came back to him of how he had hated Numirantoro to look down at him, and Maesrhon was already much taller than his mother. At least when they were all seated at the table that advantage was cancelled out. As they helped themselves to the food, he wondered how the boy had come by the scar on his lip; but then his eye was caught by the knife hanging at his belt.

'Where did you get that thing?'

'It was a present from Ardeth, sir. He made it for me himself.'

'Let me see it.' Vorynaas turned the knife over in his hands. 'What kind of an object is this? You'd be a laughing-stock in Rigg'ymvala.'

Ghentar sniggered, but Maesrhon's reply was unruffled and calm. 'It's a tool, sir, not a weapon.'

Vorynaas looked up sharply and then, noticing Ghentar watching for his reaction, raised a knowing eyebrow at his elder son. 'No sky-steel in this, eh? But I see the blade has been forged in the *sigitsaran* way, a technique that should never have been allowed to cross the border. No doubt this Ardeth filched the secret during his foster-years.'

'No sir, he learnt from Sigitsar Metal-Master. I have heard the story from him many times, how he bound himself in apprenticeship and paid for his teaching both in kind and with his own labour.'

The dark brows drew down again. 'You're very free with your answers these days. Now listen to me. I'll have no Gwentaran speech and customs brought into my house. In a couple of years' time, you'll be called up for your military service. I don't want you going off to that knowing nothing but peasant crafts, or coming back with no further skills except how to check a permit; so in the meantime, you're to make yourself useful in the business. Get yourself over to the office, they've got a programme set out ready for you to work through: accounts, stores, transport, assays and so on. Apply yourself, because you can be sure I'll be checking up on your progress.' Vorynaas handed the knife back to Maesrhon. 'You're not to wear this in Seth y'n Carad. Hedging and ditching may be all you turn out to be fit for, so you can keep it in case you need it later, but there's no need to dress for the part until it's necessary.'

Ghentar laughed openly at this, but was ignored by both father and brother. Maesrhon stood up.

'Learning is something a man can never regret. I look forward to my new course of study. May I begin immediately?'

Vorynaas shrugged, feigning indifference, but already he doubted whether he would be able to restrain himself. All his old demons came crowding back to torment him. Was the quote from Arval's maxims intended to taunt? Was that inclination of the head meant in deference or derision? Five years away had wrought some subtle change in the boy: was it that now he had something of his mother's infuriating unreachable, untouchable demeanour? Remembering not to make the mistake of looking up at Maesrhon, he dismissed him with a wave of his hand and turned back to his meal. And Maesrhon too saw something different now in Vorynaas. There was something new underneath the old contemptuous pride, something changed behind the devious smile, an extra dimension to the familiar sardonic speech and hot temper. Glancing back as he left the room, Maeshron suddenly realised what it was. Lurking in Vorynaas' mouth and eyes was a new, careless cruelty that it seemed he felt no need to conceal.

Alone now with his father, Ghentar leaned forward eagerly. 'So, what's the news? Haartell was saying something last night about a parade-ground, and reviews. What's the Open Hall? How soon can I start in Rigg'ymvala? But I'll need a new horse before I take up a commission there: Traebenard was good in his day but he's not up to my standard now. And what was all that about yesterday, sending us round to the south gate? I thought we'd have come home in style, made a bit of a show in the city and given everyone something to talk about.'

The smile faded from his face as he noticed Vorynaas eyeing him, and sure enough, next thing he was on the receiving end of his father's well-remembered sarcastic tongue.

'Really?' Vorynaas sighed in mock-resignation. 'You know Ghentar, sometimes it seems to me you don't think at all. Don't you remember why you went to Salfgard? And what I said to you before you left? You seem to have forgotten that I was forced to agree to a resolution of Tell'Ethronad, forced to eat humble pie by old fools like Arval and your grandfather! Why would I want to remind people of that by letting them gawp at you in the streets? Didn't you even notice yesterday how empty the streets were? That's because these days, things here are done the way I want them. When I'm holding a review, or a session in the Open Hall, people know they've got to be there. When I issue an order, even just a message to the city gates, that order is obeyed without question, as you found last night. Remember how I said when I make a vow, I keep it? Didn't I swear to you the council would rue the day they crossed me? Money talks, Ghentar. With a tight grip on the mine, I keep a tight grip on power. While I control the gold supply, my word is law here. Now you explain to me why I would be foolish enough to jeopardise that hold by recalling to men's minds a day when I was weak enough to be compelled against my will.'

Ghentar sat and digested all this. It seemed so obvious, when his father put it to him like that. He felt really stupid at not thinking things through for himself, and that in turn made him sullen. 'All right, I get the point. There's no need to talk to me as if I was Maesrhon, I'm not a child any more. And anyway, I do remember what you said. What about your plan to put the Gwentarans in their place? *Once and for all*, I think was how you put it? I've just spent five years there and I can't see they've got anything to worry about.'

'Mm. Well, that would certainly tally with the reports you sent. Not very informative, were they?'

'What was I supposed to do, invent things? I'll tell you what it's like up there. First you have winter, then spring, then summer, then autumn. Then again. And again. And so on. You get up, you go to bed. Maybe in a good week, you go to market. Once in a while, Ardeth takes you with him to Framstock, but you can't attend Val'Arad so you don't really know what goes on there. The feast-days aren't too bad, a bit boring but the food's good; the best thing is probably the hunting. And that's it!'

Vorynaas laughed at this. 'You should compare notes with Valestron. Or maybe Thaltor. He came back here all misty-eyed about dawn over Salfgard, until the sight of a bag of gold dust brought him to his senses. But I'll tell you what, though.' Narrowing his eyes as the laughter left his voice, Vorynaas raised a finger to emphasise his point. 'Thaltor can be quite observant. Now *he* brought back some interesting information that's going to be very useful one day.'

'Is that so?' Ghentar flared up, affronted. 'I can't say he ever bothered to share his observations with me, although he spent enough time whispering in corners with Valahald, not to mention giving Maesrhon a silver *moras* and a swollen head into the bargain! "Keep it up, and you could be as good with the sword as your father", what a joke when he couldn't even be bothered to...' Ghentar stopped suddenly, seeing the look on his father's face. Vorynaas stood up slowly.

'Thaltor said that about Maesrhon? What else did he say?' His voice was quiet, but held a note of menace that panicked Ghentar into a babble of response.

'Yes, but what I'm telling you is, after that Maesrhon didn't even have the good manners to present himself for instruction. Thaltor waited at Salfgard, but Maesrhon was off in the hills somewhere with some crony of Ardeth's, and anyway he's not *that* good. Who gave him that scar on his lip? But Thaltor has to go and tell him...'

'*What else did Thaltor say?*'

Ghentar shrank back into his seat, baffled and alarmed. 'Well, that was about it really, as far as I can remember. I never knew you were so famous with the sword! Why didn't you tell me?'

Now it was Vorynaas' turn to be confused. 'What?'

'I said, how is it you never told us you were such a good swordsman? It's what Thaltor was saying to Maesrhon, something like you were the best in the city in your day.'

Vorynaas took a pace or two across the room, looking out of the window while he composed himself. He saw now how he and Ghentar had got at crossed purposes. "As good as your father, and he was the best": Ghentar had misinterpreted the true significance of the words, but Vorynaas knew very well what Thaltor had meant by them, and by his earlier hints too. So Thaltor suspected as well! He needed time alone now to think how best to proceed, but first he must put Ghentar off the scent. He turned with a modest smile.

'Oh well, it was a long time ago. You need to remember I was a middle-aged man by the time you were growing up, I was out of practice by then and more than occupied with business affairs. Thaltor is much younger than I am; I was happy for him to look after your progress. I saw no need to harp on about my own past glory, he's an excellent swordsman himself. But what's this you were telling me about you and Maesrhon? You won a fight with him, did you? What was all that about?'

Too late, Ghentar saw that he had walked into a trap of his own making. He lied quickly. 'Yes, we, er, we had words about him missing Thaltor's visit, and things got a bit heated, so I challenged him to fight me, and I won. Of course I didn't mean him to get hurt, I, I underestimated how quick I could be with my new sword – I haven't thanked you properly for it yet, and I should have done.'

'That's all right.' Vorynaas pulled Ghentar to his feet and put an arm around his shoulders. 'And don't worry about Maesrhon, either. It's only a small scar and after all, if he's the swordsman in the making that Thaltor thinks, no doubt he'll learn from it, won't he? Now I must get on, I've a busy morning to attend to. Enjoy your first day home, and we'll talk again this evening.'

New sights in the city

He left the room and soon after, Ghentar hurried off too. He knew that Maesrhon could tell Vorynaas the truth about their fight as many times as he wanted and still not be believed, but Heranar and Valahald were a different matter. He must find them and make sure they were word-perfect in the new story. He walked up the street, swaggering slightly in his fine new clothes, making frequent unnecessary little adjustments to his sword-belt. Remembering how his father had ridiculed Maesrhon's new knife, he grinned to himself, enjoying the joke over again, and then it occurred to him that Vorynaas had made no response to the suggestion that it was time he had a new horse. Too busy ranting and raving about Thaltor – what on earth all that had been about was anyone's guess. Maybe the old boy was losing his touch; he was definitely looking older. Well, perhaps the thing to do was to take matters into his own hands. He'd go down to the horse-market first, have a look over what was on offer so that if anything took his eye, he could twist his father's arm that evening. After that, he'd look up Valahald and Heranar. They're probably still sleeping off the journey, thought Ghentar with a touch of resentment; see *their* father making them parade at an early breakfast like we had to. Turning the last corner, he stopped abruptly and gazed in amazement.

The horse-market had gone. Where once had been noise and bustle, all was quiet. Where once had stood stables and feed stores, saddlers' workshops, offices for hiring mules, livery firms, businesses selling new and used tack, now there were imposing buildings ranged around four sides of an open square. Where stalls and pens had once accommodated every kind of beast for riding, driving, draught, breeding, even racing; where vendors had shouted and men had bargained; where hooves had clattered on the cobbles or thudded on straw, all was cleared away and replaced by a vast, silent, echoing level space overlooked by the windows of barracks, by stands for spectators, by a covered dais. Where once the air had been filled with the smell of closely-packed horses and men, of leather and dung, of hot metal and burnt horn drifting from the forges, now there was nothing but a faint grittiness from the little dust-devils that twisted in a corner of the square. And where the wheeze of bellows and the roar of fire had been punctuated by the deafening clang of hammers and the regular hiss as white-hot metal was tempered in half a dozen low, blackened forges, these too were gone. In their place was a large round building of pale-coloured stone, encircled by slender pillars. These upheld the roof which extended all around to shelter four arches; Ghentar noticed that they were empty of doors and that the walls held an unusual number of large, clear windows. This must be the Open Hall that Haartell had spoken of, and obviously this huge open space was the parade-ground. He crossed the road slowly and stood at the end of one of the lowest rows of seats, staring about him.

'I see the young master has returned to us.'

He turned quickly in surprise as the light, amused-sounding voice came from behind him, and saw Valestron standing at the door of the barrack-block. 'Oh, it's you. Where's the horse-market these days?'

'Over near the wall, between the north and east gates. Glad to see you up and about nice and early.'

'Why? What do you mean?'

'Well, can't tolerate slackness in junior officers, what effect would it have on the ranks? Always like to have the day's duties well under way by dawn, if not before. I take it you're still set on a commission in Rigg'ymvala?'

'Yes, eventually.' Ghentar eyed Valestron haughtily; he was taking a pretty high and mighty tone for a man who was only chief of security at Seth y'n Carad. 'I'm in no particular hurry, especially after five years in the backwoods. My plan is to enjoy myself here in the city for a while first, if you really must know, so I expect we'll see each other in the *Leopard* from time to time.'

'I doubt it; I'll be leaving this afternoon for Heranwark to take up command at Rigg'ymvala. I'd advise you not to get too acclimatised to the delights of civilian life, and to remember the word will be *Sir*, not "Oh, it's you", next time we meet, because you'll be reporting to me,' said Valestron, enjoying the look on Ghentar's face. 'Now, if you'll excuse me? Mustn't keep you from the horse-market, after all.' With a sardonic smile, he turned back into the building.

It was getting on for noon when Ghentar called at Valafoss' house to see Heranar and Valahald. The steward showed him through to the courtyard and he sat down, looking about him. Strange to think he had been born here and spent the first years of his life in this house. It seemed very small and ordinary compared with Seth y'n Carad. Eventually Heranar emerged, yawning and looking rather bleary. He sat down, rubbing his eyes as the servant who had followed him set down food and drink on a small table, and then turned to his friend.

'Hello. Help yourself. What time is it? I didn't expect to see you this early.'

'Early! You must be joking. It's nearly mid-day, I've been up for hours. It's all right for you two, lying about in bed all morning. We had to show up for paternal inspection at the crack of dawn. Where's Valahald? I wanted to talk to both of you.'

Heranar yawned again, leaning back in his chair with his eyes closed. 'Don't know. Not sleeping, anyway. You weren't the only ones dragged from your beds, because there was a message here for him when we got in last night, telling him to meet Thaltor first thing. He must be still out.'

'Why does Thaltor want to see him?'

'Don't know. What's the matter with you? Why all the questions?'

'If you say "Don't know" like that once more, I'm going to empty this jug over you. You'd be in a bad mood too if you'd had the morning I've had. Did you know Valestron has taken over in Rigg'ymvala, can you believe it? I ran into him when I went down to the old horse-market, well, to where it used to be, because it's all changed there now – yes, thought that might wake you up a bit, you should see it – and he lost no time informing me he'll be my commanding officer. There's something to look forward to, I don't think! But before that I'd been on the receiving end of one of the old man's tongue-lashings. Honestly sometimes you don't know what to say to please him.'

'I thought it was usually Maesrhon who came in for that kind of thing. What's he up to today?'

'Well, you'd have laughed if you'd been there.' As Heranar selected a slice of cured meat, rolled it round a bread stick and began to eat, Ghentar relayed the story of what Vorynaas had had to say about Maesrhon's knife before packing him off to work in the offices. Heranar, now eating fruit, tittered appreciatively and held his cup out. Ghentar picked up the jug to pour for both of them and then leaned forward, speaking quietly. 'But while we're on the subject of Maesrhon, there's something I wanted to say to you. You'll need to be ready to back me up, because this is what I had to tell my father…'

When he had finished, Heranar shrugged easily. 'No problem. Look, give me a moment to get properly dressed, and I'll come with you to see this new horse you've got your eye on.'

They strolled off together, but headed first for the north gate to get a closer look at the huge barbican and new fortifications they had admired from a distance the previous evening. Heranar was openly impressed. He leaned into the angle between a tower and the outer wall, watching the orderly bustle of military business, admiring the arrangement of the buildings, the strategic positions of watch-stations and guard posts. He turned to Ghentar with an enthusiastic grin.

'This is all right, isn't it! I'm definitely going to try for permission to do my year's service here.'

'Oh, not really? Why don't you come to Rigg'ymvala with me? I thought we'd go together.'

Heranar shook his head. 'No, that's more in Valahald's line, I'd say. I don't want to do more than I have to. It's all right for you; Valestron was probably just trying it on with you today. He knows he can't touch Vorynaas' son and heir if he wants to stay in favour but he could make my life a misery if it suited him. No, I want to stay as near the city as I can, and not just because there's more scope to enjoy myself when I'm on leave. This is the place where everything important happens, where the big decisions are made, and I want to be close to all that.'

As Heranar talked on, Ghentar realised suddenly that his friend knew more than he did about what went on in Caradriggan now, about the changes there had been in their absence. Belatedly, it occurred to him that his father had answered none of his questions earlier that morning. He had taken a certain amount of malicious pleasure in seeing Maesrhon consigned to what he considered a menial pen-pusher's position, but now he felt faint stirrings of resentment at the way he seemed to be left out of the plans, not considered important enough to be kept informed, just told to run off and amuse himself. Coming out of his thoughts, he registered a question in Heranar's face.

'Sorry, I was miles away. What did you say?'

'I said, let's go and look at this horse and then drop in to the *Leopard* for a drink.'

Some hours later, they parted for the day, Ghentar's good humour fully restored. As they paused outside the inn, he reminded Heranar to coach his brother in the new story. 'You'll tell Valahald what to say if he's asked, right? You won't forget?'

'No, I'll mention it to him. By the way, you never told me who's taken over from Valestron at Seth y'n Carad?'

Ghentar paused, feeling stupid again. 'I don't know.'

Heranar gave him a shove, laughing. 'Now who's started saying "Don't know"! Wish I'd asked you while we were still inside there, I could have emptied the jug over *your* head!'

'Oh all right, all right!' They scuffled for a moment in friendly fashion and then went their separate ways. But when he arrived home, Ghentar found that the biggest surprise of his day awaited him at Seth y'n Carad: Valahald had been appointed to fill Valestron's post at the hall.

Reunited with Arval

Maesrhon meanwhile was finding out that someone like himself, who had devoured all the teaching he had received in Tellgard and during his foster-years, would have no problems at all with the kind of work he was now expected to undertake. Having begun early in the day, he applied himself much more diligently than the other clerks and overseers; thus by the time the morning was over, he had finished his allotted tasks and the rest of the day was his own. As fast as he could, he hurried in search of Arval, scarcely seeing the changes in the once-familiar streets as he came in sight of Tellgard at last. He noticed immediately what Heretellar had described to Ancrascaro: the old place was looking a little shabby, the wood showing silvery here and there where the paintwork needed renewing; there were cracks in one or two of the steps in the colonnade and the fluted stone of the pillars was slightly chipped in places. He was soon to discover that things could not be otherwise, when these days the cost of repairs, like all other expenses, must be met out of donations from a dwindling number of supporters instead of found by the city; but at the moment all he could think of was that at least the old place was still there, still serenely devoted to the pursuit of learning. Oh, only let Arval be still here too, he thought, his eyes darting in every direction at once, seeking a glimpse of him, as he made for the tower door.

He let himself into the high-ceilinged room next to the library, and there at last was Arval, somehow seeming smaller than he remembered; but the silver hair, the neatly clipped beard, the dark eyes in the keen, spare face were unchanged. Maesrhon felt a huge wave of relief sweep over him as he and Arval finally met once more. They were alone in the room, where Arval had been sitting at the heavy table, making notes from two large, ancient-looking books that lay open beside his work. Unable to utter a single word, Maesrhon followed Arval over to a seat under the four high and narrow windows that gave onto the central court.

'So, *Is-torar*, we have two years together before your time of service is due. We must use them well! I have received your messages: Ancrascaro works with us here now, and Heretellar visits when he is in the city.' Looking out as Arval gestured, Maesrhon saw Ancrascaro moving behind the windows of a classroom opposite. 'But for now, I am going to claim an old man's privilege, and ask you to speak first.' A knowing smile crinkled Arval's eyes. 'Tell me all you would like me to know of your life in Salfgard.'

Many and many had been the times that Maesrhon had anticipated this long-awaited meeting, had seen himself pouring out all the questions he burned to ask, had heard Arval's voice in reply though without being able to imagine his answers. How different the reality had turned out to be! This quiet room, its hushed, studious air, the subtle calm of Arval's gentle welcome, were like a haven of tranquillity in which his mind could be at peace, secure in the confidence that all would be made plain when the hour arrived. So he spoke at Arval's bidding, talked until his throat was sore, telling of his years in Gwent y'm Aryframan.

'You know better than anyone how badly I wanted not to go to Salfgard,' he said, coming to the end of the tale, 'but when the time came to leave it, I found that hard to do. I gave Ardeth the little wooden robin I made here when I was a child. It was flawed, but my heart went into its making: it was the only possession I took with me, and a part of me has stayed behind with it. Yet though I was happy, building a wall high on the hillside with only my thoughts for company, could I do this from year to year as Ardeth must, growing older under the weight of his losses?'

Maesrhon broke eye contact with Arval, hiding the next thought that came to his mind: though I remember the sunny days of swimming in the river and feast-day games in the meadows, could I have that joy again once I had seen the pain in Astirano's face? He looked up, ending instead on a different example. 'Even Torald comes down from the wild places and turns to his home and pasture again, but could I do that now I have heard Geraswic's sorrow? I'm glad that Ardeth will see Geraswic more often now; he said to me, "He's the son of my heart", and it must have been hard on them both while we were there. So though part of me pines for Salfgard, I see now what I took on trust before, that learning truly is the one thing a man can never regret. I am ready to begin again, Lord Arval.'

Arval smiled slightly. 'Your friend Torald sounds a most intriguing character, one with whom I think I would have much in common.'

Maesrhon saw with some surprise that this was not meant as a joke, and realised that here was something interesting to be thought through later. For a moment they sat in silence, then Arval spoke again.

'I see you carry the mark of your brother's anger on your face, little son.'

'But how did you ... oh ...'

Arval's thin face and dark eyes lit up with laughter at the moment of shared reminiscence. 'No, this time there is no need to suspect strange powers as the source of my knowledge: you can put it down to deduction based on information and observation.' His voice hardened a little. 'Vorynaas made sure we all heard about the sword he was sending to his son. I have seen enough of your skill to know that it would take deceit rather than strength to harm you, and enough of Ghentar's mind to know that only he would be driven to use such guile. Poor Ghentar! I fear it will not be the last mistake of that kind he makes.'

He sighed and shook his head, but Maesrhon slid to one knee, taking Arval's hand. 'Arval, reveal to me what is the choice you told me I must make.'

'When the choice is upon you, you will know without my telling you what it is; but before then, there is yet more knowledge you need to acquire. I have that knowledge, and we will work together for you to receive it from me. But I am still in doubt as to the way forward.'

Arval stood, and raising Maesrhon to his feet drew him over to the table where the books lay. Closing the two heavy tomes, he picked up the thick pile of handwritten notes and ran his thumb across the edge of the pages, flicking through them. 'One never reaches the end of learning, as I think we have agreed before. Every day that you have been away, I have worked at my researches, yet still I have not reached my goal. But I promise you that when the time comes for you to hear what you must, I will be ready, and I will speak.'

Maesrhon hung his head, biting his lip. He felt that his whole life trembled on the brink of some half-guessed revelation, but it seemed the wait was not over yet. He turned to go, assuming his audience with Arval was over, but the old man called him back. Sorrow and a surprising bitterness showed in his face as he indicated that Maesrhon should sit again. After a moment of thought, Arval began to speak.

'You will have noticed already that there have been many changes in the city during the years of your absence, but I imagine that you do not yet know how great those differences are. They go much deeper than the visible veneer of wealth, the new buildings, the large houses that one sees in every street. When you learn more about what has been happening here, you may wish to question my part in it: indeed, I am sure you will. I have answers to those questions, but they are painful to give, and they will be painful to hear.'

Arval gathered up his books and replaced them on the shelves, then perhaps feeling that silence hung heavily between them, he turned to Maesrhon once more. The golden eyes were locked on his, the loose dark locks flowing back from a face that was more angular now that the softness of childhood was gone, stronger now that the bone structure began to show. Memories flooded Arval's mind, and suddenly his heart lifted. 'I am so glad you are back, little son. It has been a long time.'

The cloud sailed off Maesrhon's brow immediately, his smile of joy smoothing out the slight twist of the lip which the sword cut had inflicted. 'Oh yes, indeed it has, Lord Arval. Five years is a long time.'

Arval laughed almost merrily as he left the room; he felt new life run through him like wine as hope revived. 'I have waited much longer than five years, *Is-torar*, but the wait is nearly over.'

Left alone, Maesrhon glanced out of the window again and saw that Ancrascaro was still busy. He thought he would go down and wait for her on the bench outside the tower door where she would see him when she left her class, then they could talk and catch up with each other's news. Frowning, he pondered the hints of trouble in Arval's words, then as he wandered around the room, savouring the pleasure of being in Tellgard once more, his eyes fell on the books Arval had been using. Intrigued, he took them down from the shelf and looked to see what they contained. One was an ancient volume of lore concerning the Starborn: no surprises there, although he had never seen this particular book before. It was clearly extremely old and he turned the pages slowly, fascinated, hoping that maybe he and Arval could study it together. The other work was a medical textbook, more advanced than anything he had read before he went to Salfgard. It must be for use by the senior students who were going to specialise in the arts of healing, so why was Arval using it? Surely he was already an expert in this field. Then Maesrhon noticed that Arval had left a page marker in the book, and opened it at the place. So far as he could understand it, this section appeared to deal with the boundary between different stages of consciousness: whether either the mind or the body could truly live without the other; the difficulty of precisely defining life and death. There was a page reference written by hand on the marker and turning now to this chapter, Maesrhon saw complex formulations for drugs and medicines together with much theorising about their uses and effects. He closed the books slowly and replaced them on the shelves with a slight shiver, wondering why Arval had been using them together. But then, hearing children's voices as they spilled out into the exercise court, he hurried to catch Ancrascaro before she left, smiling to himself. *Never too soon to start, and no need ever to stop*: there was no-one who could say Arval failed to follow his own precepts about learning! And no-one is going to say of me that I shied away from knowledge that was put before me, whatever the subject-matter, vowed Maesrhon. I must make sure I humour Vorynaas, so that there is no interference with my free time over the next two years; and with that, he was through the door and calling to Ancrascaro as she walked towards the colonnade.

CHAPTER 26

New loyalties forged

'You're going to be late if you don't leave that now and get changed.'

Maesrhon looked up from the calculations on his desk to see Valahald, smartly turned-out in parade kit, leaning in through the doorway of the office. 'I won't be late, because I'm not coming at all. I can't see how my presence will add anything to the proceedings and anyway, Ghentar's home on leave from Rigg'ymvala. No doubt he'll be there.'

'But today's an Open Hall day. You know your father's orders are that everyone attends.'

Maesrhon put his pen down and laughed shortly; he noticed the two junior clerks eyeing the scene warily from their stools in the corner. 'Well, then perhaps he'd like to explain how I can be in two places at once, because he's left me in no doubt that I'm not to leave the office until I've finished my work for the day. I've got all these statistics to analyse yet, and then the results have got to be set out in a graph and attached to this report, and *that* has to be finished in time to be tabled for discussion at a meeting later this week.'

Valahald hesitated; he was annoyed at being belittled like this in front of witnesses, but on the other hand was unsure whether his authority extended to actually issuing an order to one of his employer's sons. He decided to beat a strategic retreat. 'Well, I've done my bit, I'll have to get on or I'll be late myself. All I can say is, on your own head be it.'

'Yes, I expect it will be.'

Pushing himself away from the doorpost with a dismissive snort, Valahald strode off and Maesrhon returned to his papers without further comment. The two young clerks exchanged glances, open-mouthed, and then hastily applied themselves to their work. At mid-morning, one of them approached Maesrhon timidly to ask what refreshment he would like. This had not happened before and for a moment he was surprised until he realised that today, the rest of the staff being at the Open Hall, he was the senior person present. As he was not usually included in the managers' break-time, he was about to say there was nothing he required, when a sudden thought struck him. The warm months of the year were beginning and it was hot and stuffy in the office. He sent the youngster to fetch biscuits and a jug of iced mint cordial, but told him to bring extra glasses. When the tray arrived, he called the boys over.

'We'll have a break. Here's a drink for you, and eat these biscuits. You can take them outside for a few minutes' fresh air – well, fresher than it is in here, anyway.'

They backed off. 'Sir, we're not allowed, we don't get a break.'

'If they find out, I'll be dismissed,' added the smaller of the two.

'Don't worry. You'll only be doing what I've told you to do, so if anyone's going to get into trouble, it'll be me, won't it? I've already been told once this morning that there's a storm brewing over my head anyway, so a few more clouds won't make that much difference. Come on now.'

Hesitantly they came forward again and took a biscuit each, but made no move to eat them. Anger stirred in Maesrhon, that they should be so downtrodden. Children, he thought, they're just children. What are they doing in here, how can they be capable of much more than ruling lines in ledgers?

'How old are you two?' he asked.

'Sir, I'm twelve, and he's thirteen.'

'Where do you live?'

The younger boy had begun nibbling at his biscuit; he seemed the bolder spirit of the two, and now spoke up readily enough. 'Here, of course, sir. In the compound, here at Seth y'n Carad. But when I'm a man, maybe I'll be able to go back home to the Lowanmorad, maybe by then they'll need somebody new to teach in the village. My father's dead, he went to the mines away south to look for work, and he was killed in an accident. In the Red Mountains, that was, and then my mother couldn't keep us all, but she thought I would make a clerk, because I was doing well at my lessons in the village, so she sent me to the hiring market here in the city.'

Throughout all this, his fellow had been nudging the boy, hissing in his ear, trying unsuccessfully to silence him. Maesrhon turned to the older of the two now.

'And do you live here, too?'

The boy hung his head and blushed. 'Sir, I'm a bondsman. I'll always live here, unless Lord Vorynaas instructs Haartell to sell me. My father signed for the gold mine, so when he tried to leave and take us all away, they said he was a deserter. They brought the whole family to the Open Hall, and he was sent to Arval. I came here, and I don't know where my mother and sisters are now.' Then he raised his head and looked Maesrhon in the eye. 'When he found out what it was like in the Lissa'pathor, my father said he'd sooner go to Arval than go back to the mine.'

Maesrhon looked down at the two earnest faces, old before their time. 'I am truly sorry, but listen to me now. I'm going to trust you with a truth the rulers of this city cannot know, for if they did, they would prevent it. Arval would never send innocent men to death, uncomforted. He cannot save them from death, but he must have some means to spare them pain, though what could be so powerful that it gives them strength to face their fate, I don't know. I have seen men die, who have been sent to him from the Open Hall: not one of them showed fear. Arval holds some key to joy beyond this darkness.'

I must be insane, Maesrhon thought, to risk telling two children this; then he looked at them again, their eyes fixed wide upon him, and once more his heart overruled his head. 'Now we have told each other secrets, but we will all three keep close what we have heard today, yes?'

'Oh yes, we swear it, sir, we swear faithfully. You won't run into trouble because of us, sir.'

'There's no need to call me sir when we're on our own,' said Maeshron, smiling slightly. 'After all, I'm not long turned seventeen myself.'

They glanced at each other, then stepped forward together. Breathlessly, the words tumbled out. 'Lord Maeshron, we are your men.'

The smile left Maesrhon's face. 'I am no lord. There are few in Caradriggan worthy of that dignity, but the first among them is Arval; and I am his man. But we've shared food and drink, and that makes us brothers. Now, take your drinks outside, and make sure you eat up all the biscuits.'

The day wore away, and by late afternoon street life in the city was busy once more, and in Seth y'n Carad people returned to their work. Maesrhon finished his analysis and began drawing up the graph on which to plot his results; he was just filling in the headings when the chief accountant came in and told him to stop. Putting down his pen, he waited for the message that he was to present himself before Vorynaas immediately, but to his surprise the summons never came. As the man muttered his way over the sheets of figures and calculations, Maesrhon wondered what was afoot and whether he was really going to get away with not being called to account for his non-attendance at the day's public proceedings.

'Right, that all seems fine. You two, tidy up and clear off.'

The youngsters scrambled to put away their work, clearing their desks and pushing their stools tidily underneath as the accountant turned to Maesrhon again. 'Are you going to carry on with this now, or what?'

'Yes, I thought I'd get ahead with it.'

With a shrug, he handed the paperwork back to Maesrhon and made for the door, chivvying the little clerks ahead of him. 'Come on, hurry up there, I want to get home.'

They exchanged fleeting glances with Maesrhon and then all three were gone, leaving him alone. He turned back to his task, the scratching of his pen and the small noise as he replaced the ruler on the desk the only sounds now in the quiet office. Two hours later, all was done and he stood up and stretched his bent back and stiff limbs. Putting out the lamp, he headed for the kitchens, noticing that the windows were illuminated in the private upper room of the east wing of the hall. Presumably Vorynaas was holding court up there, which would account for the fact that he had been left alone. He had never been invited to join the inner circle, although nowadays Ghentar was included in the meetings when he was home on leave. In the kitchen he ate a quick supper of grilled meat with a portion of cold roast vegetables and bread and then walked up to the fountain gardens, enjoying the exercise after being cooped up all day. As he turned into the gardens, he was watched by the men who loitered there. Maesrhon smiled grimly to himself as he strode away from the lanterns and into the deeper darkness that lay on the further side of the gardens. They would report having seen him, but they could not follow him in case there were untoward doings at Forgard's house, when one would need to remain at his surveillance post while his fellow took a swift message to Vorynaas. For the time being Maesrhon could be sure of solitude and quiet and he badly wanted both. Now walking, now running, now loping easily, he went round and round a wide circuit in the dark.

Justice in the Open Hall

As his feet ran, so his mind ran also. During two years back in Caradriggan, he had never been able to reconcile himself to the changes wrought by the unscrupulous ambition of a few men upon the greed and lethargy of the many. He had gone unsuspecting to the Open Hall that first time, and sat aghast at the sight of Vorynaas lording it over a complaisant council, watched horrified as the miserable procession of unfortunates had been herded in to await their fate. No doubt there had been wrongdoers among them, but many had simply been down on their luck, reduced by necessity, or runaways who had fled from what they could no longer bear. After the most cursory examination of the facts, Vorynaas instructed the council to vote, and it was obvious that every time the majority was overwhelmingly in favour of what he wanted. Valafoss stood forward and announced the verdicts, and at first Maesrhon had thought that *tan vigu* was a sentence of death until he understood that to say a man or woman used to live simply meant that henceforward they were to be enslaved; until he saw what happened to a man who was accused of attacking an overseer at the gold mine. *Tell'ethronad hir rossana starfach*, intoned Valafoss: the council commands him to die. And between each case, Thaltor's soldiers, who were drawn up at regular intervals both within and without the Open Hall, had moved the crowds round so that different faces appeared at the wide windows or were ushered through the doorless arches to that all could see and hear what went on.

Round the gardens again ran Maesrhon. Before this mockery of justice dispensed openly before all men, those to be tried were held in the stronghouse behind the Open Hall while troops from Rigg'ymvala and from the civic force stationed at Seth y'n Carad performed manoeuvres on the review ground as Vorynaas looked on. Afterwards, they too were paraded there before the general gaze, prior to being taken away to their various fates. As Maesrhon had looked along the rows and rows of tiered seats, it had seemed to him that all he saw were faces avid for enjoyment of others' misery, eyes devoid of pity, mouths agape in greedy excitement. He had been sickened, and then had noticed Vorynaas. Again, and much more clearly, he saw the cruelty he had marked on their reunion, the careless cruelty he felt no need to hide because now there were none to check him.

Shame had burned in Maesrhon, as he sat there beside Ghentar who was applauding, catcalling, shouting, clapping, clearly loving every moment of the spectacle. Since then he had managed somehow to avoid ever attending again: his duties while learning the business had involved a certain amount of travelling around the country, and once in desperation he had made himself vomit by swallowing down quantities of salty water and pretended to be ill. Until today, he thought; today I have no real excuse, nothing at least that will be accepted by Vorynaas. Will his wrath fall on me? He jogged to a halt, leaning against a tree to get his breath, wondering whether any had been condemned to die. If so, they would be in Tellgard now, which was why he had not gone there himself. He would go down to the *Sword and Stars* and scratch on Isteddar's window. He could sleep on his floor and not go back to Seth y'n Carad until mid-morning, whatever the consequences. That first time, he had been unprepared for the sight of a man facing a squad of archers, a man set in bonds against a wall, a wall of the building he supposed he must call his home. He knew now what had caused that bloodstained smear at the east side of Seth y'n Carad, facing the compound, but he would not be caught unawares again.

A new idea

'Look, I don't care whether you can manage without or not, I'm going to get them.'

With a grin over his shoulder at his friend, Isteddar ducked out of the room, leaving Maesrhon sitting on the edge of his bed. After a few moments he was back, bringing a thin pallet and a couple of blankets. 'There you are. That's basic enough, surely it won't interfere too much with your endurance programme.'

Maesrhon peered at him suspiciously, and then both of them burst out laughing. 'What *do* you mean?'

Isteddar was twenty now, with a self-reliant air and, as often happens with those who must begin earning their own living when young, he seemed older than his years. 'Go on, you know all right. I've never forgotten that night we talked in the stable loft, before you went away. Always setting yourself tests, making yourself do things that scared you. Not to mention scared me, too, by the Starborn! It won't be long now before you go off on service and I'd wager you're going to apply for one of the scouting units. And I've heard bits and pieces about your time in Salfgard, as well as what you've told me yourself. You know my family live with Lord Forgard now. It means I can call in without too many remarks being passed, and sometimes I see Heretellar and Ancrascaro there. Plus, of course, I pick up a lot, working here at the *Sword*. People talk about you, Maesrhon.'

After a long pause, Maesrhon spoke from the pallet where he had settled himself. 'I've got to make another trip to Staran y'n Forgarad first, before I go off for basic training in Rigg'ymvala. But you're right, I'd rather be out on patrol than stuck on a border crossing. Up north is what I'd really like, as near to the forest as I can get.'

There was a rustle of blankets as Isteddar shuddered. 'Whatever for? Honestly, who but you would want to see the forest.'

'Well, I *have* seen it, if only from a distance. My uncle Ardeth used to say he could never understand why folk in Caradward were so wary of it, and I'm inclined to agree with him. I think it's a case of fear filling the space left by ignorance. But anyway, I'd like to find out for myself, and if I could, I'd like to visit my grandfather at his work. Since I came back from my foster-years I've only seen him once, briefly, here in the city. He's a sick man, by rights he should be spending his final years in ease and comfort, but he's not welcome in Seth y'n Carad.'

'Yes, you told me before.' Isteddar tossed and turned in his bed for a while, and then spoke again. 'Maesrhon, are you still awake? I've heard it said that Vorynaas will send you to the Lissa'pathor once your year of service is over. Men say he would never trust anyone in charge up there who wasn't family, that's why he keeps Arythalt there although he hates him. The rumour is that he'll make you take over, as soon as he can. I mean, we all know he'd never send Ghentar there.'

A rather mirthless chuckle came from the dark corner where Maesrhon lay. 'He hates me much more than my grandfather, but I don't think he'd let me anywhere near his gold, even if it did mean he could send me to a slow death far away that could never be laid directly at his door. Having said that, you can be sure he has something fairly unpleasant in mind for me. He was closeted with all his cronies tonight, maybe they were planning it then.' He laughed again.

'Maesrhon, stop it! Don't joke about things like that. Listen, you don't seem to realise that just because your father doesn't rate you, it doesn't mean that everyone thinks the same way. Not everyone goes willingly to the parades and the Open Hall, you know.' Isteddar lowered his voice to the merest whisper. 'People talk about you, Maesrhon. They would follow, if you gave them a lead.'

'People should follow Arval. If they had heeded his wisdom, things would be very different today,' said Maerhon rather shortly; and then after a pause, 'Will it be all right for me to use the bath-house here in the morning? Good, then let's go to sleep now.'

But it was Maesrhon, rather than Isteddar, who lay awake far into the night. He thought over their conversation and realised there was truth in what Isteddar had said. It was not only prominent citizens like Forgard and Issigitsar and a few others who held to Arval's word: though it had seemed otherwise to him on that first, never-to-be-forgotten experience of the Open Hall, there had indeed been faces in the crowd where dismay and displeasure were plain to see. He frowned in the darkness, remembering other things Isteddar had said. When men stirred in the early morning and the fires were lit in the bath-house, the two of them hurried over and disappeared into the steam. After a few minutes' soak in the hot tub, they climbed out one after another.

'Ready?' Isteddar was standing dripping on the tiles, waiting to turn on the cold fountain.

'Yes. Go on.'

Maesrhon gasped as the icy jets of water hit him, and then as Isteddar ducked under in his place, an idea came to him. No-one would be able to overhear them over the noise of the water, if they were careful. He spoke quietly into Isteddar's ear.

'You told me twice last night that people talk about me. What exactly do they say?'

'Well ... no disrespect to your mother's memory, but ... well ... for one thing, they say Vorynaas isn't your true father.'

When Maesrhon showed no surprise at what he heard, Isteddar assumed these whispers were not new to him. But when he made no reply, Isteddar began to shiver with more than the chill of the water, afraid he had gone too far, said too much. He stepped aside, reaching for a towel, huddling into it, watching Maesrhon, wondering what he was thinking. The torrent poured onto Maesrhon's dark head, flowed over the lean body with its hard muscles and white scars, splattered on to the floor beside him and ran noisily down the drain, but he neither heeded it nor noticed its numbing cold. Far from jumping to the same assumption others had made, his mind was possessed by the question which had leapt into it with his friend's words: *could Arval be my father?*

Blackmail

In Seth y'n Carad, a heated exchange was taking place between Ghentar and Valahald. Later in the morning, Ghentar would be travelling back to Heranwark to re-join his unit in Rigg'ymvala, but at present he was pacing up and down attempting to extract information from Valahald, who was calmly eating his breakfast.

'I've a right to know!' shouted Ghentar furiously. 'I'm an officer, I'm the first-born son, I attend all the meetings, one day I'll inherit everything! You've got to tell me!'

Valahald took his last mouthful of bread and honey, replaced the lid on the pot, rinsed his fingers in the waterbowl and politely waited to speak until he had swallowed, enjoying how this short delay in response infuriated Ghentar further.

'Well, let's just think about this. Yes, you're an officer, but I'm in charge of the garrison here at Seth y'n Carad, so I outrank you there.' He glanced around the room with his curiously colourless smile; he was well pleased with the suite of rooms he had taken over from Valestron. 'And, by definition, you certainly don't attend all the meetings, otherwise you wouldn't be in such a state over the fact that your father wanted to talk to Thaltor and myself privately after the general discussion last night. True, you're Vorynaas' first-born, but until you do inherit, it's his orders that count, not yours, so let's have less of what I've got to do, hm?'

Ghentar swung round on him with an oath; he was armed and in full uniform but would have been more formidable had he not been so flushed in the face with anger. 'By my right hand! You want to think carefully about things!' He made a sweeping gesture and the rings on his arm jangled together. 'When all this *is* mine, you'll be sorry for it if you cross me now. Tell me what my father wanted with you and Thaltor!'

'You know, you really should try to calm down a little. A powerfully-built man like you, with your temper you'll be dropping dead before you're into your fourth ten years.' Valahald wiped his mouth on the napkin, drained his cup and dabbed his lips again before pushing the tray aside. 'Get this through your head. I was bidden to a confidential meeting, and what was said and done there is going to stay confidential, whether you think you've a right to know what went on or not. I'd concentrate on making sure you *do* inherit, if I were you.'

'Oh? Meaning just what?'

'Well, your father isn't the most tolerant of men, and one of the things he hates most is being lied to. I'm sure you wouldn't want him to know the truth about your fight with Maesrhon up in Salfgard, for instance.'

The first course of Valahald's breakfast had been a dish of eggs with smoked fish; he favoured his eggs very lightly cooked, and the smell of them lingered in the room, making Ghentar feel slightly nauseous. His stomach churned as he stared at Valahald.

'You promised I could count on you about that. Are you going back on your word, then?'

'I wouldn't go that far. Let's just say a little sweetener every so often would help me to remember your version of things.'

'You're blackmailing me.' Pallor crept into Ghentar's face as Valahald merely smiled a little without reply. 'What do you want from me?'

Valahald moved to open the door, ushering Ghentar out with over-done courtesy. 'I'll think about it and let you know. Have a safe journey, now.'

Left alone, he reflected on his good fortune. How glad he was that he had waited for Vorynaas himself to show his hand, rather than acting on Thaltor's word. He might have ruined all his prospects, but as it was now, he had a position of authority close to the centre of power, he had been entrusted by both Thaltor and Vorynaas with the tricky task of getting rid of Maesrhon, and on top of all that, he had a hold over Ghentar that could prove very valuable in days to come. A servant tapped at the door and came in to remove Valahald's breakfast tray; his uniform was laid out for him in the bedroom, the metal trappings brightly burnished, his boots polished. Yes, life was good.

Ruthless decisions

Hearing shouting and the clatter of hooves, amplified by the confined space of the compound, Vorynaas glanced out of the window, breaking off from his conversation with Thaltor. He saw Ghentar and his entourage preparing to leave for their journey back to Rigg'ymvala, watched for a moment and then turned back to Thaltor with an expression that was half grin, half grimace.

'The way he treats his horses, he'll be pestering me to buy him yet another before the year's out.'

Thaltor had heard the note of indulgence creep into his old friend's voice and tailored his reply accordingly. 'We were all young once, you were a tearaway yourself at twenty. The lad was badly put out last night: after all he and Valafoss' boys grew up together so it must have come as a slap in the face to see Valahald party to something from which he was excluded. He'll feel better when he's cleared his mind with a wild gallop. You're pretty tough on him, you know. Why not include him in things more? Let him know you've got confidence in him?'

'He knows his position's secure.' Vorynaas gave a short laugh. 'I worked my way up to where I am now, I don't want him to think it's all going to be handed to him on a plate. Funny, when you think of it. Things came easy to Valafoss, he'd be nowhere now if he hadn't thrown his lot in with me, yet *his* sons take nothing for granted. Very keen to make their mark, the pair of them: didn't you tell me Heranar had signed on as a regular once his year was over, and Valahald's a real find.'

'That's right, he's at the armoury in the barbican. Heranar, that is. I heard he showed quite an aptitude for metalwork while he was away; he's working in the specialist development section now.'

Vorynaas grunted: it was the elder brother who was on his mind. 'Listen, Thaltor, you're to keep an eye on Valahald. It's got to look like an accident, and it's got to happen soon, well away from the city. Can I be sure he's up to it?'

'Absolutely. But can *we* be sure you won't have second thoughts?'

Vorynaas jumped to his feet. 'Listen, I've had seventeen years to make my mind up! When I swear to do something, I do it, no matter how long it takes. Remember that, Thaltor – and make sure Valahald knows it, too.'

Thaltor muttered a few words of agreement and then, conveniently remembering some task which he must see to without delay, lost no time in hastily leaving the room. It seemed his intuition had been right, when he'd spoken to Valahald about getting rid of Maesrhon, but it was just as well the younger man had failed to act at the time. He had just had a forcible reminder of how ruthless Vorynaas could be and promised himself now that no matter how much Valestron and others might enjoy sly innuendo on the subject of Maesrhon's parentage, he would take no further part in such sport himself. One look at the savage expression on Vorynaas' face had convinced him that it would be far too risky. Vorynaas glared at the door as it swung shut behind Thaltor, breathing rather heavily. That's right, he thought, you take yourself off and chew things over! Got a bit of a fright there, didn't you? Thought you could indulge in a laugh or two at my expense, mock me behind my back? Think again, Thaltor! He sat down, relaxing a little, unclenching his fists and smoothing his hair. Arval and Arythalt, Numirantoro and Arymaldur, they all thought they could cross me, but I have broken them all. A smile of implacable hatred played on his lips. Let Maesrhon make himself useful for a few months more; soon I need never see his changeling's face again.

Only a week left. Methodically working his way through the routine of settling his horse at the journey's end, Maesrhon was thinking about the strange tricks that time could play with a man's mind. In some ways it seemed only yesterday that he had arrived back in the city from Salfgard, in others it seemed an age had passed since the happy days with Ardeth and Fosseiro. Going much further than just those two years back, it seemed no time to him since he had been a small fearful child, about to leave for Gwent y'm Aryframan; and now here he was, on the brink of yet another departure. He paused in his work to rub Traebenard's nose, speaking to him quietly, and the horse's ears turned to the sound of the familiar voice. The old fellow was getting on a bit now. His father and brother might scoff at him riding Ghentar's cast-off, but Maesrhon paid no heed: Traebenard's quality still showed. He would be sad to leave him, but conscripts were not permitted to bring their own equipment with them to base camp, and that included horses. When all was done, he shouldered the saddlebags and turned to find Vorynaas confronting him at the door of the building.

'You took your time. You should have been back two days ago, so you've only yourself to blame if you're late to bed tonight. We've an important meeting in the morning: Haartell's off north the day after tomorrow, so we need your report straight away. Make sure you're on time with all your facts and figures sorted, and a copy prepared for everyone.'

'That won't be a problem, sir. How many copies am I to provide?'

Maesrhon hid his anger when he heard Vorynaas' reply. Clearly there would be no sleep at all for him tonight; he would need to work right through to make sure he was ready on time. He called in to the kitchens and collected some cold food to eat as he worked, and then settled in the silent office. Cleaning up after the journey would have to wait; he could wash and change tomorrow morning early after he had got everything set up for this meeting. He knew perfectly well that Vorynaas had timed it to annoy and harass him: there was no reason at all why it could not have been scheduled for the afternoon and still not interfered with Haartell's travel arrangements. But as he set out his working documents on the desk, collating the papers into neat piles and preparing to begin on his report, he reflected that the past couple of years could have been a lot worse. True, he had been on the receiving end of many a sarcastic comment and barbed jibe, but that was nothing new; generally speaking, Vorynaas had seemed curiously uninterested in his doings, even after Ghentar went off to Rigg'ymvala. Maesrhon had been astonished to be entrusted with various business trips, and was now quite well-travelled within Caradward. He had on several occasions been based for a week or two in the mining district of the Somllichan Ghent, had visited Staran y'n Forgarad, seen the ever-expanding development of the Cottan na'Salf, journeyed through the Lowanmorad and across the Ellanwic.

Laying his pens, the sharpening knife, coloured inks, ruler, blotting sand and various geometrical instruments readily to hand, his mind played over his recent dealings in Staran y'n Forgarad. He had come to rather enjoy this city; its down-to-earth commercialism and vibrant industrial activity made a bracing contrast to the somewhat effete air of decadence that tainted life in Caradriggan. He found he got on well with the *sigitsaran* he had encountered; the Outlanders made up a significant part of the southern city's population and he admired their independent spirit, even attempting to pick up some of the language they spoke among themselves, whose pronunciation was so difficult for others to master. Then there was the arrangement he had come to with Heretellar. Maesrhon smiled to himself. He had made several purchases now, using Arythalt's gift of silver which Arval held in trust, leaving them then with Heretellar whose estate in the Ellanwic was most conveniently placed for an overnight stop, knowing that in due course either he or Meremvor would be coming to Caradriggan, and could deliver items to Tellgard for him with no-one the wiser. But the smile faded from Maesrhon's face. Time was short now: only days were left before he was off to Heranwark with the others of his year and whatever else happened, he must somehow make himself ask Arval the questions that gnawed at him, the questions that time and again he had nearly voiced only for his courage to fail him at the last moment. He wanted to think over his most recent talk with Heretellar and the friends who gathered around him, needed to order his thoughts on the matters that burned in his mind. Instead, with the cool detachment that reminded Vorynaas so forcibly of the two people he most wanted to forget, he sat up straight, stretched, and composed himself to the task in hand.

Arval's counsel

'Now!' The shout came in a high, clear, young boy's voice, and was followed by excited shrieks and much clapping.

'Do it again! Please, go on, show us again!'

Half a dozen lads were scuffling around Maesrhon in the exercise court at Tellgard; one of them, clutching a catapult, ran to pick up a strange feathered object which had just fallen to the ground. Maesrhon's demonstration of decoy-shooting with the sling was a Salfgard speciality which had proved wildly popular with some of the youngsters in Tellgard: too much so initially, for the boys were clumsy still and a couple of windows had been broken by errant sling-shots. Maesrhon had paid for these himself, but had thought it best that for the time being, he did the shooting while the boys took it in turn to fire the decoy.

'Well, all right then,' he said now, 'but remember, while I'm away, if you want to try this yourselves, don't do it here. Go up to the fountain gardens, or even outside the city if you can. We don't want any more broken windows, or broken heads either, come to that. Right, ready?'

He loaded a stone into the sling and turned his back, waiting for the boy with the catapult to fire the decoy again. On the shout, he spun round, aimed and shot all in one movement; a cloud of feathers spun back to earth as the battered decoy finally disintegrated with the impact of the slingstone.

'Oh, no!' The boys ran to assess the damage and then turned as laughter and clapping came from the colonnade. Meremvor and Heretellar were advancing into the court, waving at Maesrhon. He waved in reply, tucking the sling back into his belt.

'Now, you lads can set about making a new decoy,' he said to the boys, 'and remember what I explained to you, the skill lies in offsetting the weight and the feathers so that its flight is unpredictable. If you hurry up with it, we'll have time to test it before I have to go off to Heranwark.'

They scurried off, and Maesrhon joined his friends, taking the bundle which Meremvor handed to him. 'Thanks. I didn't expect to see you here so soon.'

'No, but we've been talking things over since we saw you, and we thought we should come to Arval now, before you go off. My father says there's no point, that we should trust Arval to know what best to do, but we feel we want to see him face to face.'

Maesrhon noted Heretellar's serious manner, so like Forgard's; with a strand or two of silver in his hair even though he was only in his early twenties he looked set to follow his father in appearance also.

'I expect there's something to be said for both points of view,' he said, while hoping that his own plans for private discussion with Arval would not now be prevented. Private they would certainly need to be: there were things he wanted to say to Arval that were for only the two of them to hear. 'Let's go and wait for him in the small hall; he usually eats in there at mid-day.'

Ancrascaro joined them, and Arval welcomed his young friends, inviting them up to his study. Much of what was said was predictable to Maesrhon, its background no longer the mystery to him it had once been; his mind ran on its own track as he half-listened to the conversation in the room. At the first opportunity on his return from Salfgard, he had challenged Arval to tell him the full story of what had happened at the Spring Feast of his birth, and Arval had confirmed what Heretellar had told them all that evening in Framstock: that a lord of the Starborn had lived among them until they raised their hands against him, and that Vorynaas had been the leader of those who had tried to kill him. He had pressed Arval to say what had happened to Arymaldur, if he had indeed avoided death; to explain how this could be, to say where he went, why he had left them. The answers to these questions had been harder to understand.

'The Starborn may walk unseen,' Arval had said, 'and if you would learn more of their nature and powers, there are many volumes in Tellgard that treat of the As-Geg'rastigan. You may read in them as you will. As to where Lord Arymaldur went, you know as much as I, or any to whom his own words are known: he departed whence he came. But where that may be, or how to travel there, is not known to the Earthborn. The reason for his going is easier to comprehend. You have heard how among men, the Starborn must fulfil whatever part the Earthborn put upon them; they are not permitted to wield the power of the As-Geg'rastigan. If that part should tend towards evil, they will warn, but they cannot, and will not, ward. Arymaldur did indeed warn us, but not enough of us heeded. We drove him away and now we must endure what may follow.'

'...and there are many in the south, not *sigitsaran* only, but men of note in Staran y'n Forgarad...' Heretellar was leaning forward, emphasising the extent of the support Arval would be able to draw upon. Meremvor prompted him with a couple of names. '...and I believe we could count on Poenmorcar and his people, certainly his son, and there are others in the Ellanwic like my father, who refused to negotiate the sale of their land... Here in the city too, Isteddar brings word of those who would be with us, though they keep their heads down now, and the slaves would surely rise to grasp their freedom...'

But Arval was shaking his head slowly, and Heretellar faltered into silence.

'You reason that the end will justify the means, that to bring about good will be worth the risk of more evil. There has been strife already among us, but how many more deaths would there be this time, how many left widowed, maimed, ruined, bereft, even if you carry the day? Could you build again on sorrow such as that? And supposing you do not succeed, what do you think would happen then? Even with a lord of the As-Geg'rastigan to show them the way, men followed Vorynaas, and he has tightened his grip since then. If you do not prevail, he will be ruthless. Yet think of this: Vorynaas has never achieved universal support, neither then nor indeed today, as you have been telling me. Arymaldur renewed the pledge for the sake of those who knew him for what he was; he promised me that there is always hope, if men know where to find it. All those you speak of, those who have stayed true, they are keeping alive our chance of finding that hope. The more numerous they are, the more time we will have, the more likely we are to achieve our quest.'

After a pause, Heretellar spoke again. 'Very well, Arval na Tell-Ur. We came here for your wisdom, and we will abide by it. But it goes against the grain to stand by as wrong is done, to raise no hand to prevent it.'

Arval smiled; he had always been fond of Heretellar and chose his words carefully to bring approval and comfort. 'You should take heart from what you have heard, for there is indeed a work to be done, and you are already engaged upon it by making your own lives an example. But you can do more, if you will. Remind men of Arymaldur, and their minds will turn again to the light.'

Through all this, Ancrascaro had said little, but she had been listening intently and now she had a question of her own. 'Arymaldur promised us hope, yet he is gone from us and you say we cannot find the Starborn, who walk unseen. But he spoke as if that hope was there to find, if we knew where it lay hidden, and you speak to us of a quest. What is that quest? How is it possible to set out in search of hope, as a man might ride to seek an unclaimed valley for a new land-take? Where does our hope lie? Can't you tell us more of this? For I think none of us here would hesitate, if we saw a clear path before us.'

There was a murmur of agreement from the young people, and they watched Arval eagerly, awaiting his reply; but he had seen the way their eyes first turned to Maesrhon, as the boy lifted his head suddenly. He forced himself to hold Ancrascaro's gaze, not to look at Maesrhon, to keep his voice calm and steady.

'You have a sharp mind, *is-gerasto*, your questions are shrewdly put. But you must be patient, my friends, although I know this is not easy, when one is young.' He gestured at the books stacked high on shelves all around the room. 'Every day, I work to acquire the knowledge I need. Doubts still cloud my mind, but I promise you that when I see the way forward, I will speak.'

Even as he formed the words, he realised that he had used them before; in spite of himself, his eyes went to Maesrhon's face and he saw that he too had recognised phrases from a well-remembered conversation. Arval's pulse raced; he could hear the blood rushing in his ears: no, not yet, his heart spoke within him, not yet, not yet, it is still too soon!

The burning question

On the old bench seat outside the tower door of Tellgard, Maesrhon and Arval sat side by side. Arval was reading and Maesrhon was busy with some leather-work; it was his last chance to finish it, before he left for base camp early the following morning. Beside him on the bench were the tools of his craft, together with bits and pieces of cut-off skins and hide, and more scraps were scattered on the ground at his feet. He was stitching steadily, inserting a series of pockets and pouches into two long straps that lay across his knees, but his mind was turning over the two questions he most wanted to ask Arval. He stole a sidelong glance at his companion, who seemed engrossed in his book. Maesrhon shifted on the bench. He told himself he was being ridiculous: Arval had never, ever, rebuked him for putting any question, yet here he was, after two years and with only a couple of hours left to him, and still he had not asked what he had burned to know ever since Ardeth's casual remark all those years ago in Salfgard. As for his other question, that was of more recent origin yet it haunted his mind no less. It would have to be now, or it would be too late. He turned to Arval, but the old man spoke first.

'I see not all your time in the south was occupied with business affairs.'

'No, I've made friends and contacts in Staran y'n Forgarad through whom I have learnt new skills and improved old ones. I've been spending some time among Issigitsar's metalworkers, and in the tanneries too. I bought this leather on my most recent trip and left it with Heretellar, as usual; but when he and Meremvor came up to the city earlier this week, they brought it here for me so I thought I would take the chance to try out some ideas I had during my time with Torald – I told you about him, didn't I?'

'You did indeed. A master of his chosen arts, and a wise man too.'

'Yes. Well, I often think over what I learnt from him, and…' Maesrhon broke off, biting his lip for a second or two. 'Lord Arval, I want to ask you something,' he blurted out.

Arval had been expecting this ever since the afternoon in his study and was unsure how he intended to respond.

'It was something Ardeth said to me.' Maesrhon kept his eyes on his lap, running a hank of waxed thread through his fingers. 'He said he thought, that is, he wondered whether you, and ever since then I've wanted to ask…'

This did not sound like the question he was expecting, thought Arval as he slowly closed his book, an intuition confirmed when Maesrhon suddenly looked up and said quickly, not giving himself time to change his mind, 'Ardeth said he thought you might be *as-ur*.'

To Maesrhon's surprise, Arval chuckled softly. 'Well, well! I always said there was more to Ardeth than met the eye. Those who think him a simple countryman are much mistaken.' Then the laughter faded from his voice. 'I cannot number myself among the As-Urad, yet it is true that I share a small part of the life of the Starborn. You know from the old tale *Maesell y'm As-Urad* of the danger to any of the Earthborn who hazard a union with one of the Starborn. My father's mother was of the As-Geg'rastigan, or so I have deduced, for I scarcely knew my own parents. My mother's hold on life failed once my father was gone, and I was still a child when he disappeared, driven in spite of himself to seek what he could never find upon this earth.' Arval sighed.

'It was long ago, and far from here, in the high valleys of the Somllichan Asan, looking westward over Ilmar Inenad. Yes, I was born in Gwent y'm Aryframan, though as soon as I was old enough, I made my way here, for the fame of Tellgard as a seat of learning had travelled far afield. It seemed to me that here I might find answers to my own questions, and here I have remained. The years have passed, and I have taught, and learnt: always learnt. And waited. To endure the wait, I have succeeded in distilling a fiery spirit, potent with life: none know of it but I, and latterly those whom Tell'Ethronad send to me.' Arval's voice carried a new burden of bitterness.

'For them, the tiny drop which moistens their lips is not enough to stave off death, but it gives them strength and joy so that they feel no fear or pain. But for myself, though I have made my own means of delaying it, and my own reasons, yet you see that age lies now upon me, as it must upon all men: the years cannot be held back for ever. Time is running out; I feel the end of days coming.'

Moments passed, and Maesrhon sat silent, almost overwhelmed by what he had heard. Sounds of sudden activity in the stables beyond the exercise court reached him but he paid no heed. Eventually Arval spoke again. 'Are you answered?'

'I am more than answered, Lord Arval, I am honoured: honoured that you trust me with such an answer. Yet somehow, always the more I learn from you, the greater the number of questions which arise in my mind, so that now I would know the purpose of your waiting.'

Arval noticed how the light from the lamp beside the door shone obliquely into Maesrhon's eyes, kindling all the sun-sparks in the amber, and remembered a long-ago conversation with Numirantoro when she too had thanked him for his trust. He smiled slightly, wrapped in the memory. 'When your mother was born in this city, and grew daily in wisdom and grace, I knew she was one of the reasons.'

Maesrhon made a sudden, involuntary movement, and the old man turned to him.

'I see her in you, little son.'

Maesrhon gripped the edge of the bench: it was now or never. He heard his own voice, as if from a distance. 'Do you see my father in me, also?'

This time, Arval looked at the high brow, the dark hair flowing back, the hollows under the high cheekbones, the otherworldly air that was daily more marked. Surely all must see what he saw? Three men hurried through the archway, the foremost calling for him, the other two carrying some burden between them, but he ignored them. 'Yes, I do.'

'Lord Arval. Arval.' It was no more than a whisper. 'Arval, are you my father?'

The newcomers were almost upon them now, but Arval and Maesrhon stared at each other with painful intensity, oblivious to the world about them. Arval felt as though he had stepped onto ice that cracked and slid beneath his feet: he had one instant left in which to speak. 'No, I am no man's father. But you are the child of my heart, *Is-torar*.'

Breathless with haste, the first man now panted up to where they sat. 'Arval, please help! I have Lord Arythalt here, he is ill!'

Arval jumped up with an exclamation, seeing that the other two men, who now approached, carried between them a litter designed for horseback and in it, eyes closed in a gaunt, grey face, lay Arythalt. 'Merenald! What has happened? Why are you here in the city?'

'Lord Arythalt has been ousted from the Lissa'pathor by Vorynaas and the rest of them. Haartell arrived without warning about five days ago. He produced authorisation for taking charge, and turned us out. I have been in service with Lord Arythalt these thirty years: though I followed him to the forest, I could not obey his command to leave him there to his fate. A man in failing health should not have had to make such a journey, but we have made him as comfortable as we could and brought him straight to you; he is too weak to protest. Give him refuge here in Tellgard, bring him healing! I will work for you to repay the debt, you have only to name any task.'

Merenald plucked at Arval's robe in his urgency, and then as Arythalt groaned faintly he seemed to notice Maesrhon for the first time and turned swiftly to where the young man still sat, numbed from the shock of disappointment. 'Sir, forgive me, it is some years since I last saw you.' He seized Maesrhon's hand and pulled him across to the litter. 'Lord Arythalt, see who is here! Look, Maesrhon is with you! Now all will be well again.'

Maesrhon dropped to one knee and took Arythalt's thin hand in his. 'Sir, can you hear me? You are safe in Tellgard with Arval.'

Slowly Arythalt's eyes opened; his glance wavered over Maesrhon's face and his other hand reached up to touch his hair. 'Numirantoro?'

'No, no.' Maesrhon bent a little nearer. 'It's Maeshron, sir. Do you see me now?'

'Ah.' The eyes closed again, and the voice was weary, but the hint of a smile lit Arythalt's wasted features. 'You can call me grandpa, you know.'

'Take him into the guest wing, we will have the first two rooms arranged for his private use.' Arval nodded to Merenald, and his two companions lifted the litter again. 'Maesrhon, go with them and help; it will do your grandfather good to know you are with him.' He began to move off towards the medical wing. 'I must arrange for his nursing requirements.'

'But… I must leave at dawn tomorrow, and there are things which surely we should finish speaking of, now we have begun, Lord Arval!'

The old man turned back to where the boy stood, bereft; his heart ached within him, although the dark, deep-set eyes were as steady as ever. 'I am sorry, little son. You must wait again, but it will not be for long, this time.'

CHAPTER 27

Military service

Most of the lads who were called up to Heranwark that summer went reluctantly, some resenting a year taken from their usual way of life, some apprehensive at the prospect of military discipline, some fearful at leaving their homes for the first time. Somehow they scrambled their way through the four-week basic training period, constantly running from one task to the next, shouted at by officers, laughed at by the regulars, always tired, often hungry. Their conversation consisted almost entirely of complaints, of wishing themselves anywhere else, but as they became more used to their new surroundings, talk turned more often to speculation on where they would be sent once their training was completed. Those who hailed from Caradriggan or the districts nearest to the city all hoped to be posted to the urban garrison in the barbican barracks; most of the others thought border duties would be a bearable prospect. There was only one option which was open to choice, and that was service with the auxiliaries, the specialist troops who formed mobile, lightly-armed scouting units: even the regulars were all volunteers, for conditions were harsh and the training intensive. The drop-out rate was high and those who made it through were held in some awe, enjoying a well deserved reputation for uncompromising toughness. It was almost unheard-of for any of the conscripts to put their names forward and Maesrhon smiled ruefully in the darkness, remembering the reaction of his fellows to the news that he and Sigitsinen had done so.

He was lying wakeful as usual on the hard, narrow bed in the bare dormitory. When he had first come to Heranwark, tired out though he had been at each day's end, he had been unable to sleep for the bitter disappointment that flooded his mind as soon as his body was at rest. The other lads had groaned at the pain of their aching limbs and complained about the unremitting pace of the work, but he had lain silent, alone with the emptiness that gnawed at him. He had so hoped he was Arval's son; he realised that, wanting it so much, he had persuaded himself it would be so, and now he felt lost and desolate. Yet as the days passed, though time and fatigue had dulled the sense of loss and disappointment, new preoccupations had arisen to disturb his rest. He knew for certain now that Arval could tell him who his father was and he cast about in his mind for likely candidates. Forgard? Could he be half-brother to Heretellar? But Forgard seemed happily married, surely he would not have betrayed his wife… and from all that he had heard of Numirantoro, he found it impossible to imagine that she had been involved in some secret liaison however much she might have hated Vorynaas. If only Merenald had not appeared with Arythalt just at the moment when Arval had seemed about to speak!

Now his thoughts turned to his grandfather and he wondered whether he would see him again. At least in Tellgard Arythalt would have the benefit of Arval's healing and care and need never go back to the Lissa'pathor. And now that Haartell had taken over, presumably he himself need worry no longer that Vorynaas would pack him off there, as rumour had suggested he might. I still want to see the forest, though, thought Maesrhon. He remembered what his grandfather had said to him about it, years ago when he was still a child. *Dark and full of secret life*, those had been the words. Maybe he should talk more to Arythalt, there could be much he might reveal; he seemed a man of education and experience, perhaps it was just his cloak of sorrow and regret that hid the inner self. Whether he would live long enough for them to get to know each other better was a moot point, especially as conscripts got so little leave during their year of service.

Maesrhon turned over yet again. One thing he would certainly do, next time he was in Caradriggan, was speak privately to Isteddar and charge him with an errand to Heranwark on his behalf. He realised that Sigitsinen's father and brother, though they had thanked him for his praise of their work, had been secretly a little disappointed that he had not bought from them. He was sorry he could not be more open with them, but it would not be long before they had cause for celebration. More of Arythalt's silver would be well spent, soon.

This Sigitsinen was someone with whom Maesrhon had become quite friendly. He too stood out as slightly different from the other young men, being, as his name implied, of Outland stock. He had their dark colouring, with glossy black hair, but his eyes were an unexpected greenish colour, very pale and bright with a hazel ring around the iris. He had been born and bred in Heranwark itself, where his father was in business supplying weaponry to Rigg'ymvala; but having an elder brother who would take over in due time, and a whole brood of younger brothers also destined for apprenticeships, he had decided to make his own career in the military. During training camp there were only two free days, and today on the second of these he had invited Maesrhon to meet his family. Heranwark was a busy, thriving place, but a typical army town. As the two of them walked down the hill from Rigg'ymvala, Maesrhon thought the streets and buildings were drab and charmless; but the interior of Sigitsinen's home surprised him with its elaborate decoration and intricately-embroidered and worked fabrics in the dark, richly glowing colours favoured among the *sigitsaran*. He could barely tell the little boys apart: they all took after the man of the house who was dark and stocky, a typical Outlander; but his wife, although also very dark, had Sigitsinen's pale eyes and was noticeably taller than her husband. They made Maesrhon welcome, chiding the children's giggles at his attempts to thank them in their own tongue, using some of the phrases he had picked up in Staran y'n Forgarad.

After they had eaten, he asked whether he might see any examples of the weaponsmith's craft. Everything he was shown was the work of a master, but what impressed him most were the smaller items: hunting knives, daggers, spear heads, axes, throwing-knives, arrowheads in various styles, spurs, buckles and arm-guards, sheaths, scabbards, shield-bosses; there were even hooks, ranging in size from grapples down to fish-hooks; needles, buttons, coils of wire in various metals and gauges; uniform brooches and badges, harness decorations. Maesrhon examined a set of needles, perfectly-matched in graduated sizes; the light flashed on their brilliant polish and winked on the invisible points. He laid them carefully down again and picked up a slender throwing-knife, admiring the sheen of the narrow blade and feeling the balance in its weight.

'These are all works of art,' he said warmly. 'I have never seen such skill in small pieces such as these.'

'Well, they say you do best what you most enjoy doing, and I've always taken most pleasure in what you might call the miniature side of my craft. Must run in the family or something, take a look at these now. This is my eldest son's work.'

The man directed Maesrhon's attention to a workbench at the side of the room, and opened a wooden case. Inside it were small boxes in different shapes and styles, most in metals of various kinds but some also in turned wood, carved bone and horn.

'I'm a metal man myself, but you can see he wastes his time on wood and suchlike.'

He exchanged a grin with the young man, who returned it while watching for the visitor's reaction to his own work. Maesrhon opened a square pewter box, noting the tiny hinges; a round silver container had a lid which screwed off; and a small, cylindrical horn tube simply pulled apart but was so exactly finished that the join between top and bottom was invisible when they were matched together.

'A man would find it difficult to choose between these, they are all so beautiful. If I had the means to do so, I would purchase widely among your wares. I have never seen better quality, neither in Caradriggan nor Staran y'n Forgarad, nor during the time I spent in Gwent y'm Aryframan.'

Being aware of who he was they had assumed he must have wealth at his disposal, not realising that Vorynaas wasted no generosity on his younger son, and they locked everything away with a slightly crestfallen air, though they did their best to hide it; but as he and Sigitsinen headed back up to the fort, Maesrhon was already mentally compiling an inventory of items for purchase even while chatting with his friend. Two throwing-knives headed the list, but it also included more surprising items such as hooks, needles and wire and a selection of the small boxes in bone and horn. They reached the gate, gave the password and made their way back to quarters. There was some banter as everyone returned from their free day, but soon the order came for lights out and all was quiet. Arval, Arythalt, Sigitsinen's home and family, the events of the day, the mysteries of the past, the unknown future, all circled in Maesrhon's thoughts in a seemingly endless round. What was he to do with his adult life? He squeezed his eyes more firmly closed, willing sleep to come. The gruelling training for which he and Sigitsinen had signed up began tomorrow: it was vital that they made a success of it. The other lad had set his heart on a full-time military career, but Maesrhon, mindful of Arval's mention of a quest, felt again the strange call of the north that had haunted him for as long as he could remember. He had learnt from Torald, now he must be ready to take every advantage of this new form of instruction.

Problems for Ghentar

The sordid little room was heavy with the smell of cheap scent and stale drink. A tangled heap of clothes spilled from the one chair and in the corner on a small table was a jug that still held a couple of inches of wine. On the bed lay a sleeping girl and a young man whose bleary eyes refused to close, weary and drunk though he was. Dim light was shed by a glim burning on the wall: it fell on the girl's slender arms, lying outside the coverlet, on her thin shoulders under the dark, loosened hair. Too thin for my liking, really, thought the young man; and a voice in his mind that he seldom heeded added that she was far too young to be selling herself. But what do I care, a more strident inner voice asked; I've got enough problems of my own to worry about. He heaved himself on to an elbow and reached out to pour the remaining wine; misjudging the distance, he knocked over one of the cups, which rolled on the table-top, spilling dregs on to the floor. Cursing under his breath, the young man looked over his shoulder but the girl slept on as he took a swallow at his new drink. He pulled a face: the wine was sour and of poor quality, and had already given him a severe headache. How much worse was he going to feel in the morning, if he drank the rest of it now? Not bothering to consider an answer to this question, he raised the cup to his lips again. He would have to spend the rest of his leave here in Heranwark; the thought of turning up at Seth y'n Carad with a hangover like the one now gathering force in his head was unbearable. Propping the lumpy pillow against the wall, he leaned back and closed his eyes. What was he going to do? What could he do? Anger at his predicament swept over him, a rage all the more destructive because he knew he had brought his trouble on himself. Then self-pity took him, and he dropped his head onto his knees with a groan. To think that Ghentar, elder son and heir to Vorynaas of Caradriggan, should be reduced to skulking in a filthy doss-house like this!

By mid-morning next day, he was wandering listlessly around the weekly street-market, feeling like death and at a loss as to how to fill the rest of his time, when he was hailed by a familiar voice. Looking round, he saw Thaltor heading towards him through the crowds.

'No need to ask what's the matter with you,' grinned Thaltor, taking in the dark circles under Ghentar's eyes in his pallid face. 'Come on, you need my patent hangover cure.'

'Don't talk to me, I'm not drinking any of your lethal concoctions. I'm never drinking anything again. In fact I don't think I'm ever going to eat anything again.'

Thaltor laughed, too loudly for Ghentar's bruised senses, and steered him by the elbow around a corner or two. 'Yes, I know what it's like. Done it myself, more times than I care to remember.'

They went into a small eating-house, where the smell of food made Ghentar shudder even though he was grateful for the fact that the room was dark, lit mainly by firelight. He sat down in a corner, staring in front of him, too withdrawn into his self-inflicted misery to take any notice of what Thaltor was ordering from the stout woman who came forward to serve them or even to wonder what Thaltor was doing here in Heranwark. When the food arrived he attempted to push it away from him, but Thaltor divided it up and made him eat. The bread was warm, crisp on the outside and soft within, drizzled with oil and garlic and dusted with salt crystals. With it came a vegetable broth, thickened with roots and grain; two poached eggs nestled in the bowl. Afterwards, a hot infusion of camomile and a plate of sweet biscuits was put in front of him. As the starchy food began to enter his system, the fog in Ghentar's head cleared a little; he felt warmer and less shaky and life seemed marginally more worth living. He sat back, taking a deep breath.

'Thanks, that's a bit better. I can't tell you how terrible I felt.'

'No need: I told you before, I know all about it.'

A shout from the doorway made them both look round. Valahald was on his way into the room, and with him a young man in junior officer's uniform who was speaking with some heat.

'Hey, Ghentar! What are you doing in here? I thought you said you were going home for the week.'

Thaltor saw how Ghentar shifted in his seat, the colour rising once more in his face. The newcomer pressed his point. 'You said you'd get the funds when you went back to Caradriggan. It might be all right for some of the others, but I'm not made of money. How long am I supposed to wait? I want my winnings, there's things I need to buy. You owe me, when are you going to pay up? Are you having the money sent on to you, or what?'

'Er, change of plan, I'm just … Excuse me a minute.'

Ghentar, pushing out past Thaltor, nodded briefly to Valahald and took the other man outside. So, thought Thaltor, he's gambling again. And obviously losing again. I wonder how much debt he's run up this time. He exchanged a quiet, urgent word with Valahald. Ghentar came back after a moment or two, frowning and chewing his lip, furious that the other two had witnessed his discomfiture, panicking at the new lies he had just told.

Valahald stood up and made to leave again immediately, to Ghentar's immense relief.

'I'll see you soon,' he said with a nod of farewell; Ghentar could only hope that the words were meant for Thaltor and not himself.

'What's Valahald doing here in Heranwark?'

'He's with me,' said Thaltor. 'I'm over here on business, so he's left his second in charge back home and we travelled together. He's staying with Valestron up in his quarters in the fort. Who was the other young fellow, by the way?'

'Oh, a friend of mine from Rigg'ymvala. He's in the third watch, they're not on leave this week like we are in the seconds and fourths.'

He sat there, grimly waiting for the inquisition, but Thaltor appeared to change the subject. 'What's Maesrhon up to these days?'

'Surely you must have heard how he put his name forward for the auxiliaries, him and some dirty little Outlander.' Ghentar spat the words out. 'Trust him to do something like that. Why is there always all this fuss about Maesrhon? I can't understand my father; these days he seems to let him get away with anything, even not turning up to the Open Hall. Then he comes here for his year's service and all I hear is "Maesrhon's your brother, isn't he? He's really good with the sword, isn't he? Did you know he came first in the archery? Did you see him on the climbing wall? Maesrhon's put his name down for the patrols, didn't he tell you? Why didn't he tell you, he's your brother isn't he? Do you think he'll make it through the training?" Maesrhon, Maesrhon all the time. I'm an officer, *he* should be telling people I'm *his* brother. But no, he goes about with his nose in the air, making friends with an Outlander, if you don't mind! By my right hand, I hope they're really putting him through it, wherever they're holed up.' He laughed derisively.

'Do you know that fellow Atranaar? He's got a touch of the *sigitsaran* about him too, by the look of him, but apparently he's a big noise in the auxiliaries, and they say he's a real fanatic about keeping up tough standards in his command. He turned up *in person* to look over Maesrhon and his pal, and I heard he made some crack about it being a real test for two misfits like them to see whether they could stick the pace with his boys. Ah well, there's one good thing about it: they're out there crawling about through the undergrowth or whatever it is they do for months on end; they only get one short leave break during the training, so at least I don't have to see him here in Heranwark any more for the time being.'

'Yes, I know Atranaar all right. Known him for years. He takes no prisoners, as they say.' Thaltor laughed heartily at his own joke, and raised a quizzical eyebrow at Ghentar. 'That was quite an outburst! You're obviously beginning to feel more like your old self.'

'Oh, well.' Ghentar brooded for a moment or two, trying to stop his mind automatically totting up his mounting problems. 'It's just that I feel people should show me more respect, you know? They should take more care to keep in with me, I'll be number one when my time comes. Even the old man treats me like a child half the time, he should have seen me in action last night!' He nudged Thaltor with a suggestive smile; then the frown returned as he peered gloomily into the dregs of his camomile drink, wondering if he was sufficiently recovered to risk a shot of something stronger. Hair of the dog and all that, after all.

A new debt

That evening, a message from Valahald was delivered to Ghentar's rooms, proposing that they should ride out together the following day with their hunting bows. Feeling he had no option but to agree, he presented himself at the meeting place. The morning was chilly and silent, hardly anyone being up and about at this early hour, and there was little conversation between the two of them as they rode off westwards towards the more broken ground where the foothills of the Somllichan Ghent began to rise. In all the time since their argument at Seth y'n Carad, no word had come from Valahald naming his price for silence, but Ghentar was acutely aware of the veiled threat hanging in the air between them. He was expecting some move from Valahald at any moment, but the morning passed and the subject was not mentioned; the strained atmosphere eased in the exertion of the chase and by the time they stopped to rest and eat at mid-day all seemed friendly once more.

'Not much of a bag, is it?' said Valahald, chewing on bread and cold beef and poking with his foot at the single hare they had managed to shoot.

'No, but that's the problem round here. Too many of us coming out from Heranwark and Rigg'ymvala, it's spoiled the hunting from what it used to be like, they say.'

'Right.' Valahald took a swig of water from his bottle and then rinsed out his mouth and spat. 'You know, I could use a real drink. What say we go and find one? Do you know of anywhere nearby, to save us lasting out until we get back to town?'

Within the hour, they were warming themselves in front of a roaring fire with mulled drinks on the table before them. The village where the inn was situated lay at the mouth of a wide valley winding back into the mountains; it had grown up originally at the meeting-place where the valley road crossed the main north-south route on the eastern side of the Red Mountains, but these days its prosperity was owed more to the fact that Heranwark was only a half-day's ride away. Officers from Rigg'ymvala had found it a pleasant and convenient place to spend leave when they wanted a little privacy to enjoy female company, and the compact old stone buildings of the original *gradstedd* had been extended several times by the addition of new wings. Ghentar stretched his legs out to the hearth and leaned back in his seat, feeling a glow spread through him as the drink took hold. Strong stuff, this, he thought, or maybe I still haven't cleared my system from the last time. He chuckled to himself at this idea, but his mellow mood was suddenly and unpleasantly dispelled.

'What are you going to do about your money problem?'

'Leave it, can't you. I don't want to talk about it.'

'No doubt. But that's not going to make it go away, is it? How much do you owe, anyway?' Valahald already knew the answer to this, but whistled with convincing shock when Ghentar sulkily told him. 'That's more than two months' pay! Better avoid narrow streets and dark corners for a while.'

'Oh, very funny. Anyway, I've said I'm expecting an advance from home, so that gives me a few days to sort something out.'

'Ghentar, have sense. I know what you're going to do, you're going to gamble again in the hopes of winning. But what if you lose? You'll be in a worse mess than ever, and if the heavy boys come calling, your father will find out what's been going on.'

'Look, will you just shut up about it!' Ghentar banged on the table with his fist, swearing. 'What else *can* I do? My luck has to change some time, surely. It doesn't help to keep going on about it.'

After a pause, Valahald spoke softly. 'All right, we won't talk about it. But maybe I can help some other way.'

'Huh.'

Ghentar reached for his drink and turned away, feeling as though all the woes of the world were settling on his shoulders. He heard Valahald stoop and open the saddle-bag he had brought in with him, and then a tiny metallic chink as something was set on the table between them. He looked round and saw Valahald watching him.

'What's that?'

'It's for you. Have a look inside.'

Ghentar opened the leather pouch and stared incredulously. 'Who is this from?'

'From me, of course. I'm evidently more careful with my money than you are with yours. There's enough there to clear the debt, and some more to tide you over. You can say it came through from Caradriggan.'

Although his fingers had closed tightly round the top of the bag, Ghentar pushed it from him with an effort. 'I can't take this.'

'Listen.' Valahald stood up. 'I'm going through to order something to eat now. If that pouch is still on the table when I come back, I'm taking it home with me. That gives you about three minutes to make your mind up what to do about it, so it's up to you.'

When he returned, the table was bare. 'Well, that was fairly painless after all, it seems.'

Ghentar could not meet his eyes. 'I'm very grateful. I don't know when I'll be able to pay you back.'

'Don't worry about that, you can owe me. There'll be a chance for you to repay me in due course, I'm sure.' Valahald smiled. 'Ah, here's the food.'

Mine slaves

With a shrill blast on his whistle, the gangmaster gave the signal to his labourers that they should down tools. There was a clatter as picks, shovels and heavy mallets were dropped to lie where they fell, and the men threw themselves to the ground beside the section of paved road they were repairing. Dull eyes blinked in faces streaked with sweat and dust; they all had a narrow strip branded into their hair, the mark of mine-slaves. A water-bottle was passed among them and they drank with desperate thirst, too tired to waste energy on resenting how the overseer alone had water to spare for splashing on his face and head. Flies swarmed around them, settling on their throats and around their nostrils. The gangmaster sat on a tree-stump, looking down the valley: sizing up mentally how much more work there was to do and how long it was likely to take. They would need to press on;

autumn was half-over already and the road needed to be fully restored before winter weather began to take its toll. Hearing voices from the opposite direction, he turned and saw a group of men approaching, among them Haartell. With a muffled curse, he stood up quickly. There were tools and loose stones all over the road, and Haartell had already made his mark as a cruel and capricious overlord with an inventive capacity for finding fault. If he and his party had to step over a dirty shovel, or pick their way round a pile of stones and muck, there'd be ructions, guaranteed.

'Hey you, Vigurt! Clear this mess out of the way before the boss gets here. Jump to it, now.'

None of the men moved; they were all experts in delaying obedience just long enough to gain an extra moment's rest without risking a beating. With a curse, the overseer grabbed the slave nearest to him, a middle-aged man whose face was grotesquely disfigured by an old wound. 'Deaf as well as ugly, are you, Vigurt? Get those tools gathered up. And you there, shovel up this loose stuff on to the heap, and be quick about it, the pair of you.'

He pushed a second man to his feet, but the job was not quite done when Haartell and his companions arrived on the scene. Haartell stopped, pushing fastidiously at a mud-encrusted mallet-shaft with an expensively booted toe.

'Why are these men lying about resting when all this clutter is blocking the road?'

'I'm sorry, my lord, we'll have it clear for you in just a couple of minutes. These useless idiots are so slow...' The gangmaster cringed in front of Haartell and then rounded on the slave who was gathering up the tools. He was limping slightly, but the overseer kicked him viciously on the lame leg. 'Speed it up there, can't you, you idle bastard!'

The man stumbled under the blow, and a rake fell with a clatter from under his arm. Fists raised, the overseer stepped forward again, but with an exclamation a young man detached himself from Haartell's party.

'There's no need for that. He's working as fast as he can with that leg of his.'

He picked up the rake, gathered up two or three remaining shovels and hefted a pick with his right hand. As he straightened from piling them with the other tools at the side of the road, he suddenly saw that under the grime of sweat and dirt on the man's arm, a tattooed design was visible on the skin. Faded though it was, the pattern was unmistakeable: the sign of the springing corn. His gaze flew to the man's horribly damaged face where one eye and half the nose was missing and a twisted scar pulled one side of the mouth aside. The surviving eye was blue and was now staring back at him with a strange fixity, but the gangmaster was shouting again, chivvying all his men to their feet, urging them back to work.

'Just a moment.'

Haartell raised a hand for silence and walked over to the young man. 'You have no authority to interfere in the work of the Lissa'pathor. You have the tokens you came for: now get out.'

'With the greatest pleasure.'

The weary labourers were taking notice now, all right; they all heard what the young man said as he turned again to the disfigured slave, speaking quietly. 'I am sorry. May the As-Geg'rastigan keep you.'

Then as they gaped in amazement, without another word he walked straight into the forest, disappearing soundlessly into the trees where the mixed, muted colours of the heavy-duty fatigues he was wearing caused him to vanish from sight almost immediately. Every man there stared open-mouthed, some gazing at the road where the speaker had stood, others at the place where it seemed as though the darkness of Maesaldron had swallowed him without trace. Haartell was the first to recover.

'Listen to me very carefully, all of you. Yes, you too, overseer. One more repetition of the kind of slackness I have seen today, and it will take more than the so-called Starborn to protect you. If I have to send you back there, you will not be so lucky on your second appearance in the Open Hall. Finish these repairs on schedule, or face the consequences. Now get on with it.'

Locked in the sleeping-cage that night, the slaves whispered among themselves for a while. One of them had heard a rumour that the mysterious young fellow who had melted into the forest was a son of Lord Vorynaas, but the others were inclined to scepticism.

'Go on, Haartell wouldn't have spoken to him like that if that's who he was.'

'Well, they say the younger one's never been in favour. And him that we saw today was in some kind of uniform, and I heard he's in the army these days.'

The one-eyed slave spoke, clearing a rusty throat. 'What did Haartell mean about the Open Hall?'

There was a rustle in the darkness as men rose to their elbows, peering into the corner where he lay: none of them could remember him uttering a word before tonight.

'Hey, our friend with the gammy leg's found his voice. What do you think he meant? You can't have forgotten your first time in there.'

After a pause, the unfamiliar voice came again from the shadows. 'I have never been there. I was taken in Gwent y'm Aryframan and sent straight here as a captive.'

Even through the distortion in his speech made by the damage to his face they could hear the bitterness in his voice, but there was no room in their world for sympathy.

'You want to make sure you stay here, then. Haartell meant it would be death for us, next time. Now listen, you, whatever your name is. You've kept your mouth shut up till now so keep it shut tonight too, can't you? Some of us want to sleep.'

With the auxiliaries

Some weeks later, away south in the Lowanmorad, Atranaar sat writing up his report on the exercise that his dozen or so new men had recently completed with varying degrees of success. The final test of their initial period of training was always the same: to spend a set number of days away from their unit, alone and reliant on their own resources; to return to base with proof of where they had been; and to regain their own lines without detection from the experienced men, who were deployed in a wide screen with orders to watch and intercept. As usual, the success rate was about one third of the total, although quite a few more had got close enough before being picked up: it had been one of the better intakes. That young fellow Sigitsinen was acquitting himself well; there was officer material there in the making. Atranaar chewed at the end of his pen, staring at the paper in front of him. The problem was what to say about the other one. How had he done it? If his account was to be believed, Maesrhon had gone into the forest, passed through the Lissa'pathor, and returned to camp from an easterly direction. As proof he had handed over leaves from the *salleth* tree, an affidavit from Haartell, and signed statements from half a dozen village elders.

Atranaar marshalled the evidence for and against. The *salleth* tree was only found in the forest, and the leaves had been still comparatively fresh; they must have been recently picked. But they might have been passed on to Maesrhon by arrangement, and Haartell was an employee of his father, after all. The mine seal on the document was genuine enough, but could it have been prepared in advance? Maybe... but surely it would have been impossible to organise all this from within base camp. And it must be conceded that none of the scouts had picked up so much as a trace of his movements, nor, apparently, had he been recorded using the bridge even though he must have crossed the river twice. Then there was the way he had materialised out of nowhere at the very door of Atranaar's own quarters, having got past all the perimeter sentries. So if all was genuine, it seemed that Maesrhon had gone of his own will into the forest, travelled much further than any of his fellows while deliberately showing himself from time to time to gather his witnesses, evaded all attempts to apprehend him, and penetrated what was supposed to be an impassable guard. Oh, and got across the river twice by some unknown means. Abruptly, Atranaar bent to his task again, writing swiftly and then signing off his report with an almost angry flourish. Maesrhon was not given to boasting or flamboyance. If he had been going to cheat, he was far too clever to have attempted it on such a scale: his story must be true. Atranaar felt his skin creep as the hair rose slightly on his head. If he was inclined to superstition, he might almost be wondering now whether there was something *as-geg'rastig* about Maesrhon.

But Atranaar was not a man given to superstition, or indeed belief in anything at all. He saw midwinter as a time for practising manoeuvres in harsh conditions rather than for feasting or observation of rites, which was why he always scheduled a period of relaxation for his men now, at the end of autumn. For his new recruits, it was their first break since beginning training, but it could hardly be described as leave, since everyone remained in camp. This was all one to most of the regulars, the majority of whom had left their past behind, like Atranaar himself. Some of them might well have had children scattered about Caradward, but they were not family men. And it was a theory of Atranaar's that he could learn as much from observing his troops at leisure as under orders; he liked to note what they did, how they interacted with each other, officers and rankers, rookies and veterans. So here they were, based for the moment in the Lowanmorad, the central uplands of Caradward, where the morning air retained a touch of bracing sharpness and the hunting was still good. A supply train had brought in plenty of fresh and preserved meat, casks of ale, and new bread; tomorrow they would have a hog roast, and after that might ride out onto the moors and up into the hills. The drovers with the wagons had brought word that a hunting party from Rigg'ymvala was nearby and apparently heading in their direction. Parade-ground peacocks, thought Atranaar, headquarters officers who would last no more than half a week in the field: it would be amusing to see how they matched up to his men if it should happen that their paths did indeed cross.

Calling in a favour

A few miles away in a different valley, Ghentar exchanged goodnights with his friends and headed towards his sleeping-quarters. He could scarcely remember when he had last felt so happy, although in truth his main emotion was relief. At last, at long, long last, his luck seemed to have changed. It just goes to show you, he thought; it's right what people say, fortune favours the brave. His winnings that evening would easily cover what he owed Valahald, and then he'd be clear. Well, clear of everything except whatever Valahald was going to want for keeping his mouth shut: he'd never mentioned that again. Before Ghentar could get started on worrying about this, he tripped heavily over a tussock hidden in the darkness and almost fell. The stumbling and cursing attracted the attention of four or five men sitting drinking around a small fire of their own, away to his left.

'Hey, Ghentar! It's too early to turn in, come over here and join us.' He hesitated, and they began to egg him on. 'Don't say you're too mean to risk your ill-gotten gains! If lady luck is with you tonight, you could double your winnings before morning, and we've plenty of drink here still.'

'You're on.' He sat down with them, grinning. Quit while you're ahead? Not likely! He was on a winning streak tonight, how could he lose?

It was the following evening after they had all returned from the day's sport when Valahald came calling. A servant admitted him to the living area of Ghentar's tent and then withdrew. Valahald's colourless eyes roved briefly around the rich interior of the pavilion, hung with expensive embroideries and furs and lit by three silver lamps, and came to rest on Ghentar who was already drinking heavily. Without looking at his visitor, Ghentar gestured loosely to indicate that he should serve himself.

'Thank you, I won't, just for the present,' said Valahald, sitting on a soft couch covered in fine-grained leatherwork. 'An excellent day, today. Most enjoyable. Anyway, I thought I would just drop in while supper is preparing, to say I'd like my loan repaid now, please.'

Ghentar bit his lip as foreboding gripped him. 'Look, just give me until we get back to Caradriggan, can you?'

'No, I'm afraid I can't, I've a commitment of my own to honour. There's surely no problem, after the amount you won last night.'

'Well, I …' Ghentar cleared his throat, and tried again. 'Actually, there is a problem. I, I was invited to join another game later on, and things didn't go so well … Luck seemed to run out on me …'

He tailed off and Valahald let quite a silence develop before he spoke again. 'How much did you lose?'

With an oath, Ghentar jumped to his feet and paced up and down a couple of times, coming to rest with his forehead resting on one of the carved tent-poles; his eventual reply was muffled and reluctant.

'I see.' Valahald moved to a more comfortable position on the couch. 'So let me just be clear about all this. Not only can you not repay me, you're in debt to others as well, since last night. Plus, of course, you owe me on other counts too.'

'What do you mean?'

'Surely you remember that story about yourself and Maesrhon that you peddled to your father, the one you want me to back you up on? And in Rigg'ymvala, they think you settled your debts yourself. Didn't you tell them you'd sent for an advance from Vorynaas? Just imagine how you're going to look, if they find out you had to borrow from me; and how your father is going to react if he finds out you've lied to him, you've lied to fellow-officers, you owe money right left and centre, and on top of all that, you couldn't even beat Maesrhon with a sword of sky-steel when all he had was a sparring-stave. If I was to let any of that slip out, then you'd really know all about having problems.' Valahald laughed briefly. 'So you need me to keep my mouth shut, don't you?'

'Kick a man when he's down, eh? Some friend you are,' said Ghentar bitterly, his voice rising.

'Remember we're talking in a tent. I'd keep it quiet if I were you, you don't want to be overheard. Well, have you got any suggestions to make?'

Ghentar sagged in his chair. 'Look, I've told you I don't have the money. If you could just give me time...'

'I've already explained that I can't wait. But I'll tell you what. Here's an idea for you to think over. I'll waive the debt, in fact I'll lend you some more to cover what you lost last night, and I'll say nothing about the other things – but you'll need to do something for me.'

He waited, watching, and slowly Ghentar raised his head. 'What do you want me to do?'

Valahald spoke very quietly. 'Get rid of Maesrhon, and we'll forget all the rest.'

Disappointment registered on Ghentar's face. 'Oh, my father will pack him off to some pen-pusher's desk in the Lissa'pathor. I thought you were going to come up with some serious idea.'

'I am serious. Absolutely serious.'

'Oh, for...' Ghentar gave a short, almost exasperated laugh. 'Believe me I don't think there's been a day of my life when I wouldn't cheerfully have got rid of the little...' Suddenly he caught sight of the expression on Valahald's face, and the laughter left his own; his eyes widened. 'Just a minute. Get rid of Maesrhon... you don't mean... when you say get rid of him, do you mean *permanently* get rid of him?'

'That's exactly what I mean,' said Valahald pleasantly. 'Remove, take out of the equation, eliminate, get rid of, you can use whatever term you prefer. It all comes down to the same thing: kill him.'

'But...' Stunned, Ghentar sat staring at Valahald. 'What will people say? And then there's my father... and what about you? Why do you want him dead?'

'Listen. He's already got his eye on you: remember what he said after you had that go at him in Salfgard? "You made a *mistake*." That's a threat; as long as he's alive, he'll be a threat to you. Didn't you tell

Thaltor you were sick of hearing people talk about him? Men will gather to him, you'll never be able to rest. As for your father: he hates him, he wants him got rid of. And he wants it doing soon, away from Caradriggan. What better opportunity? Don't you know Maesrhon's unit is in camp not five miles from here?'

Ghentar stood up again and wandered distractedly about; then he realised Valahald had left a question unanswered. 'Where do you come in to all this?'

'Well, I'm the one who was commissioned by Vorynaas to get the job done. I told you, your father wants him dead. But the time, the place and the method were left to my discretion; and although obviously I could get rid of Maesrhon myself, somehow I find it suits me better to have you do it.'

Footsteps and laughter came from outside the tent walls and Valahald stepped across and lifted the flap, looking out. 'Supper's almost ready, I see. So there it is: you take this on for me, and we'll say no more about all the rest of it. If you don't feel you can do it, that's fine; but of course then you'll have to face up to what I could tell everyone, including your father. And I would, naturally.' He smiled. 'Think it over, during supper.'

As the servants busied themselves clearing up after the meal, Valahald headed for his own sleeping-tent. He had kept on eye on Ghentar in the meantime and had noted how he sat silent, scarcely touching his food, pale and preoccupied. Footsteps sounded behind him now, and a voice calling his name quietly. He turned and sure enough, there was Ghentar. They went into Valahald's quarters together and the younger man spoke abruptly, without preamble.

'All right, I'll do it. But you'll have to give me a day or two to work out how I'm going to manage it.'

Valahald raised those curiously colourless eyebrows of his and placed a hand on Ghentar's shoulder. 'Don't worry, I'll tell you exactly what you have to do. Your father's instructions are that it's to seem like an accident, and I have it all worked out.'

246

Ghentar pushed him away and left without answering. Well satisfied with his evening, Valahald retired to rest, a smile spreading across his face as he contemplated the future. Ghentar might set great store by his position as heir to the wealth and might of Vorynaas, but as usual he had not stopped to think beyond his immediate predicament. The real power would lie in Valahald's hands, with the man whose secret knowledge meant that from now on his hold over Ghentar would be unbreakable.

CHAPTER 28

War games

Heranar was feeling mildly put out. He had been really enjoying himself for the past week, riding out in the early morning, returning at evening more than ready for feasting on the spoils of the chase, laughing and drinking with his friends. There were about twenty of them in the party, not counting the grooms, cooks and other servants; Valahald had taken leave from his post at Seth y'n Carad at the same time as he and his fellows from the barbican garrison, and then along had come Ghentar with half a dozen junior officers from Rigg'ymvala. But a couple of days ago their progress through the Lowanmorad had taken them close to where a unit of auxiliaries was in rest camp. He had been surprised by several things: the quantity and quality of their provisions; the readiness of these hard-bitten irregular troops to accept any challenge put to them; and the presence of Maesrhon among them. Glancing around as they all sat at supper together, he realised that he would be glad when his own party moved on. There was an air of effortless superiority about these temporary comrades, and especially about their commanding officer Atranaar, that made him feel uncomfortable. He found casual conversation with them difficult and was annoyed that Ghentar apparently had no time for him. They had been friends from boyhood, but now it seemed that Ghentar preferred Valahald. For the past few days they had been inseparable: look at them now, sitting there slightly apart from the rest of the crowd, heads together. He wondered what they were talking about, although now he came to notice it, it was a rather one-sided conversation. His elder brother was speaking urgently into Ghentar's ear while he ate and drank, but Ghentar, only picking at his food, merely nodded from time to time with downcast eyes.

Helping himself to more meat, Heranar walked over to where Maesrhon was sitting and settled beside him. He gestured at his loaded platter appreciatively. 'You fellows know how to look after yourselves. Do you often come here for the hunting?'

'I don't know, you'd need to ask one of the regulars. This is only our first leave.'

Maesrhon turned to draw Sigitsinen into the conversation, noticing that Heranar had ignored him. He introduced his friend, but Heranar merely nodded in acknowledgement without offering to shake hands.

'None of us went after waterfowl today,' he said now, stripping the remaining flesh from a duck leg with his teeth, 'so this must be part of Ghentar's bag.'

'No, you've got Sigitsinen to thank for that.' Maesrhon saw how Heranar, with his gingery colouring, began to blush. 'There's a little upland lake a mile or so to the north of here. He's an expert with the throwing-stick, it's not unusual for him to get several birds with one cast.'

Heranar, red to the roots of his hair, stood on his dignity. 'That doesn't sound very sporting to me.'

'We don't do it for sport,' said Sigitsinen, 'we do it for the pot. And when your efforts are directed at feeding yourself, it makes sense to get the best return for the least effort.'

This was exactly the kind of thing that had already irritated Heranar. He tried to be polite, but the words came out with a sardonic edge to them. 'The old self-sufficiency, eh? Yes, we've all heard the stories about how you lads can stomach extraordinary things when you have to live off the land. So, do you think you'll enlist permanently then, Maesrhon, when your year's up?'

'I doubt it; but anyway,' Maesrhon frowned, looking down at the ground, thinking of his earlier conversation with Atranaar, 'anyway, there's no point in even considering it unless I can get through the rest of my year successfully. Sigitsinen here is set on it, and I'd say he has a good chance.'

Looking up again, he caught Valahald and Ghentar watching him from the other side of the fire; Ghentar quickly turned away and Maesrhon felt an unaccountable chill run over him in spite of the warmth from the embers. He fell silent, barely heeding as Heranar and Sigitsinen indulged in some verbal baiting about the outcome of the various contests scheduled for the morrow. It had been decided earlier that instead of going hunting, the two camps would match up in games and sports in what was intended as friendly rivalry.

Early the following afternoon, Maesrhon was leaning on his sparring-stave, looking on as an archery target was set up. The morning had passed pleasantly enough, although like Atranaar he had noted what bad losers the visitors tended to be. However, in some matches they had had the victory: although he himself had won his sword bout, the overall contest had been won by a young officer from Heranwark where they set more store by swordsmanship than was usual among the auxiliaries, who mostly fought with other weapons and used their own swords with ruthless efficiency rather than flair. The maimed slave he had seen in the Lissa'pathor came back into his mind: it was surely a sword-cut that had injured his face. He switched his weight to his other foot, noticing Heranar among the crowd. He had behaved so petulantly when beaten by Sigitsinen, who had challenged all comers to wrestle him in the Outland style, that bad feeling had threatened the whole gathering. Maesrhon had already been trounced by his friend, who had been practising this style since childhood, but had deliberately allowed Heranar the victory when they squared off for third place so as to restore the general good humour of the day.

The archery contest was well under way now. Maesrhon was not taking part in this, and his gaze fell on his commanding officer. Several times during the morning he had seen that Atranaar was watching him, but now it seemed he had his eye on Valahald and Ghentar. Maesrhon wondered whether Ghentar was unwell, or, more likely, feeling the effects of excess food and drink. He seemed unusually pale and had not so far participated at all in the activities. Valahald had done a certain amount of strutting, but apart from riding in a couple of tests of horsemanship had also spent most of the time spectating – and muttering into Ghentar's ear, which was what he was doing now. Maesrhon's mind drifted back again to the conversation he had had with Atranaar. The latter had been probing for more information about his time on exercise, and in the course of their exchange Maesrhon had mentioned the disfigured slave with the Gwentaran tattoo. Atranaar had recovered himself very quickly, but his immediate reaction, before retreating behind his most impenetrable veil of inscrutability, had made Maesrhon strongly suspect that he knew something about the man; and now his mind was considering several most unwelcome and unsettling theories. A round of applause jerked his attention back to the present: a young man whose name he had missed, on leave from the barbican garrison, had won the shooting contest. Suddenly he heard his name being called. Valahald was strolling over, smiling broadly.

'I must be mad to do this, but maybe this will be the one time I'll win, and that'll be something to tell the grandchildren, eh?' said Valahald, pointing at the stave on which Maesrhon was leaning. 'Somebody lend me a stave, I challenge our winner here!'

It had been more or less inevitable that Maesrhon would emerge as the victor with the sparring-stave, but some of his colleagues in the auxiliaries had not heard of his prowess and had put themselves up during the morning, all to no avail. Now they laughed and clapped, anticipating the drubbing he would surely mete out to this popinjay from Caradriggan: Valahald had not endeared himself to many of them. Even Maesrhon was smiling with incredulity, wondering what on earth had come over Valahald. Turning away to strip for action, as men thrust forward to offer Valahald his choice of stave, Maesrhon again noticed Atranaar staring hard at Ghentar. His brother appeared oblivious of the general fun, and was pouring himself another drink with hands that were visibly shaking. Maesrhon felt his hair lift slightly, as if a cat's paw of icy wind had run over his skin; a faint presage of something very wrong suddenly came to him. But men were clamouring for them to begin, and a ring of grinning spectators formed around himself and Valahald; those nearest sitting on the ground, others further back standing so as to see over their heads. The three arbiters took up stations, one counting aloud, one marking the time by thumping the packed earth with his own stave, the third alert for foul moves.

Predictably, it was over very quickly. Valahald's stave was wrenched from his hand and he stood there with arms outstretched, smiling, as the rest of them milled about laughing and calling in their wagers.

'Ah well, it was worth a try. Here's Ghentar, now. Hey, keep it down a bit! Ghentar's got something to say.'

Valahald was shouting, trying to make himself heard above the noise, but as everyone turned in curiosity Atranaar noticed that he had to surreptitiously push Ghentar to get him to come forward into the midst of the throng.

'Well speak up, boy. You're coming between me and the ale barrel,' urged a leathery patrol-leader to the accompaniment of laughter from his men. Colour stood out on Ghentar's cheeks and then ebbed away. He licked white lips.

'Maesrhon. Well done. I, I'd like to offer you a challenge myself, now.'

That chilly breath of warning passed over Maesrhon again as he looked at his brother. 'No, let's leave it,' he said. 'Match up with someone else if you want a bout.'

This got a mixed response, in which jeering from some of Ghentar's cronies could be heard. Maesrhon glanced round at them and the barracking died down; he turned again to Ghentar, who had Valahald at his shoulder. Ghentar took a deep breath.

'I want to make things right between us. I've felt bad ever since that time in Salfgard, so here's what I suggest. I'll take the stave, today, and you can have my sword.'

In spite of himself, Maesrhon's eyes dropped to the sword at Ghentar's side. He had never in his life had the opportunity to handle such a weapon. Everyone seemed to be shouting in approval, jostling forward. Valahald was pushing his borrowed stave into Ghentar's hands, again speaking privately to him; then he stepped across to Maesrhon.

'Here, I'll look after that for you.'

He took Maesrhon's own stave and sat down in the front row. Slowly Ghentar drew his sword and turned it around, offering the hilt to his brother; and slowly Maesrhon took it, noticing that Ghentar did not meet his eyes. Again an icy feather seemed to brush his neck. Slowly the ground was paced out, slowly they took their stance facing each other. Everything seemed to be happening slowly, so slowly. Maesrhon was able to consider his tactics: he would have to simply play out the allotted time, parrying his brother's strokes. Ghentar had never been much good with the stave, and nowadays must be completely out of practice: he would never be able to disarm a swordsman. With the tail of his eye, Maesrhon caught a glimpse of three faces. Sigitsinen, Heranar and Valahald, all sitting next to each other. From nowhere the thought came to him that only the first two were innocent of complicity in some double-dealing. Sigitsinen simply wanted him to win; and Heranar, perhaps genuinely uneasy about his part in the fight at Salfgard, now saw the slate being wiped clean: but Valahald wore a calculating, watchful look, like a cat crouched beside a mousehole.

The first round ended and the second began. The onlookers began to shout encouragement, many voices calling out Maesrhon's name. The colour rose in Ghentar's face at this and Maesrhon was vividly reminded of their dawn encounter on the misty islet. Today he was holding the very sword with which his face had been marked, and again the ruined face of the mine slave passed before his mind's eye. Could what he suspected be possible, could a force from Caradward have infiltrated Gwent y'm Aryframan? This thought seemed to lend him impetus and he momentarily abandoned his defensive tactics, pressing forward. Men yelled, engrossed in the scene before them; no-one noticed how Valahald shifted in his seat as if to make himself more comfortable, nor that when he settled again, the stave which rested across his lap into the crook of his arm was now sticking out into the fighting area. For the first time, his voice was heard above the clamour, urging Ghentar on. Ghentar's eyes flicked quickly across and back; Maesrhon saw him swallow. Had they exchanged some signal? Ghentar was wading in now; Maesrhon began to give ground. He realised he was still thinking about the mine slave, remembering the stories he had heard in Framstock about people disappearing, and was angry with himself for not concentrating. With a frown of renewed determination, he looked into his brother's face and for the first time their eyes met. A strange sound, a cry almost of anguish broke from Ghentar: that golden gaze was unbearable. He lunged forward, Maesrhon took another step back and something caught at his heel. He stumbled, the stroke meant to parry missed its mark, the sword flew from his hand. In a last, lightning-swift instant of time before the darkness, his senses registered a storm of images and impressions: he felt his ankle give as the outstretched stave tripped him from behind, saw the flash of the falling swordblade, the sudden horror on Sigitsinen's face, the secret satisfaction in Valahald's eyes; heard an intake of breath, a ragged shout rising, a whistle of air as the stave hurtled down; then there was a vortex filled with searing white light, and a black tide of oblivion. A stupefied silence was broken by Heranar, who threw up helplessly at the vile sound of an iron-hard wooden stave smashing into bone with sickening force, by Valahald's smooth protestations of dismay, by Ghentar's convulsive shivering as he stood trembling, white-faced once more. But Maesrhon heard nothing, saw nothing, felt nothing: he had dropped like a stone and lay sprawled where he fell at their feet on the trampled ground, his mouth slightly open, his hands flung wide, his limbs tumbled in the dust that dulled his dark hair and settled on the huge, bloody wound in his head.

Between life and death

Arval climbed the tower stairs heavily, his head bowed. As he entered his darkened study, he caught himself sighing and smiled wryly. This is no time to give up, he told himself. Your greatest test is near, you will need all your resilience to face it; but here you are, you old fool, wasting your strength, debating within yourself whether the weight of your many years, or the fear that their end is approaching, is the greater burden to bear. He crossed to the open window and sat down, sighing again in spite of himself. A robin was singing in the tree beside the light. Arval listened to the sweet, wistful notes as they drifted across to him in the dark. Strange how easy it was to persuade oneself that it was always the same robin, even though one knew quite well that the little birds lived barely a season or two. He remembered so clearly hearing that plaintive whistling many times before, years back, even before Arymaldur had come to him; and then again when Numirantoro... and now Maesrhon... With that, Arval stood up abruptly and leaned his forehead against the window-frame. Ah, Maesrhon, *Is-torar*, little son! How eagerly you asked if I was your father; and believe me, I thought of you as a son, I tried to take a father's place. But though I promised your mother I would guard and guide you, yet I failed to keep you from harm. A tear spread out into the deep wrinkles around Arval's eyes, and he hastily brushed it away as a scratch came at the door. Meremvor stood there.

'Come in, young man. Sit there, I will light the lamp.'

Arval closed the shutters and sat opposite his young friend; the flame burned up and then steadied, casting a soft glow that left the corners of the room in shadow. Gold lettering on the spines of some of Arval's myriad books glinted here and there.

'Now, I believe you will be setting out for the south tomorrow, and I would be grateful if you would take word to Heretellar for me.'

'Of course, Lord Arval. Do you have it ready, or should I write it down now?'

'There's no need, the message is very simple. I want Heretellar to come to the city before midwinter, and to stay for the days of the feast. I hope I've not left it too late for him to arrange this?'

'No; well, not with regard to the journey – but he won't be expecting this, so...'

'Listen, Meremvor.' Arval interrupted, leaning forward so that the lamplight threw his thin face into sharp relief. 'Tell him, I want him to lead the rites for me, here in Tellgard. This year, of all years, a voice from a new generation must be heard. I want it to be Heretellar's voice that renews the pledge, whether I am able to be present myself or not.'

Meremvor's eyes searched Arval's face anxiously. 'So, you think you may still be keeping watch? Could there still be some hope, even then?'

'There is always hope, if men know where to find it.' Arval clenched his fist on his knee. 'We must cling to that! But in any case, even if, if it should happen that,' he paused briefly, and then, mastering himself, continued, 'whether I am in the hall or not, I want Heretellar to recite the *Temennis*.' He stood up. 'I cannot stay longer, I must go back down now. You will ask Heretellar, then; do you think he will do this for me?'

'Lord Arval, I promise you on his behalf, we will be there. And I can assure you also that our thoughts are always with you both.'

'I know, I feel it. Good man! Safe journey now, and my greetings to Heretellar.'

Arval stood, ushering Meremvor out, and then dimming the lamp he left the room and hurried down the stairs himself. Walking swiftly through Tellgard, he lifted the worn latch of a plain wooden door and passed silently through a narrow archway.

As the weeks went by and the time of the feast approached, the whispers began to spread. The murmurs seemed to start among the Outland community, but soon the tale passed far beyond the streets and taverns where *sigitsaran* were accustomed to meet. Men said that what befell Maesrhon was no accident, that Ghentar had acted knowingly with murderous intent. Some claimed that he had made an earlier attempt on his brother's life while they were living abroad during their younger years; but whatever the truth of this, what was plain to all was that Ghentar was still in favour, that he had not been called to account for himself in any way. He and Vorynaas were seen together on the stand at the parade-ground, on the dais in the public hall in Seth y'n Carad, riding out on exercise, walking the city's walls: always side by side, laughing and talking together, close companions. And though Maesrhon lay insensible and it seemed impossible that he could ever wake again, he was not actually dead; yet while his fate still hung in the balance, neither Vorynaas nor Ghentar once came near him in Tellgard where it was said that Arval was calling upon all his skill in a sleepless battle to sustain that last tiny flicker of life. The message was plain for all to read. *Vorynaas wants Maesrhon dead*, so ran the rumour; men muttered under their breath that a father could be so ruthless, and wondered how merciless Ghentar might prove to be when his time came. Then they would look sidelong at one another and fall silent, some fearing to say more, some thinking it prudent to show their loyalty to Vorynaas before the head-counting began. But others whispered of Numirantoro and reminded each other of how Arval had tended her long ago; they began gathering to Tellgard by ones and twos, and at the Midwinter Feast the ancient hall was more thronged than it had been for many years.

As for Arval, though his heart wept for Maesrhon and raged at those who had hurt him, he forced himself to be calm, to concentrate all his power on the task before him. He and his medical colleagues had worked on that battered, apparently lifeless form for hours: they had clipped out the matted hair and washed away the blood, finding

257

that unbelievably the skull seemed unbroken although the flesh was crushed and split open. They stitched the ugly wound and dressed it, applying cooling compresses and lotions to the damaged area. There was a large area of swelling above Maesrhon's right temple; the angry, purple bruising had spread down across his forehead and into his cheek and he had a black eye on that side; but both eyes were closed now, closed in an otherwise white and waxy face. There was a small wound with a trace of blood showing where he had bitten his lip as he fell. At last they were finished and Arval stood back. Thank goodness the boy's commanding officer had had the sense to act quickly, he thought. That young Outlander, Sigitsinen was it, had been sent off immediately, riding like a madman, to bring them early warning; and the patrol medic had obviously known his business. He had seen to it that Maesrhon was moved as little as possible, strapping him into thick wadding to minimise the jolting of the journey. Arval glanced around at his colleagues but they all busied themselves tidying up after their work, not meeting his gaze; he could see that not one of them thought Maesrhon would pull through. Speaking quietly, he thanked them for their efforts.

'I want you to know how much I appreciate your skill and support. Whatever happens, you may be sure I realise that you have done everything you could for him. I think it unlikely that anyone from Seth y'n Carad will enquire for him, although others may seek to know how he fares, so we will confer daily on his condition; but science can do no more for him now and I must ask you to trust me enough to leave him in my hands alone.'

They murmured their assent and approval, and Arval heard the grief and love in their voices. The boy had touched many hearts in his short life, and he himself was revered by a staff more devoted to him than he knew. They took his hands or gripped his shoulders as they went; one or two embraced him briefly.

'The Starborn keep you both, Arval.'

The heart of the mystery

So Arval the Earth-wise took Maesrhon through the secret door in Tellgard that only those who shared in the life of the As-Geg'rastigan could find or pass, and there he watched him day by day, and night by night. Time passed, and when Arval judged it was safe to remove the stitches, he saw that though Maesrhon's hair was reappearing where they had had to cut the congealed blood away, now it was no longer dark in that place, but white as a swan's feather where the blow from the stave had caused some permanent damage to its growth; and though the bruising gradually faded, and the swelling on his head diminished, yet he never woke or moved. Arval looked into Maesrhon's closed, pale face. The resemblance to his mother was not now nearly so marked; it had faded as the bloom of childhood had been gradually replaced by a man's strength. He would need all that strength from now on: strength to deal with what all would see in him, if he could live; strength to bear the knowledge he must hold in his heart, if he could wake. If he lived, if he waked! Not even in my mind must I use such words, thought Arval, settling once more to the purpose of his lonely vigil. He must live, he will wake.

After Maesrhon's birth, and while he was still a small child, Arval had spent many an anxious hour wondering how he could explain the boy's parentage to him. The bare facts of it would be difficult enough for him to endure, for Arval knew well himself that to be numbered among the *as-urad* was not an easy heritage. But how could he convey to him the mystery and meaning of what had happened? Then, wakeful one night, he remembered how in the very moment Numirantoro had slipped away from the life of the Earthborn, a part of his mind had been keen to follow, eager even in the midst of his sorrow for this new knowledge which he sensed was there for the learning. He could see himself now, the baby in his arms, but distracted by Forgard's distress, by the unrest in the streets, by the unwelcome appearance of Vorynaas. Thinking of all this, he had embarked on researches lasting many years: years in which as Maesrhon grew, he had been encouraged by the boy's own obvious intuition that some mystery surrounded his origins. And gradually, hour by hour, midnight by midnight, shelf by shelf, volume by dusty volume, page by page, he had followed where the trail of learning led until he had the answers to the questions he sought. Eventually Arval found himself faced with one final stumbling-block: the actual means of expressing to Maesrhon what he needed to know. Like Numirantoro before him, he realised that a large part of his difficulty lay in the attempt to use words, for there were no words in any human tongue known to him that could do justice to the tale he had to tell. If only they could speak with each other mind to mind, as it was said the As-Geg'rastigan were able to do.

But surely, thought Arval, if Arymaldur felt the touch of Numirantoro's thought upon his heart, and she heard his voice in her mind, she was half withdrawn from us into his world even as she walked in this: how else could she have passed through the secret door? Pondering on the mystery in solitary meditation over the years, gradually he arrived at a possible solution. In memory he saw again Numirantoro lying before him, withdrawn and remote, touched with the same unearthly beauty that lit Arymaldur. Was there some way in which Maesrhon too could be lulled to rest, some way in which both body and mind could be stilled so that only the hidden life remained awake: could they somehow then exchange thought directly, one heart to another? During the months following Maesrhon's departure for his year of military service, Arval had cast about with increasing urgency for the means to achieve his aim; but he had not foreseen the brutal circumstances in which the boy's battered and insensible body would indeed one day lie before him. Yet now as the time drew nearer to midwinter, he allowed a tiny seed of hope to flower within him. Maesrhon's physical hurts seemed to be mending, and sustained as he had been solely by the nourishment contained in the spirit of which only Arval knew the secret, maybe his inner self would lie open to receive the truth. So now on the night of the feast itself, Arval sat beside Maesrhon and summoned all his powers of mind; he drew on the deep well of his accumulated learning and lore, and called upon the As-Geg'rastigan to aid him: and then he set free his thought to dwell upon Numirantoro and Arymaldur.

He looked into the still, white face that lay before him, scarred already by wounds and faintly lined by the marks of sorrow and loss; he held the cold hands, now wasted of strength and loosed of their hard-won skills; and inexorably, but with infinite gentleness, Arval unlocked his memories and poured them into the young mind he had always loved so tenderly. Widely his thought ranged, resting softly on the child Numirantoro: the grace of her inner life, the radiance of her outward loveliness; her thirst for knowledge, her instinctive longing for the As-Geg'rastigan, her fateful wish to behold the Starborn. Sadly it settled upon Numirantoro of the silver daisies, bereft of her mother, cheated of Geraswic, torn from the suns of Salfgard, betrayed by her father, shackled to Vorynaas. With longing and regret, and a kind of humble pride, his mind gazed on Arymaldur: his austere beauty, his air of ageless integrity, his authority in advice and command and in the words of the rites; his warnings, and his promises. And now Arval approached the central mystery of the tale his heart silently told. His thought conjured into being the intolerable love that woke in Numirantoro when she knew Arymaldur for what he was; her despair, so great, so unendurable for a daughter of the Earthborn, that from her sorrow a call had arisen to reach out and touch Arymaldur himself. In his mind he re-created Numirantoro's yearning for the life of the As-Geg'rastigan, ever more intense, more unassuageable, until it seemed she walked between their world and this, hearing Arymaldur's words in her heart, heedless of what was past or to come if only she could know his majesty and might.

Arval leaned forward and laid his hands on Maesrhon's pale forehead. The deepest, most enduring human love is a weak and feeble thing compared to the fire that burns in the Starborn, little son. Be it body to body, or mind to mind, or a mingling of both, yet that

261

is but a meagre embrace when set beside the all-consuming loss of self that is the love of the As-Geg'rastigan, whose union is a radiance of light. None from among the Earthborn could abide such glory and live, yet your mother went willingly to her fate when Arymaldur laid the choice before her. Thus she was able to pass the secret door, stepping from her world into his; but though she looked into his eyes, she was helpless to endure their power. Arval drew a deep breath. If my thought is reaching you, *Is-torar*, forgive my halting words: these are mysteries I cannot ever fully explain. Together Arymaldur and I watched over Numirantoro, so that the life which had kindled within her should not be lost. She spoke but once again, to name you and leave you with her love; and I promised her, as I had also promised Arymaldur, that I would be steadfast for your sake. Who knows where Arymaldur or Numirantoro walk now, but we have you with us: Artorynas, man of the sun, born of the star.

Exhausted by the effort he had expended, Arval closed his eyes, leaning back once more. I promised to guard you, guide you and love you, he thought; but if you never wake again, I will have failed in the first of these duties. Moments passed. They would have doused the lamps in Tellgard's ancient hall by now; it must be about the time for the light to flower anew. Suddenly he felt again that once-familiar stir of life in the air, a tingle of energy that hovered at the edge of hearing. His eyes flew open, and there at last was Maesrhon watching him with his amber, sun-flecked gaze. A silence beyond words enveloped them, vast and profound: it stretched away to an unfathomed distance of time and space, immeasurable yet undaunting, bringing a peace past reckoning, unknowable, infinite, deep and comforting. Eventually Maesrhon spoke; and now it seemed to Arval that not only did he see Arymaldur again, but faintly once more he heard him also.

'So the heart of the mystery is revealed at last.'

'I am sorry if the wait seemed long. If I have ever appeared harsh in refusing to speak, I ask you to pardon me now for it, and for my failure to protect you from harm.'

'Arval.' Maesrhon smiled a little, now bringing Numirantoro to life in his face. 'There is nothing to forgive. You promised me you would tell me the truth when the time came: the moment arrived, and you have spoken. As for the injury I have suffered at my brother's hands, you need trouble yourself no more. I have survived the hurt, and it has been the means for you to bring me to an understanding of what I need to know. Many things are plain to me now. I see why Vorynaas has always hated me, why he can scarcely tolerate my presence.' Then glancing about him, and looking up towards the stars that burned blue above, Maesrhon laughed softly. 'I recognise this place; I know what happened here. But shall I tell you what it brings to my mind? On the night before Heretellar left Ardeth's house, we young folk argued amongst ourselves about the Starborn, until Heretellar and Ghentar quarrelled over the fate of Arymaldur. I realise now why this disturbed me so much; but then, all I knew was that I was unable to rest. I walked down to the bridge in Framstock and wrestled with thoughts that were too confused to set in order. The darkness rang with frost and stars, brilliant jewels that sparked and flashed both overhead and underfoot, and I was stung with pain to think that you waited for me here in Caradriggan's gloom, denied the beauty that the night above me wore. I am glad to know you had the solace of this secret court. Numirantoro and Arymaldur walk in my mind like figures from an old tale, ardent and bright yet remote beyond my reach: but you have been my refuge all my life. Arval, to me you have been more than guard and defender, more than teacher and guide. You have stood to me for friend, brother and sister, parents and family. No matter what I have learnt from you here today, you will keep the father's place in my heart which has always been yours.'

With bowed head, Arval bit his lip; he could not have spoken.

'I think this is the night of the Midwinter Feast?' Maesrhon stood up slowly, and Arval hastened to help him, knowing how weak he would be until his strength was rebuilt.

'Yes, I asked Heretellar to take my place at the rites. All will be over by now.'

'Well then, let us go in and rekindle the light ourselves. Arval and Artorynas, we will renew the pledge together, we two alone.'

Valahald's second chance

Days passed, and word was quick to spread around the city that Maesrhon lived and was likely to recover. Arval kept him close in Tellgard, to have an eye on him while he regained his health, where his friends and other folk who saw him began to call him *Alfossig,* for the white lock in his hair; only between themselves did Arval and he use his true name. Ghentar rode off back to Heranwark after the holiday feasting was over, relieved to get away from Caradriggan and glad to leave Valahald behind, but tormented by the complications of the position he found himself in. He had been left with no option but to maintain to his father that it had been his own wish to despatch Maesrhon himself: he could hardly confess that Valahald had forced him into it, for this would have meant explaining how Valahald came to have such a hold over him. And Valahald, knowing this perfectly well, had been ready with a smooth account of events, telling Vorynaas that he felt he must defer to Ghentar in consideration of his birth and status.

'I hoped to fulfil all your instructions in such a way, my lord,' he said, when Vorynaas tackled him as to why he had not proceeded directly and removed Maesrhon himself. 'Circumstances brought us together far from the city, with the chance to make events seem accidental. And I may say I think I was successful in this; I am sure, from the reactions I observed in those who were present, that none of them could have known that any hurt to Maesrhon was intended or planned. Indeed Ghentar's own dismay seemed absolutely genuine: if I had not heard him earlier, assuring me privately of his implacable desire to get rid of his brother, I would have been in some doubt as to his stomach for the task. Although, once I had shown him how his aim could be achieved, what should have been the decisive blow was convincing enough; it amazes me that anyone could have survived it. It is still possible, after all, that Maesrhon may fail to recover, or be left permanently disabled in some way.'

'Maybe.'

Vorynaas studied Valahald in silence for a moment or two. His instinct told him that there was more to all this than met the eye, but he could not detect where the falsehood lay. He would bide his time and meanwhile it was true that there was still a chance that Maesrhon might die in the end. So in public he took care that both Valahald and Ghentar were seen to have his favour, and every so often he would turn the conversation without warning to see what reaction he got; but both of them stuck to their stories although he noticed that they avoided each other's company. And then, immediately after the feast-days of carousal in Seth y'n Carad, his hopes had been dashed by the unwelcome news that Maesrhon had regained consciousness. Once Ghentar had left for Heranwark, Vorynaas sent for Valahald once more.

'It seems that all is to do again, then.'

'It would appear so indeed, sir.'

Vorynaas narrowed his eyes. 'You seem to have a somewhat flippant attitude to all this. I entrusted you with an extremely delicate mission, for three reasons. One, from my own observation I saw that you were a young man with ambitions to rise in my favour. Two, you were recommended to me by a person whose judgement I value. Three, I also noticed that you have a very high opinion of yourself with the composure both to disguise this self-satisfaction when you think it prudent, and to back your confidence when you think it advantageous. You need to realise something: I will only tolerate this third characteristic so far and no further, and the critical point is success. I have had a lifetime's experience of reading men's minds and motives, and I know that there is something about this business that you are concealing from me, so don't waste your breath denying it. For the moment, we'll look at it this way: you have tried to hoodwink me, and have been partially successful, so that's one to you. But I know that you have tried, so that's one to me, too, and a rather more important point to score when you consider how many other aces I already hold. It's my opinion that you've botched the job I gave you to do by over-complicating it for some obscure reason of your own. Although I won't forget it, I will overlook it this one time only, provided you are successful at your second attempt. And remember this. If you still want my favour, you should know that I don't give third chances.'

More than a little shaken inwardly by this, Valahald inclined his head with the best imitation of equanimity he could muster. 'My lord, I do not presume to answer except to assure you of my complete attention to your words and commands.'

'You've got some nerve,' said Vorynaas with a snort of laughter. 'Well now, you cheeky young pup. The last thing I want is that cuckoo in my nest being hailed all round Caradriggan as a man with a charmed life. "Maesrhon, the man they couldn't kill", I can hear it now being whispered in drinking dens and hovels where peasants and Outlanders lurk. So get that devious mind of yours working, and tell me what you think our next step should be.'

'Well sir, Maesrhon was only part of the way through his year of service when he sustained his unfortunate injury. We have still three months before he will be eighteen, and his own man, and I will be much surprised if he is not fully recovered by then given that apparently he is personally tended by Arval. I would suggest that as soon as ever he is sufficiently fit for it, you send him straight back to the military to finish his due time.' Valahald's confidence began to rise again as he saw that Vorynaas was listening to him closely; he allowed the suggestion of a smile to touch his face. 'It seems he is well-named, in view of the way misfortune does appear to dog his steps. And of course, by its very nature, service in the auxiliaries, particularly under Atranaar's command, does lend itself to the possibility of unlucky accidents occurring.'

East, or north?

In Tellgard, Maesrhon was oblivious of all this but would not have cared, now, had he known. Now he was not only Maesrhon, hated changeling son of Vorynaas; *Is-torar*, devoted pupil of Arval the Earth-wise; Alfossig, who had been pulled back from the brink of death: he was Artorynas, born to Numirantoro and Arymaldur, Artorynas of the As-Urad. *Maesell y'm As-Urad.* As he followed Arval's every instruction in order to recover his physical health and strength, in his heart he could not help but ponder the words of the old tale. Was he too fated to know the sorrow of his kind, one day? This was but one of a host of questions which flooded his mind as he and Arval talked together daily. With no secrets between them any more, the young man's keen intellect had no reins to restrain it and roved ever more widely, soaking up everything Arval could impart. Often his thought was so swift it would race ahead, opening up new areas for debate, new ideas for consideration, new landscapes of the mind where even Arval himself had never trod. The old man would never have been happier, had it not been for his foreboding of grief and darkness ahead, of danger and parting drawing ever nearer.

There came an afternoon when the two of them were deep in conversation where they had so often talked before, on the old wooden bench seat outside the tower door in the corner of the exercise court in Tellgard. It was very quiet, for the day was chilly and most of the windows were closed; a faint murmur came from the street outside, occasional sounds from the nearer workshops, and sometimes the opening or shutting of a door and a snatch of voices; but mostly there was nothing to hear except their own words and a fluttering of wings as the doves of the court rose and settled again.

'Are you quite sure, Arval, that Arymaldur did not mean he would take my mother with him when he left us?' said Maesrhon.

'Indeed yes; in fact I asked him that very question myself,' replied Arval, 'and one has also to remember your mother's own words to me. The arrow was almost the last thing she ever spoke of.'

'So, if Arymaldur took the arrow, but I was left here among the Ur-Geg'rastigan, then it must be for me to seek the arrow, if his words of hope returning are to be fulfilled. And my mother too said I must follow the arrow's path, if light is to shine again. It seems therefore that the quest is to find the arrow; but if the arrow is with Arymaldur, how can one succeed? What was it Ancrascaro said: one cannot simply set out on such an errand, as a man might ride to seek an unclaimed valley for a new land-take. Do you not know whence Arymaldur came to us?'

'No. To have a lord of the Starborn among us was a thing so great and solemn: one day maybe you will feel the same awe, and perhaps then you will be able to understand how it was that I failed to form the questions I should have asked.' Arval sighed heavily. 'Yes, I should have asked, and not given in to weakness; although who knows whether Arymaldur would have answered me. Perhaps it is for us to seek this knowledge ourselves. I remember that he said he came to Caradward to try the truth of whether the As-Geg'rastigan might return to love the earth anew, as they had begun to hope. Ah, Artorynas, *Is-torar*, what shame this city should feel!' Mastering himself, after a pause Arval continued more quietly. 'It seemed to me from his words that others of the Starborn might have moved among the men of other lands, but I have heard no rumour of this from elsewhere.'

The afternoon was drawing to a close, and as the gloom thickened, a boy emerged from a door at the far end of the courtyard and began to light the remaining lamps. Golden circles twirled and tilted across the ground as the lantern beside the tree swung to and fro, gradually rocking back to stability; and then from the bare branches next to it, the first sweet, plaintive notes of the robin rang out in the twilight.

Maesrhon looked up, his face alert to the sound, brightening from its preoccupied expression to a smile of pleasure.

'There's the robin. I love the way he whistles and warbles right on into the dark, even in the winter, even on the coldest days when no other birds are stirring. Brave little fellow! You know, Arval, I often think, if the world were to end, if men were no more, still the robin's voice would ring out unheeding.' Arval suppressed a shiver and Maesrhon went on. 'I wonder if Ardeth still has the little wooden carving I gave him. But what I was going to say was, during all my years in Gwent y'm Aryframan, though they are remembered with honour there, I heard no word of the Starborn returning; and since then I have been among the *sigitsaran*, many of whom are my friends, but no hint that the Starborn walk in the Outlands has ever reached me. That leaves us with the east and the north to consider, and both are wide and pathless.'

As he said this, his heart leapt suddenly at the thought of the north, but Arval shivered again and Maesrhon turned with quick concern. 'Arval, it's too cold for you out here. Let's go inside now.'

'No, no,' said Arval, reaching for his cloak and wrapping it around himself. 'We'll stay just a little longer and enjoy the lamplight and the robin. But you are right that we must urgently decide whether to look north or east.'

'Is it such a pressing question?' asked Maesrhon. 'Surely we need more time: time for you to seek the knowledge that will let us make the right decision, and time for me to prepare myself to carry it out. You know I have sent word to Atranaar that I must go back to my unit, as soon as I am fit for it, so that I can complete my training.'

It seemed to him that he had foreseen, all his life, that one day he would have to set out on some weighty enterprise; but though he knew now what this would be, he realised that he was not yet ready for it. With the mystery of his parentage revealed to him at last, he felt an inner serenity, a newly-discovered certainty that he could achieve the quest; yet in spite of this, he had barely escaped death and had not yet regained his full strength. He knew he had much yet to do to build the endurance he would need.

'We cannot delay too long, little son. I feel that time runs on to the end of days coming.'

A door opened half-way down the workshop wing, and a crowd of youngsters spilled out, laughing and chattering, illuminated by the beam of light that fell from the doorway across the courtyard.

'And as for going back to the auxiliaries…' Arval broke off as a movement caught his eye.

Through the colonnade from the street came a young man in the uniform worn by the garrison at Seth y'n Carad; he was fully-armed and came striding across the courtyard towards them, clanking at every step. The youngsters all stopped talking to stare at him. The newcomer had now arrived in front of them and announced baldly that he brought orders from Vorynaas. No doubt he was doing his best to appear impressive and intimidating, but he was undermining any hope of creating this impression by allowing his eyes to flick anxiously from Arval to Maesrhon and back. He looked about nineteen or twenty, and though tall was rather lanky and underweight; his uniform hung on him and his throat wobbled visibly in a nervous swallow.

'The As-Geg'rastigan keep you, young man,' said Arval with a smile. 'What is it that you have to say to me?'

Clearing his throat, the lad half-nodded an acknowledgement and turned to Maesrhon. 'Er, actually, the message is for Maesrhon here. Lord Vorynaas says you're to report back to your unit to finish your year's service. He says you're to go back as quickly as may be and he wants to know how soon you can be ready.'

Maesrhon looked up at him. He flinched slightly and there was a small metallic noise as his armour and accoutrements rang to the movement; but Maesrhon spoke quietly. 'I have already been in contact with my commanding officer to make the arrangements for re-joining my unit.'

Arval noticed how the youngsters were edging nearer, gazing from the trooper to Maesrhon and back again, open-mouthed.

'Oh. Oh, I see.'

One of the boys sniggered and the messenger's face flushed. 'So, when will you be leaving? I have to find out, you see. Lord Vorynaas wants to know when you're going.'

Maesrhon stood up and the young man immediately stepped back a pace, swallowing again, audibly this time. 'You may tell Vorynaas that I shall be returning to my unit in two weeks' time as of yesterday,' said Maesrhon. 'Now if you will excuse me, I have matters to finish discussing with Lord Arval. Thank you for your message, which I have heard and understood.'

'Right, I'll tell him that then.'

Suppressed giggles came from the group of youngsters as they enjoyed the messenger's inability either to dominate the exchange or to find a snappy exit line. In the end he drew himself up in a half-salute aimed somewhere between Maesrhon and Arval. 'Thank you, sir. Good day to you both, Lord Arval. Sir.'

Turning, he tramped off, looking like a man who knew his feet were too large for him.

Sitting down again, Maesrhon shooed the boys away, although he was smiling himself. 'Run off now, you shouldn't laugh at him like that. You don't know how good his memory is, and you might be serving with him one day.'

They laughed and scampered off, fooling about as they went, saluting and swinging their arms in exaggerated imitation of a march, mimicking the young trooper's tongue-tied speech. It struck Arval that in other circumstances the whole scene would have been richly comic; but he said nothing. Alone once more, he and Maesrhon looked at each other. The afternoon had passed into evening now; if it had not been for the lamps, the twilight would have deepened to full dark. Suddenly the robin, invisible among the branches, burst forth in a sequence of cadences that fell like quicksilver into the quiet air. Maesrhon laughed softly.

'Listen to that! But it is more like something one sees, rather than hears: like a spattering of garnets winking brightly from a rock, or like drops of blood flung down in the dust, gleaming red as they scatter and fall.'

Once more a shiver ran over Arval, and he caught his breath. 'Artorynas, little son, what a thing to think! But we were talking of the patrols. I am uneasy that you are going back. You will be more of a marked man than ever, now.'

'Arval, have I not always been a marked man? But there is no need for you to worry. No-one from Caradward will touch me again, somehow I know it.'

CHAPTER 29

An uneasy interlude

It was with mixed feelings that Atranaar saw Maesrhon return to his unit for the completion of his year's military service. As the young man stood to attention before him, he studied him carefully, his face inscrutable as usual. How he had survived such a murderous blow to the head was a mystery of which presumably only Arval knew the secret. Atranaar had heard him being greeted here and there by his new nickname of Alfossig, appropriate if not particularly original, for the white lock at his temple, startlingly white against the rest of his dark hair, did indeed lie like a feather at the place where he had been struck. And yet Atranaar saw other differences in Maesrhon. He seemed taller, which was no great matter: at his age he might well still have some growing to do. But there was something else, something that showed in his face, in those strange golden eyes... not simply confidence, more than just composure... there was an air of inner peace, of quiet authority, that fitted him almost like a garment. Maybe it was the serenity of a man who had been to the brink of death and found it held no terrors for him – or was it the assurance of a man who felt himself somehow untouchable? Atranaar was used to reading men for qualities of leadership and command, and he saw that there was an allure about Maesrhon which could attract followers to him.

Had circumstances had been different, Atranaar might have been pleased and proud that a son of Vorynaas had chosen to train with the auxiliaries, especially as Maesrhon was obviously both skilled and dedicated; but as things were, it would not do for him to become too closely associated with a man so clearly marked out for elimination; for he was in no doubt at all that Maesrhon's injury had not been accidental and that an attempt had been made on his life. Like everyone else, he had noted that retribution had failed to fall on Ghentar; and having been present at the time, he had also drawn his own conclusions as to Valahald's involvement. But what do I care for Vorynaas, or his sons either, come to that, thought Atranaar. This one before me now: if he has had a difficult time of it, were my own young years not unhappy also? I made my own way in life without help, let him make his own destiny too, if he can. And as for Ghentar, he has lacked for nothing, all his life: he has wealth and status, and his father's favour, yet he has turned out a drunken wastrel who will be unchancy to deal with if he inherits. If it ever does come to a struggle for power, it will not be easy to choose which side to back! But whichever of them gains the upper hand in years to come, I must be ready to take advantage of it; so meanwhile, there will be no more incidents that may allow any man to question the grip I have within my own command. Atranaar's main emotion was anger that the whole incident had occurred within what was effectively his jurisdiction and he was absolutely determined that nothing similar should happen to tarnish his command during the three more months or so that Maesrhon would be under his orders.

Signing his name to the document that lay before him on the desk, Atranaar closed the file with a snap and handed a docket to Maesrhon.

'Here. Go to the store and they'll issue you with this list of kit. I'm sending you out tomorrow on reconnaissance patrol. You'll go with my senior scout: he's had his orders from me, and you'll do what he tells you. I hope you're fully recovered, because take it from me you're in for a tough time. We don't carry passengers and if I'm to stamp your discharge certificate with my seal, you'll need to come up to scratch over the next few weeks. And if you've any ideas about enlisting permanently after that, I'll want to hear that your performance has been outstanding rather than just satisfactory. No questions? All right, you can go now.'

So time passed, and though Valahald racked his brains for the means to assail Maesrhon, he had no success. Several times he sent men to spy on Atranaar's camp, or even to enquire for Maesrhon on some pretext; but always the word was that he was away from base, out on some exercise or patrol: no, he could not be recalled, he was taking part in some final test of his service; no, his whereabouts could not be divulged, he was on a high security exercise; no, he would not be eligible for leave, having already missed so many weeks through injury; was there a message for him? No message: well in that case, the guard begged to be excused, he had his own duties to attend to... and so it went. Ghentar remained in Heranwark. Revulsion at what he had tried to do, relief that no punishment had followed, apprehension at the news of Maesrhon's recovery, all these emotions battled together within him, to be gradually replaced by an ever-increasing unease at the hold which he saw that Valahald had achieved over him, a grip which was now tighter than ever. Temporarily at least this was keeping him away from his gambling cronies: the fear of incurring further debt and obligation was sufficiently strong for that, but on the other hand he was seeking the solace of strong drink more and more often. Valestron warned him that his behaviour had not gone unnoticed, and he pulled himself together to embark on a combat fitness course; but dropping out before he had completed it did nothing for his self-esteem or the respect in which others might have held him. The men in his company began muttering about his uncertain temper and he went about his business glowering with resentment against everyone and everything.

Vorynaas scents victory

In Caradriggan, Vorynaas brooded on how matters had turned out and considered his next move. If Valahald succeeded in removing Maesrhon as he had proposed, well and good. But time was moving on towards the Spring Feast and the window of opportunity was closing fast. The thing to do was to know how to handle the situation if the young cuckoo returned to the city. Vorynaas conducted a brief mental audit of how things stood at present. On the plus side, all was going well at the gold mine. Haartell was sufficiently greedy to risk his health for the sake of continuing in charge there, and was doing a good job. By all accounts that old fool Arythalt was only holding to life by a thread, so let him linger in Tellgard as long as Arval could keep him alive: he had long ago served his purpose with Vorynaas. While the gold flowed, there was no risk to his position. Even the temporary loss of face caused by his rash promise concerning the climate had been forgotten: his opponents had achieved nothing better themselves, when they forced him to humble himself before the Gwentarans, and in any case the successful gold strike had changed everything. No matter that there were still other wealthy men: whether they held lands in the Ellanwic, or shares in the Cottan na'Salf, or businesses in Staran y'n Forgarad, or metalworks in the Somllichan Ghent, he controlled the money supply, so the real power was his. So far, so good. But not all was satisfactory, and Vorynaas now turned his mind to what he saw as the negative aspects of his position.

First, there was no point in pretending that agriculture in Caradward was not in irreversible decline. The technology employed to create the Cottan na'Salf had been successful, up to a point: acre upon acre was now covered with growing-houses and livestock shelters in a vast project which produced fruit, vegetables, and meat from such animals as could be reared indoors. But though ingenuity had triumphed so far, it had been unable to counteract the effects of failing sunlight upon the wide plains where grain had once grown and cattle grazed. Those who had held out, refusing either to buy in to the growing-house scheme or to sell their land for its development, were now falling on hard times, their estates worth a mere fraction of the former price and only of use, if they were lucky, as ranches for breeding mules and low-quality pack animals. Horse-meat makes tough eating for a feast-day, Forgard, but you have only yourself to blame, thought Vorynaas with a flash of mirth. Then the laughter left his face. How long was it now, eight, more than ten years since he had been forced to buy grain from Gwent y'm Aryframan? And the price kept rising. True, the fact that it was his gold that put bread in their mouths increased his hold over his fellow-countrymen, but it galled him to think that those peasants across the border should benefit. Then there was the other cloud on the horizon: the next generation.

It would all be for nothing, if Ghentar did not inherit. Yet somehow, Vorynaas had to admit it to himself, the boy was not shaping up as he should. Look at Valahald: with all his faults, and it certainly seemed as though he had made a mess of his first major assignment, he was ambitious, hard-working, keen to succeed. Maybe I have been too soft on Ghentar, thought Vorynaas, maybe he has had everything handed to him too easily. But surely that cannot be true: look at the times in his childhood when I had to chastise him, or even beat him, even though I loved him; look at how I was forced to send him away for five long years, even though he begged and pleaded with me not to. And yet even though he is assured of his place beside me, though he has men under his command and a status that none can challenge, it is as though something eats at his happiness, as though demons whispered in his ear. Vorynaas' brows drew down in a scowl. Perhaps that changeling has put a spell on him. Yes, what to do about Maesrhon, if he returned in one piece from service? As his thought turned this way and that, an idea began to form in Vorynaas' dark mind. Maesrhon would be of full age when his year was up, and in a position to defy any of Vorynaas' orders if he wished. That was not to be tolerated, nor would it be a good idea to retaliate by disinheriting him and turning him out so that he had nothing to lose by causing trouble and unrest. No, thought Vorynaas, I need to keep him under my eye for just a little longer, however much I may wish never to see him again. If he stays under arms, he may attract a following; and if I cast him off, he will fly to roost in Tellgard and men will gather to him. I will make a place for him here, offer him scope within my affairs: not too much, just enough so that my indulgence will not seem feigned. Because meanwhile…

Meanwhile, it is time for me to plan the last move in the game I began so long ago. And now I see how making it will bring down all the birds with one cast! Vorynaas thumped his fist into his palm and sprang up as energy flowed into him. Walking up and down, he remembered the idea that had come to him in this very room as Thaltor sat making his report, remembered the meticulous planning, the choice of that fellow Atranaar to lead the mission, its audacious execution, its complete success. He was confident that an incursion into Gwent y'm Aryframan could be so far over the border before it was detected that invading forces would be able to sweep all before them like a storm. Victory would be swift, and then the Gwentaran lands would be theirs, together with the corn they produced. Or rather, they will be mine, thought Vorynaas. Never again will I pay for grain! And now I will fulfil my vow to settle with the Gwentarans, as long ago I was revenged on Arymaldur. By my right hand, never again will any man laugh behind my back because Arymaldur came from Gwent y'm Aryframan to cuckold me with Numirantoro. Their changeling son shall go to war when I give the order for men to muster, and I will take care that he does not survive the battle. And if he refuses to go, then by his own choice he shall meet a traitor's fate here in the city. Caradward is mine, and Gwent y'm Aryframan will be mine also; I will have both vengeance and satisfaction. The reins of power will all be in my hand and the future will belong to me alone, and to my true son after me. All that remains is for me to find or devise a pretext for war.

Patience and haste

The day of the Spring Feast came, with revelry and lavish entertainment provided by Vorynaas in Seth y'n Carad to bind his followers to him in loyalty and obligation. To Tellgard gathered any who held to the old ways and some who had turned again for solace to the traditions of their forefathers: there was Arval, and those who kept the lamp of learning alight with him; families of Gwentaran origin; *sigitsaran* both wealthy and less so; many city folk of lowly estate who served in other men's houses; and lords such as Forgard who had never wavered. And as the flame flowered into light, as the people turned to greet each other in the joy of leaf and life returning, there among them stood Maesrhon.

'Maesrhon is with us again, he's here, look! Maesrhon has come back to us, Maesrhon Alfossig, Lord Maesrhon!'

The murmurs ran round the hall, and the people pressed forward to touch him, to take his hand, those behind craning round the heads of those in front to catch a glimpse of what was happening. The light fell on his face as they gazed at him, as they reached out smiling with a kind of unformed joy and hope; and he smiled back in turn, touched by their welcome. Arval looked down from his place beside the Spring Fire and saw that with maturity, Maesrhon's true nature was there for all to discern who would: there could be no going back, now. He wondered how much time was left to them, time in which to prepare for the quest and to determine whether its direction lay east or north. In the midst of these reflections, Maesrhon turned and their eyes met. How strange it was, thought Arval, that Maesrhon had not yet asked him again what the choice was that he was destined to make.

Stranger still, and more disquieting, was the news that reached him a few days later: Vorynaas had actually installed his younger son in a place prepared for him both at Seth y'n Carad and in his various commercial enterprises! As Arval sat with Maesrhon one evening over a private supper in Tellgard, he voiced his fears.

'I cannot believe this is a change of heart, or an arrangement to be taken in any way at face value.'

'No, I'm sure you're right. But so long as I act as though I trust it as genuine, it gives me licence to operate within Seth y'n Carad, and to travel about on business, to look about me, talk to people, hear what men may be saying. Who knows what I may learn or find out? After all, how many in Caradward apart from myself know the truth about the forest? If I hadn't ventured into it, that time I went up to the mine while I was in military service, I would still have thought what I was brought up to believe, that it was a black wilderness where demons or worse might lurk. "Maesaldron" we all say, even those who labour there; even my own grandfather, when as a child I asked him. Yet the darkness clings only to the Lissa'pathor. Climb out of that valley of slavery and death, and the woods are as green and wholesome as any in the hills and dales of Gwent y'm Aryframan.'

Maesrhon paused, and then added the thought that had been growing in him ever since he had made his daring foray. 'Arval, this surely must mean that the shadow hangs only over Caradward, or where the hand of Caradward falls. I see why you say time may be short. I must have freedom to go about, and if this means I must play at deceit with Vorynaas, then so be it.'

Arval sighed heavily, pushing his plate away from him. His meal had been frugal, even by his standards: bread with curd cheese and radishes, and a small portion of grilled vegetables.

'Well, you may be right. But be wary, Artorynas. He won't have given up hope of getting rid of you. I would be happier if you were not living in Seth y'n Carad; you know you're welcome to come here to Tellgard.'

'I know. Believe me, I would rather be here.'

But Maesrhon had seen what Heretellar and Ancrascaro had noticed before him: the dilapidation creeping over the buildings, the shabbiness of their furnishing, the air of make-do and mend; he had noted the short commons both in the small hall and at the high table. No meat had been served tonight. When finding the means to keep going at all was so hard, when holding aloft the torch of knowledge was such a struggle now in Tellgard, he would not add to the difficulty by using up meagre resources in lodging there, especially when he could be fed and housed in Seth y'n Carad. Smiling now at Arval, Maesrhon said nothing of all this, but gave his other reason instead.

'As you have been like a father to me, so Tellgard has been my refuge and sanctuary. But if I must soon set out on a search whose end is doubtful, it will be easier to face the journey if I don't have to begin it by leaving the one place in the world that seems like home to me. Meanwhile, I'll be here as often as I can, to learn from you still and to help in whatever way you wish.'

In Seth y'n Carad Maesrhon was allocated office space in a suite of rooms set around an inner courtyard: his remit was to analyse the workings of the commercial side of Vorynaas' enterprises and to improve their efficiency where appropriate. And so almost a year went by, while Maesrhon worked for Vorynaas and went about in Caradward; while Arval in Tellgard studied deep into the night hours, seeking still for any word of guidance that might steer their quest; while Vorynaas bit his nails and forced himself to ignore what he knew was murmured in secret. 'Maesrhon is a son of the Starborn' said those who remembered the days when Arymaldur walked in Caradriggan; 'Maesrhon surely is one of the As-Urad' said those who believed the old tales; 'Maesrhon would set us free, we would follow him, if he would lead us' said those of Gwentaran stock, the downtrodden, the dispossessed, the young and reckless, the old with nothing to lose. Wait, wait, said Vorynaas to himself, you will find a way, you will have revenge yet. Hurry, hurry, Arval bade himself as he turned the pages, you must find the answer, time is running out. Yet matters moved, despite them both, and the signs were there to read, had either of them looked higher or lower: but seldom did Vorynaas take into account true friendship and loyalty; and Arval's mind was more attuned to lore and learning than to the weary toil of daily drudgery.

Vorynaas had derived much amusement from setting Maesrhon his task: he knew that enquiring into their accustomed ways of working would be resented by those under review and it gave him great satisfaction to think that he would benefit while Maesrhon gained only unpopularity. But so far there had been no trouble: Maesrhon had gone about his work quietly and with great tact, beginning by consulting with those who headed up their departments. He had listened to them with respect and noted down their comments carefully; and had had his notes worked up into a summary of the present standing of the business, a report which had been mostly produced by the two young clerks he had befriended in earlier days and who formed part of the small staff he had been permitted to make use of. All this had taken up the first six months or so, forming the basis of his work since then. He was due now to leave for another trip south, and wanted to check that all would be ready for him later that day. Getting up from his desk, Maesrhon had a word with the servant in the outer lobby as he left the office to walk over to the stables and transport yard; noticing, as he crossed the compound, that Valahald turned suddenly on his heel when he saw him and went back into the guardroom. The two of them rarely spoke, these days, for Maesrhon had little to say to a man who he was sure had plotted his death, and Valahald avoided him as far as he could. Maesrhon felt his spirits rise, and a new lightness in his step: soon he would be free of the city, riding out on the roads, and suddenly the certainty came to him once more that none from Caradward could harm him again.

When he returned to his office, the servant had just come in from the kitchens with refreshments for the mid-morning break, and everyone was gathering to help themselves. Maesrhon had learnt many things from his time with the auxiliaries, and some of them were being put into practice here. He made it a rule never to require any subordinate to perform a task that he was not able to do, or prepared to do, himself; and he claimed no privileges of seniority or rank. If he was to have a break from his labours, then all would enjoy the same. His eye fell on Haldas and Valisar as they laughed quietly at some joke together, remembering the almost pathetic gratitude they had shown him for his kindness those years ago. When he had asked for them to be seconded to his staff, he had seen that dogged devotion still in their eyes and been shamed again, as he was each time he thought of it, that the older of the two of them was enslaved. Well, at least he had been able to find out their names and use them. No man will shout for Haldas by yelling *Vigurt-is* at him, not while he works for me, thought Maesrhon. I wonder if there is any way in which I could buy his freedom. Perhaps I could arrange something with Heretellar, when I see him. It would have to be done indirectly, like so much else: if Vorynaas suspects my hand in the matter, Haldas will be as good as condemned to the Lissa'pathor.

Good intentions gone awry

Dealing indirectly was something in which Maesrhon had developed a skill that sometimes surprised even himself. A week or so later, he was riding slowly at the end of the day, having spent the afternoon with Heretellar and Meremvor while the latter worked with half a dozen estate hands to put a consignment of mules and other pack animals through their paces. Maesrhon had made his selection, but the buyer would be a dealer in Staran y'n Forgarad who was party to the arrangement: he would then sell on to Maesrhon's agent later. All the prices were agreed beforehand, although nothing was committed to paper. It was one way in which Maesrhon could put money into Heretellar's hands right under Vorynaas' nose, money which, however much Heretellar might dislike having to take it from such a source, was badly needed. Maesrhon had never visited Forgard's estates in the Ellanwic in the old days, when they had been sown with grain and other crops and supported herds of cattle and sheep, but he could see that it was a struggle now even to sustain the rough grazing which was all that was left to them. The three of them arrived back at the house, attended to their mounts and then headed for the bath-house. Before supper was served, a visitor arrived who was warmly welcomed by Heretellar and introduced to Maesrhon.

'This is Rhostellat,' said Heretellar, 'a nephew of Poenmorcar from Staran y'n Forgarad, and now engaged to be married to Ancrascaro! There's a piece of news for you.'

'Oh, congratulations! May you never know sorrow.'

Maesrhon gripped Rhostellat's shoulders in formal greeting, and then shook his hand with a smile. He was a reserved, rather shy young man, some years older than Ancrascaro by the look of him, tall and slightly-built with dark hair and eyes. His hands were narrow, with long delicate fingers, and he had a bookish, rather short-sighted air. This turned out to be an accurate assessment, for Maesrhon gathered that Rhostellat was a teaching member of the academic establishment in the southern city.

'But after we're married, we plan to live in Caradriggan,' he said. 'Ancrascaro wants to stay near her parents, and to continue working with Arval in Tellgard; and if he will take me too, I would be honoured to be his colleague. I'm hoping to purchase a suitable house for us in the city, and as soon as I can arrange to move my goods and household, then we can begin to plan for the wedding.'

'I'm sure Arval will be more than pleased,' said Maesrhon. 'It sounds as though you know him, but though I was in and out of Tellgard from my earliest years, I don't remember seeing you there as a student.'

'You are too young,' said Rhostellat. 'When I left Tellgard, you can't have been more than four, or at most five, years old. I remember you, though.'

So he was rather older than Ancrascaro, but they made a good match: both quiet and studious. If children were born to them, Arval would have a ready-made supply of intellectuals for another generation at least. Then with a sudden lurch of the heart, Maesrhon remembered that unless he and Arval found the key they searched for soon, there might be no future generation. For a moment or two he lost the thread of the conversation, as his companions continued with laughter and bantering talk; although when he looked up he saw that Rhostellat's dark eyes were still fixed upon him.

'No, no,' Heretellar was saying now in answer to some remark of Meremvor's, 'I'm not looking to marry yet. But is it true, Maesrhon, what rumour says, that Ghentar may be wed soon?'

Maesrhon shrugged. 'You probably know as much as I do. I may live in Seth y'n Carad but I'm not included in the inner councils of its grandees. But I'll wager Valafoss lies awake at night wishing he'd produced a daughter as well as sons: there's a man who would let ambition take pride of place over a father's love. The Starborn pity any woman who finds herself tied to Ghentar!' Bitterness crept into his tones: he was thinking of his own mother, sold to Vorynaas: much of what Arval had imparted to him, mind to mind, had indeed been difficult knowledge to live with. 'But yes, I've heard it said that Vorynaas is putting pressure on Ghentar to choose a wife; it seems he's anxious that the heir should have a successor of his own as soon as possible. Where they will find a suitable girl, who knows.'

'Not in Gwent y'm Aryframan, that's for sure.' Meremvor's voice was hard and Maesrhon remembered that although he had lived in Caradward from boyhood, his home was over the border. No hint of what Maesrhon intended to tell Heretellar must reach Meremvor's ears; and Rhostellat he had only just met, he had no means of knowing how far into Heretellar's confidence he had been taken: somehow he would have to shake them both off.

'No, nor among the *sigitsaran* either,' he said, smiling at Meremvor, who looked back, his heart in his face. Wrapped in the memory he cherished more dearly than any other, here for this one evening he saw that memory before his eyes, walking in the world again. But all three of them were looking at Maesrhon now; he saw that they had all heard and believed the whispers about Arymaldur and Numirantoro. Heretellar changed the subject.

'Would you not rather have stayed with the auxiliaries than returned to Seth y'n Carad? At the time, all the talk was that you would enlist as a regular, when you passed out with such high honours.'

Into Maesrhon's mind came the memory of what he had discovered on his final field exercise, the shameful knowledge he had not shared with anyone, even Arval. He wished Heretellar had chosen any other topic, here in open conversation, and his reply was somewhat terse. 'I was there to learn, not to make a career out of soldiering.'

An awkward silence greeted this, and Maesrhon groped for something else to talk of. They were still sitting around the table after finishing their meal and he noticed the flowers standing in a tall jug, beads of dew glistening on their petals and an ethereal perfume stealing from them under the warmth from the lamplight. An idea came to him, and he turned to Heretellar.

'Are you still working on the development of night-blooming flowers? Good: I wonder whether I might see the growing-house where you raise them? It will be something new to bring to Arval and I know he would be interested.'

Heretellar's dark eyebrows lifted fractionally under his silvering hair, but he nodded in agreement. 'Of course. We can go over there now, if you like. Would you like to come with us, Rhostellat?'

To Maesrhon's intense relief, the young man excused himself and said he thought he would retire to bed. They all went out into the darkness together, and then Meremvor led Rhostellat off towards the guest wing, lighting his way with a torch. Waiting until he was sure they were alone, Maesrhon turned to Heretellar, interrupting him in the midst of a long explanation about irrigation and pollination techniques.

'There's something I think you should hear. I found it out during my second stint with the auxiliaries, although I had begun to suspect earlier. It was already on my mind, so you caught me by surprise when you mentioned military service to me earlier this evening; I'm sorry if I seemed a little sharp with you. I've told no-one else this, not even Arval; but Heretellar, did you know that after we came home from Salfgard, Caradwardan troops invaded Gwent y'm Aryframan?'

'What! I've heard nothing of this! How do *you* know of it?'

The two young men stood in the growing-house staring at each other, the flowers forgotten. Then Heretellar sat down behind the open door on the wooden locker in which the tools and hoses were kept, and Maesrhon came to sit beside him.

'It was like this. For my final test I had to go out with a senior patrol leader: I won't bore you with all the details of what was expected, or what I had to show I could do; but towards the end of the exercise, we were lying hid within an easy bowshot of a group of travellers who were setting up camp beside their wagons. We'd been trailing them all day, getting closer and closer, but you could see they had absolutely no idea we were there. My instructor must have thought I knew all about what had happened; maybe he simply assumed I was in the know because of who I am. He turned to me with a grin and whispered, "Sitting targets, eh? It was just like this in Gwent y'm Aryframan away back. They never stood a chance, we picked them off like flies."

'Well, I had to think quickly what I should say, so I said that I supposed he was talking about, what, four years previously? Because it was after you had left Salfgard, in fact it was not long before Ghentar and I came back with Valahald and Heranar: Framstock was alive with rumours that people had been disappearing by twos and threes. I could see that Ardeth was worried, although he discounted the stories and no-one seemed to be able to prove them one way or another; but that's hardly surprising in view of what my patrol leader said. "Yes, that's right. Across the border and dug in all over the place we were, with none the wiser. And let me tell you, Atranaar doesn't mess about. When he has orders, he carries them out and makes sure everybody else does the same. If you're going to stay in the military, you won't go wrong if you stick by him. We came in, we rounded them up, we packed them off to the Open Hall and the gold mine, and then we pulled out leaving never a trace; and I'll bet you none of those peasants know to this day what it was that hit them."'

'By the Starborn!' Heretellar sat staring before him as the silence lengthened and the heady scent of the flowers drifted around them. 'Meremvor's family live in Gwent y'm Aryframan, but they can have heard nothing, or he would have mentioned it. Yet you were saying that you had already suspected something like this. Why was that?'

Outside in the darkness Meremvor, returning from bidding Rhostellat goodnight, had extinguished his torch, not needing it himself here where every step was familiar to him. As he approached, silent in his soft indoor footwear, he caught his name amid the murmur of conversation and paused, listening.

'I saw a man in the Lissa'pathor. This was while I was out alone on a different exercise, before I was wounded. He was lame, and moving too slowly for his overseer's satisfaction, so I stepped in to help him and I saw that he had the springing corn traced around his arm. That means he'd been raised a free man in Gwent y'm Aryframan, even though now he had the mark of the mine-slaves branded into his hair. He was only of middle years, and it seemed to me that there had not been time enough for him to have lived in his own land until he was a man and was tattoed with the sign, then come to Caradward for whatever reason, and fallen into misfortune sufficient to have condemned him to the mine.'

Heretellar was silent for a moment or two, frowning. 'Yes, I see,' he said eventually. 'Well, I see your reasoning, at any rate. But I still don't understand how Meremvor has never heard any rumours,' he added.

'When was he last over the border?'

'He came with me when I went up to Framstock to bring Ancrascaro home… I think that was the last time.'

'There you are, then. Wasn't that five years ago? This has all happened since then: it was when *I* was on my way back that the muttering started about folk disappearing. And didn't you tell me once he was raised in a *gradstedd* away up in the Rossanlow? If that's where his family are from, they'd be far enough away to be out of danger themselves, perhaps; that might account for it.'

Hidden in the darkness outside, Meremvor strained his ears as Heretellar said slowly, 'But still, it all seems rather inconclusive, somehow.'

'Wait though, there's more.' Maesrhon got to his feet and Meremvor shrank back into his hiding-place behind the water butt under the eaves. 'This fellow I saw, he'd been hurt. He was badly disfigured, he'd lost an eye and part of his nose, half his face was torn up by an old injury. I saw things during my year of service, Heretellar, and learnt things too. He'd taken a sword-cut to the face, and received specialist treatment for it. Now, he wouldn't come by a wound like that without being in a fight; and furthermore, the only place where they've got the expertise to pull a man through such an injury is in the military. The medic with Atranaar's troop was exceptionally skilled. In spite of what my instructor claimed, I don't think all the prisoners were "picked off like flies". I think the slave I saw in the Lissa'pathor had been taken in a raid, but made a fight for his freedom first. And what makes me even more sure of it is the way Atranaar reacted. When I mentioned my encounter, he pulled the shutters down straight away, and believe me he can be completely inscrutable: he's part-*sigitsaran*, they say. But he wasn't quite quick enough, and before he could hide it, I saw that he knew who I was talking about. He'd seen the man before, I'm certain of it.'

When Heretellar spoke again, his voice was heavy. 'I remember Ancrascaro saying, in my father's house one evening after we came home from Salfgard, that we got no good from our gesture of renewed friendship towards the Gwentarans, the time when the council voted that Valafoss and Vorynaas must send their sons for fostering, because the move was made gracelessly and under protest. And before that, when I brought her across the border and she saw all the troops, she was horrified and asked me what they were all for; and I said my main fear was what they *might* be used for. But I never imagined bad faith such as you have revealed.' He sighed and shook his head. 'This Atranaar, you have mentioned him before. Until now I had thought him an honourable man: you always seemed to speak of him with respect.'

'I respect his expertise, which is what I went to him to learn. But he's a ruthless man, as hard on himself as on others, a career soldier who has made himself the best at his chosen trade. He's got where he is by obeying orders, not questioning them, whatever his private thoughts. And what those might be, I think no man would ever know. He puts me in mind of what you said to me once about Geraswic, that he was damaged inside. Remember that?'

'Yes, I do, now you come to mention it.' Heretellar looked thoughtfully at Maesrhon. 'You said you'd not told Arval about all this. Why is that?'

'Arval has enough to worry about. Of course, it's possible that he knows without my telling him. He is Arval na Tell-Ur, after all. But if not, and you think that he, or other men, should hear the truth when I am not here to tell it, then you can reveal what I have told you now.'

Heretellar's glance flicked from the scar on Maesrhon's lip to the lock of white hair at his temple. 'Do you think another attempt may be made on your life?'

A faint smile touched Maesrhon's amber eyes. 'No. But who knows what else the future may hold.'

'Maesrhon, why not go back to Salfgard?'

'I can't do that. You saw what it was like when Ghentar and I were there: my presence would only cause Geraswic more pain. At least now Ardeth and Fosseiro and he can get on with the life they have made together.'

'It's almost unbelievable,' said Heretellar. 'I mean, that all this should happen and no-one know anything about it.'

'Well, it's obviously been kept a closely-guarded secret, hasn't it? Even when I was with the auxiliaries, I never heard so much as a whisper until the time I've been telling you about. And I could see that the man I did hear it from wasn't disobeying his orders in order to drop me a heavy hint: he let it slip because he assumed I already knew.' Maesrhon dug moodily with his toe at the cinder-path around the raised beds; a small chunk flew up and hit a watering-can with a doleful clang. 'Listen, Heretellar, you'd better give me some quick details about these flowers, in case Rhostellat wants to hear about them from me over breakfast tomorrow.'

Heretellar got up slowly from his seat on the locker and joined Maesrhon; together they moved off down the growing-house examining the flowers in the various stages of blooming. Meremvor waited until their voices had receded, then crept from concealment and melted into the shadows, stealing back to the house as quickly as he could. He was trembling with shock and rage, his fists clenched; but he had already made up his mind what he was going to do. As soon as he could think of a plausible reason, so as not to attract too much comment, he was going to Gwent y'm Aryframan. Suddenly it occurred to him that he had overheard only a part of the conversation. Perhaps he should tell Heretallar what he had accidentally learnt and ask him for the full story? But no: it was important not to implicate a man he respected so much, and to whom he owed so much. Heretellar might take action himself, anyway; but whatever he might resolve, Meremvor's decision was made. He would ask Heretellar for leave to visit his family in the Rossanlow, but his family could wait: he was going straight to Framstock, to speak to the first member of Val'Arad he could find.

The next morning, Meremvor busied himself making sure that everything was in order for Maesrhon's return to Caradriggan, and while the animals were readied and the baggage checked and loaded, Maesrhon took the opportunity of another quiet word with Heretellar. This time, he briefly outlined his concerns about the two young clerks he had taken under his wing.

'I'm not so anxious about Valisar,' he said; 'even though he's the younger of the two. He's a perky, resilient sort of character, more outgoing than Haldas, and in any case, he's technically a free man. As long as he does nothing stupid, he stands every chance of going back to his home one day, and that's what he says he wants. I think he would make a very good village teacher, and I'll do what I can to help him, although it worries me that both of them may have made their attachment to me too obvious. But Haldas: well, according to what he's told me, his father was put to death and his mother and sisters were enslaved at the same time as himself. He'll never see them again: another family destroyed by Vorynaas. Oh yes,' he added as Heretellar looked at him in enquiry, 'tricked into signing up for the mine and then punished for trying to leave when they saw the reality of the Lissa'pathor. But anyway, I can't help him directly, so I wondered whether you would take him, if I can think of some way to arrange things so that he is sent for sale? Then once he gets to you, I will buy him back and together we will give him his freedom.'

'How old is he?' asked Heretellar.

'Probably about fifteen now. You'd find him useful to have around, he's a good worker and a pleasant lad even though very quiet and shy.'

'I'll be happy to take him,' said Heretellar. 'You make the arrangements and find some way to let me know, and then I will do what's necessary. Come on now, it looks as though they're ready for you to start. Give my greetings to Arval and take care, Maesrhon. Have you got Rhostellat's letter for Ancrascaro?'

'Oh yes, it's in here.' Maesrhon grinned, patting his saddlebag. 'Quite a letter,' he said, for Heretellar's ears only. 'They've got plenty to say to each other!'

And so he set off for the city, well pleased with how his journey had gone, and looking forward with every mile to talking with Arval again. Arriving back at Seth y'n Carad late one evening, he turned over the transport to the yard staff and headed first for the bath-house and then, after a hasty supper in the kitchen, went straight to his bed. But when morning came and he entered his office to begin work, the tense, subdued atmosphere hit him like a blow in the face. He glanced swiftly round, but no-one spoke; and then he noticed that two familiar figures were missing.

'Where are Valisar and Haldas?'

The senior clerk answered, his eyes lowered. 'Sir, I was told to ask you to report to the chief accountant as soon as you came in.'

Maesrhon turned on his heel and made for a room in the next block of buildings. He had never liked the accountant, an unpleasant man who lost no opportunity to vent his sarcasm on his subordinates while toadying to those higher up the chain of command.

'Those two little trouble-makers?' he said dismissively in answer to Maesrhon's question, laying down his pen with a sneer. 'They won't be working with *you* any more, for one thing. You're clearly not much of a judge of character, asking for them in the first place, and it's obvious from the way they seemed to think they could behave that you weren't able to exercise any authority over them; let's hope it wasn't from you that they got their subversive ideas.'

Maesrhon ignored all this. 'Where are they?' he repeated.

'There's one of them now.' The man jerked his head towards the window, and Maesrhon saw Valisar crossing the courtyard, walking slowly and stiffly. 'He's been transferred to duties that will give him less time to waste.'

'Why is he moving like that? What's happened to him?'

'He's been flogged for insolence and disruptive behaviour. And before you ask, the other one's been packed off to the mine.' As Maesrhon looked at him in horror and fury, the man leaned back in his seat and laughed. 'I gather that's where he came to us from in the first place, so it should be quite a home from home for him, shouldn't it?'

CHAPTER 30

Slavery

Without another word, Maesrhon left the room and was halfway across the transport yard almost before he was aware of what he was doing or where he was going, men scrambling to get out of his way as he strode through with set face. Near the inner gate, a shift in a group of workers revealed Valahald in front of him, heading towards the officers' quarters. He must have come out of the guardhouse and was strolling along, unaware of Maesrhon rapidly catching him up; but his pleasant reverie was suddenly interrupted as Maesrhon overtook him to stand in his way.

'I have just been told that while I was away, you have had one of my staff flogged.'

Valahald was taken aback by this unexpected confrontation and for an instant made no reply. Yet though he felt uneasy under the scrutiny of those uncanny golden eyes, his agile brain was working at high speed.

'Your information was incorrect. Well, incomplete would be more accurate. I have had two clerks flogged. One was a slave and has now been sent to the Lissa'pathor.'

The premature frown lines between Maesrhon's widely-spaced brows deepened. 'They were scarcely out of childhood! And they were answerable to me. If they'd done wrong, why didn't you wait until I returned to the city, so that I could decide what punishment they merited?'

'You're too soft, Maesrhon, they were old enough to know better. "One of my staff", indeed!' Beginning to recover his composure, Valahald sneered slightly. 'We're all in the employment of the same master, you know. You want to remember that all your workers are only seconded to you. But if they were answerable to you, maybe they got their ideas from you? Me, I'm answerable to Lord Vorynaas. When he issues an order, I obey it.'

'Yes, I have reason to know that.' Though Maesrhon spoke quietly there was menace in his voice and in spite of himself, Valahald could not quite prevent his glance flicking to the white lock at Maesrhon's temple. 'So making slaves of our fellows satisfies us no longer, now we beat those whose mere words displease us.'

Valahald lifted an eyebrow. 'You know, I remember once warning Ghentar about the trouble his hot temper could bring him.' With a meaningful laugh, and a hint of emphasis, he added, 'I wouldn't have thought it would run through *both* sides of your family, but there you are,' and made to move off, but Maesrhon blocked his path and his laughter died.

'Never say anything like that to me again. Never.'

Alarmed, Valahald took a step back, but covered it with bluster as best he could. 'Are you threatening me? Touched a raw nerve, have I?'

Maesrhon came after him; he gave back another pace. 'I am warning you. If you read a warning as a threat, I must draw my own conclusions.'

Leaving Valahald standing rooted to the spot with his heart beating uncomfortably fast, Maesrhon walked swiftly away. Apprehensive faces looked up as he returned to his workplace, but by then his long-standing control over his emotions had reasserted itself. He sat calmly at his desk, beckoning over two other clerks to instruct them in how to continue with the work from which Haldas and Valisar had been forcibly removed. There was nothing to be gained by mentioning the youngsters, or by asking questions: that would only put others at risk.

He would wait until evening, and seek out Isteddar. Maesrhon knew well that some of those who worked at Seth y'n Carad frequented the *Sword and Stars* and Isteddar had told him once that one of the stable-hands there had a second cousin or marriage-cousin or some such in Vorynaas' stores. He would find out later what had reached Isteddar's ears of events unfolding in his absence.

Far away in the forest, Haldas lay wakeful in the dormitory for office slaves, hopeless tears sliding one after another from his closed eyes down his cheeks. This was the nearest thing to privacy he had, when black night settled over the Lissa'pathor and hid him from his fellows. Even so, he could hear the small tell-tale sounds which told him others beside himself wept, alone with their despair in the dark hours. He turned to lie on his back: he could do this now that the pain and discomfort of his flogging had finally subsided, and at least it meant that his face was not pressed into a clammy pool of tears. How many weeks had he been here now? But there was no point in trying to count the weeks, when years of the same stretched ahead. Rumour had it that those who laboured in the Lissa'pathor did not live long and he hoped it was true. He wondered how many hundreds, thousands maybe, now endured in drudgery here, most enslaved like himself, but many others tied by the chains in which they had unwittingly bound themselves, duped like his own father had been. When he had lived here as a child, he had been housed with the other families, nearer to the mine itself in the workers' village which had been constructed. Here, further down the valley, although there was a distant rumble of industrial noise, he was more aware of the sounds made by the river as it flowed by, and the whisper of the trees. The administrative buildings where he worked now were adjacent to the overseer's house, a handsome building once occupied by Arythalt; these days it was Haartell who lived there. Haldas set his teeth, but fresh tears flowed as he reflected sadly on the contrast between reporting to Maesrhon and toiling for Haartell.

Arythalt too had lain awake at nights, bitterness and regret keeping sleep away. Haartell had no such problems: he much enjoyed lording it over his empire of human suffering and his nights were not spent alone, as Haldas was to discover to his cost. One morning he had not been at his desk for long when his section-head sent him across with a message for Haartell. The servant who admitted him told him curtly that he would have to wait, and left him in a small room opening off the corridor that ran the length of the house on the first floor. Haldas sat there, looking about him. His days were spent poring over columns of figures and closely-written text, calculating, copying, page after page. Early in the day though it still was, his eyes were already tired, pained by the close work and the gritty air. No such problems for Haartell though, he thought, noting the fine mesh grilles at all the windows. With the natural resilience of youth, Haldas had already, even without being consciously aware of it, begun to recover somewhat from his initial despair. Now he found himself wondering whether there was any chance he could be moved to duties on Haartell's personal staff, and maybe from there even hope for a transfer back to Caradriggan. At that moment, he heard a door open and close further down the corridor, and looked up, expecting to see Haartell come into the room. Instead, to his surprise he caught a brief glimpse of a young woman who walked past the open door.

Haldas was on his feet and out into the corridor before he had had time to think. His body had reacted quicker than his brain and even now, although he saw that the girl's long hair, dishevelled though it was, had been elaborately arranged and she was only scantily dressed, he failed at first to register what this might mean. In the instant during which she had been visible as she passed the door, his mind had flooded with long-buried memories.

'Asanardo!' His voice sounded breathless in his own ears.

The girl whirled around, shock etched onto her face under the stale make-up. She stared at him as though not really believing he could actually be there. 'Haldas? What are you doing here? Who…'

The next moment her words were cut off as he rushed at her, hugging her fiercely. There were so many things he wanted to say, so many questions to ask; somehow he could not utter a single syllable except her name.

'Asanardo, Asanardo,' he groaned, oblivious to the sound of a door opening again. The most urgent question managed to form itself into words. 'Is our mother here, too?'

Looking over his head in sudden alarm, Asanardo bit her lip. 'No.' She began trying to free herself from his embrace. 'Haldas, I'm sorry, she's dead.'

'No, oh no!'

A wild cry of anguish broke from Haldas as tears started once more from his stinging eyes; but suddenly a hand seized him roughly by the shoulder and he was spun round, staggering against the opposite wall. Haartell was standing there, dressed in an expensive night-robe.

'You have already disturbed me with an unnecessary intrusion into my leisure hours,' he said, his glance flickering between Haldas and the girl, 'but now I find you shouting like some brat off the streets and pawing at my property. Don't you know the penalty for handling what belongs to me?'

As he spoke, he put his hand up to Asanardo's face and touched her cheek with his finger; she jerked her head away and he laughed.

'Leave her alone! She's not your property, she's my sister. Don't touch her again!'

Haldas, scarcely aware of what he was saying or doing, pushed himself off from the wall and started towards them, but suddenly froze in his tracks. With an abrupt, violent movement, Haartell wrenched at the girl's garment and the thin material tore, revealing that beneath it she was naked.

'Steward!' Haartell shouted, and there was the sound of a slamming door followed by rapidly approaching footsteps. Lowering his voice to a conversational level once more, Haartell turned to Haldas with an unpleasant laugh.

'Your sister, is she? I don't know what things are coming to, when I find a young man embracing his own sister.'

Haldas was staring, aghast; he had not seen his sister naked since they were children together and now he was confronted by her woman's body. Haartell began to fondle her breasts and she flinched from him, her eyes filling with tears. The steward had arrived on the scene and was waiting, his face studiously blank. Haartell indicated with a nod that he was to stand beside Haldas, and then pulled Asanardo round towards him.

'Allow me to correct you, Vigurt-is,' he said to Haldas. 'She most certainly is my property; let me show you what that means.'

Pinning the girl to the wall with his forearm, he forced his other hand between her thighs as she began to weep audibly. With a scream of incoherent fury, Haldas came back to life and launched himself at Haartell, but the steward was too quick for him. There was a brief struggle as Haldas fought to get at Haartell, fists flailing, but after a moment or two he found himself gasping for breath, arms clamped to his sides in the steward's iron grip. A curious pause fell on the group. Haartell let go of the girl and she stood hopelessly, head bowed. He smoothed his hair and adjusted his night-robe, his eyes roving coolly over his companions.

'Go back to my room and wait for me there, and do try to make yourself a little more presentable.' He dismissed the girl and she walked away without a word. 'It's still quite early. I think I might permit myself a little more pleasure before attending to the business of the day, but first I'll deal with you.'

Haldas had been watching in horror as his sister disappeared, never looking back; somehow he knew they would never meet again. He turned back to Haartell, impotent hate rising in him like a black tide, and spat in his face. Very slowly and deliberately, Haartell removed a fine handkerchief from the sleeve pocket of his robe. Wiping his face, he dropped the soiled fabric carelessly to the floor for a servant to gather up and stepped closer to Haldas, who braced himself, expecting to hear that he was doomed to death. However, Haartell looked at him in silence for a few moments, a cruel smile on his lips, and then spoke very quietly.

'I think you are wasted in a desk job, Vigurt-is. You have so much spare energy, you could be much more efficiently deployed elsewhere. Steward, hand this man over to the guard and tell them to take him to the mine.'

And so the wheel of misery came full-circle for Haldas, who now found himself condemned to the sinew-racking labour from which his father had once tried to escape. He had run only to death, but Haldas knew that for himself it was only a matter of time before death came to find him in his chains. The work was dangerous and unrelenting, and accidents were not uncommon; but always there was a new pair of hands to replace the unfortunates whose wasted bodies were dragged off for unceremonious disposal. Sometimes though, Haldas thought it might be better to go suddenly, dispatched by a misplaced blow of the pick or crushed in a rock-fall, rather than suffer from one of the mysterious wasting sicknesses that seemed to afflict so many of those whose fate had brought them to the Lissa'pathor. Once they began to cough up blood, or had difficulty keeping down their meagre rations, it was only a matter of time. They would be pulled out from the gangs and set to lighter duties, their food allowance cut still further, but they never lasted long. Their eyes dulled and sunken, they got ever thinner until morning found another spent, emaciated body lying huddled, never to move again.

The sweet taste of revenge

At first even his exhaustion was not enough to prevent Haldas weeping openly over his food bowl at the day's end, tears tracking through the grime on his cheeks whether his fellows ridiculed him or not. And there was plenty of bullying among the slaves, who would fight among themselves like dogs for an extra morsel or a warmer sleeping spot in the cage. When brutality was all they knew, any sign of weakness was despised and picked upon. Then Is-Avar had befriended him and beaten off his tormentors, who were caught off-guard by sudden action from the strange, bitter man with the wounded face who had been silent and unresponsive for so long. Haldas was unsure why Is-Avar had taken to him as he had: it could hardly be from pity at his story. The tale of mother dead, father killed, sister degraded, the son of the family enslaved, was not so unusual. But something in his plight had touched the other's heart sufficiently to make him break the silence of years, although he had refused to tell Haldas his name, saying he had lost this along with his freedom. Haldas called him Is-Avar just between themselves, for friendship and in gratitude for the little acts of kindness one slave had shown another in their mutual hopelessness, not knowing what pain his words renewed when, as he poured out his story, he described Maesrhon's virtues with fervent devotion.

Tonight, in the pitch blackness of a corner of one of the slaves' sleeping-cages, Haldas fidgeted restlessly, his stomach rolling with hunger; for weeks now their evening rations had consisted of chewy beans in thin, tasteless gruel. All the slaves knew that their bread ration had been stopped because the Gwentarans were now refusing to sell any grain at all to Caradward and Haldas was worried that Is-Avar was not yet shut in the cage with the rest of them. Was he sleeping somewhere else, or still at work in the stables, or had something happened to him? It was generally known among the slaves that he was from Gwent y'm Aryframan and even though he had been captured in a raid, it would not be surprising if some of his fellows had set upon him, taking out the frustration of their hunger by beating him in revenge. Suddenly Haldas heard voices outside the cage and then a rattle of keys. Next there was a stir among the sleepers, muffled cursing in the darkness, and then even over the stench of sweat and dust he detected the strong smell of horses and animals that always hung about Is-Avar.

'Here, eat this. It's probably rotten in the middle, so watch out if it smells bad.'

Haldas took what his fingers recognised as a misshapen, leathery apple. His mouth watered nonetheless. 'What about you? Have you got one, too?'

'I ate mine in the stables.'

Haldas wondered if this was true or not, then a wonderful trace of sweet apple scent reached his nose and he wasted no more time on speculation. Biting into the fruit as quietly as possible, he ate it as slowly as he could bear. He tasted mould at the core, but ate it all anyway, just as he had eaten the carrots which his friend sometimes filched from the fodder-store. What did he care if his stomach ached tomorrow? It would be nothing compared with the heart-ache he suffered every day.

'Thanks, you've been really good to me.'

'Every maggot-infested horse-apple the less is a small way of getting back at these accursed Caradwardans, may the blindworms of Na Naastald take every last one of them.'

The other man's voice already had a strange, twisted tone to it, caused by the injury to his face; but bitterness dripped from every syllable that was breathed on a whisper into his companion's ear. Pity stirred in Haldas and he wished there was some way to show how grateful he was for companionship and kindness. He gripped his companion's arm in the darkness, and whispered back.

'You know that's not the only reason. I wish you would tell me what your name is. I told you mine.'

'I am Vigurt, I have no name.'

'Well then, I'll just have to keep on calling you Is-Avar.'

There was a long silence, and Haldas thought the other man was not going to reply. Then slowly an answer came. 'Why not? Though I have no child of my own, I am of an age to be a father to you. And you have done for me what a son should: you've given me back a reason to live.'

'Oh?' Surprised and pleased, Haldas waited for more; but the silence grew again. 'What do you mean, Is-Avar?' he asked eventually; but his companion turned over as if for sleep.

'It's best you don't know,' was all he would say.

But long after Haldas was himself asleep, he lay wakeful among his fellows as they muttered and moaned in exhausted dreams. He remembered his youthful vow that nothing would ever again make him set foot in Caradriggan, and his ruined face moved in a mirthless smile. He was going to break that vow when the moment came, now that he had found a reason to tread the city road once more. Parts of Haldas's story had reinforced other whispers he had heard circulating in the Lissa'pathor. Rumours of all kinds frequently swept through the enslaved workers: often wildly improbable, usually unattributable, they served to provide brief talking points of interest amid the grinding monotony of toil; but a persistent theme over the past couple of years had been the hint of a faction growing around this Maesrhon, the growing feeling that Vorynaas' younger son was becoming the focus for those disenchanted with the way power was exercised in Caradward. A day had come when, during the long hours of shifting earth and stones, he had suddenly realised that his mind had awoken and his brain was alive once more: without being conscious of it, he had begun planning a long-delayed revenge. He had watched his moment, and when the opportunity came in the form of a commotion among a passing mule-train, he had been ready to throw himself into the melee, calming the animals and bringing them under control. For a man with his background and experience, it had not been particularly difficult: he had been noted, once, for his way with horses and transport animals and he had not forgotten all his skills. After that, a campaign of finely-judged dragging of his lame leg and diminishing of his work output had finally taxed the patience of his gangmaster. One day an overseer had brought up a strapping young man to take his place, and marched him off to the stables and transport yards where he could still be of some use.

As he lay now, thinking things over, a guard passed by outside carrying a torch; its light briefly raked the darkness of the sleeping-cage and waked a spark in his one good eye. He heard small sounds as Haldas beside him whimpered and chattered his teeth together, probably dreaming of food as hunger gnawed at him in sleep. If his plan succeeded, it would perhaps trigger strife between the supporters of

Maesrhon and those of the favoured son, Ghentar; maybe Caradward would destroy herself and his own homeland could step in to reap the benefit. He would not be there to see it, but the thought brought a satisfaction to warm his bitter heart. But though his vengeance would be partly for Gwent y'm Aryframan, betrayed and then raped by a friend and neighbour, partly for Haldas and others whose families had been destroyed, yet in the last analysis, vengeance was mostly for himself, for his poisoned happiness, his ruined hopes. And his plan would succeed, because he had a weapon the hated Caradwardans had not taken into account. Had he not himself told Atranaar that he had no interest in living, and no fear of dying? They could not touch him again, who was *vigurt*, already as dead; his blow would be struck before they had so much as laid a hand on him. They would not be able to stop him; they would have no defence against a man who was prepared to throw his own life away in order to take that of another. He lay in the darkness, savouring the taste of revenge, feeling strength flow into him. Soon the chance would come, he knew it, for him to attach himself to a consignment of wagons going south to Caradriggan; and when he got there, he had made up his mind what he was going to do. How many years had it been? His twisted face moved as he bared his teeth in a grimace of anticipation. Somehow he must make time for Vorynaas to know him, first; and after that, they could do what they would, it was nothing to him. Oh yes, he would make sure, before they both died, that Vorynaas knew who it was who assailed him; knew who the avenger was, who had come out of the past to take his life, as Vorynaas had stolen his future.

Hard times

Wintertime in Caradriggan that year was a dark and doubtful season, troubled by hardship and unease. When the days of the feast came around, cheer was in short supply in most men's houses: most, but not all; in Seth y'n Carad, Vorynaas held court as usual and wanted for nothing. Nothing, that is, in a material sense; although it took all his willpower to bide his time when he burned for action, all his reserves of guile to feign compliance with Tell'Ethronad even though it was only for a few months more. He stood at an upper window late one morning, stroking his beard as he looked down at the last couple of dozen men in the long line of those who waited under guard in the compound each day, shuffling forward one by one for their dole of corn from his store. Noticing Valahald standing in the doorway of the guardhouse, his gaze darkened slightly and he turned from the window to survey the young man's father. Valafoss was seated on the couch, helping himself from a tray loaded with savouries. There was a glass of spiced wine at his elbow and he lifted it to his lips as he leaned back again. These days Valafoss' belly was broad and bloated, and fat lay in rolls from his well-padded shoulders up to the back of his head. He was not so much seated as propped against the back of the couch, leaning into the corner of it behind his vast paunch. Vorynaas' lip curled in distaste behind his hand, but as their eyes met, Valafoss gestured towards the window.

'Sure you're not being over-generous? I've no intention of opening my granaries for the world and his wife to take advantage of.'

'It's only for the holiday period. And of course my stores are considerably more extensive than yours.'

Vorynaas paused to let that sink in while he poured a drink for himself and privately savoured the thought that all those who queued for his charity were obliged to pay a nominal sum for the privilege 'to save their pride', as he had expressed it in council. Valafoss was becoming a little tiresome. His support had been useful, but was scarcely needed now. Having done very nicely out of them, what was he contributing these days to Vorynaas' plans, apart from through the services of his sons? And Valahald had turned out to be something of a disappointment, in the end; all froth and no beer, to use one of Thaltor's favourite phrases from their young days together. Vorynaas came to a sudden decision and straightened up from the wine table.

'If you'll excuse me now, I've some business I want to talk over with Thaltor.'

Valafoss heaved himself to his feet, sweating slightly from the exertion and looking rather put out.

'You want to lose some weight, old friend. You could be seeing action, come the spring,' said Vorynaas as he ushered him out, enjoying the alarm that registered in the piggy little eyes, sunk in the fleshy face.

He was still smirking slightly when Thaltor arrived some minutes later, but came straight to the point.

'I want you to take over from Valahald here at Seth y'n Carad. You'd have Ghentar as your second; I'm bringing him back from Heranwark. He'll live in the house but report to you, and you can take over the commanding officer's quarters. How do you feel about that?'

Thaltor stared, drink in hand. He was reaching middle-age now and had spent most of his life acting as a kind of roving enforcer for Vorynaas. He had never married, preferring to keep some girl or other installed in his house across the city, but had often grumbled privately at how often his assignments took him away from home. Today's proposal seemed too good to be true, but though he wanted to jump at the offer, he could foresee plenty of potential problems.

'I feel fine about it, in fact there's nothing I'd like better. But what about Ghentar, and what about Valahald?'

'Listen, Thaltor. I've known you too long to bother pretending. Ghentar is going to the bad in Rigg'ymvala. I've got to get him back here under my eye, and I've got to do it in some way that doesn't make him lose face. Between us, we'll sort him out. As for Valahald, I made it quite clear to him that I don't give third chances when those I trust let me down. He needs a dose of reality and that's exactly what he'll get when he finds himself reporting to Valestron over in Heranwark. With a bit of luck, both he and Ghentar will shape up yet; and I need them both to be ready when it's time to make our move.'

There was a short silence in which Thaltor wandered over to the window, glanced out and then turned back again. 'And when will that be, do you think?'

'I'd say soon after the Spring Feast. I meant what I said to the council, Thaltor.'

They sat for a few moments, both remembering the events of early autumn. Not since the old days had so many members of Tell'Ethronad turned up for a debate, but that was hardly surprising. When the convoy had come back from its fruitless journey to Framstock, bringing not just clattering wagons empty of the expected grain but also the incredible news that none of the year's harvest was for sale, there had been consternation. The negotiators who had travelled over the border could offer no explanation to the council other than that they had been told that Val'Arad had voted to sell no grain at all to Caradward. They had tried to bargain, to reach some sort of accommodation, they said; but the answer had always been the same: the decision of Val'Arad was final, there would be no sale of corn. Vorynaas had been so sure this was the opportunity he had racked his brains to engineer: he had risen to his feet insisting that such an insult was not to be tolerated, that Caradward should take what it needed by force, if the Gwentarans refused to sell. Of course that old fool Arval had spoken against this, together with his usual band of hangers-on, not to mention that young bastard Maesrhon. It had been all Vorynaas could do to restrain himself at that point, but curiously he had calmed down as other men too spoke against his proposal. It seemed that many even of the younger members of the council were too faint-hearted to follow him now, and shrank from war as an option, and he had been unable to obtain a majority. Recalling the scene, he smiled at the memory. If they have no stomach to endure a fight, let them see if they have the stomach to endure a famine, he had thought as he stood once more to concede the debate, secure in the knowledge of his own full grain-stores. Catching Thaltor's eye upon him now as they sat, he smiled more broadly and echoed the words he had used to Tell'Ethronad.

'Yes, it was all very well to be high-minded at the end of the summer, but we'll see how they feel by the time the Spring Feast comes around, after a winter spent tightening their belts with no prospect of a following harvest.'

Thaltor grinned and drained his cup. 'There's something else I meant to ask. What about Maesrhon?'

'That changeling! Either he goes with the troops, in which case I guarantee you he'll die in the fighting; or if he refuses to go, I promise you he'll die here instead – so the choice will be his.'

There was a rather tense pause in which Thaltor digested this, and then Vorynaas changed the subject slightly. 'I'd give quite a lot to know what prompted those yokels in Val'Arad to turn so intransigent.'

'Yes, I've wondered about that, too,' said Thaltor. 'It seems so out of character, certainly not in the style of any of the worthies I encountered in my various trips over the border.'

'Do you think they've got wind of our, how shall I put it, our earlier little foray into their back yard?'

'No, no. I told you at the time they'd no idea, so how could they find out now?'

'Maybe Ardeth's started throwing his weight about.'

Thaltor shook his head. 'Well, I suppose it's always possible, but I'd say not. Perhaps that other fellow, that Geraswic, the one you crossed all those years ago? I never met him, maybe he's stirring them up at last.'

'Mm. Well, if so, he should enjoy his moment while he can. Because understand this, Thaltor.' Vorynaas leaned forward with narrowed eyes. 'Come the spring, I'm going to wipe Gwent y'm Aryframan off the map.'

Demotion

Vorynaas, always a shrewd reader of the baser side of human nature, noted with satisfaction how accurate his prediction of the public mood had been as the winter's end approached in shortages and privation. As stores and stockrooms emptied and faces became thinner and more pinched, so the mutterings became louder; and sullen resentment against Gwent y'm Aryframan turned day by day to ever more open aggression. Maesrhon, demoted to manual labour in the transport yard, worked in grim silence and kept his thoughts to himself until those times when he could slip away to Arval in Tellgard. He blamed himself for what had happened to young Valisar and Haldas: according to what Isteddar had heard, the two of them had complained when in his absence they had been curtly excluded from the small privileges he had allowed them to share; his own name had been dragged into things, tempers had flared, and at the very time when he, far away in the Ellanwic, was trying to make secret arrangements to improve their lot, the youngsters had flung caution aside, bravely but unwisely defying their masters to proclaim their loyalty to himself. Then he had voted against Vorynaas in Tell'Ethronad and an ugly scene had followed after he was summoned to Vorynaas' private apartments in Seth y'n Carad.

'I put you in charge of an operation which was supposed to increase efficiency, but you introduce slackness and insubordination!' raged Vorynaas. 'Have I reared a wastrel, as well as a cuckoo in the nest? You have the arrogance of your grandfather, and now you dare to defy me in council, disloyal as your mother was!'

Maesrhon's eyes widened. 'My mother?' he said quietly. 'My mother's loyalty cost her her life.'

With a snort of exasperation and disgust, Vorynaas flung himself back in his chair. 'What would you know about it?' he sneered.

'I know more than you could ever understand.' The amber eyes were burning now; Maesrhon was on his feet, glaring down at Vorynaas.

'Sit down!' he bellowed.

Vorynaas had taken the precaution of making Maesrhon sit facing the lamp, while he walked to and fro; but unnerved by the way the lamplight accentuated the boy's resemblance to Arymaldur he had made the mistake of retreating to the chair behind his desk, and now found himself on the receiving end of the old, hated, height disadvantage. Breathing heavily, he fought for calm by gloating at the thought of the fatal choice he would shortly be laying before Maeshron. Jabbing his finger in the air for emphasis, he spat the words out.

'I forbid you to defy me again. Next time there is a debate in Tell'Ethronad, you will vote for what I propose.'

'I am of full age now. I will vote for whatever I believe to be right.'

Vorynaas clenched his fists. That uncanny air of unreachable serenity, how it maddened him! 'You will do as I say, as a son should – though when have you ever been a true son to me, you insolent changeling?'

'When have you ever been as a father to me? I will do what is right, you cannot compel me otherwise.'

Shock registered momentarily on Vorynaas' face and the high colour in his cheeks paled a little. Maesrhon wondered what was passing through his mind, not knowing how his words had unconsciously echoed Numirantoro's old, wounding disdain. Casting about for a way to regain the upper hand in their altercation, Vorynaas leaned forward.

'I will have my own way in my own house. As of now, you are dismissed from your position.'

Maesrhon's mind worked at speed. He could not expect food and a roof over his head at Seth y'n Carad without contributing towards it, nor could he add to the burden of its upkeep by taking refuge in Tellgard. Yet he needed to stay in the city while Arval and he still sought for guidance on the direction of his quest. He shrugged.

'Very well, I will work for my keep at the *Sword and Stars*.'

'You will not.' Vorynaas smiled unpleasantly; he was not going to have word spread all over Caradriggan that Maesrhon was out of his control, or allow the boy to remove himself from under his eye. 'You underestimate my authority. There is no man in this city who will employ you, if I say he must not. From tomorrow you will work with the labourers on the transport teams in the yards. And you can sleep with them in the loft above the stables; I don't want to see your face under this roof once your brother is home. Now get out.'

The hours were long and the work hard in the stables and around the yards, but Maesrhon made the best of it in the knowledge that he would need all the strength and endurance he could build when the time came for him to set out on his journey. Wondering when that time would be, he slipped away to Tellgard as often as he could, but was sometimes too tired to do much reading or research at the end of an exhausting day. As spring drew on, convoys of wagons arrived more and more often from the mine, sometimes two in a week rumbling down through the north gate and into the compound of Seth y'n Carad. Clearly, production had been significantly stepped up; and the increased revenue was being put to immediate use: other transports being despatched with men and material to Heranwark or the border zone, and orders for every kind of commodity being sent out to Staran y'n Forgarad and the south. The yards were a constant ferment of men, horses, mules and carts of every kind, the soldiers' quarters in the compound bulging with troops in transit and the labourers obliged to make room in the stable-lofts for all the extra men and lads passing to and fro from the Lissa'pathor.

Sometimes Maesrhon saw Ghentar lounging in the guard-room or talking with Thaltor; and although he was too busy to take much notice, he did occasionally wonder how his brother and Valahald had taken to their switch of postings, which each of them must surely have seen as demotion. In point of fact it had actually suited them both; for Valahald had been glad to get away from Vorynaas' baleful presence, and Ghentar was more than relieved to be leaving the complications of his life in Heranwark behind. Back on home ground he felt more like his old, cocksure self; and even if he was subordinate to Thaltor, he told himself he was only nominally second while he still enjoyed his father's indulgence. Valahald meanwhile had ridden off, determined to impress Valestron and make his mark in Rigg'ymvala. His time would come, he was sure of that still. There would be another chance to prove himself to Vorynaas and if not, there was still the hold he had over Ghentar. Thaltor indeed had not failed to notice how alarmed Ghentar had been at first, thinking he would be reporting to Valahald once he was back in Caradriggan. Something was going on between those two, no doubt about it. He smiled to himself, visualising the stresses and strains likely to develop between Valestron and Valahald, two ruthless and ambitious men both straining after power. It struck him that both were actually more like Vorynaas than his son was: Ghentar might resemble his father physically, but the other two were more of a match for Vorynaas in cunning and guile. He resolved, with an eye to his own future, to watch them all carefully at the festival, especially if Valestron was there too. And sure enough, in the week before the Spring Feast, Maesrhon spotted Valestron heading towards the hall doors, a servant at his heels carrying bags and bundles. He frowned to himself: did this mean that Valestron was on leave from Rigg'ymvala and visiting the city for the festival, or was his presence, like the unusual level of activity, part of some new machination from Vorynaas?

One morning he was standing in the yard, unloading straw bales from a cart and reflecting ruefully, as he lifted them with the fork and pitched them up to his workmate on the stack, that at least he had had plenty of practice at this sort of thing during his years in Salfgard. He heard shouts and noise from the compound, and then with a great creaking of harness and thunder of heavy wheels on the cobbles, half a dozen wagons rolled slowly through the inner gate. Yet another load from the mine, thought Maesrhon as he stepped aside to let the newcomers manoeuvre into position. The day was warm for the time of year, and in the enclosed area of the yard the heat soon became stifling for those working there. Maesrhon propped his hayfork and took off his jerkin, and then jumped from the empty cart, scrambling up to help build the stack. From his more elevated viewpoint he saw that many of the men who had arrived with the mine wagons had already stripped to the waist; but one of them, although the sweat was rolling down his back, had not removed a thick felt cap from his head. Scarcely had he noticed this and thought it odd when he registered that the man was lame; his eyes flew to the man's arm and he saw some sort of tattooed device. Without thinking he paused in his work, waiting for the man to turn and show his face, but was suddenly knocked off his feet by a falling bale, not correctly stacked and now dislodged; when he regained his position and looked again, the man had moved off into the stores and did not reappear. Could this possibly be the man he remembered from the Lissa'pathor, the man whose face was maimed by a sword-cut? If so, why should seeing him in Caradriggan fill him with a faint foreboding? That evening Maesrhon lingered near the kitchen door and strolled among the braziers where men were gathered for talk and leisure, but the fellow was nowhere to be seen and eventually he dismissed him from his thoughts.

CHAPTER 31

Greetings from the dead

Later that week, Vorynaas threw open the doors of the great hall in Seth y'n Carad with a welcome to all comers. As usual, his generosity was finely calculated. Ignoring the Spring Feast itself, which fell the following day, his own revels had several purposes. His followers and adherents were rewarded in style, and very publicly, for their loyalty; his wealth and resources were flaunted for all to see; and most importantly, although he kept this motive to himself, those who were feeling the pinch as stores and granaries gradually emptied were able to fill their bellies at his expense in an evening of warmth and conviviality. He sat now at the top table on the dais looking down on the scene, his mouth hidden behind the hand that stroked slowly at his beard. Yes, the moment he had waited and schemed for was very close now. This time, when he called for war to take by force what he desired, they would rise up and follow and he would sweep all before him. Lost in his thoughts, he barely heard the din of voices all around him, or noticed details as his eyes roved idly over the throng below. He and his guests were served directly by the passage that linked the dais with the kitchens by a private side door; but lower down the hall the huge doors which divided off the feasting-chamber from the cooking area had been folded back, and here there was much shoving and pushing as servants thrust through from the bustle of the kitchen with dishes and platters, while in the opposite direction men pressed forward to help themselves from the ale and wine barrels which had been set up. Even though the hall was crammed with long tables full of revellers, it was still a sea of movement as folk passed constantly to and fro from kitchen to table, from friend to friend, out to the privies and back again.

Excluded these days from the family rooms where he had eaten as a child, Maesrhon was accustomed to taking his supper in the kitchen; but tonight when he let himself in through the service door as usual, he was shown out again in a hurry by a red-faced and flustered cook, who told him apologetically that she couldn't be doing with him, he'd have to eat in the hall. Reluctant to claim hospitality at Tellgard, because he would be attending the ancient rites there the following evening at the festival itself, he resigned himself to joining the crowd at the lower end of the hall. He would get a bowl of stew and some bread and find some private corner in which to eat them. As he stood waiting his turn, he felt someone pulling at his sleeve, and looking round saw a youngster wearing the livery of the Seth y'n Carad house-servants.

'Lord Vorynaas wants you to bring another barrel of ale up to the high table, please,' said the boy.

Maesrhon glanced up to the dais, noting Vorynaas' malevolent stare: it was a fair bet that he wouldn't thank the lad for that 'please' if he knew about it. With a sigh he left his place in the line and began to push through to the kitchen so as to gain access to the connecting passage, but was stopped in his tracks by a shout from Vorynaas that rose above the general hubbub, temporarily quieting it slightly.

'Not that way, we can't wait all night! Bring it straight here, and make it quick.'

Vorynaas was pointing at the barrels stacked beside the folding doors, ready for instant replacement when those in use by the floor of the hall ran dry. Maesrhon saw through the trick immediately. Vorynaas, assuming he was not strong enough to lift a full barrel, planned to humiliate him by making him roll it on edge through the crowded hall and struggle with it up the steps to the dais. There they all were, grinning in anticipation: Thaltor on Vorynaas' right, with Valahald next to him; Valestron at the left and next to him Ghentar and then Valafoss. Maesrhon turned, took hold of a cask from the top of the stack and swung it to his shoulder. Never taking his eyes from Vorynaas' face, he walked steadily up the hall, up the steps, and along the table. Behind him the sounds of approval broke out, as those who had noticed the incident banged on the boards in appreciation. Vorynaas glared down, and men returned hastily to their food. He jerked his head at Maesrhon.

'Well don't just stand there, get it set up.'

Maesrhon moved round behind the table and lowered the cask to the floor. He was bending down, settling it onto its chocks after removing the spent barrel, when he heard a new voice, a strange voice: quiet, but somehow arresting, it cut through the confusion of all the other voices.

'Vorynaas!'

Looking up, Maesrhon saw a man standing below the dais right in front of Vorynaas. He was roughly dressed and wearing a felted hat, but like everyone else who was facing him, Maesrhon could stare at nothing but his disfigured face. One eye only shone blue in the lamplight from the ruin left by a sword-cut which had slashed across, taking with it the other eye and part of the nose. The mine-slave! What was he doing here? Time seemed to stand still as the part of Maesrhon's mind that continued to work raced with the thought that it would be easy for anyone to ease their way through such a throng without attracting much notice. The man smiled, a terrible, twisted smile. He lifted his left hand and removed his cap, shaking out hair with the mine-mark branded into it; he kept his right hand hidden, below the level of the dais floor. Then he spoke again.

'Last time we met, you pressed me to eat and drink. Will you not invite me to join your table?'

Beginning to react to the situation, Thaltor and Valafoss started to bluster and shout. 'It's a *vigurt* from the mine! What's he doing here?'

But Vorynaas put out his hand for silence. His eyes were fixed on the man's face. 'Who in the name of the Waste are you?'

316

'Don't you know me yet, Vorynaas? Has my face changed so much?'

With a wild laugh, the man threw down his cap, placed his left hand on the dais and in one move vaulted on to it, landing on his sound leg in front of Vorynaas; Maesrhon saw how strong his shoulders and arms were compared with his lower body and the injured leg.

'Your marriage-cousin has come to join your feast.'

Vorynaas gaped as the man took a slow step forward, his one eye burning with hate. 'Geraswic of Framstock brings you greetings from the dead.'

He waited for a split second, to be sure that Vorynaas had heard the words, had understood them, knew him for who he was, realised what he was going to do; then his right hand moved out from the folds of his tunic, revealing a dress-dagger with a short, wicked blade.

Valestron alone seemed untouched by the shock that kept the rest of them staring in their seats; smirking, he leaned across Ghentar to whisper into Valafoss' ear. 'Numirantoro certainly wasn't too fussy, was she? She'd been behind the cowsheds with this one before she ever met Arymaldur.'

For the briefest moment, the slave's eye flicked to the two of them, then back to Vorynaas; but Maesrhon saw how even as Geraswic hurled himself at Vorynaas, a terrible fury took him as he realised what Valestron had said; in the very act of lunging forward, he changed direction to leap at Valestron instead. But with the lightning reactions of a serving soldier, Valestron threw himself out of harm's way, backwards from the path of the knife-stroke into his own seat; and carried forward by his own momentum, Geraswic buried the razor-sharp blade right to the hilt in Ghentar's throat.

It was only afterwards that Maesrhon realised what a short time had passed. Although an eternity seemed to stretch between Geraswic's first appearance and the time when the fatal blow was struck, in reality it was no more than a few seconds. He stared in disbelief at his brother, the young face still fresh and high-coloured, the eyes open, but bloody froth bubbling from the corner of his mouth, dead between one breath and the next. Ghentar's wine cup had fallen from his hand and the stain was spreading over his clothes to mingle with the blood that welled from the gaping tear in his neck. Maesrhon looked back at Geraswic, who made no attempt to retrieve the knife for use on Vorynaas, but simply stood blankly as if he too could not believe what had happened. No-one except those on the dais had yet realised anything was amiss; then suddenly uproar broke out. Vorynaas began raving incoherently, men were shouting, jumping to their feet; tumult spread rapidly through the hall. Valahald and Thaltor sprang from their seats and ran round the table towards Geraswic who still appeared dazed, even though Vorynaas was now screaming for his death. As Thaltor drew his own dagger, Maesrhon came to his senses. Leaping over the table, scattering food and utensils and sending plates crashing to the floor, he grabbed Geraswic and manhandled him out of Thaltor's path.

'No! Not like that! Arval, Arval!'

Scarcely knowing what he did, Maesrhon shouted above the clamour, amazed to hear the ring of authority in his own voice. Momentarily taken by surprise also, the others paused; but with a blow of his fist that set the broken crocks rattling, Vorynaas began to yell again.

'My son is dead, murdered in front of a thousand witnesses! We need no old fool from Tellgard here: hold this Gwentaran vermin still for me, I will kill him myself!'

He advanced upon Geraswic and Maesrhon, but suddenly the clamour began to falter and die away, heads turning towards the strange silence that spread towards them from the doors of the hall. Relief and astonishment swept over Maesrhon as he saw Arval approaching between the tables, Arval who had never before entered Seth y'n Carad. He could not possibly have heard his desperate cries, so how was it that he came here? He walked calmly towards the struggling group below the dais and put out his arm, moving Geraswic away from Vorynaas. Then he spoke, quietly but clearly.

'This man has taken a life before you all and will now be subject to our laws.'

Vorynaas stepped forward, his face distorted with rage. 'This *slave* has murdered my son! *Murdered my son*! Get out of my way, you meddling pedant, or by my right hand, I swear I will kill you both!'

Arval looked around him steadily. Men stared back, scarcely breathing; some lowered their eyes, unable to meet his gaze.

'Is this a den of savages, or a city of civilised men?' said Arval. 'Geraswic of Framstock will come with me now. There is no possible doubt about his guilt, but he will spend his final night of life in Tellgard as is our law and his right. Vorynaas, only another father can truly understand your loss. But rather than clamouring for blood, you should mourn for Ghentar in a more seemly way; and remember, though you grieve, that you have another son.'

'Him? This cuckoo in the nest, a son to me? *That* for him,' snarled Vorynaas, striking Maesrhon across the face and turning furiously away.

Geraswic's tale

Maesrhon showed no emotion, but his eyes met Arval's briefly.

'Come,' said Arval to Geraswic, and leading the way, with Geraswic stumbling behind like a sleepwalker and Maesrhon bringing up the rear, he turned towards the doors. They passed out of the hall, across the compound, through the gates of Seth y'n Carad and away up the street to Tellgard. Maesrhon looked back as they went. None had attempted to hinder them or to follow them and the streets seemed deserted; the same strange silence that had fallen in the hall attended their echoing footsteps. Questions jostled for space in his mind, emotions battled in turmoil in his heart. How could this man be Geraswic? How did he come to be in Caradriggan? Did Ardeth know what had happened to him? What would he and Arval say to each other? What would Vorynaas do now that Ghentar was dead? *Dead*!

He had still not taken in the stark finality of the fact; the night's events seemed completely unreal, like things seen in a dream.

No word was spoken until they paused in the shadowy porch of the tower door; then Arval turned to Maesrhon. 'Arythalt must have this news broken to him gently. Go across now, tell Merenald what has happened and ask him to speak to his master. He will know best how to deal with the situation.'

For the first time, Geraswic seemed to take notice of his surroundings. He watched Maesrhon walking away from them across the courtyard and then looked back at Arval. 'Arythalt is here? So that is why his house is so neglected.'

'Yes, Valafoss has lived there for many years now. But Arythalt is a sick man, and I fear that the death of his grandson, on top of the other losses he has suffered, may accelerate the decline of his health.'

When Maesrhon returned, Arval began to climb the stairs and then opened a small door on the second landing. In single file they went along a narrow corridor. Maesrhon guessed by its direction that it ran along above the workshops within the thickness of the wall, although he had never been this way before nor seen the small room into which they eventually emerged. It had another door, opposite that by which they entered, but no windows; yet still and utterly silent though it was, secret and enclosed, it had no feeling of close confinement, but rather an air of peace and calm. A small lamp burned, giving off a faint breath of flowers as if from perfumed oil, and in a recess in the wall were two locked caskets. Another niche held high shelves on which rested a crystal flagon and a second, larger lamp wrought of ancient silver. Maesrhon's eyes widened when he noticed it, and Arval smiled very slightly in acknowledgement of the unasked question.

'Yes, we are behind the sanctuary of the hall.' When they were all seated, he turned to Geraswic. 'I assume that it was not your intention to kill the son of Vorynaas.'

An appalling sound broke from Geraswic: part groan of grief, part bitter laugh, it raised the hair on Maeshron's head.

'I came to Caradriggan to take Vorynaas' life as the price of my own, but it seems fate has betrayed me once more. Even the pain I have caused him is as nothing compared with the hurt I have done myself: there is no death he can inflict upon me tomorrow that will be more bitter than the knowledge that I have killed Numirantoro's son.'

'Be assured that I will not permit Vorynaas to prolong your suffering. The condemned of Caradriggan face the arrows of trained marksmen, the end will be swift. But,' added Arval with a glance up at the flagon on its shelf, 'I can ease your death, if you will.'

'What do I care, old man? My life ended long ago, in this very city.' Geraswic leaned forward and dropped his head to his hands, running his fingers into his hair. 'I would have done better to give myself to the blindworms of Na Naastald then, rather than return to blight Ardeth's hopes with barren sorrow. Twice already I have cast his kindness in his face, although not of my own will; but this time... Now my only hope is that he never hears of what I have done today.'

'Does Ardeth not know you were taken captive?' Arval turned in surprise as Maesrhon spoke.

Geraswic's reply was muffled by his hands. 'He may suspect it; I was not the first to disappear. But I left no message or word, he will never know for certain. Day after day, night after night of fading hopes: I brought that on him, a weariness of regret and grief almost like that I myself have suffered.' Suddenly he sat up, his ravaged features contorted still further with a terrible mixture of torment and anger.

'The ruin of my own life is a small thing, to all but me; some mocking destiny must have made the pattern that set the paths of Numirantoro and Vorynaas to cross with mine. But what evil drives Caradward on? You have poisoned the very sky above you, will you spread the darkness still further? Why did you turn from the old ways of friendship and trust? Wasn't it enough to close your borders, to raise barriers between us, to set family against family, friend against friend? Weren't you rich enough, with your lands and your lords and your gold, that you must creep into our fields like a pestilence, killing and enslaving? What did we in Gwent y'm Aryframan ever do, to turn the fury of Caradward upon us?'

A heavy silence fell. Arval rose to his feet and turned away from his companions; with his finger he traced the chasing on the ancient lamp used for the rites, then sighing he began to pace softly to and fro in the tiny sanctuary.

'I have little to offer in explanation, and even less in comfort,' he said. 'I could blame Vorynaas, but that would be too easy; for though his heart may have been a fertile nursery for hate, where did the seed come from that quickened there? Yet he himself is like the kind of pernicious weed that every farmer dreads, the kind that scatters its myriad fruits broadcast to germinate wherever they fall; for his greed and ambition, his lies and schemes, have taken root in other men's minds to grow and flourish and spread again. Indeed it sometimes seems to me that the seedlings of evil spring up faster, the more we try to cut them back. And Geraswic, some here *have* tried: not all in Caradward have followed Vorynaas, or been duped by him. But we must all share some of the blame; for we have failed to prevent him, and cannot now succeed in wholly thwarting what may follow.' Arval stood motionless for a moment, staring sightlessly into the darkness beyond the lamplight. Then, almost as if he felt a touch, he turned back to see Maesrhon watching him intently.

'However,' he continued, holding that golden gaze from the depths of his own fathomless dark eyes, 'there is always hope, if men know where to look for it. Even now, we seek guidance in our search. But Vorynaas is a skilled manipulator of men; he has played upon their prejudice and fears, blaming Gwent y'm Aryframan for disasters such as the spring sickness many years ago, and making it the scapegoat for more recent misfortune of our own causing. I fear he may point to tonight's events as the clinching evidence in his argument.' Arval dropped his gaze and pushed his hands into his sleeves as if forcing himself not to tremble.

'Your sorrow is not a small thing to me, Geraswic,' he said, sitting down again beside him. 'Would it comfort you to know what Numirantoro said to me, when she told me of you, and her years in Salfgard? "*I wish I could have stayed, I wish I had never come back here.*"'

'No. There is no comfort you can bring me; but then, there is none that I look for.' Geraswic seemed to withdraw into himself, staring blankly at the floor and though he spoke aloud, his words were so quiet and pensive it was almost as though he was alone.

'Our firstborn son would have been Cunorcar, named for my father. It was always like that in my family, Geraswic and Cunorcar in turn, all down the generations. But right from the beginning I feared it would never be and here in Caradriggan I found out the reason. Vorynaas took her from me against her will, but there was another before whom both he and I were as powerless as Numirantoro.' He lifted his head and found a pair of amber eyes upon him. 'I think that Maesrhon cannot be the true name of one whose face and bearing so recalls Arymaldur.'

'You have seen Arymaldur?' exclaimed Arval, urgency leaping into his voice. 'When was this?'

Geraswic answered without taking his gaze from Maesrhon's face. 'Yes, indeed. As I sat beside Numirantoro at the fountain he came walking towards us up the street and I saw how she had no eyes for the things of this world when she looked on him. But I had seen him once before, long before that day, and far away from here.'

Maesrhon's eyes flew to Arval. 'But I thought...' He turned back to Geraswic, frowning. 'Far from here! You saw him in Gwent y'm Aryframan, then?'

'No, not there.' Geraswic laughed briefly. 'You failed to recognise me in the Lissa'pathor, but am I right that you knew who pursued you, the day you fled from me into the wilderness? Yes, I thought you had realised. When I came closer, I saw Numirantoro in your features and understood in my turn who you were. You are not so like her, now. Will you not tell me your true name, while there is still time?'

Wondering where this was leading, Maesrhon answered slowly. 'My workmates sometimes call me Alfossig, and Maesrhon is the name Vorynaas gave me at my birth. But my true name is Artorynas, though none know it or have ever used it except Lord Arval the Earthwise.'

A bitter smile twisted on Geraswic's lips when he saw the trust and loyalty in Maesrhon's eyes as he looked at Arval. 'You are fortunate to know friendship and love. Well, man of the sun, born of the star, cast your mind back to that day we spoke of. Under the birches beside the lake in that little upland dale, there once I spoke with Numirantoro. The flowers that bloom there now grow in memory of that time; they have spread year by year until they fill the whole hillside. When I first set them, to mark the place where we had stood, I climbed up and looked out on the wilderness; and what I saw gave form to the foreboding of sorrow that already shadowed my heart. I see that you know what I speak of. Yes, I saw Arymaldur as he came out of the north.'

'The north!'

'Yes; alone, untouched and untroubled by Na Caarst as one of the As-Geg'rastigan would be. I watched him to see where he would go, and he passed from the wilderness into the foothills of the Somllichan Torward.'

'How long ago was this?' asked Arval.

'It was in the autumn of the year before the spring sickness; about eighteen months before I arrived in Caradriggan to discover Numirantoro not two weeks wed to Vorynaas.' Arval and Maesrhon heard the pain seep back into Geraswic's voice. 'Failure has haunted me: I lost Numirantoro, I disappointed Ardeth's hopes, I could not bring back my warning to Framstock, I have not even succeeded in my revenge on Vorynaas. My life has been worthless.'

'You are wrong to think any man's life is worthless. Your own has been blighted, and I cannot right the wrongs that have been done to you, or remove the causes of your pain. But you should remember with pride how you helped others, how you passed on your skills to them, how Ardeth and Fosseiro loved and trusted you.' Arval spoke forcefully, but when Geraswic only shook his head, he stood up and took the crystal flagon down from its shelf. 'This spirit has a potency the corrupt rulers of this land cannot guess at. Let it merely moisten your lips, it will ease your pain.'

'I told you, no. I know you mean well; I appreciate your mercy. But I have walked through the world as a dead man these twenty years and more. All I care for is that in a few more hours I need no longer drag myself from day to day.'

'Well, before that hour strikes, there is a thing you should know.' Arval's voice trembled slightly and Maesrhon, who knew him so well, would almost have said it shook with elation. 'You have solved a riddle which has thwarted me for too long. What you tell us of Arymaldur gives us the answer I have sought: the direction of the quest that draws near. Artorynas will journey to the north in search of hope for men; and if he succeeds, your name and Numirantoro's will be always remembered with his.'

Geraswic made no reply, merely shrugging hopelessly. Maesrhon's heart wept for him; he wanted desperately to bring him some final shred of comfort. He stared down at his hands, hesitating, not sure whether when he spoke he had found the right words.

'Geraswic, there is something I want to say to you. It must be a bitter thing for you, that I even exist. It is bitter for me that I never knew my mother, I have not even one memory of her. But everyone I care about who knew her speaks of her with love. I saw what happened, there in the hall. Your aim was spoiled when you turned from Vorynaas to punish Valestron for his filthy taunts. It was your loyalty to Numirantoro that brought you to death, and I will remember this, and also how you loved her.'

The damage to his features made Geraswic's expression hard to read, especially when his one good eye was dull and blank. But his words had a hollow, weary tone as heaviness dragged at his voice.

'A final failure, since Valestron lives still, with Vorynaas. But you tell me his archers do not miss their mark, so the end will not be long delayed, now. Let it all be over, and soon.'

North, but not yet

Without Maesrhon to cling to, Arval thought that Arythalt might very well not have survived the shock of Ghentar's murder. Merenald hovered constantly, attentive and solicitous, begging him to eat and drink, trying to make him take an interest in life again; Arval and his medical staff tended him with concern; but at first it seemed that their efforts would be in vain. For days Arythalt was prostrated by grief, unable to leave his bed, racked with tears. It seemed to Maesrhon that his grandfather was tormented by remorse as well as sorrow: his broken mutterings hinted that he blamed himself for past events, but it was difficult to be sure when sometimes he appeared not even to recognise his grandson. He lay and wept, or sat shivering in his chair, rocking to and fro while murmuring Salfronardo's name; then he would hold on tightly to Maeshron's arm, or stroke his hair and talk to him as if he thought he saw Numirantoro. But Arval insisted that Maesrhon's presence would do him good, so as the days went by he sat with him for hours on end. He remained in Tellgard when men came for Geraswic, being present neither when Geraswic faced his death nor when the funeral rites were held for Ghentar. When he snatched a bite to eat in the small hall at mid-day, he gathered from the talk that there had been more than two deaths in Seth y'n Carad. In the renewed commotion after Arval and he had escorted Geraswic from the feasting chamber, Vorynaas' fury had become uncontrollable. They had tried to restrain him, at least until the body of his son was composed and removed from the hall, but he had lashed out, spreading havoc among those closest to him; and several of his servants and followers had fallen at his hand while the blood still dripped from Ghentar's throat to the table and his eyes stared sightlessly down on the mayhem below.

Maesrhon was burning to talk to Arval privately about what Geraswic had told them, but they were never alone for long enough while Arythalt wasted in decline and Maesrhon was sleeping on a pallet in Merenald's room so as to be available during the night if necessary and to allow the other man to take some rest. Then after almost two weeks, there came a day when Arythalt was more lucid. He asked for the fire to be built up and called for mulled wine; when Merenald gently insisted that he must eat something first, he forced down a little broth with some bread. They helped him to dress, and settled him beside the hearth. Arythalt looked about him, and beckoned Maesrhon over. The old man's eyes were sunk in a face that was more gaunt than ever, and his voice was weak, but his wishes were clear.

'I want to talk to Forgard. Have someone take a message to ask him if he will come to me here.'

Wondering very much what lay behind this request, Maesrhon was nevertheless greatly relieved to see Arythalt taking some interest in life again.

'I'm sure he will be pleased to talk to you, grandfather. I'll go round to his house myself and tell him you would like to see him.'

Having delivered his message, and received the assurance that Forgard would set out within the hour, Maesrhon made haste back to Tellgard, hurrying along side streets and alleys in the hope of avoiding anyone from Seth y'n Carad. He had not been back there, since it had all happened; surely he could never go back, now. Vorynaas would never tolerate his presence, even in some lowly capacity in the yards, now that Ghentar was dead. A little shiver of apprehension ran over Maesrhon's skin. It was as certain as anything could be, that Vorynaas would not be content with merely having Geraswic put to death. His whole life had been devoted to his relentless ambition for himself and for Ghentar after him. With his son snatched away, what would he do now? Maesrhon felt sure that black days and evil deeds lay ahead; should he not set off on his quest without delay? He walked faster, almost breaking into a run. If Forgard was going to visit Arythalt, that meant he would be free for the rest of the morning, at least; if only he could find Arval, now was their chance to talk. He sprang up the worn stone steps two and three at a time and knocked softly at Arval's study door, drawing a breath of relief when he heard a voice bidding him enter.

'I've just returned from Forgard's house: he's on his way to talk to my grandfather, so I have come straight to you. Arval, what must we do now?'

'Tell me first what you know of the raiding into Gwent y'm Aryframan, and how you know it.'

Briefly Maesrhon outlined how he had begun to suspect something of the kind, had actually seen Geraswic previously in the Lissa'pathor and had had his suspicions confirmed during his second stint of service with the patrols.

'Why have you not mentioned this to me before?'

'Well, I suppose for two reasons. Partly because I still clung to the hope that somehow I could be wrong; and partly because I was unwilling to add to the burdens you already carry, although I also thought it likely that you knew without my telling. But, in case you didn't, and to make sure that you would hear of it if anything… if I… if for any reason I wasn't able to tell you myself, I told Heretellar what I knew and suspected.'

'Heretellar!' After a moment or two of thought, Arval's deep-set eyes crinkled in a smile. 'And he will have said nothing to his father, because he deals as gently with Forgard as you do with me, little son. You should not be so concerned, *Is-torar*, after what I have told you of myself. Remember when you were ten years old, how I promised you I would still be here when you returned from Salfgard? I promise you now, I have the strength, and the means if strength should fail, to endure to the end: provided the end is not too long delayed. But the end is coming… if we can only succeed in time…' He broke off, his words overtaken by his speed of thought.

Maesrhon waited for a moment or two, but when it seemed that Arval was not going to continue, he was unable to contain himself longer.

'You think then that my grandfather's wish to speak with Forgard has nothing to do with what I told Heretellar? But why should he want to see him now, of all times? He only dragged himself from his bed this morning; he is so spent with grief he looks like a man who will scarcely last through the day, yet he asks to talk to someone with whom by all accounts he has never been on particularly friendly terms.'

'It is not only illness and sorrow that eats at Arythalt. He is a man consumed by regret and guilt. He blames himself for being deluded by Vorynaas, for not seeing him in his true colours from the start, for compelling his daughter into marriage with him, for closing his eyes to the truth even after he had realised his error.' Arval sighed. 'These are not guesses, I have heard all this from Arythalt himself, both privately and even in council. He spoke openly, and bravely too, to Tell'Ethronad before your foster-years, acknowledging what he views as his faults. I think he wants to see Forgard now because he is the only person still alive with whom he can retract past deeds and words. Poor Arythalt! He torments himself with the thought that if only he had, or had not, done this or that, then how different things would be today. And in a way he is right, but his reasoning is flawed; or at least, he does not see what I see: which is that today we have you, who would never have been born, if Arythalt could turn back time.'

'Which brings me back to what I first asked: what must we do now? Should I not leave without further delay, now that we know I must travel north?'

'Soon, yes, but not immediately. This will be a journey like no other, following a road into the unknown. We must take at least some thought for its length, both in distance and time; try at least to make what preparations we can to ensure your safety, whether you succeed in the quest or not; consider where in the north to aim for and how to keep secret both the reason for and the direction of your going. Vorynaas will try to prevent you leaving, and if he fails in that, he will pursue you. You will be unable to go openly through Caradward or the Lissa'pathor; you cannot walk blindly into the wilderness; and you will not be able to cross into Gwent y'm Aryframan.'

The frown lines deepened between Maesrhon's eyes. 'I know that Vorynaas wants me dead, although somehow I'm sure that it will not be his hand that takes my life, nor will his commands have power to thwart my quest. But why do you say that I cannot travel north through Gwent y'm Aryframan? After what Geraswic told us, this seemed to me the best way to pick up the trail of what I seek. And I have the skill to pass the border undetected.'

'I do not doubt it, *Is-torar*. But though you have heeded Geraswic's words, you forget his deeds. Gwent y'm Aryframan will be engulfed by war long before you are ready to leave Caradriggan.'

Maesrhon stared at Arval, horrified. He felt sick. 'But I thought... last autumn, when Vorynaas pressed for war, and was voted down... You mean Tell'Ethronad will do what he wants, now? Because of Ghentar?'

'Not so much that, although it will give him an extra lever; but more because everyone has a reason to vote with him now. Even when he was a young man, Vorynaas never missed an opportunity to speak against Gwent y'm Aryframan, although it was subtly done because he was also determined to obtain your grandfather's favour – and remember that Arythalt was married to the daughter of a leading family from Framstock. Yet a poisoned hint here and there will often do more harm than outright hostility, and in any case Thaltor and Valafoss were always ready to provide the bluster and aggression that both backed Vorynaas up and also made his own attitude seem more reasonable. I cannot see that there was ever any basis in experience for the original prejudice, but for many years now a personal enmity, all the more potent for being unspoken, has fed his obsession. While he lived among us, Arymaldur became the leader of those who stood in Vorynaas' way, and was therefore the main focus of his hate even before he suspected that your mother loved him. Arymaldur was known to have reached the city by the northward road, and for this reason, as well as for his policy of friendship and alliance, Vorynaas insisted that he had been sent here from Gwent y'm Aryframan, or at least must have come to us with their knowledge and backing. And then there was Numirantoro.' Arval sighed.

'I have shown you how it was with Numirantoro and Arymaldur: do you think a mind like Vorynaas' could ever begin to understand? He deludes himself that he rid us of Arymaldur, but this has never been enough for him. He knows that Valestron and others of his associates suspect, and laugh at him behind his back; and as you have grown, and Arymaldur is there to see in your face and bearing, so he torments himself with the thought that all men call him cuckold. His pride will not let him speak of this, or even acknowledge it: and so his desire for revenge has burned itself ever deeper into his heart. He has sought your death, but you live still; and now Ghentar has been taken from him. And on top of all this, the Gwentarans have played into his hands. I do wonder very much what prompted Val'Arad to stop all sale of corn to Caradward after last year's harvest. It occurs to me that they may have discovered what you tell me of the slave-raiding. Do you think this is possible?'

'How could it be? None in Gwent y'm Aryframan suspected it while I was still living there, though we know now it had begun even then. Heretellar said no word had reached Meremvor from his family, and I have told no-one but him and yourself. Even here, it must be a well-guarded secret: the council have never been informed, have they?'

'No, but if a stray word reached your ears, even within the military, there is always the possibility of another loose tongue wagging. But be that as it may, the grain shortage has caused widespread hardship among us. Vorynaas knew he had only to wait, when Tell'Ethronad drew back from his warmongering in the autumn. Men have had time to think, as they tighten their belts month by month. If we are hungry now, runs the whisper, how will we feel after another half-year of scrimping, with no prospect of harvest to fill the empty stores? Surely, men reason, surely we should act now, while we still have the strength to take what we need? I think the council would vote to follow Vorynaas now even if Ghentar had not been killed. I have reported the truth to Tell'Ethronad, while you tended Arythalt: that Geraswic acted without accomplices, that his motive was vengeance for what he had suffered, that his target was Vorynaas alone; but I fear this will make no difference. The fact remains that Vorynaas' heir was murdered at the hands of a Gwentaran. Now that the funeral rites are over, Vorynaas has called another meeting of the council and he will use the death of his son to rouse them in war against our neighbours and kin.'

For the third time that day, Maesrhon appealed to Arval. 'What must we do?'

'We will do again what we have done before: we will stand up for what is right, and speak against him. I have no hope that this time we can prevent the fools from bringing disaster on themselves as they wreak ruin on others, but we must make our voices heard on behalf of all those who cannot or dare not speak out. And then I will stay here, so that the doors of Tellgard stay open and its work continues; but I will look to the north and count the days until you return to bring us hope once more.'

Sons-before-the-law

Before the week was out, it all befell in council as Arval had foreboded. The chamber was so crowded that not all had a chair; many were forced to stand two and three deep behind those seated at the huge, heavy table. Everyone knew that great matters were afoot and men who normally would only have attended perhaps once in a year had made the effort to come to Caradriggan. Even Arythalt was there, having insisted on being brought in his litter; and standing together next to those who had journeyed up from the south were all the *sigitsaran* who were members of Tell'Ethronad: Maesrhon had overheard Thaltor and Valestron exchanging derogatory remarks on the subject of Outlanders. He glanced around the handsome room with its high, elegant windows and was ashamed to think of the wise men and measured debates the old walls must once have looked down upon. Today's proceedings could scarcely claim the name of debate, consisting as they did mainly of ranting from Vorynaas and an undignified scramble by most of the delegates to be the first to endorse his demands. Having obtained, by an overwhelming majority, the backing he wanted, Vorynaas had called upon Valestron to outline the situation with regard to troops, supplies and strategy. So this was what all the extra activity at the mine and in Seth y'n Carad had been leading up to, thought Maesrhon dully. Arval had been right, the plans had all long been laid; Ghentar's death had simply served to tip the scales. He felt a sudden pang of regret for his brother, whose life had been so short, and so brutally ended. It occurred to Maesrhon now that Ghentar had never really seemed happy, in spite of all the pampering and privilege he had enjoyed; but his attention was suddenly diverted by a stir at the top of the room as Valafoss moved to stand before Vorynaas with Valahald and Heranar behind him.

'I call upon the members of Tell'Ethronad to be the witnesses of my words,' began Valafoss, pausing to make sure everyone was listening. 'Lord Vorynaas, as always, you put the interests of Caradward first, before you think of yourself. You have taken up the burden of leadership once more, allowing yourself no time for private grief. As a father, I can imagine only too clearly the sorrow you must feel, and it is as a father that I speak now. Although I know that nothing and no-one can take the place of Ghentar, let me offer you my own sons.' Turning, he took their hands and ushered them forward.

'Valahald and Heranar shall be sons rather to you, than to me, from now on; let their duty and service be to you as to a father. Use them as you will, I yield my first place in their hearts readily to you, as I acknowledge your first place among us all.'

He stood back a pace, and the two young men both sank on one knee before Vorynaas.

For a moment there was a buzz of muttering as astonishment swept the room. Maesrhon, watching closely, saw from the expression on the faces of Thaltor and Valestron that they were surprised by this move and did not welcome it. He saw Valafoss wipe his forehead, sweating not just from overweight but from nervousness at how his gesture would be received. He noted the difference in the brothers' stance. Heranar, with his sandy colouring, was blushing in embarrassment, no doubt wishing himself anywhere but here with all these eyes upon him. Valahald in contrast had knelt with a certain flamboyance and had a confident tilt to his head. Yes, thought Maesrhon, there is a man who senses another door of opportunity opening: whatever the reason for his demotion, it did not last long. Then he looked at Vorynaas, who was leaning on an elbow stroking his beard, gazing intently from Valafoss to the two brothers; his expression was wary but with more than a hint of knowing cynicism as his eyes fell on Valahald. As the murmur of comment died away, Vorynaas sat up straighter in his seat.

'Valafoss, old friend,' he said, 'never fear that I might misinterpret your gesture of support. You may be sure that I know the value of your generosity.'

Wiping his brow again, Valafoss visibly relaxed, but Maesrhon noticed Haartell and Valestron exchanging smirks: the ambiguity had not been lost on them. Vorynaas paused, waiting until the silence became uncomfortable. His dark eyes passed over the many faces turned towards him and came to rest on Maesrhon. A dangerous, cruel little smile touched his lips as he began to speak again.

'I was reminded not so long ago, while my heir lay dead before me – butchered by a Gwentaran! – that I have another son. Since this is so, perhaps I should not yet declare myself a father to Valahald and Heranar. But is it so? There he stands. He has defied me again today in council. He has ignored my warning, voted with my enemies, intervened to save his brother's killer from my wrath. Let this son of mine tell me now: will he take upon himself Ghentar's duty after all, will he follow me to Gwent y'm Aryframan?'

Every head turned towards Maesrhon. He took a step forward to stand beside Arval's chair, placing his hand on its high, carved back.

'I came between you and Geraswic to prevent you breaking the law of your own land. Why do you speak of enemies? Our law says that all members of Tell'Ethronad are equal; each man's vote is of equal worth, and I have told you before that I would vote for what I believe to be right. As for Ghentar, from my earliest days we have both known that his place in your heart would never be shared or given up to me. But to answer your final question: yes, I am willing to go to Gwent y'm Aryframan.'

Several of those present cried out in astonishment, but the colour rose in Vorynaas' face as Maesrhon continued.

'I will go, if I may go in peace. Let me go to Framstock, to treat with Val'Arad; let me go to Salfgard, to speak once more with Ardeth my mother's uncle. If I may go with words rather than weapons, then I will go gladly. But there is no threat you can make that will persuade me to go with war.'

There was a moment or two of complete silence, then a quiet sound began and grew in volume as men found the courage to applaud Maesrhon's stance in the traditional way of Tell'Ethronad, giving the old, understated sign of approval that had rarely been heard in recent years when raised voices and dramatic posturing had become more usual. The curiously dry, strange little drumming noise welled up in the room as Forgard and Heretellar, Arythalt and Issigitsar, Rhostellat and Poenmorcar, Arval and Merenald and no few others tapped on the edge of the great table; the Outlanders and some of the men who had not found seats pushed forward between the chairs in order that they too might reach the polished wooden surface. But soon the sound faltered and died away, men exchanging glances, moving back again, their hands in their sleeves, as Vorynaas rose glaring to his feet, his eyes hot with anger. When he spoke, they could hear how his voice shook with the rage that gathered in his throat.

'Oh, fine words! But do not be seduced by their sound, think of their substance! He will go before Val'Arad, will he, he will negotiate on our behalf? What arrogance! From Framstock we have endured sickness, insults, famine: down that very road have travelled incomers to take our substance, troublemakers to disturb our council, even an assassin to murder my son; yet he will go that way to talk with the ringleaders of these peasants. What treachery! Listen to me, you lover of Gwentarans, and think carefully before you answer. I warned you not to defy me again, but you have done so. You have spoken insolently to me before this assembly, and thought fit to lecture me on its procedures. However, I give you one last chance. You are no longer in military service, but you are my second son, and all the second sons of Caradward have been called to arms today. This council summons you to stand forth for your country; will you stay or go?'

'I have already given you my answer. I will not go.'

'Then you declare yourself a coward and a traitor before us all. When we return, we will deal with you accordingly.'

'I will not take the name of traitor from you, or any man here. Nor am I afraid to face the consequences of my action.'

Vorynaas beat on the table before him with his clenched fist, his voice rising to match his temper. 'We'll see how brave you are when the day comes! By my right hand, I will make you regret that you refused to follow your father!'

'No doubt there will be many things I shall regret before death takes me, but I assure you that refusal to follow my father will not be among them.'

Vorynaas had been on the point of turning away in contempt, but at this he seemed to freeze. Behind him, Valestron lifted an eyebrow at Thaltor, and a rustle ran round the chamber as men drew in their breath or moved sharply, wondering if a double meaning lay hidden in Maesrhon's words. Vorynaas gripped the edge of the table, his knuckles white, as if fighting to master himself. Then with a fierce stare that challenged any man to speak at his peril, he put a hand out to the shoulders of Valahald and Heranar and with a swirl of his robes made for the door, pushing them before him, and his henchmen and supporters followed; without looking back they pressed forward on the fatal path they had chosen and the room emptied as swiftly as water pouring from a breach in a dam, leaving behind Maesrhon with Arval and the small group of those who still stood beside them.

CHAPTER 32

Preparations

'No, I need the time to prepare and plan. My mind must be clear and free of doubt when I go. And I want no suspicion of helping me to light upon anyone; if I disappear while Vorynaas is away, he would say I must have had fellow-conspirators.'

'And that you were afraid to face him.'

'He has already called me a coward, but I don't care about that. He knows I'm not afraid of him, that's one of the things that's always infuriated him about me.'

Maesrhon and Arval were talking one evening in Tellgard; there were books and rolled-up maps on the table where Arval sat, and Maesrhon knelt in a corner of the room, methodically checking and packing tools and equipment as they spoke together. He looked up, shaking the hair out of his eyes.

'What worries me is what he might do to you. He'll be certain that you can tell him where I've gone.'

'Artorynas.' There was a subtle change in Arval's voice as he spoke Maesrhon's true name. 'Neither Vorynaas nor any other man in Caradriggan can hurt me. But be careful for your other friends. You are being watched.'

As he heard the authority in Arval's tones, a thrill ran through Maesrhon as he realised now that he too possessed something of the same power within himself, some legacy of the As-Geg'rastigan. He had heard it in his own voice on the night of Ghentar's death, and he felt it now, buoying him up, steadying him when otherwise he would have trembled at the task facing him.

'I know. That's one of the reasons I am spending as much time as I can at Tellgard: there's nothing new for them to notice in that. It's fortunate that everything except my provisions has already been quietly gathered together here and kept secure, mainly thanks to Heretellar and Isteddar. And thanks also to my grandfather's money, of course. Thaltor's spies can lurk at street corners all they like to note my comings and goings from Tellgard, but they can't see through the stones to watch what I do within the safety of its walls.'

He busied himself once more with his preparations, and for a while Arval watched him in silence. He was working his way along the length of two broad leather straps that were sewn with a series of loops and pouches. Arval remembered sitting beside Maesrhon in the courtyard on the day he had made these – the day he had asked if Arval was his father. Now he was carefully storing small items in their special places along the straps: fishhooks, thongs, a whetstone, many other pieces of equipment selected for their use in sustaining life. The lamplight sparked briefly on a set of needles as Maesrhon fitted them into a tiny bone container before placing this in turn into its own pocket on the strap. On the floor beside him lay a belt-pouch, already packed and its contents double-checked; a spearhead and various other tools in their own leather holsters, including the knife Ardeth had made for him; some larger objects awaiting stowage in his pack; and a neat pile of folded clothes. The thigh-pockets in the breeches were already filled with lightweight survival equipment in water-tight wrapping, and the throwing-knives which, like many other small items, had come from Sigitsinen's family business in Heranwark, were secure in their holders on the side of the boots. Finishing with the straps, Maesrhon arranged everything carefully in sequence along the wall and then, getting to his feet, he lifted a bale of fabric from the corner where it had lain. It gave off a rather rank, pungent smell as it was unfolded; glancing up at Arval, Maesrhon smiled apologetically.

'Sorry about the smell, it's the proofing. Are you sure you wouldn't rather I took this somewhere else to assemble?'

'No, it's all right. Is this another tip from Torald?'

'Well, yes and no,' said Maesrhon, now fitting slender metal rods down tubes which were sewn into the fabric for them. 'I learnt how to use proofing from him, and worked with Ardeth to develop the most effective mixture, but the fabric is something I found out about on one of my visits to Staran y'n Forgarad. We tend to think of the *sigitsaran* as a people of the warm, dry south only, but some of the Outlanders roam much further west and have ties of trade and kin with others who live in the Haarnoutan, the wetlands south of Gwent y'm Aryframan. There's a marsh plant that they gather for its fibres; when they're teased out and dried, they weave them into fabric that's much stronger than cloth and has its own natural water-resistance. When the proofing's worked into it, it's almost completely impervious, and a good wind-blocker as well – see how I've used it for my hood, too? And it's light in weight, which is one of the most important points to consider. Everything I take has to justify its inclusion, preferably twice over, and this is my own design: now it's a shelter, but fold it like this and fasten it here, here and here, and there's my pack!'

With that, Maesrhon began putting into it some of the bundles lying ready on the floor.

'One might almost imagine that you had always known that this journey lay before you, *Is-torar*,' said Arval.

Leaning his pack up against the wall, Maesrhon turned to look at the old man. 'Yes,' he said slowly, 'it's a strange thing, but all my life I have felt that the north called to me, although I never knew why. It seems to me now that I have been preparing for this quest for as long as I can remember. Anyway,' he continued more briskly, moving to sit across from Arval at the table, 'that's everything ready now, except the perishable stores.'

'You have some food already packed, though,' said Arval.

'Oh yes, I have basic provisions, and the tools that will enable me to get more, stored separately in four survival kits so as to minimise the risk of losing everything if I should meet with an accident. And they are already packed, in case I have to leave suddenly for any reason, without time for further preparation. But if all goes well, later I'll collect meal and other staples. It will seem as if I make the purchases for Tellgard, but I'll use more of Arythalt's silver. Meantime I will work for my keep at the *Sword and Stars* in the mornings, so that I can eat there at mid-day; and at evening I will consult with you so that your wisdom can guide me on my way when the time comes.' He glanced at the maps strewn across the table. 'How much easier it would have been if I could have started from Salfgard! Now I have a long road to tread before I even begin to pick up the trail. And then I think I must strike out for Rihannad Ennar.'

Arval smoothed out a sheet of parchment and held it flat with his hands. 'The Nine Dales? Yes, probably. But where they lie, and whether men still live there, maps do not show and I cannot say.' His finger traced a path northward through Caradward, into the forest, beyond Maesaldron to the wilderness, and out beyond Na Caarst, on into a vague indication of mountains and a guess of vast distances where the mapmaker's knowledge had given way to fancy. He lifted his hands and the parchment sprang back into a roll.

'Every step of your way is likely to be both long and hard, and it must all be trodden twice if you find what we seek.'

Fitting the roll back into its case, Maesrhon shook his head with a smile. 'I will return, even if empty-handed. I will not leave you to face the darkness alone, Lord Arval.'

'Well, well, we're running ahead of ourselves here,' said Arval slightly gruffly to hide the emotion he felt. 'We have to get you safely out of Caradriggan first. If you're determined to wait until Vorynaas returns from Gwent y'm Aryframan, how long would you say that will be?'

Into Maesrhon's memory came pictures of the day the invading force had set out, and his smile faded as he remembered the shame and horror he had felt.

'Probably before the month of midsummer is out. They had surprise on their side; I think they will have met very little resistance.'

A heavy silence fell as Maesrhon tried hard not to imagine what might even now be happening across the border, and Arval scoured his mind for all the lore he could recall of Rihannad Ennar.

Fatal tidings

The long twilight of midsummer lay over Salfgard, a soft, blue evening with stars overhead and a lingering glow in the west. Mag'rantor and Ardeth paused in their leisurely progress, stopping to savour the moment in companionable silence. Ardeth had formed the habit of taking a stroll before rest and Mag'rantor very often accompanied him, sitting beside him now on a rough-hewn wooden seat. A low bank rose behind them, giving back the day in a breath of warm flower-scents. Stretching his legs out into the path, Ardeth leaned back with his hands behind his head.

'You know, I think this is my favourite time of year.'

Mag'rantor laughed quietly. 'You say that about every season.'

Ardeth chuckled but made no further reply; after a moment he rummaged in his pocket, took out the little robin carving and began absently turning it over and over in his fingers. Mag'rantor wondered what he was thinking about. The loss of Geraswic had hit Ardeth hard: he had said very little, but Fosseiro had confided to Mag'rantor how anxious she was about him. He had been aged by the long wait for any news of what had happened to Geraswic, the gradually fading likelihood that he would ever return; the strain had taken its toll. Mag'rantor thought that Ardeth would have never quite given up hope, had it not been for that fellow who said he worked for Heretellar. It was strange, really. After refusing stubbornly for so long to accept that Geraswic was lost, Ardeth had finally decided to face reality and had made Mag'rantor and Gillis his heirs, the one in Salfgard and the other at Framstock, and at the very meeting of Val'Arad where the change had been recorded and ratified, they had been stunned to hear that the Caradwardans had betrayed the fragile renewal of friendship by raiding for slaves. It still seemed barely credible to Mag'rantor, but the informant had risked his life to warn them, and claimed to have found out by overhearing no less a person than Maesrhon telling Heretellar. Others had also been inclined to scepticism, especially when the witness admitted under questioning that he had heard only a part of the conversation between Heretellar and Maesrhon; but Mag'rantor was not the only member of the council who remembered these two young men from their foster-years, and reluctantly Val'Arad had been forced to acknowledge that they at least were trustworthy: if they believed the story, it must be true. No need to wonder after that what had happened to Geraswic. Ardeth's had been the loudest voice calling for reprisals, and among the first to vote for the ending of the corn trade; Mag'rantor had never seen him so angry. Although how, thought Mag'rantor, as he had wondered many times before, how on earth had the Caradwardans managed to do their evil work without being detected?

Ardeth broke in on Mag'rantor's reverie with a belated reply. 'It's because the world is so beautiful, so lovely, so… I can't find the right words. How fortunate are the Starborn, if it's true they need never leave it.' There was another long silence and then Ardeth said, 'You know, Mag'rantor, I've been a very lucky man.'

Mag'rantor turned towards him in the gloaming, secretly amazed. Lucky? Childless, bereft of his sister whose own daughter was dead and her sons in turn lost to him, his chosen heir snatched away?

'I've known sorrow and loss, yes; but all those I loved have loved me in return: no man can take that from me. And I've spent all my days in the place I love best in the world, with the woman I have loved from childhood by my side. Happiness like that is beyond price, and a blessing which too few ever know.' Ardeth stood up and leaned for a moment on his stick. He looked slowly round at the familiar fields and trees now blending with the dusk, and took a deep breath.

'Well, we'd better get back I suppose.'

They had taken barely half a dozen steps when Mag'rantor stopped, listening. 'Somebody's riding late this evening.'

'I can't hear anything… Wait, I hear now.' Ardeth turned towards the sound, exasperation in his voice. 'Can anyone explain to me why Cunoreth has to ride like a madman? If that's one of my horses he's taken out, he'll get the rough edge of my tongue when I see him.'

'That's not Cunoreth. I saw him in the village, he said he was going to walk down for a chat with Fosseiro.' The sound was getting louder, the hoofbeats nearer in a wild, headlong gallop. Mag'rantor felt suddenly afraid; he heard it in his voice when he spoke again. 'And anyway, Cunoreth wouldn't… no-one would risk his neck by riding like that in the dark without need… Something must have happened.'

He ran towards the road and Ardeth, forgotten for the moment, put out his hand and gripped the fence, catching his breath as the pain began in his chest.

'Hey! Who is it? What's the big hurry?' Mag'rantor shouted as the horse swept up the track from the valley.

A cloud of dust billowed away as the hooves skidded to a stop, and the rider slid to the ground.

'Over here,' called Mag'rantor, his nose detecting something over the smell of horse and sweat, something more than dirt and leather: something wrong. 'Who are you? By the Starborn! Ardeth, it's Ethanur!' he shouted over his shoulder towards the dark shape of the old fellow now leaning heavily against the fence. He turned back to the rider. 'Since when have you been able to ride like that? Come over here, Ardeth and I were just on our way home.'

He put his hand out to Ethanur and snatched it back again. Even in the deepening dusk he could see the dark stain on it, feel the stickiness: now he knew what it was he could smell.

'You're hurt! What's happened?'

'That's nothing, it's just started bleeding again because of the riding. No, never mind that, listen!' Ethanur cut across Mag'rantor as

344

he made to speak again. 'I've come to warn you. I gave them the slip but they're after me, we've not got much time. May the Waste take them!'

He paused, fighting to get his breath back, brushing at the strands of sweaty hair that were stuck to his dirt-streaked face, waving aside Mag'rantor's stammered questions.

'The Caradwardans, man, that's what I'm telling you! I don't know how they did it; we got no warning. Suddenly they were at the gates of every village; their army roared up to Framstock like a flood, we'd no time to organise properly. We tried to hold the bridge, but it was hopeless. That's when I was hurt, and Rossanell was killed.' He laughed rather wildly. 'Imagine Rossanell being sober enough to even find a sword! But at least he tried.'

'What about Gillis?'

'Gillis was already dead by then. The streets are choked with dead, trampled by the stampede to get away. But those bastards from Caradward are rounding them up, looting, taking prisoners… and they're coming this way. They'll likely be at Rihannark by now, we've got to get a move on!' Suddenly he seemed to notice Ardeth, and moved swiftly across to him. 'What's wrong here? Oh, no! Quick, Mag'rantor, Ardeth's ill, we'll have to get him up to the house.'

Part of Ardeth's mind heard him, but distantly; so too, as if from far away, the tale of disaster had fallen on his ears. But all his strength was concentrated on fighting the pain that deepened and worsened with every word of woe, spreading up into his jaw and pressing all the breath from his chest. Now the pain was in his arm as well, and as Mag'rantor and Ethanur reached out to him he began to slide down the fence, the carved robin falling unnoticed from his hand to lie on the ground, his stick clattering beside him. Somewhere within himself, Ardeth knew that nothing was going to make the pain go away: only moments were left to him. Why could Mag'rantor and Ethanur not stop fussing? They were good lads, both of them; but they were wasting time, and he had no time. Somehow, he managed to push at them, make them move back and give him space. Ah, that was better! The sky, he had to see the sky. With a huge effort, he marshalled his thoughts and tried to form them into words. 'Fosseiro.'

'Don't worry Ardeth, we're going to bring you to Fosseiro. Lie quiet now…'

He closed his eyes and frowned, shaking his hand at them for silence. 'Salfgard. Keep Salfgard, stay here. Fosseiro knows.'

Ardeth stretched out his hand and touched the ground. It was still warm and spoke to him of the life springing within it as the year turned. His eyes opened once more and wandered towards the last traces of sunset. The earth, the sky! If he could only have seen Fosseiro again, but it was too late for that now: how bitterly his wish had been granted.

'Another one to Caradward's account. They've killed him, as surely as if he fell in battle.' Mag'rantor spoke through angry tears as he got wearily to his feet. 'Come on, we'll have to take him up to the farm. I'll go in and break it to Fosseiro.'

They brought up the horse, lifted Ardeth and gently placed him across its back; then they set off slowly and carefully, but neither of them noticed where the little wooden robin lay and it was left where it had fallen, tramped into the soft earth of the path and forgotten.

Those who fled from Salfgard and lived never forgot that night. Fosseiro took charge, staying steady and calm as if she knew her grief would have to wait. She sent Mag'rantor and Ethanur to rouse the folk, bidding them abandon everything they could not readily either carry or stow in barrows and carts and to leave immediately so that by morning they would already be on the upland paths, heading for the remoter valleys and hidden glens high in the Gillan nan'Eleth. Weeping as he remembered the desperate circumstances of his own arrival in Salfgard, Mag'rantor wanted to stay beside Fosseiro, but she would have none of it.

'You've got a wife and children to look after, and Ethanur's hurt, he can hardly use that arm. He'll do more good convincing people that the tale he brings is true. Cunoreth will help me, we'll catch you up before tomorrow's out.'

Soon the darkness was ablaze with lights and torches as men ran from house to house and women shook sleeping children from their beds; dogs barked, cattle lowed and everywhere there was the sound of wheels, hurrying feet, slamming doors. Cunoreth gazed sadly down at Ardeth where he lay now in peace, far beyond the reach of all the tumult. When they were alone, Fosseiro spoke to him quietly.

'I know what Ardeth wanted. The buildings, our possessions, they don't really matter. If we live, we can get more and start again. But Salfgard was always more than just a village or a farm, and Ardeth will keep its heart safe for us now that we have to leave it.' She put her hand up to Cunoreth's shoulder. 'Find one of the lads to work with you, and dig him a grave where the pasture levels out on the south slope while I pack up food and gear for the three of us.'

And so as the early dawn of summer broke over Salfgard, they laid Ardeth to rest in his home place; and leaving him to watch over the fields he had always loved so dearly, they fled away after those who had already disappeared into the silent hills.

The victory parade

It was always fairly quiet at the *Sword and Stars* in the middle of the morning. There would be a bustle of activity at dawn, as the staff fired up in the kitchen and men worked in the stables; hooves clattered on the cobbles of the yard, boys worked the water pump; any merchants or travellers who were staying in the inn milled about as they organised their onward journeys. But when all the accounts were paid, the goods taken from store and loaded, the pack animals harnessed and away, then the staff took their own breakfasts and after that things would settle down again until business began to pick up once more towards mid-day, as customers arrived in search of food and drink. Work went on, of course. Maesrhon was fetching water in two buckets and sluicing the yard down, cleaning up the paving and cobbles with a stiff broom. The rhythmic swish of the bristles against the stones, the clank of his pails as he set them down, the squeak of the pump handle, the splash of the water against the metal and then the gurgle as it flowed away into the gully, all these sounds blended in his mind into a background against which his other thoughts floated free as he brushed steadily on, up and down, side to side. He could smell the smoke that wisped from the kitchen chimney as the mid-day food was prepared; smell the cooking, too, although he tried to ignore that. In his mind's eye he saw his ten-year-old self, turning down the offer of cheesebread in a bid to toughen himself up. Hadn't been such a bad preparation, had it? Bread was still available at the *Sword*, although these days only the wealthiest patrons could afford to order it. His own meal would probably be some kind of lentil broth, maybe with some smoked fish in it if he was lucky. He attacked the cobbles a little more vigorously with the stiff yard-brush. Better get in as much practice as he could at hard physical labour on meagre rations.

By late morning he had finished, and was working in the woodshed, sorting and stacking. People began to drift in from the street by ones and twos, heading towards the inn; he heard the clatter of dishes and a burst of laughter from the open door. He paused for a moment, wiping the sweat from his face. It seemed even darker than usual today, a mockery of midsummer noon, but it was oppressive too: heavy and threatening, as if a storm was brewing. The man working with him embedded his axe in a log and sat down on the block for a breather, blowing out his cheeks. Maesrhon nodded at him sympathetically.

'Hard going today, isn't it?'

'You've said it.'

Picking up his axe again, the man hesitated, not knowing quite what else to say. Like all his workmates at the *Sword* except Isteddar, he found it difficult to know how to talk to Maesrhon. How was it that he appeared so unworried, when according to what you heard, it was only a matter of time before, well, before what? Would Vorynaas really have his son executed as a traitor when he came back from the war? But then everyone said Maesrhon wasn't really his son… Taking a sideways peek, he returned to his task. He seemed sound enough, pleasant sort of young man, always pulled his weight; what a waste to make him face the death squad. By the Starborn, thought the fellow as he chopped away, I don't think I could stack firewood as calmly as that if I was in his shoes! As cool as you like, and he might only have days to live, surely it couldn't be much longer before they all came home again from Gwent y'm Aryframan. At that moment, a boy came tearing into the yard from the street and dashed into the inn. They heard his voice, high-pitched and excited, and then a clamour of men's voices. Within seconds, he ran out again. Seeing them staring, he paused just long enough to shout before pelting off to spread his news.

'They're on the way! An outrider's come to the west gate, he says they'll be here before the day's out. We've won!'

The *Sword and Stars* began to empty as men hurried out towards the street, where the noise level was rising as already people surged from their homes and workplaces towards the walls and the gates, hoping to find good vantage points. It was the best chance Maesrhon was likely to get for a decent meal, but he was no longer hungry. Grimly he worked on into the afternoon, unwilling to join the throngs in the streets, ashamed to take refuge in Tellgard; but it was impossible to ignore everything he heard or to be unaware of what was happening beyond the yard entrance. After a couple of hours the initial surge of excitement abated slightly, as folk settled down to wait for the spectacle. The shouting, the clamour of people running, died away to a constant buzz of voices; the whole city seemed to pulse with a low, humming sound like a giant hive where the bees were preparing to swarm. Once or twice Maesrhon heard a prolonged mutter of thunder, and each time it was answered by a mistle-thrush, singing wildly to the dark sky above from some hidden garden. The storm-cock, he thought with a shiver in spite of the sultry heat, the storm-cock greets our ruin.

And now a restless note arose from the crowds, children called out in excitement, and a new noise grew from outside the city walls: the relentless sound of hundreds of men marching, drawing ever closer. Maesrhon gathered up the tools he had been using, cleaned them, put them away, and then went into the deserted bath-house. Water could not wash away the feeling of guilt that oppressed his heart, but at least he would confront what was coming with the grime cleaned from his face and hands. For he had to see, must force himself to look at what he was desperate to hide from in shame.

Soon enough, the first riders were passing by, the horses dancing and fretting a little, nervous at being hemmed in by so much noise and so many people. Maesrhon saw Thaltor with Valahald, and Valestron too had returned at the head of a column of his men from Rigg'ymvala. The crowds cheered and shouted, men whistling and clapping, children whooping, women smiling and waving. After the mounted troops passed, there was a pause; then all the faces turned, craning to see what was coming next. A sound Maesrhon had never heard before began to roll towards him along the street, a sound in which rumbling wheels and the shuffling of many feet was mixed with an uneasy growl from the watching crowds. It was an ugly noise, in which mocking laughter and catcalls were underlaid with uncertain muttering: the watching faces showed a curious mingling of greed and defiant embarrassment. At the very moment when he realised with a lurch of the heart that a parade of captives was approaching, a shift in the bystanders suddenly revealed Ancrascaro only a few paces away from him, pale with horror. He elbowed men aside to reach her, drawing her back with him to the gateway of the inn yard.

'What are you doing in the middle of all this? Where is Rhostellat?'

'He's in Tellgard.' She clutched at him, on the brink of tears. 'I was at home, but when everyone started shouting that they were coming back, I wanted to be with him; but I got swept along by the crowd, so I tried to turn off to make for my parents' house instead, but there were too many people and this was as far as I could go. Oh, Maesrhon, I'm afraid to look! What if we see someone we know?'

'Don't look then. It's all right, I will watch.'

Putting his arms around her, Maesrhon turned Ancrascaro's face into his shoulder and looked over her head. For what seemed an age, the sorry procession passed by: carts piled with loot, some also carrying frightened children too small to walk; lumbering grain wagons to which sweating, half-naked men were harnessed, straining to pull them under the goading of foot-soldiers who patrolled the line; and hundreds of prisoners, men and women, young and old, footsore and weary, some obviously wounded, shuffling along with dead eyes, moving as if they walked in a dark dream. Sick with shame, Maesrhon watched them pass. He could feel Ancrascaro's heart beating against him and his own too was racing in dread that he might recognise someone among the captives. He scanned the hopeless faces, but though he saw none he knew, this brought no comfort. Had those he loved escaped, or were they dead? At last the final stragglers trailed by; they were followed by troops on foot, swaggering along with a tramp of mailed feet and the crash and jingle of arms and accoutrements, and after them there was a pause, an expectant hush. Then more cheering began. All too soon Maesrhon realised who it was who next approached, as the crowd cried out for Vorynaas. Abruptly he gripped Ancrascaro's hand and pulled her into the deserted courtyard of the *Sword and Stars*.

He turned under the overhanging eaves where the straw was stacked and they sat down on the bales. They were only a few yards from the street, but shielded from the tumult, here in the quiet under the hayloft where the sweet smells of fodder and animals lingered, they could have been a hundred miles away.

'We could almost be in Salfgard,' said Ancrascaro with a sad smile.

'Yes.' Maesrhon looked at her; what was it he noticed that was different? Something in the shape of her face, the look in her eyes? He touched her hand. 'When is the baby due?'

'Oh!' Ancrascaro blushed slightly. 'We've not told anyone yet, not even my parents. How did you guess?'

'I just knew, somehow.' Shrugging, Maesrhon laughed and then became serious again. He jerked his head towards the clamour from the street. 'Listen, Ancrascaro. When all this is over, I'll take you to your house and wait with you there until Rhostellat comes home. Then I must go to Arval. Promise me you'll look after yourself, and the baby; and take care of Arval for me too. Will you do that?'

'Yes, of course, but Maesrhon,' she was white-faced again now, staring at him, 'what do you mean? You don't think, now that Vorynaas is back …'

'I mean that the time has come when I must set out.'

They sat in silence for a moment, as another long growl of thunder rumbled overhead. The white lock of hair at Maesrhon's temple gleamed like a feather in the gloom and a spark of fire waked in his eye as he turned his head to a new sound.

'But one day I shall return: I have promised Arval. Vorynaas would do well to heed how the storm-cock sings.'

A choice and a vow

It was evening by the time he came back to Tellgard to find Arval alone in his study. As Maesrhon came into the room, he saw in surprise that Arval was turning the pages of one of the books that Numirantoro had made; the volume was open at the picture of the standing stones. He paused in the doorway, disconcerted by the way Arval looked up at him. Far from holding the contemplative gaze of an attentive reader, the old man's dark, deep-set eyes had been smouldering with wrath; but when he saw Maesrhon his thin face changed as a strange, unfathomable expression passed across it.

'What is it?' asked Maesrhon as he shut the door and moved forward.

Arval sighed as he closed the book. 'For a moment it was as if Arymaldur stood before me again. It seems beyond belief to me that we should have acted as we have done today, we who not so many years ago saw a lord of the As-Geg'rastigan walk among us. It was in this very room that Arymaldur revealed himself to me as one of the Starborn, and renewed the pledge.'

Maesrhon looked about him. Was it his imagination, or could he see an extra radiance globed around the flame of the lamp? He felt his hair lift slightly as if some hidden energy had filled the room, a strange shift in the feel of the air as he had sometimes noticed immediately before a flash of lightning. He turned swiftly to Arval.

'That's it, isn't it? The choice I will have to make, some day: whether to belong to the Starborn, or the Earthborn?'

'*Is-torar*, didn't I say that when the time came, you would know what the choice was without my telling you? I was right, you see.'

'But of course.' For a moment they smiled at each other, sharing the memory of a small boy's dogged devotion. Then Maesrhon sat down beside Arval, his face serious once more.

'But that's not all you said, nor all that I remember. You also warned me that the choice would be difficult to make. More than ten years have gone by since then, years in which I have tried always to remember your advice that knowledge and learning are not the same thing. I have let time pass and experience accumulate, as you told me to, my mind has built up its strength; but the choice would still be too hard, if I had to make it today. And though as you said I would, I do indeed understand it better for having waited to hear it, I think I also see where the difficulty lies. I have increased my knowledge of the Earthborn, but the As-Geg'rastigan are still as pictures in my mind. Surely, before I can make my choice, I must know more fully the life of the Starborn. Is it possible that this is where my journey leads me?'

Arval stood up abruptly and moved away to the window. He pushed it open and leaned out into the heavy evening air for a moment. Faintly the sweet notes of the robin floated across from its perch in the lamplit tree. Then Arval turned back into the room, his black eyes wide with yearning.

'Ah, the life of the As-Geg'rastigan! We had Arymaldur and Numirantoro among us, but they are gone; and now we must lose you also, little son. Your thought is like the arrow, Artorynas: swift and sure. Yes, I think you go on a twofold quest. I have shared with you the words that Arymaldur spoke to me: *There is always hope, if men know where to find it. Know that I will leave something of myself with you when I go; but also I shall take something away. Let that which is left seek for that which is taken. When the two are united, hope shall return.* You are what he left among us: it is for you to seek the arrow which he took, to bring us hope. And though I have spoken before of your mother's words on the day you were born, I have not told you all. Now it is time for you to hear everything she said when she entrusted you to my care: *Let him follow the arrow's path and light will shine again: upon the earth, upon men's hearts, upon the choice that lies before him.* If you succeed, you will bring not only hope to men in light returning, but also peace to your own heart.'

For some moments, Maesrhon said nothing. He pulled his mother's book towards him and leafed through it, obscurely comforted by the thought that her hands had made it, her mind brought it into being. But then his eyes fell on a page with the words *As wide as a windy sky* and a picture of a huge, cloud-tossed skyscape stretching over a vast sweep of empty land below. How wide the world was also, he thought; how endless the miles that lay before him. He closed the book and put it away from him, raising a bleak face.

'Successful or not, there is no knowing the length of the journey I may have to make. I could be away for years, Arval. I am prepared for this, but are there years left to us? You must tell me now how much time I have for the search.'

When Arval replied, Maesrhon saw immediately that this was a question he had expected and had already considered.

'You have seven years,' he said, 'at most; I do not think that either Caradriggan or I myself may endure for longer. But the time has already begun running. A message came from Vorynaas late this afternoon. Tomorrow evening he holds a victory feast in Seth y'n Carad, but the morning after, they will bring you to judgement in the Open Hall.'

Maesrhon heard the anger and bitterness in Arval's voice, heard his contempt for Vorynaas mingled with dread at what he might do; but he himself laughed as sudden elation filled him.

'Arval, I promise you as a son to his father, whether my quest be achieved or not, I will return to you. Before seven years are passed, I will stand beside you again. But as for Vorynaas, why do him the discourtesy of waiting another two days to greet him? Clearly, Maesrhon is not bidden to share the celebration, but I think Artorynas must attend his feast.'

Fire and ice

With all the preparations for his journey now made, on the following evening Maesrhon set out for Seth y'n Carad. The great gates were open, the compound thronged with revellers: Seth y'n Carad had been thrown open to all, for who was there left now for Vorynaas to fear? Softly Maesrhon threaded his way through the crowds, laughter and merriment ringing in his ears, smells of roasting meat and woodsmoke tickling his nose. None seemed to heed him and at the doors of the hall he paused, surveying the scene before him. The huge chamber blazed with light and colour; the faces before him were full of joy and mirth. He saw young men, second sons who had been marched off to war whether they would or no; here and there a middle-aged couple sat beside them whose happiness was easy enough to understand. But not so readily forgiven was what he saw further up the hall, where the tables were filled with those who had advanced in the wake of Vorynaas' rise: military men, landowners, merchants, all now claiming the rank of lords. Corruption, duplicity, greed, and hunger for ever more power and wealth was what showed in these faces; and behind them in the corners of the hall were piled great heaps of trophies, the riches brought back from the rape of Gwent y'm Aryframan. The lamplight fell on weapons and jewels, finery of all kinds, items of wrought silver and bronze. And now Maesrhon noticed that other men and women moved among the tables, or stood back in the shadows against the walls. There was no need to wonder who they might be: these faces were downcast and without hope. Every man bore the device of the springing corn on his arm, and every woman's left ear had been pierced, but not a single amber drop winked and swung there now. Already the liveried servants were treating them harshly, forcing them to perform the more menial tasks. Maesrhon felt a fury beginning to burn in his heart, but his mind was as cold as ice. He walked slowly through the doors and part of the way up the central aisle of the hall.

Suddenly his presence was noticed by those nearest and the roar of voices began to subside in whispering and muttering. His senses at full stretch, it almost seemed to Maesrhon that he could see even what was happening behind him. Further up the hall he walked, and the silence spread around him; with the tail of his eye he noted that even the slaves were watching him now. When he reached the centre, where a wide space between the tables crossed the aisle, he stopped and waited. One by one, then more and more at a time, the faces at the top of the hall turned towards him and conversation faltered here too. He watched as realisation reached those seated on the dais, as Vorynaas' eyes widened in surprise and momentary fear. Maesrhon, imagining that Vorynaas was reminded of how Geraswic had brought death to his table, had no means of knowing that to those who remembered him, it was as if Arymaldur had suddenly appeared among them once more; but now he began to hear the name being muttered all around him and the heads turned this time towards Vorynaas, carrying the hated name up to him on a breath of whispers. Complete silence fell as Vorynaas stood up.

'How dare you walk in here, traitor and coward! We will see whether you are so bold tomorrow when they bring you to the Open Hall.'

Maesrhon smiled slightly and again a whisper, almost a shiver of tension, ran round the hall. 'But why wait? Let men judge between us now. Who is the traitor here? Who has betrayed his family and his marriage-kin, his friends and his country? Those who follow you do well to enjoy themselves while they can, for you have deceived them and your ruin is all they will share.'

He looked around him, noting what the faces showed, whose eyes could not meet his own. Then as his gaze swept across those who sat behind Vorynaas on the dais, he saw the cup that Valafoss held, a two-handled horn cup in a silver holder whose intricately worked handles and polished amber insets caught the light as Valafoss nervously lifted it to his lips. Anguish such as he had never before imagined flooded through Maesrhon as he recognised Heretellar's gift to Ardeth. So Salfgard had been over-run and looted! Pain pierced his heart as he stood speechless, fighting to keep his head clear of the poisonous rage that threatened to overwhelm him. Vorynaas was speaking again; was he calling for his guards? Disregarding him, Maesrhon raised his own voice in a cry that cut through the shouting.

'No, now you will listen to me!'

Suddenly he felt it, heard it in his voice once more, the authority that was his heritage from the As-Geg'rastigan. That other-worldly force of life was in the hall with him; they could not touch him and they knew it, he saw the fear in their faces. He sprang forward to the great pillars that rose at the centre of the chamber and seized two of the torches that had been fixed there, adding their brighter lustre to the glow of the lamplight.

'How many stolen harvests do you think you will gather in Gwent y'm Aryframan? I tell you now, the bread you eat will taste bitter in your mouth; it has been more dearly bought than you know. The darkness deepens and spreads and you are powerless to prevent it.

The day will come when it will engulf you, and your deluded followers will be dragged down with you.'

Maesrhon swung the torches high, and in the rush of air they flared up, blazing; then he flung them into the soft sand of the firepits below the brackets and instantly they were quenched. Some of those who sat gaping at him rubbed their eyes, momentarily confused by the sudden dousing of a light that was still imprinted on their sight in a blinding dazzle. Dark, acrid smoke drifted through the hall from the blackened sand.

Walking forward to the second pair of huge pillars that supported the mid-point of the roof span, Maesrhon took down two more torches. Then without warning he ran suddenly up the hall towards the top table, the torches streaming behind him. Chairs and benches scraped on the floor as men and women scrambled to move away from him, afraid for what he might be about to do. Standing in front of Vorynaas, his golden eyes lit by the flames he carried, Maesrhon passed the torches swiftly about himself, so close that the flames licked at his clothes and touched his face and hands. There was a panicked intake of breath, but though he stood at the centre of a sphere of fiery light, he appeared unscorched and unharmed. From within the whirling arcs of flame, his voice rang out in power and might.

'Bring me to the Open Hall? Neither you nor any of your henchmen will lay a finger upon me.' He laughed into his adversary's face. 'Reach out to me: I am ice at the heart of the flames, ice which will burn you like fire. Stretch out your hand to take me: I am fire at the heart of the ice, fire which will freeze you to the bone.'

Holding the torches high now, he surveyed all points of the hall; and then began slowly walking back towards the entrance.

'You have raised your hands against the Starborn, but here also Vorynaas has deceived himself and lied to you. No man takes the life of the As-Geg'rastigan, who may walk unseen.' At the doors, Maesrhon turned again.

'I hear the name of Arymaldur whispered among you.' An audible gasp greeted these words, and he smiled. 'How do you know whether or not Arymaldur treads the streets of Caradriggan even now? I see in your eyes that none here can tell me. Keep to your homes tonight! There is a power you cannot guess abroad in this city. And what of Artorynas? You have not heard that name before, but you will hear it again. Yes, when the sun next rises over Caradward, you will hear it again.'

Swinging the torches so that they flamed up once more, Maesrhon pushed them into the wrought ironwork of the elaborate bolts and latches; then gripping the edges of the heavy oak timbers, he cried out, 'Remember Artorynas!' and vanished into the night, crashing the doors to behind him.